Kate's Turn

OTHER BOOKS AND BOOKS ON CASSETTE BY
CHERI J. CRANE

Kate's Return

The Fine Print

Forever Kate

Following Kate

Kate's Turn

A Novel

Cheri J. Crane

Covenant Communications, Inc.

Published by Covenant Communications, Inc.
American Fork, Utah

Copyright © 1994 by Cheri J. Crane
All rights reserved
Printed in the United States of America
First Printing 1994

99 00 01   10 9 8 7

Library of Congress Cataloging-in-Publication Data
Crane, Cheri J. (Cheri Jackson) , 1961-
Kate's turn : a novel / Cheri J. Crane.
p. cm.
ISBN 1-55503-715-1 : $11.95
1.Mormons—Utah—History—Fiction.   [1. Mormons—Fiction.
2.Time travel—Fiction.]   I. Title
PS3553 . R2696K38   1994
813' .54--dc20
[Fic]   94-31946
                                                    CIP
                                                    AC

Dedicated to the Bennington Ward Young Women.
Never forget who you are!

ACKNOWLEDGMENTS

A big thank you to the people of Covenant Communications. You've been great!

Special thanks to my husband, Kennon, our three sons, Kris, Derek, and Devin, and those wondrous family members known as my siblings, Tom, Heather, and Trudi, for the encouragement and support they are constantly giving me.

I would also like to extend my gratitude to Shelley Burdick for the advice, proofreading, and friendship that made this book possible.

Last, but certainly not least, I'd like to thank my mother, Genevieve Sibbett Jackson, whose pioneer spirit has kept all of us going through our own trek across the plains of tribulation.

To all of you: Je t'aime!

PART 1

Behold, I stand at the door, and knock: if any man hear my voice, and open the door, I will come in to him.

Revelation 3:20

CHAPTER ONE

Susan Mahoney Erickson sat cross-legged, pulling at the weeds that had invaded her strawberries. It was good therapy, working in the rich soil of her garden in the cool of the evening. It offered comfort and a sense of peace, the elements missing in her life lately.

As she moved along the row, she silently berated herself for going to work meeting tonight. If she'd stayed home, then the unpleasant scene afterwards would have been avoided. She paused long enough to wipe at her eyes with the back of a gloved hand. Dirt mingled with the tears, drying in muddy streaks across her face.

As she labored, the conversation overheard earlier replayed in her mind. A conversation not meant for her ears. The topic, her sixteen-year-old daughter, Kate.

"Isn't it a shame, the way Kate Erickson carries on, and her father in the branch presidency too? I heard her mother has given up, thrown her hands right in the air. It makes you wonder what went wrong with that girl. Of course, we all know apples don't fall too far from the tree," Sister Rhoads had said as she'd cornered the first counselor in the Young Women's presidency. "Maybe her parents were a little on the wild side growin' up. I was watchin' one of those talk shows the other day. They had experts on the panel, people who know all about raisin' children. It makes you wonder. Maybe Greg or Sue . . ."

"Greg and Sue Erickson are wonderful people," Lori

Blanchard had replied. "They have tried everything they can think of with Kate," Lori had added, glaring at the older woman. "We all have," she had stressed. "Sometimes, kids have a mind of their own. Kate has always been a little independent."

"Don't I know it," Sister Rhoads had complained, shaking her head. "I taught that girl in Primary. I knew then she was headin' for trouble. Always makin' light of the lesson. Actin' up to beat the band."

"I thought she was a well-behaved little girl."

"Did you teach her in Primary?"

"Well, no. But from what I saw . . ."

"You just didn't know her then. She was full of the devil from the time she could walk."

"Look, I really have to be going now," a nervous Lori had interrupted, fearing Sue Erickson was somewhere nearby. She had failed to notice Sue, frozen in place behind the door of the room used by the Relief Society.

"If I were you, I'd be a little more concerned. That young lady will drag the other girls down with her, you just mark my words," the older woman had persisted.

"I really don't think . . ."

"You should discourage Kate from comin' out to Mutual, or whatever you people call it these days."

"Sister Rhoads, Kate needs the Young Women's program. She needs . . ."

"I'll tell you what that girl needs, a good swat on the behind! If Kate was my daughter, she'd be singin' a different tune! There would be none of this wild hair, clothes too short and too tight, garish makeup smeared from here to here," she said, gesturing across her face. "No sir, that young lady would know what's what! None of this runnin' around with a bunch of hooligans. Delinquents who think it's great sport to throw eggs at a person's car!"

Sue had flinched, knowing Sister Rhoads had referred to the egg and water balloon spree several high school students had indulged in the last day of school. At the time, she'd hoped Kate had steered clear of the incident. Later, she found the telltale signs in her daughter's room. An empty egg carton stashed inside a jacket on the floor of Kate's bedroom. Several suspicious balloons on her daughter's dresser.

"Kate has some problems, but I still think . . ."

"I'll tell you what I think. I think you'd be ahead to write that one off. It's better to lose one girl than the entire bunch!"

That was when Sue had snapped. Coming forward, sparks flying from livid green eyes, she had asked Sister Rhoads what gave her the right to pass judgment on others. Lori, a peculiar shade of red, mumbled a hasty apology as she tried to make amends. But waves of anger and frustration surfaced, causing Sue to say things she now regretted.

Frowning, Sue reached for another weed, pulling it free from the fertile soil. She knew eventually she would have to call both women and apologize. Lori had been an innocent victim of her hot Irish temper. It wasn't Lori she was mad at. And she was more irritated than mad at Sister Rhoads. Edith Rhoads was notorious for gossiping. It was a well-known fact in their small branch. Most ignored or tolerated the bitter widow, realizing she was angry with life in general.

Sue knew her own anger stemmed from the deep sense of helplessness she felt concerning Kate. A part of her feared Sister Rhoads was right. There were times when Kate seemed to be a lost cause. Not that Sue would ever write her off, as Edith Rhoads had suggested. She would persist in the continuing battle to reclaim her daughter.

Kate's face came to mind. Her daughter's flashing green eyes. The long auburn hair with the slight reddish cast. The defiant expression shared with anyone who cared to glance in her direction. A sneering frown had replaced Kate's smile since her thirteenth birthday.

It hadn't always been this way. The fighting, tears, and door slamming hadn't been a part of everyday life. There had been laughter, hugs, and harmony. Good times had been shared as Sue had taught Kate about sunsets, birds, and hot fudge sundaes. Together, they had experienced flowers, swinging in the park, ballet, piano lessons, Primary, and shopping.

Shopping had remained a favorite pastime until resentment had emerged against Sue's advice concerning makeup, hair, and clothes. Kate no longer came to Sue for approval or advice. Instead, she enjoyed the shocked expressions each time she bounced down the stairs in an outfit that declared her independence. Sue usually sent her right back upstairs to change, refusing to let the world see the tiny skirt, the shorts that were too short, the plunging neckline, or the clinging blouse that revealed too much.

Memory of the outfit Kate had chosen to wear last night sent a hot stab of rage through Sue. She grabbed at a fierce-looking weed, pulling it out by the roots. Too late, she saw that a strawberry plant had become entangled with the weed. Dismayed, she pried the plant loose from the weed. She set it aside and reworked the soil, carefully replacing the strawberry plant in its rightful place. "Watch it wilt and die now," she muttered under her breath.

Removing the glove from her right hand, she ran frustrated fingers through her short red hair, forcing out an insect that had chosen to land there. As it flew away, she glanced toward the house, her eyes wandering to the upper story, settling on Kate's bedroom window. She wasn't sure, but thought she could hear wailing guitars and the muffled sounds of thumping drums. *Kate's choice of music leaves a lot to be desired*, she thought, sliding her hand back inside the glove. But, if she said anything concerning the inappropriate lyrics, or the nerve-wracking squeals and pounding, Kate became more sullen than usual, taking her foul mood out on everyone around her.

With a sigh, Sue wondered how she had managed to become the enemy. The metamorphosis had taken place without her knowledge or consent. In her daughter's eyes, she had somehow fallen from grace. No longer considered a loving confidant, she found herself classified as an ornery hag. The closeness once shared with Kate had evaporated, fading with the friendship that had once thrived.

In the beginning, Sue had attributed this shift in Kate's attitude to the hormones raging in her daughter's maturing body. Some of Sue's friends, expert mothers of teenagers, had offered sympathy, and the promise that things would return to normal when Kate's emotions had caught up with her physical development. Thinking this made sense, Sue had tried patience, until Kate had tried hers without mercy. Kate's behavior continuously changed, and not for the better. Sue barely had time to adjust to one surprising transformation before another surfaced.

One such change involved Kate's rotating circle of friends. During junior high, she began ignoring the girls who had been her friends since first grade, gradually replacing them with others, most unknown to Sue. To Sue's way of thinking, this was a cause for concern. There were very few Mormons in Bozeman. And, though most nonmembers were very fine people, there was often a difference in standards. Sue had been relieved to learn that one of Kate's new friends was a member of the Church. That was before she had actually met the young lady named Linda.

Linda was tall and slender, her blonde hair hanging down past her shoulders, the stiff bangs flipped up in an outrageous fashion. She dressed in wild colors, choosing to decorate herself with bracelets and earrings that usually clashed with whatever she was wearing. Sue thought the entire look was overdone. This included the bright makeup, applied in layers.

Kate thought Linda was sophisticated; after all, she was nearly a year older, and much more knowledgeable about these things. Because Linda was sophisticated, she referred to Kate's mother as Sue, not Sister or Mrs. Mahoney. Sue didn't think this was sophisticated. She thought it was rude, but she put up with it, hoping Kate would see how hard she was trying to accept this new-found friend. She drew the line when Kate began imitating Linda, calling her Sue instead of Mom. Trying not to make an issue out of it, she'd very politely asked Kate to refrain from using her first name. When Kate persisted, Greg had threatened to cut off their daughter's allowance unless Kate cooperated. Kate now called her Mother. Sue had never considered this to be an insult, but the way Kate said it, offense was implied.

As time passed, worried about the continuing influence of Linda, and a young man named Jace, Sue had encouraged Kate to start spending more time with her former friends—the girls from the neighborhood, and the young women in their branch. But, according to Kate, these people were total dweebs. Jace was Mr. Wonderful, and Linda, Ms. Perfection. The sun rose and set in everything Linda or Jace said or did.

Kate became a Linda clone. The two girls dressed alike, talked alike, and Sue shuddered when she thought about the other things the two friends might be doing alike. As a result, Sue decided to take a firm, bold stance. She made it perfectly clear what was and wasn't acceptable behavior. When this failed miserably, she turned to others for help. Greg suggested that she relax and give their daughter more space. Sue informed her husband that if she gave Kate any more space, the girl would be in orbit. Greg then suggested prayers on their daughter's behalf. A certain amount of inner peace was attained, but Kate's rebellious attitude thrived. A firm believer in the power of prayer, Sue had nevertheless continued in this practice on a daily basis.

She took her concerns to the branch president. He recommended that she continue to offer Kate unconditional love, and ask the Young Women leaders for assistance. These women had made several valiant efforts, but hadn't gained much ground with Kate. The Church was simply beneath Linda, and Kate was a devout believer in her friend's philosophies concerning just about everything.

Linda said, "Too many rules are stifling."

Kate agreed.

"What has the Church ever done for us?" Linda presented for contemplation.

Kate could think of nothing.

"Who are these people?" Asked by Linda the one time she agreed to go to church with Kate.

Sue had asked Kate to invite Linda, hoping to sway her daughter's friend toward the gospel. When Linda later informed Kate she'd hated every minute of this adventure in boredom, Kate had apologized profusely. She in turn was furious with her mother for proposing such a thing in the first place. Sue was told that she had once again tried to ruin her daughter's life.

"Linda hates going to church. Don't you have any couth, Mother?" Kate had asked, looking extremely pained.

It was the same question Sue often longed to ask Kate.

Sue was aware that Linda's attitude toward the Church stemmed from her parents' divorce. Linda lived with her mother, who was a member, but the woman hadn't been to church in years. Linda couldn't even remember being baptized. Not that being baptized was important. This according to the Book of Linda, chapter 5, verse 14.

It hurt when Sue saw that Kate believed Linda concerning this matter. It was frustrating to know another plan to jump-start her daughter's waning testimony had disintegrated into bitter nothingness. Linda had turned her back on the Church, and Kate was leaning in the same direction.

Sue returned her attention to the garden and tugged hard at an uncooperative weed. It refused to give. Determined to remove it, she focused intently on the root, digging with her fingers until a firm handhold was obtained. Straining with the effort, she finally pulled it free. Grim satisfaction replaced determination. She stared at the weed, wishing it was as easy to free Kate from the negative influences in her daughter's life. Heartsick, she quietly wept among the strawberries where the weeds bore the brunt of her pain.

CHAPTER TWO

K ate awoke with a start. It was the dream. Again. She rolled
onto her side and peered through the darkness at the digital clock.
The numbers blinked at her, the red light casting an eerie glow on
her dresser. It was only 3:45 a.m. She groaned, sat up, and rubbed
at her eyes. Then, slipping quietly out of bed, she moved to the
window and scowled at the darkened sky. Clouds had moved in,
obscuring her view of the stars. She shrugged and walked out of
the bedroom, heading for the bathroom down the hall.

Several minutes later, she wandered downstairs to the kitchen
for a snack. She felt her way to a switch and reluctantly flipped it
on. A bright light responded to her touch. She preferred the
darkness, the light hurt her eyes, but she was trying to dispel the
bitter fear lingering from the dream. The light was comforting in
an irritating way. She blinked, impatiently waiting for her eyes to
adjust.

She selected a banana off the counter, pulled herself up onto a
nearby bar stool and slowly removed the yellow fruit from its tight
wrapping. As she ate, she tried to make sense of the nightmare that
had been haunting her for nearly a month.

The problem was, she could only remember bits and pieces.
And none of it made sense. It always started the same. Screams.
All around her. Then a strange darkness. Slowly, the darkness
faded and she was alone in the middle of what looked like a desert.
The rest of the dream was a jumbled mess. People reaching toward

her. People she'd never seen before in her life, dressed in strange clothes. The women in long dresses and bonnets. The men in loose-fitting pants and baggy linen shirts. Tears streamed from their pleading eyes as they held out their hands. Linda and Jace were on the other side, taunting her cruelly. And always, there was her mother's face, hovering near her own. As the dream ended, everyone faded from sight, leaving her alone with a pain that was foreign. An overwhelming fear crushed her, causing her to wake in a panic. She shuddered now at the memory.

She'd tried explaining it to Linda once. But Linda had laughed. Her friend thought it was funny. *"Get a grip, Kate, it's only a dream."* But, this dream was different. It was much too real, and it stayed with her longer than any dream she'd ever had before.

Years ago when a nightmare plagued her, her cries had always brought her mother to her side. In the sanctuary of her mother's arms, the nightmares were quickly forgotten, and she was lulled to sleep with a sense of secure love. She grimaced, knowing that would not be the case now. Now, her mother would give her lectures instead of comfort. Tell her helpful things like maybe it was her conscience bothering her, or something she ate.

She swallowed the last of the banana, then slid down from the stool to walk to the kitchen sink. She opened the cabinet beneath and hesitated, staring at the garbage container. Everything in its proper place. Just as her mother preferred. It was tempting to leave the peeling on the counter. Leave it, and watch as her mother lost her cool over something so trivial it didn't even matter. But it did matter to Sue Erickson. Everything mattered. Everything counted. Her mother had ingrained that philosophy into her head for so many years, it had taken a while to realize Sue Erickson didn't have all the answers. No one did. Life posed too many questions. Too much of it didn't make sense. She sighed and discarded the peeling.

Kate knew what her mother would say to her questions. "Open your heart to the gospel." Yeah, right. Like the Church made everything peachy. She'd seen it in action. The way members looked down their noses at anyone who was different. If that was being Christlike, then she didn't want any part of it.

Shivering, she wished she'd thought to throw on a robe. The

clinging nightshirt she was wearing didn't lend much warmth. She opened a cupboard and reached for a glass. Moving back to the sink, she filled it with water and hurriedly quenched her thirst. As she set the glass in the sink, she wondered what it would take to quench the thirst she felt inside. Shaking her head, she knew what her mother would suggest. *"You need a testimony, Kate."* Yeah, right, like she needed a face full of zits!

Testimonies were bunk! The ramblings of misguided people who thought blubbering or lecturing into a microphone during fast and testimony meeting was the proper thing to do. All of it was just for show! A chance to exhibit religious prestige. As far as Kate was concerned, a testimony was nothing more than an illusion. Something people sought in frustrated desperation and deluded themselves into believing. Linda had even said as much. There wasn't anything to be found in the Church. Kate had never felt the wonderful glow inside that her parents, leaders, and teachers were continuously glorifying.

She didn't pray anymore, realizing what a farce it all was. No one listened to prayers. She'd discovered this when she was eleven. Her cat, Buddy, had disappeared. She'd prayed for days. Buddy had never come home. Two years later, when Grandpa and Grandma Erickson had been in that bad car accident, she'd tried again, begging Heavenly Father to spare their lives. Grandma had died three days later. Prayer didn't work.

Linda agreed with her. Linda had prayed when her parents were fighting. They still got divorced. Prayer didn't work. Testimonies weren't real. The gospel was nothing more than somebody's idea of how the world should be. And none of it mattered.

Kate opened the cabinet beneath the sink. She reached down inside the garbage, retrieved the banana peel and closed the wooden door. Turning, she threw the peel on top of the counter. Satisfied, she moved across the kitchen to flip off the light and silently left the room.

CHAPTER THREE

With purposeful stride, Sue approached the door that led into Kate's bedroom. Loud, screeching music escaped under the door, the blare echoing in the hall. She took a deep breath and knocked. After waiting several seconds for the answer that wouldn't come, she twisted the brass-colored knob and entered the room.

"Mom!"

"I knocked first." Sue quickly closed the door behind her. "If you wouldn't crank up the volume, maybe you'd hear something once in a while. If your ears aren't already permanently damaged," she added, pointing to the CD player. Her green eyes flashed a warning. The sixteen-year-old had better cooperate if she wanted to avoid a session of Irish wrath.

Kate shuddered, recognizing the look. She knew all too well that when her mother lost her temper, casualties were commonplace. Reluctantly complying, she pushed a black button. Silence enveloped the room. "Now what have I done?" she asked sullenly.

"Tyler tells me you've decided to stay here in Bozeman for the next two weeks." Sue frowned her disapproval as she stepped around piles of clothes, papers, and shoes. She carefully made her way to Kate's cluttered bed.

Her own green eyes glittering, Kate silently fumed as she imagined how she'd get even with her younger brother. She'd give Tyler's ant farm a burial at sea, compliments of the upstairs bathroom! As she pictured his horrified reaction, she smiled.

Misinterpreting the smile, Sue raised one eyebrow. "Well?" she persisted, moving a stack of CDs before sitting down on the end of the bed.

Kate refused to meet her mother's challenging glare, choosing instead to play with her stiff auburn bangs. Doing her best to ignore the woman sitting across from her, she offered a half-hearted shrug.

"Katherine Colleen Erickson, if you think I'm going to stand idly by while you ruin your life, you've got another think coming!"

Kate cringed. She hated her middle name. Colleen, in honor of a distant grandmother. Like that really mattered or something. "Oh, Mom, lighten up! It's my summer vacation, too. Can't I spend it the way I want?"

"We've been planning this trip since last summer. And I'm not about to leave you here to do heaven knows what with Jace while we're gone!"

"Mom! I can't believe you sometimes!"

Images of Jace with her daughter sent chills up Sue's spine. If only Kate could see him for who he really was. A cold manipulator who lived for worldly pleasure. She'd heard about his wild parties. Friends had told her how he'd treated other girls. And she'd seen for herself the way the eighteen-year-old looked at her daughter. The hungry desire in his eyes. It filled her with revulsion. She knew he would only hurt Kate. Use her and hurt her, but getting Kate to believe it was another story. "Kate, I know you have feelings for Jace, but he doesn't have the same standards . . ."

Kate's tone changed from protest to sarcasm. "Oh, I get it. He's not a Mormon. He's not good enough!"

"I didn't say that. I'm saying . . ."

"That you don't trust me!"

"Honey, I don't want to see you get hurt. He . . ."

"What's with you and Dad? You both treat me like a baby. I'm sixteen! I'm an adult! I can make my own decisions."

"I'd hardly call you an adult!" Sue's temper had gotten the best of her. She took a deep breath and held it, struggling for control.

"Thanks!" Kate retorted.

Softening as angry pain became apparent in her daughter's

eyes, Sue sighed. "Look, believe it or not, I didn't come in here to fight with you."

"Yeah, right." Kate scowled and turned away from her mother's pleading gaze.

"And if you want to be treated like an adult, then start acting like one. Prove to us that you can be trusted. That you are responsible."

"Are you saying I'm not responsible, that I can't be trusted?" Kate asked, whirling around to confront her mother.

Sue stared down at her hands and remained silent.

"Well?" Kate demanded.

"I'm not blind. I know all about the nights you've left work early to sneak off with Jace." She glanced up, meeting her daughter's surprised stare with a look of sadness.

Kate shifted her gaze to the carpeted floor. She hated it when her mother gave her that look. The look that indicated she was breaking her mother's heart. Linda said it was a trick most parents used and was something to be ignored. Breathing rapidly, she wondered how much her mother knew about the time she spent with Jace.

Sue stood and crossed the room to Kate's dresser. She could tell she was getting nowhere with her daughter. But there had to be a way to reach Kate before it was too late. Before her daughter ruined her life.

Ignoring a twinge of guilt, Kate became defensive. "So, I've been seeing Jace after work? What happened to my free agency?" she ventured, hoping to catch her mother off guard.

Slowly Sue turned to face her daughter. "Free agency?" she quietly asked.

Kate refused to back down. She nodded. "Aren't we all promised the right to choose for ourselves?"

"Yes . . . " Sue began, wondering why her daughter only discussed Church doctrine when it could be twisted in her behalf. Kate grinned. Now they were getting somewhere.

"But . . . " Sue added.

"I knew it! I knew you couldn't agree with me, not even once!"

"Why are you so determined to defy us?"

Staring at the floor, Kate refused to answer.

Sue turned away, her troubled gaze settling on a small framed picture on Kate's dresser. A gift from Lori Blanchard, it was a rendition of the Savior knocking at a wooden door. There were no handles or visible knobs; the door could only be opened from the inside. Touched by the symbolism, she picked it up and carefully blew a thin layer of dust from the metal frame. Moving close to the bed, she held the picture out in front of her. "Okay, Kate, I'll admit you're partially right. We are all entitled to our free agency. But the choices we make are important. They determine who we are. We're given guidelines to help us. Standards that guarantee eternal happiness. Jesus has provided a wonderful example for us to follow, but we have to open our hearts if we want his influence in our lives. He won't force his doctrines on any of us."

"Unlike you," Kate snapped, ignoring the framed picture.

Sue made a valiant effort to remain calm. "I'm just saying that we need to choose wisely. Someday, we'll all have to account for the lives we've led." She paused, hoping her words would somehow penetrate her daughter's closed heart.

Kate glared at her mother. "Is the lecture over if I agree to go on this precious trip?"

Sue bristled. They were going on this precious trip for Kate's sake.

The plan was to drive through Yellowstone Park, then head down to Salt Lake City to stay with relatives for a few days. They'd heard so many positive things about the new L.D.S. film, "Legacy," and Greg and Sue were determined to take their family to see it. It was currently being shown at the Joseph Smith Memorial Building, across from the Salt Lake Temple grounds. They were hoping the film and a tour of the Visitors' Center would ignite Kate's tiny spark of a testimony before it flickered into nonexistence.

"Well?"

Sue sighed. She knew the victory was temporary. The real battle still loomed ahead. Silently nodding, she handed the picture of the Savior to Kate. "We leave in two days."

"Don't worry. I'll be ready," Kate assured her mother. She'd be ready, all right! She'd make this trip so miserable, they'd never ask her to go on another one! Cheered by the thought, she impatiently waited for her mother to leave the room. When the door was finally closed, she threw the framed picture onto a pile of dirty clothes and defiantly pushed a black button on the CD player. The room immediately vibrated with the squeal of an abused guitar.

Chapter Four

Give, said the little stream . . . give, oh! give . . . give, oh! give . . . everybody sing," Tyler boomed loudly, his voice cracking on the high notes.

"Oh, grow up, Tyler," Kate snapped at the twelve-year-old. "You sound like a bull moose bellowing for its mate!"

"I do?" Tyler questioned, as he beamed at the sister he loved to annoy. "Thank you ever so much!"

"Tyler, can you sound like an elephant? How about a bear?" five-year-old Sabrina asked, smiling at her brother.

"Glad to, Breeny," Tyler replied. He began to clear his throat.

"That's okay, son, really," Greg Erickson said quickly, sliding his wandering glasses back up his nose. He reached down to fiddle with the radio. It didn't take long to discover that static was the only thing they could pick up through the canyon. Giving up, he focused on the road ahead. "Look at that view," he said in an attempt to ease the tension in the back seat.

Tyler obediently glanced out the window on his side of the Ford Explorer. A foaming river raced along beside them. Towering mountains were covered by lush green grass and dark swaying pines. "Where are we, anyway, Dad?" he asked.

"I'm not sure, Ty." Greg grabbed the map off the dashboard and handed it to Sue. "Care to take a gander at this?"

"I'd love to," she answered, rolling her eyes as she opened the accordion-shaped paper. She tried to make sense of the numerous lines wandering across the map. "Well, it looks like we're somewhere between Montana, Idaho, and Wyoming."

"Way to go, Mom," Kate said, glaring out the window.

"Here, Mom, let me take a look at it," Tyler offered.

Relieved, Sue handed it to him, her eyes shifting to Kate. When Kate refused to look at her, she frowned and returned her gaze to the gray pavement winding in front of them.

Tyler spread out the map, unaware he had covered his little sister.

"Tyler! I'm not a desk," Sabrina protested.

"Oh, yeah?" Kate challenged, grinning at her siblings. "I've always said you had wood between your ears."

"Kate! Mama, Kate's makin' fun of me again!" Sabrina accused.

"That's enough, Kate," Sue said, turning around to glare at her oldest daughter.

"Hey, I think I've found where we're at," Tyler offered, breaking the silent tension.

"Good," Greg said, grateful to Tyler for providing a diversion. The last thing they needed was another heated argument between Kate and Sue. They'd already endured three since leaving Bozeman earlier that morning.

"According to my expert calculations," Tyler continued, "we're on the western border of Yellowstone Park. We've been on the road for a little over an hour. So, I figure we should pull into West Yellowstone in about twenty minutes. Oh, yeah, Dad's driving. Make that sixty minutes."

"All right, hot shot," Greg countered. "We'll be there in twenty minutes," he promised, pressing down on the accelerator. Thirty minutes later, they drove into West Yellowstone.

After stopping for a sandwich, the Ericksons drove around the small town for a quick tour. "We ought to go to The Playmill tonight," Greg suggested.

"How quaint. Is that where they make their bread?" Kate jeered.

"Nope. It's a theatre. It's where we're going to have a foot-stompin' good ol' time," Greg explained, his enthusiasm rubbing off on everyone but Kate. "Hey, let's check this out," he added, braking suddenly in front of the Museum of the Yellowstone.

"Hey, watch it," Kate complained, massaging the side of her head. A small lump was forming, the result of a minor collision with the window on her side of the car.

"Sorry," Greg apologized. He glanced at Sue and grinned. Their eyes linked in silent communication. Maybe they'd finally managed to knock some sense into their moody daughter.

They entered the log building, and were guided into a small, darkened room where they were shown a film that expounded on the wildlife found in Yellowstone Park. When it ended, they wandered through the rest of the museum. Tyler lingered over the Indian artifacts salvaged from the surrounding area, while Sabrina excitedly dragged her mother around to see several mounted animals on display. Choosing to lean against a wall near the entrance, Kate sighed continuously, her expression pained.

Tyler noticed his sister's lack of enthusiasm and moved to her side. "Whattsa matter?" he teased, "did the big scary animals make Katie feel oogey?" Kate's fist connected with his stomach, effectively knocking the wind out of him. "If you weren't a girl," he threatened, holding his stomach.

"Yeah, right," she countered. "Your muscles are all in your head."

"And yours fill out the seat of your pants!" he retorted.

Sensing an impending battle, Greg steered Tyler over to an impressive Indian headdress. Sue tried to strike up a conversation with Kate, but gave up when her daughter remained silent.

A short time later, the Ericksons left the museum. Greg drove the family to the Best Western Crosswinds, the motel where they would be spending the night. "It has an indoor pool and a spa," he began.

"Does it have cable?" Kate interrupted.

"I think so," he answered, raising an eyebrow. "Not that we'll be watching TV. We're on vacation, remember? We're here to experience thrills and wonderment. Not MTV or HBO."

Kate groaned and leaned her head against the window. She winced when the brakes were slammed into action, her head plowing into the hard glass. Swearing profusely, she stopped only when it was obvious that everyone was staring in her direction.

"Well . . . he did it again! I know he does it on purpose!"

"Right," Tyler smirked.

"Kate," their mother began.

"I know. You don't have to tell me. Improper language, right? I'll make you a deal. I'll quit swearing when Dad quits playing lead-foot on the brakes!" Muttering under her breath, she opened the door and slid out of the car, slamming the door behind her.

Sue and Greg exchanged a worried glance. Would their daughter ever learn to control herself? They forced themselves to leave the sanctuary of the Explorer to face the continuing war between their children.

"Dibs on that bed right there," Tyler said with an impish grin, pointing to one of the two beds in the room he would share with his sisters.

"Oh, great! I suppose I get stuck sharing a bed with her," Kate fumed, pointing to Sabrina.

"Mama," Sabrina cried out, her chin quivering with indignant pain. "Kate hates me."

Sue stepped in from the other bedroom and frowned. "She does not. Kate, there's plenty of room in that double bed for you and Sabrina."

"I will not sleep with the rug rat," Kate replied, folding her arms across her chest.

"Why not?" Sue asked, struggling to keep the annoyance she felt out of her voice. "And don't call your sister a rug rat." Sabrina beamed at her mother before turning to stick her tongue out at her big sister.

"Remember what happened in Virginia City last summer?" Kate whined.

Sue reluctantly recalled the trip they'd taken to the old Montana ghost town. They had stayed overnight at the Virginia City Country Inn, a charming Victorian bed and breakfast. Everyone had been thrilled with the antique features. Kate's only complaint had concerned the bathroom they'd had to share with the other guests.

Then, going against her better judgment, Sue had allowed Sabrina to drink a can of pop before bed. Unfortunately, Kate had been the recipient of the consequences. Shrieking obscenities Sue was still trying to figure out, Kate had declared she would never share another bed with her younger sister. At the time, Sue hadn't been sure who to feel sorriest for—Sabrina, who was devastated beyond words, Kate, who was trying to salvage the silk night-shirt that had been saturated, or herself, the lucky soul who would get to tell the Inn's owners of the accident in the soft, feather bed.

Sadly shaking her head, Sue realized that time didn't actually seem to heal all wounds.

"I won't share this or any other bed with her," Kate said stubbornly, pulling Sue back to the immediate conflict.

"Fine. Go get a sleeping bag from the car," Sue answered, thinking it would serve Kate right to sleep on the floor.

"Can I sleep in the sleepin' bag, Mama?" Sabrina asked, her eyes bright with excitement.

"Sure you can," Kate said before Sue could reply. "I'll even go get it for you," she added, moving to the door that led outside.

"How noble of you," Sue said, trying to inflict a little guilt.

Kate continued to grin, shrugging once before disappearing through the door.

Eight p.m. found the Ericksons, with the exception of Kate, enraptured with "Deadwood Dick, or The Game of Gold" a western melodrama. While the other members of her family booed and hissed at the villain, cheering on the hero and heroine, Kate slid down in her chair and pretended to be asleep. When it was finally finished, they applauded loudly. Sue poked Kate in the ribs, hinting for her to join in.

Offering a feeble pat of one hand into the other, the teenager yawned and slowly stood. "Darn. It's over. Guess we'd better head back to the motel," she said hopefully.

"The evening's young," her father answered with an annoying smile. "Let's wander around a bit. Savor the atmosphere."

"Savor the what?" Kate asked, suddenly alarmed. Now what did she have to endure? Perturbed, she sulkily followed her family out of the theatre into the crisp, summer air. She lingered behind as everyone else peered into the windows of the tourist shops. A deep masculine voice broke the silence, startling her.

"Why the frown, little lady?" a tall man in a black felt hat drawled.

Glancing up at the slender cowboy, Kate smiled, grateful for the diversion. He wasn't bad. The hat had seen better days, but there were definite possibilities here.

"All of our guests are guaranteed a good time," he said, returning her smile. "Rules of West Yellowstone."

"I see," she said, intrigued. "And just what is your definition of a good time?" She nearly laughed at the expression on his face. He seemed flustered, embarrassed.

"Well now, let me do some thinkin' on that," he finally said. "In the meantime, how about a grand tour of our fair city?" He removed his hat to bow.

Before she could answer, her mother had moved up from behind, firmly placing an arm around her shoulders.

"Sorry, she's with us, and she's only sixteen," Sue curtly informed the would-be-Romeo.

Embarrassed, Kate pulled away from her mother. Whirling around, she hurried to catch up with the rest of the family. Sue watched her leave, frustration turning into despair.

"Ma'am?"

Sue glared at the cowboy.

"I'm sorry about this. I thought . . . I mean . . . she looks older. I'd've guessed nineteen or twenty." He shifted uncomfortably from one foot to the other. "Maybe it's none of my business, but she seems bent on findin' trouble. Again, I'm truly sorry." He replaced his hat, turned, and walked away.

Disheartened, Sue knew the man was right. "Kate, what am I going to do with you?" she moaned. Forcing herself to follow the rest of the family, she fought to control the explosion churning within.

Later, when their children were all in bed, Sue cried into her pillow. Greg reached for her, pulling her close.

"It's all right," he soothed, stroking her soft hair.

"Oh, Greg, what are we going to do with Kate?" she asked in a choked voice.

"Love her. Be there for her. It's all we can do at this point."

"I've gone over it in my mind . . . I've tried to figure out where I went wrong. What I could've done better . . . "

Greg shook his head. "Sue, you can't blame yourself. You've been a wonderful mother to that girl."

"Then why . . ."

"Sometimes there aren't answers . . . and we're not the only parents who've been through this. There are others . . . righteous couples who have tried to teach rebellious children. Look at Lehi and Sariah."

"Don't cheer me up. I couldn't stand it if Kate turned out to be a Laman or a Lemuel. Why couldn't I have had all Nephis and Sams?"

"I don't know. I don't know why it has to be so hard sometimes." He rolled over onto his back and gently pulled Sue down until her head was resting on his chest. Wrapping a comforting arm around her, he tenderly kissed the top of her head.

"We named her after the wrong ancestor," Sue said quietly.

"What?"

"Her middle name. We named Kate after a distant grandmother of mine, Colleen Mahoney."

"Yeah, I remember. Why do you feel . . ."

"Think about it, Greg. Colleen was such a rock in the Church. She was one of the most courageous women in the Mahoney line. After her husband passed away at Winter Quarters, she drove a team of oxen across the plains, living through unbelievable hardships. And not once did she ever lose faith in the gospel!"

"Have you ever told Kate about her?"

Sue nodded. "I tried. She popped her gum the entire time. I don't think it had much of an impact on her."

"What did you mean when you said Kate was named after the wrong ancestor?"

Lifting her head, Sue gazed at her husband. "We should've named her after Colleen's rebellious daughter, Molly!"

"Now, Susan, you don't mean that."

"I do. Somewhere up there, Grandma Colleen is cringing over what her fourth great-granddaughter is doing with her name." She slowly sank back down into the comfort Greg offered. Tears threatened to start again. Turning, she buried her face against her husband.

As she silently wept, Greg made himself a promise. He'd talk to Kate tomorrow. They'd drive to see one of those bubbling hot springs, and if their daughter refused to listen, he'd pick her up and dip her hair in the water! Whatever it took to get her attention. No more Mr. Nice Guy! Kate had overstepped the boundaries for the last time. Tomorrow there would be a reckoning! One thing was for certain, he wouldn't let Kate break Sue's heart again. He'd never seen his feisty wife like this. Oh, he'd seen her fret and worry over illnesses, minor surgeries, broken bones . . . but a fierce determination had always taken over. She'd pulled them all through countless emergencies. Now, she was giving up. For the first time in her life, Susan Mahoney Erickson was admitting defeat. Well, someone was going to answer for that! Things would soon be put right. Smiling grimly, he reached for the box of tissue on the nightstand. Handing a wad of fluffiness to his wife, he patiently waited for her to regain control of herself. When she'd finally wiped at the last tear, she rested her head on his shoulder. Gently squeezing the woman he loved, Greg slipped into a fitful slumber. It wasn't long before Sue joined him in the world of abstract dreams.

Beyond the closed door, in the other bedroom, Tyler softly snored in the twin bed against the window. On the floor, Sabrina quietly slept in the sleeping bag, a plump, stuffed bear gripped under one arm. In the queen-size bed, Kate smiled, contentedly watching the movie she'd found on HBO. It really wasn't that bad, but was definitely one her parents wouldn't approve of. It didn't bother Kate. She was old enough to make her own decisions. Old enough to live her own life.

Linda said it was normal for parents to condemn teenagers. "They never try to understand us, so why should we try to understand them?" she had added, assuring Kate it had been the same when Sue Erickson had been younger. Somehow, Kate had a difficult time imagining her mother as a teenager. "I don't think Mom ever was our age," Kate had complained. "And if she was, she never did anything wrong."

"You'd be surprised," Linda had argued. "She just doesn't want you to know about the mistakes she made. She wants you to think she's always been perfect so you'll follow in her footsteps. I don't have that problem with Marie." Marie was Linda's mother. "Marie and I have this understanding. She lives her life and I live mine."

"Marie doesn't care about the drinking . . . or the parties or the . . ."

"Nope. And I don't have a curfew, either, like some people I could mention," Linda had stressed, gazing at Kate. "Let's face it, your mother runs your life."

That was when Kate had started leaving work early to hang around with Jace. To show Linda that Sue Erickson didn't always have the final word.

She glanced at her watch and stifled a yawn. It was late, but she was determined to finish this movie. Concentrating on the fast-moving plot, she struggled to stay awake.

CHAPTER FIVE

E arly the next morning, the Ericksons left West Yellowstone to explore the park. They gazed in silence at the blackened remains of the once great forest.

"What a waste," Kate commented, her eyes widening with dismayed surprise. She hadn't been to the park in years. She'd heard about the fire and the damage it had done, but it hadn't affected her at the time. Seeing it for herself made a difference.

"It's nature's method of purification," Greg tried to explain. "Sometimes it's the only way the forest can rid itself of harmful invasions."

"But to just stand there and let all of this burn . . ." Kate's voice faltered as she realized the extent of the damage.

"They stepped in when it started getting out of hand."

"But by then, it was too late," Kate accused.

"Look around, honey. See all of the new growth? It wasn't there before. Now there's plenty of feed for the animals who live here."

"Speaking of which, Dad, get a load of that bull moose," Tyler exclaimed.

"Your kindred spirit," Kate sniffed.

Tyler ignored his sister and reached for his camera. "Can you pull over for a second? I'd love to get this guy on film."

"Sure, Ty," Greg replied, gently easing into park. He didn't want Kate to accuse him of being lead-footed again. Smiling as his son bounced out of the car with camera in hand, he felt a stirring of pride. Tyler was a good kid. Respectful, eager to please. The way Kate had been years ago. His smile drooped into a frown as he recalled the way his oldest daughter had always rushed into his arms at the end of each day. Scooping her up, he'd teased and tickled, his heart bursting with love for the tiny green-eyed girl. The image of her beautiful mother.

Greg often wondered how the apple of his eye had transformed into the rebellious creature they now knew as Kate. What had happened to make her so skeptical and defiant? Sighing, he stole a glance in the rear view mirror. *Katie, where did you go?* he silently questioned, flinching at the sight of her wild hair. It was the latest style, according to his daughter.

"Thanks, Dad," Tyler said, panting as he pulled himself back up into the back seat. "Wait'll you see these pictures," he continued, setting the camera inside its carrying case.

"I can wait," Kate muttered.

Shifting into drive, Greg maneuvered the car back onto the road. It wasn't long before he slowed down again, turning off at a sign that announced they had reached the Mud Volcano Trail.

"Now why are we stopping?" Kate whined.

Greg pulled into a parking place and shut off the engine before answering. "We're here to look at some mud volcanoes," he announced as he took the keys out of the ignition.

"Cool," Tyler exclaimed. He reached for his camera and jumped out of the car.

"What's a mud tornado?" Sabrina asked, wrinkling her nose.

Sue smiled and turned to correct her youngest child. "That's mud volcano, dear."

"What is it?" the five-year-old persisted.

"Well, it's . . . a volcano made out of mud," Sue offered.

"Good answer, Mom," Kate sneered before sliding out of the car.

Sue turned away, but not before Greg had seen the pained expression on her face. Climbing down out of the Explorer, she slammed the door shut with such force that even Tyler raised his eyebrows. She gripped Sabrina's hand tightly in her own, and headed toward the wooden trails. Quietly shutting his own door, Tyler followed, nervously fingering the camera he'd hung around his neck.

Greg slipped down to the pavement and shut the door on his side of the car, watching as Sue, Sabrina, and Tyler started up the wooden path. His jaw tightened with the effort it was taking to control himself. The time had come for a father-daughter chat. As Kate passed by, he grabbed her arm. "Kate, we need to talk."

Kate pulled away from her father, stepping back to lean against the car. "So, talk," she said coldly, blowing at a piece of stray hair that had flipped down in front of her face.

Clenching his fists, Greg moved in front of her. He adjusted his glasses and gazed at his daughter. "Look, your mother is really trying. . ."

"You've noticed too," Kate smirked.

"That's enough of that," Greg warned. "We're all going through some changes right now," he continued. "In a couple of years, you'll be leaving home. Moving out into the world. As a parent, I can honestly say it's very hard to let go."

Kate folded her arms and stared down at the pavement. *Here we go again*, she thought. *Lecture number 687.*

"You have to understand what it's doing . . . to your mother especially. Believe it or not, it wasn't that long ago when she held you in her arms and rocked you to sleep night after night. Now, you're on the brink of womanhood. It's frightening how fast the years have slipped away." He paused to swat at a mosquito. "I know you think we're infringing on your space by enforcing rules, but we really do have your best interests at heart. The decisions you make now will affect the rest of your life." Aware that she was tuning him out, he decided to try a different tactic. "Soon, you'll be off on your own. It's only right that you want . . . need some independence . . . some time to figure out who you are."

Kate looked up, surprised her father would agree with what she had been trying to say all along.

"Hopefully, the choices you make will be based on the standards we've tried to teach you."

Remaining silent, Kate returned her gaze to the ground. She should've known. Her parents never changed. They were always trying to tell her what to do. They pretended to offer freedom, when in reality, they wanted to bind her with suffocating decrees.

"We only want what's best for you," he continued.

"Yeah, right," she said with a snort.

"What was that?" he asked.

"Nothing." Kate unfolded her arms to stick her hands in the back pockets of her tight jeans.

"Kate, I don't care how old you think you are, you will treat your mother and me with respect! We are still your parents. And if you ever sass your mother again like you've been doing this entire trip, I promise you'll be sorry!"

"Oh," she challenged. "I'm not a child anymore! You can't threaten me. And, you're right, I will be on my own in a couple of years, and it can't come soon enough to please me! Then you'll see! I'll do what I want, when I want, and you can't do anything about it!"

"Is that right?" he asked, his face reddening with fury.

"Yeah! That's right!"

"Kate, I'm warning you, straighten up or . . ."

"Or what?" she retorted.

"Or this," he growled, grabbing her firmly, bending her across his leg.

"Dad!" she protested. A large hand came down hard across her bottom. She gasped with embarrassed rage, wincing at the sharp, throbbing pain. Expecting more blows, she was surprised when he shoved her away. Shakily reaching for the car, she refused to look at him.

"Now, you just remember that, young lady, the next time you decide to smart off! I've lost count of the nights your mother has cried herself to sleep because of you! No more. Do you understand me, girl? No more!"

Unwilling to subject herself to further humiliation, she quietly nodded, wiping angrily at the tears spilling down her face.

Greg whirled around and stomped away. By the time he reached the boardwalk, his heart rate had slowed, the anger fading into regret. As he climbed up the trail, he paused to glance back at Kate. The teenager had sunk to her knees, her face buried in her hands. "What have I done?" he softly asked. He could count on one hand the number of times he'd actually struck his daughter. It was tempting to go to her, to apologize for what he'd done. But he sensed it would be better to give her some time alone first. Maybe after they'd both had time to cool down, they could talk things over. Reach some form of a compromise. His broad shoulders sagged as he slowly walked up the trail.

He caught up with Sue near the Black Dragon's Cauldron. Moving to her side, he gazed at the bubbling black ooze.

"It went that well, huh?" she asked.

"I think I made things worse."

"Oh, c'mon." She slipped her hand through his arm.

"I spanked her," he admitted, staring at the explosive spring as it erupted.

"You what?" Sue drew back to stare at her husband.

"It was just one little swat on the behind," he said sheepishly.

"Oh, Greg. She's sixteen years old. She must be so humiliated."

"I'm sorry, okay? She said . . . and then I . . ."

"You don't need to explain," she replied, squeezing his arm. "I've been tempted myself lately, only she's as tall as I am now."

"I wish I could take it back. But she made me so angry. . .with her defiant nose sticking in the air, telling me what she is and isn't going to do with her life. All of a sudden something snapped. I bent her over my leg and . . . oh, Sue . . . what have I done?"

"Something that should've been done before now. Maybe we've been too lenient with her. She never needed much discipline when she was younger. Then the teenage years hit, and I don't think either one of us knew how to handle her. The groundings haven't fazed her. She's laughed at the restrictions we've threatened her with. We've tried everything, Greg. I've held my tongue so much I think I've bitten a hole through the middle."

Greg smiled at her feeble attempt at humor. "Where are the other two?"

"Over by Sour Lake. Tyler wanted a few more pictures."

"I hope he brought enough film for this trip. At this rate, he'll be going through a roll a day."

"At least it's a good, clean hobby," Sue pointed out. Sighing, she thought of the interests Kate had at the moment. An involuntary shudder went through her.

"Cold?" Greg asked.

"No. But I'd better go down and check on our daughter."

"Yeah, I doubt she'll want anything to do with me for a while," he said ruefully. "Besides, despite the grief and anxiety she's caused us . . ."

"Not to mention all of this gray hair we both seem to be sprouting lately," she added.

"Sad, but true." He offered a tiny smile. "Anyway, despite all of that, we'd probably miss her if someone decided to haul her off."

"Greg Erickson, that's not even funny! It does happen, you know." A worried frown replaced her smile as she pictured strange men abducting their daughter.

"Quit worrying. If anyone did kidnap her, they'd probably offer us money to take her back."

"Greg!"

"Sorry. I didn't mean it."

"I know," Sue said, starting back down the trail.

"Don't you want to make the loop?" Greg called after her.

"No. I think it'll be quicker heading back the way we came up."

"Okay. The rest of us will be down shortly," he promised, turning to gaze at the turbulent spring.

Sue increased her speed, knowing she wouldn't relax until Kate was in sight. As she impatiently moved around the people who were climbing up, she had the sensation of going the wrong way on a one-way street. A quick glance at her watch confirmed that Kate had been alone for nearly thirty minutes. She was relieved when she finally reached the bottom of the trail. She looked around, but Kate was nowhere to be seen.

She stepped down off the boardwalk and approached the car, hoping her daughter was inside. One quick look shot holes in that theory. There was no sign of Kate anywhere. Whirling around, she gazed in every direction. Where was her daughter? She took a deep breath and struggled to control the panic that was settling in. "Kate!" she called loudly. "Kate Erickson!" A curious couple stared at her. She wanted to scream at them. Instead, she walked past and stared down the road that led away from the parking lot. "Kate?"

"Sue?"

Sue spun around. Greg was coming down the trail with Tyler and Sabrina. A faint hope flickered into existence. Maybe Kate had gone up the other way. Maybe she was making the loop backwards. That girl would do anything to be different or difficult! Racing to the boardwalk, she gazed up at her husband. "Did you pass Kate on the trail?"

"No," Greg replied, suddenly looking worried. "Isn't she down here?"

"No!" Sue answered, her eyes filling with tears. "Oh, Greg, what are we going to do?"

Instructing Tyler to take hold of Sabrina's hand, Greg jumped down off the boardwalk. "Don't panic, she'll turn up," he said with false heartiness. "She's not in the car?" he asked, stalling for time to think.

Shaking her head, Sue stared at Greg. Their other children were watching closely. It was the only thing holding her together. They couldn't frighten Tyler and Sabrina.

Greg snapped his fingers and pointed to the rest rooms. "Did you check those out?" he asked.

Sue shook her head again. Why hadn't she thought to search there? "I'll go look," she said with a forced smile. She hurried across the pavement toward the set of rest rooms up near the Mud Geyser, a geyser that hadn't erupted since 1871. Realizing she was about to explode herself, she wondered how the muddy geyser kept its composure, content to offer only an occasional blurp.

She entered the cramped facility and gazed intently at the strange faces staring in her direction. Just then, a familiar head of hair moved out of one of the tiny stalls. "Kate?"

Kate glared at her mother. Now what? Moving to the sink, she quickly washed her hands, anxious to leave before her mother caused another scene. She'd been humiliated enough for one day. She hurried to the door and stepped out into the bright sunlight. Raising a hand to protect her reddened, puffy eyes, she began walking away.

"Kate?" her mother called, the tone of her voice demanding a response.

"What?" Kate snapped. Then, realizing her father might object to the sharp retort, she struggled to sound more pleasant. "What is it now?"

Sue moved close to her daughter, fighting the urge to embrace her, sure that Kate would object. Instead, she gazed tenderly at the teenager and reached out to smooth back a stray piece of stiff auburn hair. "Are you all right?" she quietly asked.

Kate shifted her gaze to the ground, certain her parents had discussed the incident that had taken place.

"Your father didn't mean . . . he is so sorry about . . ." she paused, searching for a way to explain the spanking. "I hurried back when he told me what had happened. I wanted to see if you were all right. Then I couldn't find you. We were so worried. I was afraid something had happened . . ."

Something had happened, Kate silently fumed, still seething from what her father had done. She would never forgive him. Never! And if Linda ever found out about it, she'd never hear the end of it. A spanking. At her age.

"Kate, we love you so much. Don't you know that?" Sue timidly caressed the side of her daughter's face.

Kate closed her eyes. She would not cry. Even though tears were stubbornly forming. Even though she longed for the freedom to rush into her mother's arms. She steeled herself against the emotions that threatened to betray and turned from her mother's soft touch. The love offered by her parents demanded a price she wasn't willing to pay.

This love they spoke of, it hinged on whether or not she would bend to their will. If they loved her so much, why were they always trying to change her? Maybe Jace and Linda were right. Her parents didn't really care about anything but the shame she might cause them if she didn't toe the line. They couldn't love her for who she was.

She walked away, ignoring the pained look she was getting from her mother. Sue slowly followed, glancing up at Greg. He shrugged and motioned to the car. Soon they were all inside, heading down the road that would lead them around Yellowstone Lake.

They kept going until they reached the turnoff near Old Faithful. Racing to the edge of the observation border, they barely made it in time to see the geyser erupt. Sabrina giggled and pointed as the foaming white water rose higher and higher. Tyler eagerly gripped his camera. Kate wandered off, her back to the geyser, her eyes focused on the ground. Greg glanced at Sue, then at their teenage daughter. He removed his glasses and wiped them on his shirt to dry the water spots the geyser had shot in his direction. Taking a deep breath, he replaced the glasses and walked to where his daughter stood sulking.

"Kate," he said, trying to be heard above the gushing geyser.

Refusing to look up, she merely shrugged.

"Kate, I'm sorry. I shouldn't have . . . done that. I lost my temper. I'm not proud of what I did, and I'm not making excuses for myself, but, honey, you've got to learn to show us a little respect! Your mother and I are human. We have feelings that can be hurt, the same as you. We struggle with emotions just like everyone else. We try to keep a handle on things, but we do have our limitations."

He gently lifted her face until their eyes met. "I'm asking you to forgive me, sweetheart," he said somberly. "I never meant to hurt or embarrass you."

Kate glanced at the geyser. It was slowly settling into wisps of white steam.

"I'd like all of us to enjoy this trip, including you. So, how about we call a truce, okay?"

Kate didn't trust herself to speak. Fearing anger would control her words, she merely nodded.

Relieved, Greg hugged her, leaning to kiss the top of her head. "That's my girl," he said brightly, beaming at the rest of the family as they approached. "Let's go have some lunch!" Together, they moved toward the lodge.

CHAPTER SIX

They spent the night in a small cabin in Colter Bay, near Jackson Lake. Just before sunset, Kate wandered down to the lake, staring out at the blue-gray water. This trip was not going as she had planned. Her pride was still smarting from what her father had done. She was as miserable as she was making everyone else. It was time for another plan of action.

Something bobbed in the water nearby. Curious, she pushed at it with her foot. The piece of floating driftwood sank beneath the water. It stubbornly bobbed to the surface, filling Kate with a strange sense of delight. She tried it again with the same results. She knew that no matter how many times the driftwood was held under, it would always break free to the surface. Kneeling, she picked up the soggy piece of wood, her hands caressing its weathered shape. She stood, took a step back and threw it out into the lake. "Stay free," she whispered. "I'll do the same," she promised in a hushed voice.

The driftwood had inspired, had given her a new way of thinking. *Drift with the tide.* That would be her new motto. *Go with the flow.* Let her parents think she was the daughter they'd always wanted. Her time was coming. Soon, she'd be free of all of this. Smiling, she watched as the sun set behind the mountains.

After a quick breakfast at the Jackson Lake Lodge, the Ericksons were on the road by nine-thirty the next morning. They drove around the southern tip of Jackson Lake, then turned off at the North Jenny Lake Junction. Following the scenic one-way road along the beautiful blue water, they took a vote and decided on a boat ride across the lake. Greg parked near the dock at the southeastern tip of Jenny Lake, then hurried down to make the arrangements.

A few minutes later he returned, grinning with excitement. "The next boat pulls out in ten minutes," he said cheerfully. "Let's go. We have to put life jackets on before they'll let us climb aboard."

"C'mon, Breeny, I'll race you down there," Tyler challenged, purposely slowing his gait so his younger sister could keep up with him. Greg followed behind, chuckling as Sabrina beat Tyler to the tiny shack beside the boat dock. Sue lingered to walk down with Kate.

"So, what do you think about this?" Sue asked.

"The boat ride? It's a . . . great idea," Kate responded.

Glancing at the teenager, Sue was relieved to see the smile. But the frosty look in her daughter's eyes filled her with dread. Confused, she wondered what the teenager was up to.

Kate continued to smile, determined to keep this up for as long as possible. She'd bide her time, pretending to enjoy this farce of a vacation. Soon it would be over. Soon, she could be herself. The thought filled her with such pleasure, she nearly laughed out loud.

Greg helped Tyler fasten on an orange life jacket while Sue assisted Sabrina. Kate slipped hers on without a fuss, causing both parents to blink with surprise. Tyler climbed into the boat and nearly fell in the lake when the boat unexpectedly shifted. Kate steadied him from behind. He turned to help her down into the boat, and stared at his big sister. Kate hadn't helped him with anything in years. Startled by her smile, he timidly offered one in return. Blushing, he moved to sit against the opposite side of the boat. Kate grinned. This was fun.

The engine purred to life, causing Sabrina to squeal with delight. Soon the boat began cutting across the water, gently spraying the passengers with tiny beads of moisture. Kate good-naturedly wiped at her face. Sue nudged Greg. What was going on with their daughter? Normally, the girl would've cussed a blue streak. Instead, the teenager laughed, sliding a protective arm around her younger sister.

"Maybe setting her straight yesterday wasn't such a bad idea," Greg said in a low voice. "I think we've got our daughter back."

"I don't like it, Greg," Sue replied.

"What's not to like?" he asked, puzzled.

"Her eyes. They're cold . . . distant."

"Relax. Let's enjoy this while it lasts," he encouraged.

As Sue nodded, pretending to agree, she made herself a promise. She'd keep an extra close eye on Kate. Something wasn't right. Her mother's intuition was sending out a sharp alarm. Relaxation was out of the question.

It didn't take long for the boat to reach the opposite side of the lake. The engine was cut as it slowly pulled up to a wooden platform. One by one, the passengers disembarked, moving up out of the boat. Another group was waiting for a ride to the other side.

"Now what, Dad?" Tyler asked, gazing at a trail that led uphill.

"Well, we can either wait here for the next boat, or we can use the time to climb up to Inspiration Point. I hear it offers a wonderful view of the Tetons."

"Let's go," Tyler said, eagerly starting up the trail. His camera swung wildly from the strap around his neck.

"What about you three?" Greg asked, glancing at Sue.

"Oh, let's play mountain goat, just for kicks and giggles. It'll be great!" Kate said brightly.

Raising an eyebrow, Sue stared hard at Kate. Her teenage daughter batted her eyes and continued to smile. Sue shifted her gaze to Sabrina. "Do you want to walk up this trail?" she asked the five-year-old.

"Uh-huh," Sabrina said, her blue eyes darting around with excitement.

"How far is it to Inspiration Point?" Sue asked, wondering if their youngest child would be up to the hike.

"Oh, only a mile or two I think," Greg answered. "It might be a little steep, but I could always carry her on my shoulders if she gets tired."

"No, thanks, Dad, I can walk," Kate teased, starting up the trail.

Greg chuckled as he gripped Sabrina's hand in his own, moving to follow Kate.

Frowning, Sue brought up the rear. What kind of game was Kate playing? Not that she was complaining. It was great seeing the teenager in a good mood for a change. If it was a good mood. It had been so long since her daughter had actually smiled and meant it, it was hard to know how to react. She looked up and saw that the others were leaving her behind. Accelerating her pace, she hurried up the trail.

After hiking for nearly half a mile, Sabrina begged to stop. "Bears live up there," she insisted, glancing fearfully around at the forest.

"It's okay, Mom, I'll stay with her," Kate offered, her smile pleasant.

Sue's eyes narrowed. She didn't like this arrangement at all. Leaving Kate behind was one thing. Entrusting her with Sabrina was an entirely different ball game. As unpredictable as the teenager was, there was no telling what would happen. "I don't know, maybe I'd better . . ."

"C'mon, Sue, Sabrina will be all right with Kate. Let's go take a look at the Tetons," Greg said, grabbing his wife's hand.

"But . . . " Sue stammered as her husband dragged her up the trail. "Greg!" she protested.

Waiting until they couldn't be heard by either daughter, Greg finally stopped to answer. "Look, honey, Kate keeps hitting us with how we don't trust her."

"That's because we don't," Sue snapped, glancing back down the trail.

"Maybe if we'd start meeting her half-way, things would improve. If she feels that we do trust her, then maybe she'll start acting trustworthy."

"But, Greg, if anything happens to Sabrina . . ."

"What can happen?"

Giving him a look that could turn stone to jelly, Sue finally gave in. "All right. But let's hurry. I don't want to leave those two down there alone any longer than we have to."

Greg agreed, leaning down for a quick kiss before he dragged her up the rest of the trail.

Below, Kate walked back down the dusty path, hanging onto Sabrina's hand. She'd loved the horrified look on her mother's face. Humming to herself, she stopped when Sabrina tugged on her shirt. Annoyed, she glared down at her younger sister. *Careful,* she warned herself, *let's not blow it now.* "What is it, Breeny?"

"Why are you being nice to me?" the small blonde asked as she gazed up at Kate.

Flinching under the young girl's scrutiny, Kate hurriedly changed the subject. "Hey, look at those flowers."

Sabrina giggled and moved off the trail to explore. As she touched a colorful blossom, Kate pushed her away.

"Watch it! Bees are all over the place," Kate warned the five-year-old. A dull buzzing sounded near her ear. Waving her arms above her head to ward off the pesky intruder, Kate winced as a sharp prick pierced through her skin. She howled, slapping at her arm. She pulled a face and brushed the mangled bee from her right arm. "Da . . . ang it!" she said, barely controlling her language. Sabrina always told on her when she didn't. As a painful throbbing settled in, she silently went through every obscenity she knew.

"Are you okay?" Sabrina asked, her eyes wide with fear.

"No! Yes. Look, why don't you go play for a minute?" she snapped, pointing to the other side of the trail.

Sabrina skipped off to investigate some bushes while Kate moved to sit under a tree, away from the flower patch. She inspected the red welt raising on her upper arm. "Just what I needed," she muttered.

"Kate, I found some berries," Sabrina sang out.

"Good," Kate replied, gritting her teeth. She wondered if her parents had thought to bring along the first aid kit. She pulled a face, sure it was sitting across the lake in the Explorer.

Nearly seventeen minutes went by. The pain was so intense Kate had closed her eyes to shut it out. It didn't work. She could still feel an intense burning each time the blood pulsed through her arm. For once, she was glad when she finally heard her mother's voice.

"Kate, Sabrina?"

Slowly rising to her feet, Kate gripped her wounded arm. "Mom . . ." she started as Sabrina ran out onto the trail.

"Sabrina! What have you been eating?" Sue demanded, staring at her daughter's purple mouth.

"Berries," Sabrina replied. "Kate said I could eat 'em."

"I . . . what?" Kate asked, glaring at her younger sister. "I did not!"

"I told Kate I found berries and she said 'good,'" Sabrina insisted, bursting into tears.

"Honey, it's all right," Sue soothed as she gathered the young girl into her arms. She gave Sabrina a big hug, then gently eased back to gaze at her small daughter. "Show Mommy and Daddy the berries you were eating," she said, trying to keep the panic she felt out of her voice.

"There," Sabrina pointed. Gripping her mother's hand, she pulled her down off the trail. Greg followed, his face a combination of rage and concern.

"Smooth!" Tyler said, glaring at Kate.

"It wasn't my fault!"

"Yeah, right! Dad said they'd left Breeny with you. Way to watch her!"

"I did," Kate said, fighting tears. She'd sacrificed herself to keep Sabrina from being stung. But did anybody care? No!

"You sat under a tree snoozing while Sabrina ate berries that could be poisonous, for all we know!" Tyler continued, looking angrier than Kate had ever seen him before. She knew how fond he was of their little sister, but it still hurt to realize he cared more about Sabrina than her. Well, fine! It was obvious everyone else felt the same way! Storming off, she ran down the rest of the trail.

Greg chuckled as he swung Sabrina up onto his shoulders.

"You're sure they're huckleberries?" Sue asked doubtfully.

"Positive," Greg replied as he popped another one into his mouth. "Want one?" he offered.

"No, thanks!" Sue said stiffly.

"Oh, c'mon, Sue, it turned out all right. Sabrina's fine."

"This time," she returned, glaring at her husband.

"Let it go, honey," Greg warned. "Kate didn't mean any harm."

As they walked back to the trail, Sue glanced around. "Tyler, where's Kate?"

"Is Sabrina okay?" Tyler asked.

"She'll be fine," Greg answered. "They were huckleberries. Here, try one," he said, throwing a purple berry to his son.

Grinning with relief, Tyler caught it, throwing it into his mouth. "Mmmmmm. No wonder Breeny went down on these."

"Tyler, where's Kate?" Sue repeated.

"Oh, she got into one of her snits and ran down to the boat," he replied.

"Kate was screamin'," Sabrina informed them.

"What?" Sue asked, raising an eyebrow. Had they been concerned about the wrong daughter? Come to think of it, Kate had looked a little pale. "Why, Sabrina? Why did Kate scream?" she probed, glancing up at the five-year-old perched high on her father's shoulders.

"I dunno. I was pickin' flowers. Kate pushed me. She said there were bees. Then she screamed. She said bad words. She didn't think I heard her, but I did."

Sue looked down toward the wooden platform. Someone was helping Kate into a boat that had just arrived. A piercing shriek shattered the air. Helplessly she watched as her oldest daughter fell into the lake. Saying a few bad words herself, Sue ran down the rest of the trail. Kate didn't know how to swim.

By the time she reached the platform, someone had already fished her sputtering daughter out of the water. A soggy Kate shivered as they helped her into the boat. Sue quickly moved to her daughter's side. "Kate, are you okay?" she asked as someone handed her a blanket.

"Wwhat ddo yyou ththink?" Kate retorted, her teeth chattering violently.

Ignoring Kate's furious glare, Sue wrapped the blanket around her daughter. "How did this happen?" she asked, not caring who answered.

"I'm not sure, ma'am," a masculine voice admitted. "I reached to help her into the boat and when I gripped her arm, she screamed bloody murder. I let go and she fell in. I'm real sorry about this," he added, smiling ruefully. "This gentleman here helped me scoop her out of the water."

"Thank you," Sue said quietly. Pulling back one corner of the blanket, she gazed with dismay at the swollen welt on Kate's arm.

"Why didn't you say anything about this earlier?"

"N-none of y-you c-cared. Y-you w-were too b-busy blam-m-ming m-me," Kate stammered, sitting on a wooden bench.

"I'm sorry, honey. We had no way of knowing."

Kate sneezed in response.

"We'd best get her to the other side," the captain of the boat suggested. "Everyone hurry aboard that's goin' to the dock. We're pullin' out of here as soon as I fire this little lady up."

"W-what?" Kate chattered.

"He means the boat," Sue said as she sat next to the shivering teen. Putting both arms around Kate, she pulled her daughter close. She'd learned in a Relief Society emergency preparedness workshop that shared body heat could prevent hypothermia.

"W-what ar-r-re y-you d-doing?"

"Trying to keep you from turning into an icicle. Now quit wiggling before you fall into the lake again," she warned.

"Wow, what a dive," Tyler said as he stepped down into the boat. "I give her a 9.6!" One stern look from his mother silenced him immediately. He moved to the back of the boat to sit next to his father and Sabrina.

Sue shivered as Kate's cold, clammy face pressed against her chest. A glowing warmth surged inside. Despite everything, she loved this girl dearly. Kate was a part of her, whether the teenager was willing to admit it or not. Leaning down, she softly kissed the wet head. She wasn't sure, but almost sensed the warm tears streaming from her daughter's eyes. "It's okay, Kate," she soothed. "We'll get you out of these wet things. Then we'll do something about the bee sting," she promised.

Several minutes later, the boat pulled up to the shore. Sue guided Kate to a tiny shack near the dock and asked the tanned blonde behind the counter if there was a place where Kate could change. The young woman nodded and quickly led them into a tiny supply room in the shack.

Greg hurried to the car, Sue's instructions ringing in his ears. "Find the first aid kit. Bring it down with Kate's suitcase. Grab the makeup bag." It didn't take him long to return to the dock with the requested items. He handed them to the blonde behind the counter, concluding it would be best to remain on the dock with Tyler and Sabrina.

Twenty minutes later, Sue led Kate out of the supply room. Aside from the wet hair, the teenager looked her normal self, which included the stubborn glare she shared with everyone.

"Well," Greg said, slapping his hands together, "I guess we're off again. Where to now?"

"Let's just head into Jackson. Kate could still use a shower," Sue said, giving Tyler a warning glance. Clamping his mouth shut, Tyler marveled at his mother's perception. It had been such a good zinger, too. "And I think we could all use some freshening up before we have lunch," she added.

"You mean we're not stopping at the fish hatchery?" Tyler complained, disappointed.

"Afraid not, Ty," Greg answered. "Tell you what, though, while these women-folk get the shopping bug out of their system this afternoon, you and I could mosey on up for a peek at it later."

"Deal!" Tyler said excitedly.

"Me too," Sabrina insisted. "I want to see the fish butchery."

"That's hatchery, Breeny," Tyler said. "It's where they raise fish."

"Oh," Sabrina replied, wrinkling her nose.

"Race you to the car," he challenged. Off they ran, leaving Kate alone with their parents.

"Quite a spill you took, young lady," Greg commented, reaching to pat his daughter's arm.

"I wouldn't do that, Greg," Sue warned as Kate quickly pulled away from him. "That arm is pretty sore."

Puzzled, Greg glanced at his wife for an explanation.

"She was stung by a bee," Sue informed him.

"Oh. I'm sorry, Kate," Greg apologized. "I didn't know. Let's see your arm."

Kate sulkily held it out for inspection.

"The stinger's still in there," he observed. "It'll have to come out."

"I know," Sue agreed as Kate paled considerably. "I wanted to wait until we reached Jackson. I didn't want to risk getting infection in it."

"Good idea," Greg said.

"Don't I have any say in this?" Kate grumbled, pulling her arm away from her father.

"It won't hurt, at least not much. I promise it'll feel better once the stinger's out. Then we'll fix you up with some calamine lotion. You'll be a new woman, you'll see," Greg assured her. He watched as Kate sullenly walked up toward the car. "Lost her newfound zest for living, hasn't she?"

"I told you it wasn't real."

"I know," Greg sighed. "I guess I was hoping she'd finally had a change of heart."

"That'll be the day," Sue sighed.

"It'll happen," he promised as he slipped an arm around his wife's waist. "It may not be in our lifetime, but it'll happen."

"And in the meantime?"

"We endure to the end," he answered, giving his wife a quick squeeze.

CHAPTER SEVEN

Despite what Kate thought, the removal of the stinger was not a dramatic event. True, the teenager squealed as though she had just given birth, which prompted Tyler to donate one of his socks to the cause. Sue appreciated the thought, but declined to wedge it in her daughter's mouth. Instead, she forced Kate to sit still while Greg triumphantly performed this most delicate of operations using Sue's eyebrow tweezers. He finally held the tiny culprit out for all to see, relieved it was over. Kate moaned pitifully, sure her arm would never be the same. Sue was convinced her ears were in a similar condition. After applying ample doses of sympathy and calamine lotion, they left their rooms at the Parkway Inn and headed over to Mountain High Pizza Pie for lunch.

They consumed two medium-sized pizzas, heaped with extra toppings, then decided to split up for the day. Greg drove Tyler and Sabrina out to see the fish hatchery, while Sue dragged Kate around Jackson.

Sue thoroughly enjoyed poking around in the small shops, mistakenly assuming Kate was enjoying it too. The expression on her daughter's face revealed the error of this line of thinking. Sue decided to cut the tour short, and led Kate to the park in the center of the town.

"What's this?" Kate asked.

"This park? I think it's called the Town Square," Sue replied, relieved that her daughter was finally showing an interest in things.

"Not the park, this," Kate persisted, pointing to a strange-looking arch.

Sue gazed at the arch. "Oh. That. It's a decorative arch made out of elk horns."

"Gross!"

"It isn't either."

"It is too! What did they do, shave the elk?"

"Hardly," Sue replied. "They gathered the horns when they fell off."

"Their horns fall off?"

"Yes. Every winter," Sue said, wondering how her daughter had managed to remain so naive concerning these matters. Bozeman, Montana, wasn't exactly downtown New York City. Surely Kate had picked up a few tidbits about the wildlife in their area. She seemed to be such an expert on the other kind of wild life that was available.

"Well, why do they fall off? How are the elk supposed to defend themselves? Why . . ."

"They grow new horns in the spring," Sue answered.

"Oh." Kate shrugged and walked off, no longer interested. Sue caught up with her and pointed out a nearby art gallery. Kate reluctantly agreed, trudging along beside her mother as they crossed the street.

They wandered through the gallery, Sue lingering over several water-color landscapes that had caught her eye. Kate stood beside Sue, sighing on a regular basis to indicate her displeasure. Giving up, Sue was about to suggest that they leave when Kate suddenly seemed captivated by a painting of an Indian warrior. Sue smiled, thinking her daughter had finally discovered the world of art.

The curator noticed how entranced the teenager was with the painting and walked over to admire it with her. "It's one of my favorites too," the older woman confided to Kate, pleased that a young person would show so much interest in culture. She pointed out the feathered brush strokes, the highlighting the artist had used to capture the vivid emotions that were so apparent. Sue moved close to get in on what promised to be an educational moment. The curator smiled at her, then turning, asked Kate what she liked about the painting.

Kate grinned and pointed to the Indian warrior. "Nice buns," she said proudly, continuing to stare at the warrior's revealing loin cloth.

Sue could've died right on the spot. The curator looked like she'd swallowed her dentures. Blinking rapidly, she turned an interesting shade of red and disappeared. Blushing herself, Sue hurriedly dragged her daughter out of the gallery.

Sue decided to let the incident pass, hoping to salvage the afternoon. She didn't want to fight with Kate. Instead, she led her daughter down the street toward one of her favorite retreats. A bookstore.

"I love this place," Sue commented, gazing around at the crowded shelves.

"Are we about done?" Kate snapped.

"I suppose," Sue sighed. "Are you sure you don't want anything?"

Kate shook her head and wandered out of the store. Sue gathered up the selections she had made and walked to where a cashier stood waiting. She set the books on the counter and began looking through a colorful display of paperbacks. She selected one and flipped through the pages. "Would you recommend this for a teenager?" she asked, searching for the author's name.

"Yes, I would. It'll snag their attention from the beginning. They won't want to put it down."

"I see," Sue murmured. "It's a mystery, right?"

"Yes. And it has a touch of romance. I nearly cried when the girl experienced her very first . . ."

Sue glanced up sharply.

". . . kiss," the woman continued.

"Does it go any further than that?" Sue asked, flushing.

Somewhat amused, the clerk shook her head. "I'd let my own daughter read it," she quietly confided.

Sue added it to the pile and opened her purse.

"That'll be $25.45, please."

Sue held out two twenties and smiled shyly at the clerk. She knew the woman had enjoyed her embarrassment, but these days, you couldn't be too careful. Books could be deceiving. She'd bought a few herself that had looked harmless. Which gave credibility to the wisdom about not judging a book by its cover. Something Kate always threw in her face whenever they had discussions concerning certain friends who looked like they were visiting from another planet.

When she walked out of the bookstore, Sue glanced around for Kate. She didn't have to look far. Her daughter was sitting on a wooden bench just down the boardwalk. As she approached, she could see that Kate didn't look well at all. "What's up?" she asked, quickly sitting beside the girl.

Kate remained silent, massaging the sides of her head.

"What's wrong?"

"Guess," Kate said sharply, continuing to rub at her temples.

"Headache?"

Too miserable to offer the usual sarcastic reply, Kate nodded.

"Why didn't you say anything earlier?"

"I was trying not to be a wimp!"

"Kate . . ."

"You all thought I was such a baby when Dad pulled that rotten stinger out . . ."

"Kate, I'm sorry. I know it hurt. But, sometimes you just have to . . ."

"Be a man?" Kate winced as the pain grew sharper.

"Here," Sue said, reaching into her purse. Pulling out a white plastic bottle, she emptied two tablets into her hand. "Swallow these," she said, placing them in Kate's hand.

"With what?" Kate whined.

"You really need something to drink?"

"What am I supposed to do? Use spit?"

Sue gave her daughter a very pained look and slid off the bench. "Wait here. I'll see what I can find." She hurried down the street toward a tiny drug store. A few minutes later, she returned, carrying a paper cup. "Here," she said, handing it to Kate.

"What is it?" Kate asked as she peered into the bubbling cup.

"Root beer."

"Root beer? Yuck!"

"It was that or orange. I chose the lesser of two evils," Sue explained, knowing her daughter hated both flavors.

"Whatever," Kate moaned, sipping just enough liquid to wash

down the rounded tablets. "Here," she said, handing her mother the cup.

Sue rolled her eyes. Her daughter was such a brave little soldier. She hurriedly drank the rest of the root beer, then walked to a nearby trash can to throw the cup away. "C'mon, let's get you back to the motel," she said, returning to the bench. She helped Kate to her feet, then retrieved her daughter's purse. Together they made their way down the street.

CHAPTER EIGHT

That night, the Ericksons headed north of Jackson. Greg had assured his family they were about to experience some of the finest food and entertainment the area had to offer. "You guys will love this," he said brightly, turning at a sign that announced they had reached the Bar-J Chuckwagon Village.

"You said we were going to eat at Vista Grande," Kate whined in the back seat. "That's all we heard, all the way to Jackson, how wonderful Vista Grande is. Now we'll never know!"

Greg forced himself to look in the rear view mirror. "We can eat Mexican food anytime," he said with a smile. "This is something different. It's dinner and a show. The guide up at the fish hatchery said tourists flock here in droves."

"He said we'll get to see a gun handler!" Tyler added, gripping his camera. "It'll be great, you'll see."

"Yeah, I can hardly wait," Kate returned.

Greg carefully eased into a parking place between a Chevy truck and a tan station wagon. Removing the keys from the ignition, he then turned to gaze at his children. "We need to make some decisions. They offer chicken or barbecued beef. What does everyone want?"

"Barbecued beef!" Tyler said, slipping out of the car.

"Barbie Q beef?" Sabrina asked, wrinkling her nose. "Why did they cook Barbie?"

"They didn't, honey," Sue said, trying not to smile. "It's

barbecued beef."

"Yeah, you know," Kate said, "cow meat. They butchered ol' Bossy the moo cow."

"Cow meat? They killed a moo cow?" Sabrina asked, her chin quivering.

"Why don't you just have the chicken?" Sue suggested, sending a dirty look in Kate's direction.

"'Kay," Sabrina said, bouncing out of the car.

"How about you, Katie?" Greg asked, purposely using the pet name she couldn't stand.

"Chicken, I guess," she mumbled, slipping down to the loose gravel of the parking lot.

"And you, beloved?" he asked, focusing on his wife.

"Barbecued beef," she sighed.

"Okay. That makes three barbecues and two chickens. Got it." Sliding down to the ground, he quickly locked his door. "Let's go, troops," he said, leading the way to the ticket booth.

"Where do we eat?" Kate asked, looking less than thrilled.

"See that pasture over there?" Tyler teased. "You'll enjoy supreme dining pleasure with the rest of the cows."

"Gee, Ty, thanks. I imagine you'll be quite comfortable with your fellow kind in the old out-house over there."

"Stop it, right now, both of you," Sue demanded, giving both of her children a fierce look.

Tyler sheepishly nodded, while Kate shrugged and moved ahead of her family.

After waiting in line for several minutes, the tickets were finally purchased and the Ericksons, with the exception once again of Kate, wandered around the Chuckwagon Village to explore. Kate sullenly leaned against a wooden pole and complained to anyone who cared to listen. "I can't believe he made us come out here at 6:30 if they don't even start serving anything until 7:30! Never mind the fact that we could be eating exquisite Mexican cuisine by now at Vista Grande. Oh, no! We have to come here and play cowboys and Indians!"

"Well, we do have a healthy selection of cowboys, but I'll have to admit we're fresh out of Indians."

Startled, Kate turned and stared at the grinning cowboy who

had moved up behind her. She guessed the attractive young man was somewhere between eighteen and twenty-one. "I . . . I didn't know anyone was standing there," she stammered.

"Just me. The professional gofer."

"Gopher?" she asked, picturing a tiny, buck-toothed animal.

"Gofer. I go for things; I run errands for everyone else," he explained. "My uncle cooks for the people who run this place. He got me this job for the summer."

"I see," Kate said, silently taking inventory. He had broad shoulders and a fairly nice build. Gorgeous blue eyes. And thick black hair stuffed under that tan cowboy hat. Not bad. Not bad at all.

"You don't seem too thrilled to be here," he observed, studying her face.

"That's the understatement of the year," she admitted. "This really isn't my scene," she added, frowning.

"And just what is your scene, if you don't mind me asking?"

"Well, it certainly isn't this," she replied dryly. "What did you say your name was?"

"I didn't." he slowly drawled.

"What?" she asked, annoyed by the way he was controlling the conversation.

"I didn't say," he answered with a grin, shoving a piece of straw between his teeth. "What's yours?"

"Kate."

"Kate," he said, mulling it over in his mind. "Nope. Doesn't have enough spunk in it. Why, with those green eyes and that red hair, I'll bet you're a regular little spit-fire."

"Red hair?" she sputtered angrily. "I don't have red hair! It's brown. Auburn."

"Nope, when the sun hits it just right, it shows your true colors, you little redhead, you."

Before she offer a rebuttal, a loud voice interrupted.

"Randy, get over here. What's keepin' you, boy?"

"Comin'," he hollered, pulling out the straw. "Duty calls." Whirling around, he walked off, ignoring the seething beauty behind him.

"Why, you egotistical clod . . . you . . ." Kate sputtered.

"Who was that?" Sue asked, moving beside her daughter,

disturbed by the way Kate stared at the young man as he walked away.

"Nobody!" Kate snapped. "Do we ever eat around this place?" she asked, changing the subject. As if in answer, someone began beating on a large metal triangle, the signal that dinner was about to begin. In response, a large crowd gathered at the building which boasted a 600-person capacity.

Several minutes later, as the Ericksons sat around the wooden table they'd been assigned in front of the stage, a man stepped up to the microphone. "Ladies and gentlemen," he boomed in a deep voice. "Welcome to the Bar-J." Thunderous applause echoed throughout the building. The man grinned. Holding a hand over his eyes, he peered out at the crowd. "Well, I'll be," he said, playing up to the audience. "I guess that son of mine was right. He counted five hundred and eighty-five head for tonight's feast." He waited until the delighted laughter died down before continuing. "Now, believe it or not, we'll have every one of you hungry hombres served up in twenty minutes." Loud cheers drowned out Kate's groan.

"As we call out the number of your table, quickly line up there at the back. And hold onto your plates, folks, 'cuz they'll be heaped high with some of our good ol' country vittles." Holding up a hand to calm the crowd, he somberly removed his hat. "First, a moment of silence for those of you who wish to offer thanks for what we're about to eat."

"What is this, Butch Cassidy gets religion?" Kate griped under her breath. She winced, quickly closing her own eyes when her mother jabbed her in the ribs with a well-placed finger.

True to the cowboy's word, everyone was served in twenty minutes. If Kate hadn't seen it for herself, she never would've believed it. It wouldn't have been so bad, if only Randy hadn't been there, handing out the foil-wrapped potatoes. Grinning at her as she stood, reluctantly holding out the metal plate, he had taken great delight in giving her the largest foil-wrapped potato he could find. "Eat hearty," he'd said, winking at her. Incensed by his cocky attitude, she would've told him a few things if only her family hadn't been standing there.

She stared at her plate, picked up the fork, and stabbed at her potato, pretending it was Randy.

Puzzled, Sue watched as Kate mutilated her potato. She wasn't sure what was going on between the young cowboy and Kate, but she didn't like it. The way he'd winked at her daughter, it was obvious the young man was quite smitten. The only thing that had calmed her was the look on Kate's face. Instead of the anticipated delight, fury had flashed from those expressive eyes, so like her own. Maybe her daughter was beginning to realize some men weren't desirable. She cut at the piece of beef on her own plate and silently prayed that was the case.

After the meal, an entertaining program was presented. The man who had welcomed the crowd turned out to be the owner of the ranch. He hammed it up with his three sons as they sang several country melodies, accompanying themselves with guitars, a fiddle, and a bass fiddle. The head cook came out to recite cowboy poetry. Kate rested her head on stiffly folded arms and refused to look at the stage.

Introducing one of the ranch hands as an expert gun handler, the owner quickly moved out of the way. Tyler eagerly snapped several pictures as the man twirled first one, then two fancy six-shooters. When he fired one into the air, Kate jumped, falling off the wooden bench. Tyler laughed so hard, he almost joined her on the floor. Kate sent him murderous look. Tyler ignored her and moved closer to the stage to take a picture of the owner and his sons when they came out to perform again.

The sons clowned around, posing for the shot. One of them leaned over to his dad, whispering in his ear.

"Say, folks, m'boy here has a request. He'd like to have his li'l ol' picture taken with the beautiful redhead here at this table."

Blushing, Sue vowed to get even with her son. Slowly rising, she was startled when two of the cowboys hopped off the stage to grab Kate. She tried not to laugh as they hauled her protesting daughter up front.

"Randy said you'd love this," one of the men whispered as they escorted Kate to the stage.

"Oh, he did, did he?" she replied. Just wait until she found Randy! Realizing there wasn't much she could do about it now, she forced a smile, baring her teeth at Tyler as he snapped several pictures. One of the men planted a wet kiss on her cheek for the final shot. Then, laughing good-naturedly, they helped her down off the stage.

"How about a round of applause for the li'l lady?" the deep voice boomed. The cowboys waited until the laughter and clapping died down, then began to harmonize on another country ballad.

Hazarding a glance in Kate's direction, Sue wasn't disappointed. Her daughter was furious. She slid close to whisper in Kate's ear. "Calm down. It was just for fun. I'm sure they didn't mean to embarrass you."

"I know," Kate quietly replied. "I'm not mad at them."

"And Tyler had no way of knowing they would . . ."

"I'm not mad at Tyler either," Kate said in a hushed voice.

"Then why do you look like you're on the verge of a stroke?"

"I'm okay, Mom. But, nature is calling. I think I'd better go find a rest room."

"There's one just around the corner," Sue whispered, pointing to the opened side door.

Kate stood and quickly headed in that direction. Sue watched until her daughter disappeared through the door. Greg laughed and nudged her, pointing to the stage. She relaxed against him and listened carefully to catch the next corny joke.

Outside, Kate angrily slapped at a wooden fence. "Ow!" she exclaimed, glancing down at her hand. Slivers! Great! Another session of tweezer-inflicted pain to look forward to. Squinting, she peered at the culprits. The sun had begun to set, making it difficult to see. Still, she could count at least five slivers.

"Quite the performance, spit-fire," a familiar voice drawled.

Whirling around, Kate glowered at Randy. "You again! You just keep turning up, like a disgusting wart!"

"Ah ah ah, temper, temper," Randy warned. "Your eyes are flashing!"

"They are not!" Kate fumed. "And as for you . . . you. . ."

"Now, now, you weren't thinking of soiling that precious mouth with colorful language, were you?" he teased, his blue eyes sparkling.

"Oh, you mean like this?" she asked, selecting some of her favorite obscenities.

"Most impressive, ma'am," he replied, looking a bit overwhelmed. "Let me shake your hand." He reached for her hand and gave it a firm squeeze. He frowned when she cried out in pain. "What's wrong?"

"Nothing!" she snapped, jerking her hand away. He'd probably permanently imbedded the slivers!

"Let me see that," he demanded, grabbing her hand again. He gazed intently, finally discovering the cause of discomfort. "Well, now, it looks like you've gone and gotten yourself a mess of slivers."

"Just never mind," she sputtered, turning to walk away.

"Hold on there, filly, I can dig those out for you. It's the least I can do," he offered, smiling.

"No way!" she exclaimed, taking another step.

"I promise, you won't even feel it. I've done this kind of thing so often, I could do it in my sleep. I've lost count of the other little kids who have come through here and ended up with splinters."

Ignoring the insinuation about her age, Kate paused. After the pain-filled attempt her father had made at removing the stinger, she was unwilling to subject herself to further misery. "You promise it won't hurt?" she finally asked, turning to gaze at him.

"You have my word as a gentleman," he solemnly vowed. "If it hurts, may I be struck down by lightning."

"At the very least," Kate agreed, deciding to let him try. She was convinced he couldn't do any worse than her dad.

"Good deal. Come with me, sweet lady, I need my professional surroundings for this type of operation."

"Professional surroundings?" she asked, giving him a suspicious look.

"My uncle's cabin. The light's better." He faced her, removed his hat, and bowed deeply. "You have my word as a gentleman that I will behave as such." He held out his arm and waited until she had slipped her good hand through, then led her to the cabin.

Rising from the wooden bench, Sue made her way to the side door. She hated to leave just now; the cook had come out to recite more of his humorous poetry. But her body refused to cooperate. She hurried outside and walked briskly toward the rest room.

Entering the side designated for females, she was grateful an empty stall was available. When she came out to wash her hands, she glanced around at the unfamiliar faces and wondered where Kate was. She'd figured her daughter had needed some time to cool off. Kate was probably off sulking somewhere outside. Still, there were always the what-ifs to contend with. What if Kate wasn't fine? What if some perverted jerk had noticed her beautiful daughter was alone and unprotected? Sighing, she knew she couldn't enjoy the rest of the show until Kate was located. She quickly left the rest room to search for her.

Kate flinched as Randy gently removed the last sliver.

"There you are, ma'am," he drawled, tipping his hat back to grin at her. "Good as new."

"Gee, thanks," she said sarcastically, rising from the wooden chair.

"You might want to put an antiseptic on it later. It'll keep infection from getting in that lovely hand of yours."

Nodding, Kate gazed around at the one-room cabin. "Quite the place you have here."

"I'll admit it's not fancy, but it suffices."

Kate pointed to the single bed and smiled. "You said this was your uncle's cabin. Where do you sleep?"

"On the floor," he admitted, gesturing to the rolled-up sleeping bag in the corner.

"Nice," she replied, turning to smile at him.

Randy blushed and nervously pulled at the blue handkerchief knotted around his neck.

"You look like you're choking. Here, let me loosen that for you," she offered, enjoying his discomfort. As she took a step forward, he stepped back, his legs bumping against the bed.

"We'd better get you back. Your folks'll be wonderin' where you're at. The show's nearly over," he added, glancing at his watch.

"Am I making you nervous?" she asked, moving closer. He deserved a little stress after the stunts he'd pulled earlier.

Coughing with embarrassment, Randy bumped against the bed again, knocking a mug to the floor. It shattered on impact. He winced, then glared at Kate. "Great, that's only my uncle's favorite mug!" He knelt and began picking up the bigger pieces.

"Randy, I'm sorry, I didn't mean . . . here, let me help," she offered, kneeling beside him.

"Oh, no, not with your luck! You'll end up needing stitches." He stood and threw what he'd gathered into a waste-paper basket. "If you want to help, go grab that broom over there."

Kate obediently went for the broom.

Sue walked out of the art gallery and tried not to panic. Now what? Kate hadn't been in the Trading Post either. She'd kept an eye on the large building where the rest of the family was enjoying the end of the show. She was positive her oldest daughter hadn't returned to the fold. *Just let her be all right,* she silently prayed. *Let her be all right so I can kill her when I find her,* she added under her breath. No wonder she had ulcers! Did Kate have any idea what it did to her each time she conveniently disappeared? Maybe. Maybe Kate enjoyed it. Maybe it was her way of getting even. For what, Sue had no way of knowing, but it was an effective plan. Sue's stomach was in knots. Just as it had been the night Kate's boss had called from Burger King to inform her that her daughter had left work early again. "Again?" she had asked, bewildered. This was the first she'd heard about it. "Again," he had confirmed. He was going to fire Kate if she kept it up. But did Kate care? No!

It was just by chance Sue had found out that Kate had been leaving work early to spend time with Jace. Lori Blanchard had taken her kids on an evening picnic at the park and had stumbled upon Jace and Kate quite by accident. Lori's seven-year-old son, Stephen, had smacked a baseball into a group of trees. When he'd gone to retrieve it, he'd discovered the young couple in the trees, involved in a passionate session of necking. Stephen had run back to tell his mother what he'd seen, but by the time Lori and Stephen had returned to the trees, Jace and Kate had disappeared. Lori had called later that night. She had decided Sue had a right to know. After all, they were in this battle together. A battle that was far from over!

As Sue reflected on all that had transpired, the anger and

frustration grew, breaking free of barriers normally kept intact. Kate knew better than this! Her daughter had no business chasing around like . . . like Linda. Like those other girls she hung around with. And as for Jace, his days were definitely numbered! Now, if she could only find Kate, she'd make a few things clear. The time had come to settle a few scores.

Moving forward, she spied a small cabin tucked back near a group of trees. A light was on. She squinted, but was too far away to see who was in the window. She stepped closer and saw two people standing together. *Kate isn't in there,* she told herself. *Kate has more sense . . . Kate might act up a little with Jace but . . .* she gasped, her heart sinking into her shoes. She'd found her daughter.

"There, that should take care of it," Kate announced, dumping the final bits of stoneware into the waste-paper basket. "Here," she said, handing the broom to Randy. "I'd better get back before my parents have a coronary," she mumbled, gazing up into his eyes. They were so blue.

"Thanks," he said softly, reaching to brush a stray strand of hair from her face. What was happening to him? His legs suddenly felt like putty. They gazed at each other, both experiencing feelings they weren't sure of. Randy nervously leaned forward, lightly brushing Kate's lips with his own.

"Just what do you think you're doing?" an outraged voice demanded, effectively shattering the electricity in the air.

Kate gaped at her mother. The woman's eyes were blazing with fury. Somewhat frightened, she gulped. She had never seen her mother like this. Quickly moving away from Randy, she looked to him for help.

Randy sensed her predicament and stepped protectively in front of her. "Ma'am, I know what this must look like, but I can assure you . . ."

"Haven't you done enough?" Sue snapped, her cheeks flushing with rage. "I don't want your assurances! I want you to stay away from my daughter! Kate, get out of here, now! No arguments. *Move!*"

Kate edged toward the door. As she slipped out, she felt the anger behind the shove she received from her mother. Her own temper flaring, she spun around to glare at the woman. "We didn't do anything wrong!" she exclaimed. "Randy was just trying to help me!"

Sue slammed the door shut, grabbed Kate's arm, and dragged her protesting daughter away from the cabin.

"You're not listening to me!" Kate accused. Her mother's grip tightened. Finally stopping, Sue released her, turning to glower at her daughter.

"You're a fine one to talk about not listening!" she snapped. "You haven't listened to me for years!"

"Have you ever wondered why?" Kate shot back. "It's because you always jump in with . . ."

"I'm not the one who has a talent for jumping into situations that are way over my head! Honestly, Kate! What were you doing in that cabin? As if I need to ask!"

"If you'd give me a chance to explain . . ."

"Explain what? I saw it with my own two eyes! My daughter, alone in a cabin with a total stranger, kissing him!"

"Ooooh! I can't believe you sometimes! You're always so eager to assume the worst!"

Sue clenched her fists. "Have you ever given me reason not to?" she spit out.

"You're not being fair."

"No, Kate. I've been more than fair. I've given you the benefit of the doubt once too often. Looked the other way when I knew all along what you were up to. No more! Do you hear me, Katherine Colleen?"

"Loud and clear! Now it's your turn to hear something. You're jumping to conclusions!"

"Am I?" Sue asked, her eyes narrowing.

"Mom! What have I ever done . . ."

"Do you want me to make a list?" Sue fumed. "All right. Let's start with the cigarette butts I found in the backyard last summer."

Kate stared at her mother.

"More? Okay, how about the six-pack of beer I found stashed downstairs right around Christmas?"

Nervously swallowing, Kate remained silent. Her mother knew? Why hadn't she said anything before now?

"And for the icing on the cake, let's not forget that

pornographic trash you delight in!"

Finding her voice, Kate hesitantly replied. "All right. Maybe I tried smoking for a while. And I'll admit, I've had a few drinks here and there. But I only looked through those magazines once or twice before you found them. I was going to burn them myself!"

"Oh, right!" Her voice trembling, Sue stared at her daughter. "Why, Kate? Why?"

"I don't know . . . I guess I was curious," she stammered.

"Then why didn't you come to me with your questions? I've always tried to be there for you."

"You've only been there to accuse me! How many times have you ever actually listened?"

"I've listened! To your lies, your excuses, your versions of the truth. Do you have any idea what it's doing to me, realizing that my daughter is a . . ."

"Slut, mother? Is what you were going to say? Heaven forbid I bring disgrace to the family name! That's all you're concerned about! You don't care about me!"

"If I didn't care, none of this would matter! It wouldn't bother me that you thrive on throwing yourself at anything that wears pants!"

Enraged, Kate allowed strong emotions to control her words. "Okay . . . fine! You're right, Mother! I desperately needed a man tonight. I seduced Randy. I dragged him kicking and screaming into that cabin, begging him to satisfy my lust!"

Sue slapped Kate hard across one cheek. Angry pain clouded both faces. Ashamed, Sue dropped her hand. "Kate . . ." Regret crept into her anguished stare.

"You want to hear the rest of it, Mother dear?" Kate asked, her voice breaking. Her mother had never slapped her before. "He wouldn't have been the first!" Sensing the lie had cut deep, she savored this moment of revenge. "Jace wasn't the first, either! I've been with more boys than you can count on both hands! Satisfied, Mother? Happy now? You've always thrived on truth. Enjoy!"

Staggering beneath the weight of Kate's confession, Sue's face drained of all color. She sank down onto the bottom pole of the wooden fence behind her. Too stunned for words, she stared at her daughter. She'd suspected things had gotten out of hand between

Jace and Kate. Lori's call a few nights ago had confirmed her suspicions. But to actually hear it, to feel the words . . . it was unbearable.

As Kate watched her mother's features twist with pain, she shuddered. Why had she let her temper get the best of her? None of what she'd said was true. Oh, sure, Jace had pressured her, but she'd never given in. An annoying surge of guilt had always taken over, forcing her to curtail his advances. Putting him off with the fear of pregnancy had gotten her out of several sticky situations. AIDS alone was enough to scare anyone away from having a serious relationship. And the more Jace pushed the issue, the more she thought about breaking up with him. Not that she'd ever admit it to her parents.

"Why, Kate?" Sue finally asked, her eyes brimming with tears. The silvery drops spilled down her face, shimmering in the soft glow of the lantern hanging above them.

Kate winced. What had she done? "Mom . . ." she stammered, her own eyes blurring with tears.

"There you two are," a familiar voice called out. Kate turned, fearfully watching as her father approached. Greg slowed, glancing from Kate's pained expression to his wife's pallid face. Both were in tears. His smile drooped into a frown. "Okay, what's wrong now?"

Sue wiped at her face, and shakily stood. "It's . . . it's nothing, Greg. You know how we females are on occasion." She turned her back to Kate. "Where are the other two?" she asked, the forced cheerfulness sounding hollow.

"Believe it or not, Tyler wanted to buy a tape of these guys. I guess they're selling them at the ticket booth. Naturally, Sabrina wanted to tag along with him. I told them we'd meet by the Explorer."

Sue nodded and walked away. Greg gazed uneasily at Kate, then at his wife. More had taken place than was being said. Deciding to wait until one of them was ready to talk, he motioned for Kate to follow. As they moved forward, they were separated by the large crowd heading toward the parking lot. "I'll meet you by the car," Greg called over his shoulder, drifting with the happy mob.

Kate impatiently moved around until she'd reached her

mother's side. "Mom . . . we need to talk."

"I don't think there's anything left to say," Sue said coldly. Taking several steps forward, she moved away from Kate.

"Fine," Kate snapped. "Believe what you want! If you actually think I'm capable of . . ." her words were lost as the crowd dragged her along with them.

"Ma'am?" a soft voice drawled.

Startled, Sue glanced around, finding herself face to face with the cowboy named Randy.

"Please, ma'am, I feel terrible about this. Could we talk?"

Sue reluctantly agreed, puzzled that she would feel prompted to listen to this jerk. She followed him away from the crowd, impatiently waiting for an explanation.

"I could tell you had the wrong idea," he began. He took off his hat and held it out in front of him. "It wasn't what you thought," he added.

Fighting the urge to scream at him, Sue somehow kept her composure. "Oh?"

"Yeah. The whole thing was my fault. I never should've talked Bryan into forcing Kate onstage tonight."

"That was your idea?"

"Yeah," he admitted, nervously running his hand through the crease in his hat. "I noticed earlier she wasn't enjoying herself. She all but called us a bunch of bumpkins. I guess it was my way of getting even."

Her face softening, Sue waited for the rest of what he had to say.

"Kate came out looking for me. I saw her slap at a board; she was so angry . . ." He hesitated, remembering the sparks in Kate's eyes. "I didn't know she'd ended up with slivers in her hand until after she'd calmed down." Randy hurriedly explained everything that had taken place in the cabin, finishing with the kiss. "I know the kiss was out of line. It kind of caught us both off guard. But, I promise, it wouldn't have gone further than that."

"I see," Sue said skeptically. "And just how do I know that?"

"Ma'am, I don't know if it means anything to you, but I'm a Mormon."

Stunned, Sue stared. This joker was a Mormon? Not that it made any difference. So was Kate.

"I've cooled things off with my girlfriend back home. I don't want any serious attachments right now. I'm leaving on a mission this fall. That's why I'm working here this summer. I'm saving money. I wouldn't do anything like you thought . . . I promise!"

Sue gazed at the young man, her opinion of him rising. "I don't know why," she finally said, " but I believe you."

Relieved, Randy smiled. "Thank you, ma'am, for listening to me. I didn't want you leaving here without knowing the truth."

Sighing heavily, Sue wished his confession could alter the truth as she now knew it. "I'm sorry for the trouble Kate has caused you tonight," she murmured, turning to walk away.

"She wasn't any trouble," he said, wondering at the expression on her face. "I'm just sorry we upset you like this."

"Don't worry about it," she called over her shoulder.

Puzzled, Randy watched her go. She seemed to believe him, but it hadn't changed the look on her face. He replaced his hat, and walked in the opposite direction.

" . . . and when he fired that six-shooter . . . I've never laughed so hard in my life," Tyler said, gleefully remembering Kate's reaction to the sudden noise.

Only half-listening, Greg finished zipping Sabrina in the sleeping bag. Leaning down to give her a quick kiss, he smiled when she planted a juicy one on his cheek.

"'Night, Daddy," she said, yawning.

"Goodnight, sweetheart," he said, rising.

"Tell Mommy to feel better," she said sleepily.

"I'll tell her," he promised. Declaring she had a horrible headache, Sue had retired for the evening, leaving him to tuck everyone in for the night.

"G'night, pardner," Tyler drawled, reaching to shut off the lamp by his bed.

"Goodnight, sport," Greg replied. He glanced at his oldest daughter who had curled up in the bed across the room. "Goodnight, Kate," he added, not expecting an answer. She had been strangely silent since leaving the Bar-J. He flipped off the remaining light, stepped into the other bedroom, and quietly pulled the door shut. He then walked to the bed, sat down on his side, and stared at his wife's back. "Sue," he whispered, "are you awake?" There was no response. He slid in between the sheets and strained to turn off the lamp on the nightstand. Lying quietly, he stared into the darkness while his wife silently cried.

Chapter Nine

The next day, Sue and Kate were still giving each other the silent treatment. This was apparent even to Sabrina, who wanted to know why Mommy and Kate were mad. Greg wasn't about to step into the middle of whatever it was. When they were ready to talk about it, he knew they would both erupt with a fierce intensity. Until then, there was scenery to see, places to go, and miles to cover.

Greg figured the best place to stop for lunch was at the Star Valley Cheese Factory in Thayne, Wyoming. It would combine history with food, two of his favorite subjects. He had just started to share his vast knowledge of the cheese factory with Tyler when Sabrina tugged at his shirt.

"Yes, Sabrina?"

"I'm hungry."

"That's why we're here," Greg replied, gazing around at the small restaurant housed by the factory. "Let's eat!"

"I'm still stuffed from breakfast," Sue said quietly. Truthfully, she'd barely picked at the pancakes ordered that morning.

"What about the rest of you?" Greg asked.

"I'm starved," Tyler exclaimed.

"I want a corn dog!" Sabrina said loudly.

"Kate?"

"I'm not hungry," she mumbled, focusing on the tiled floor.

"Well, I'll tell you what. You and your mother can order drinks while the rest of us get a burger."

"I want a corn dog!" Sabrina repeated.

"And a corn dog," Greg added, leading them to a table. He enjoyed the look on Tyler's face as the boy noticed the mounted heads hanging on the walls around the large room.

"Cool," Tyler commented, his gaze shifting from head to head.

"That one's scary!" Sabrina said, pointing to the buffalo who seemed to be glowering at them.

"He won't get you if you eat all your lunch," Tyler teased.

"Tyler, stop it!" Sue said sharply.

Tyler looked stunned. Why was their mother on his case? He always teased Breeny. Never viciously. Not like he did with Kate. "Sorry," he stammered, reaching for his glass of ice water.

Sue rubbed her forehead, trying to ease the pressure that had been building all day. Her nerves were raw. Rising, she moved out of the confining booth. "I'll be back in a minute," she said, escaping to the rest room.

Kate watched her leave. She stared down at her hands, studying her fingers. One nail was broken. It must've happened last night. She closed her eyes and wished for the hundredth time she could change what had taken place. Why had she been so stupid?

"Kate?"

She opened her eyes, avoiding her father's curious stare. "Yeah?"

"Is everything all right?"

"Yeah." She couldn't deal with this. She slid out of the booth to follow her mother.

Tyler raised an eyebrow and watched as his sister walked away. "What is with those two today?" he asked, gazing at his father.

Greg shrugged, staring into his glass of ice water. "I'm not sure, son, but it's obviously something they'll have to work out between themselves."

"Mom?" Kate called out, glancing around the deserted rest room.

Sue walked out of a stall, moving to the sink to wash her hands.

"Mom, we need to talk."

"We do?" Sue frowned at her daughter's reflection in the mirror. "You have more details to share?" she asked sharply, reaching for a paper towel. "Something you forgot to add last night?"

"No! I want to clear the air between us."

Sue slowly turned to face her daughter. Yesterday, she would've given anything to have heard Kate say those words. Even now, if she thought Kate really meant it . . . but, no. Everything had changed. Whenever she thought about her daughter with all of those boys, something inside of her closed. She wasn't sure how to open that door without freeing the pain that went with it. It was better to stay numb, detached. The anger would hold her together until she was strong enough to cope with the pain.

"Mom . . . please?"

Sue continued to gaze at Kate. This daughter who was hers, and yet not hers. This daughter who had turned her heart into shards of glass. Shards that pricked whenever she drew a breath.

"Look, I know I hurt you last night and I'm sorry . . ."

"Sorry won't fix it this time, Kate." Turning away, Sue discarded the paper towel. She rested her pounding head against the white wall. "And I'm not the only one you've hurt."

"If you're talking about Dad . . ."

"I'm not, but while we're on the subject, listen and listen good!" Whirling around, Sue scowled at her daughter. "I haven't told him about any of this yet."

Kate slowly nodded. She'd already figured that out. She wanted to straighten this mess out before it went any further.

"Your father worked hard to plan this trip," Sue continued. "I'm not about to ruin it for him, or the rest of the family."

"Mom! Would you listen to me . . ."

"I'm through listening, young lady, do you understand? That went out the window with your innocence. Now, you're going to listen because there are a few new rules that concern you."

She took a deep breath, struggling to hold onto the anger, refusing to let the tears form. She needed to be strong. Strength was the only thing Kate understood. She'd been too weak before. As a result, her daughter had ruined her life. All the love in the world hadn't made a difference. Love meant nothing to Kate. Her daughter lived only for pleasure, and self, and the present moment.

"Mom . . ."

"Rule number one . . . you will show your father and I respect from this point forward. We are your parents, not your doormats."

"I didn't mean . . ."

"Rule number two . . . if you so much as look at another boy on this trip, I'll make your life so miserable, you'll wish you'd never been born!"

Giving up, Kate rolled her eyes. Whatever made the woman happy.

"That leaves rule number three. I want you to do some serious thinking about the road you've chosen to follow in life. It's a long, hard way back, and at this point, I'm not sure you've got what it takes to make it." Returning her daughter's glare, she brushed past her and left the room.

"Why is she doing this?" Kate moaned, leaning against the wall. "Why won't she listen? She never listens!" Turning to face the wall, she hit it with her fist. Just then, an elderly lady entered the rest room and stared at her. "Got it," Kate said, sensing she wasn't alone. She forced a smile, grabbed a paper towel and pretended to wipe something off her fist. "It was a big one," she confided in the woman as she discarded the paper towel. She then quickly left the room. The older woman stepped over to where the teenager had supposedly smashed a bug. There were no traces. Taking off her glasses, she gave them a good cleaning, and muttered under her breath. She'd have to set up another appointment with the optometrist when she returned home. She hadn't seen a bug at all.

CHAPTER TEN

They spent the night in Montpelier, Idaho, staying at a place called the Crest Motel. It had been crowded; there were no vacancies. They had been assigned a single room with two double beds. A roll-away had been offered for Tyler to use, which they gratefully accepted. Sue insisted that Kate share one of the double beds with Sabrina. Greg was surprised when Kate quietly agreed. There was no privacy in this arrangement, so he didn't have a chance to question Sue about anything.

There wasn't much of a chance the next morning either, but Greg did finally corner his wife while they were loading the car.

"What's up?" he asked, closing the back of the car.

"What do you mean?" Sue asked, feigning innocence.

"Don't give me that. I know you and Kate are feuding over something in a major way."

Sue forced a smile. "Don't worry about it. It's just more of the same. It'll pass." She turned away before losing her composure. She ached to tell Greg. To let him handle it. But she was determined to spare him the pain she was experiencing until they returned home. Telling him now wouldn't solve anything. Nothing could change what their daughter had done. And nothing could be done about it until they returned to Bozeman.

It was close to 10:00 a.m. when Greg excitedly pointed out the window on his side of the car. "There it is! The famed Bear Lake!"

Tyler gaped at the aquamarine-colored water. "Wow! It's huge!

No wonder the Bear Lake Monster loves it here!"

"Bare Lake Monster?" Sabrina asked, her eyes wide with fright as she pictured a naked dragon.

"It's just a story, Breeny," Tyler replied, sensing his younger sister's alarm. "There really isn't a monster, at least not in the lake," he added, grinning at Kate. Disappointed, he saw that his older sister wasn't going to rise to the occasion. He gave up on the expected response and shifted his gaze back to the lake.

As he drove through Logan Canyon, Greg marveled at the beauty surrounding them. He glanced in the rear view mirror and saw that Tyler was appreciating it as well. Sabrina was asleep, and Kate was staring solemnly into space, remaining in her private world of silence. He negotiated around a sharp curve and sighed, knowing his wife was in a similar frame of mind. What had happened between these two? Why wasn't Sue confiding in him? Slowing down to follow another curve in the road, he decided not to worry about it. His wife would come to him when she was ready. In the meantime, he'd concentrate on making this trip as memorable as possible.

At 6:13 p.m., they arrived in Salt Lake City, Utah. Greg stayed on the freeway until they reached the Murray exit. A few minutes later, he pulled into the driveway of a white brick home and shut off the engine. Shifting around, he gazed at his children. "We'll be spending two or three days here with Uncle Stan and Aunt Paige."

Tyler groaned, picturing his cousins, the twins, Rachel and Renae. He was sure the ten-year-olds would be a royal pain. They hung on his every word, following him around with puppy-dog eyes. At last year's reunion, they'd almost walked into the men's rest room with him at Tautphaus Park in Idaho Falls.

"I expect you to all be on your best behavior, okay?"

"Okay," Tyler said, his voice lacking enthusiasm.

"'Kay," Sabrina said excitedly, overjoyed that they could finally get out of the car.

"Kate?" Greg pressured. Slowly nodding, Kate refused to look at him. Deciding it was the only answer he would get from her, he opened the door on his side and slid down to the ground.

"Hello, baby sister," Stan Mahoney exclaimed, giving Sue an intense squeeze. When she realized she was struggling for air, he finally released her, grinning as Paige embraced her in turn.

"How's the vacation going?" Paige asked, drawing back to smile at Sue. As she gazed into her sister-in-law's eyes, she saw the answer.

"Great," Greg said, wincing as Stan gripped his hand in a fierce handshake. "We've had a few adventures," he added.

"I'll bet. Come sit down and tell us about them," Stan encouraged, his blue eyes sparkling as he ran a large hand through his bright red hair.

"Don't get too carried away with swapping stories. Supper's nearly ready," Paige gently scolded, smiling up at her tall husband. At five feet three inches, she was tiny in comparison. Her soft brown eyes focused on Kate. The teenager was about as miserable as she'd ever seen her. Smiling warmly at her niece, she slid an arm around the girl's waist, guiding her toward the kitchen. "The rest of you go relax for a few minutes while Kate and I finish things up," she said brightly.

"I'll help," Sue offered, suddenly very nervous. Kate had always been close to Paige. Hoping to thwart any untimely revelations, she tried to follow her blonde sister-in-law into the kitchen.

Paige shook her head. "Sue, you look exhausted. Kate and I can handle this. Do me a favor and go visit with that brother of yours. Keep him out of my hair so I can get dinner on the table."

"Paige is right," Stan said, placing a strong arm around his sister's sagging shoulders. "Let's go catch each other up to date," he continued, dragging Sue into the living room.

Sending a worried look in Kate's direction, Sue had no choice in the matter. She watched as Sabrina raced off to play with Johnny, a red-haired six-year-old. Tyler was trying to escape Rachel and Renae as he eagerly sought out Kyle, a newly returned missionary. Greg wandered off, claiming he needed to freshen up a bit. She grimaced as they left her alone with the one person who could read her like a book.

"Wash these tomatoes, then slice them into the salad," Paige instructed, handing Kate the plump tomatoes she'd picked earlier out of the garden.

"Okay," Kate said quietly, walking to the sink.

"So, how are things with you this summer?" Paige asked, stirring the spaghetti sauce on the stove.

"Fine," was the distant reply.

Paige turned to gaze at her niece. Frowning, she watched as Kate continuously wiped at her eyes. Concerned, Paige moved across the kitchen, and gently eased the girl around. "That's what I thought," she said quietly as tears worked their way down her niece's face. "What's wrong, Kate?"

Staring at the floor, Kate held her breath. Now what?

"I'm fine," Sue insisted, glaring at Stan.

"I see," Stan said, thoughtfully studying his sister. "That explains why you look like death warmed over."

"I'm just tired."

He quietly watched as her hardened resolve disintegrated into tears. "Uh huh," he murmured, offering a wadded handkerchief from his back pocket. "What's going on, Sue?"

"I . . . I can't tell you. It's horrible . . . but . . . I can't. Someone might hear . . . I don't want Greg to know, not yet," she said, wiping the tears from her face.

Stan gently pulled Sue to her feet. "Let's go into my den," he offered, placing an arm around her shoulders as he guided his sister from the room.

When they left, Greg stepped down into the living room. "Tell him," he quietly encouraged, wearing a sad, pained expression. "If you can't tell me, then tell Stan. Tell somebody before you explode." He sat on the couch and picked up a recent copy of *Field and Stream* from the coffee table and despondently thumbed through the pages.

"I'm really okay," Kate sniffed, dabbing at her eyes with the paper towel Paige had handed her. "Things haven't been very good between Mom and me lately."

"Anything I can do?"

Kate shook her head. "I guess I just needed a good cry."

"Uh huh," Paige said skeptically. "When you decide you want to talk about it, my offer to listen still stands. You can always count on that."

Kate wiped at her nose. "I know," she said softly. She forced a tiny smile, then turned to discard the paper towel. As tempting as the offer was, she couldn't bring herself to tell her favorite aunt anything. She didn't want to hurt or disappoint Paige by telling her the truth. Shuddering, she realized how ashamed she'd feel if the woman ever found out about some of the things she had done. *Kate, you blubbering idiot,* she silently fumed, *what have you done?* She moved to the sink to wash her hands, then began rinsing off the tomatoes.

Paige sighed and moved back to the stove to check on the bubbling sauce. Kate's problem would have to wait for a time when her niece was ready to talk. She knew the girl well enough to realize her niece had inherited the Mahoney streak of stubbornness. And from past experience she had learned that a Mahoney couldn't be pushed into anything. Vigorously stirring the sauce, she reached for the garlic powder, sprinkling generously into the simmering mixture.

Stunned, Stan leaned forward in the leather chair. "Why would Kate do something like this?" he finally asked, glancing at his sister.

"Don't think I haven't asked myself that same question. I've failed her, Stan. Somehow, some way, I didn't teach her . . ."

Rising, Stan gently pulled Sue to her feet. His hands firmly gripped her shoulders as he looked her in the eye. "It's not your fault, Sue. So quit blaming yourself. Kate's old enough to know better. I've watched what that girl has put you through the past five years. We should've guessed it would come to this."

"But, I always thought we'd reach her before . . . and now . . . it's too late."

"It's never too late," he said grimly. "Don't give up on her yet. Some people have to hit rock bottom before they turn around."

"I think Kate's there," she sobbed, leaning against her brother.

He quietly held her, blocking out the images that kept coming to mind. The wild parties Kate had been attending, the drinking . . . the boys . . . Sue hadn't said anything about drugs. He hoped his niece had possessed enough sense to steer clear of them. But, if she was freely giving her body to anyone who would have her . . . he closed his eyes. No wonder Sue was such a mess.

"You have to tell Greg," he finally whispered. "You can't keep this to yourself. No wonder you're coming apart at the seams."

Sue pulled back and wiped at her face. "I can't. At least, not yet. It'll kill him."

"What do you think it's doing to you?" Stan asked, frowning severely. "You need him."

"You don't understand. Greg has put so much of himself into this trip. I don't want to ruin it for him, or the rest of the family. I want them to enjoy what's left of it. When we get home, I'll tell him. We can't do anything about Kate's situation right now, anyway."

"Oh, no?" he said angrily, snapping a fist into his other hand. "Give me ten minutes alone with that girl. We'll straighten things out in a hurry!"

"Stan, you promised you wouldn't say anything about this to anyone. That includes Kate."

"I never should've made that promise," he complained, bringing his fist down hard on the desk.

"Please, Stan, I need your support, not your anger," Sue pleaded.

"You'll always have my support," Stan said, meeting his sister's pleading eyes with a look of compassion. "And I'll try to keep a handle on my temper."

"Then you'll keep your promise," she persisted.

"Yes," he said reluctantly. "What choice do I have?"

"Sorry," Sue replied, forcing a smile. "But, you'll see. It'll be better this way. And don't worry about me, I think I can make it now. Telling you has eased the pressure I've been feeling since . . . since Kate. . ." the tears ran in silently streams down her face. "Oh, Katie," she murmured, "what have you done?"

His face softening, Stan reached for his sister, holding her close as he tried to absorb her pain.

CHAPTER ELEVEN

Supper was a quiet, strained affair. Paige tried to brighten the mood by sharing an amusing story about one of the sisters in their ward, but gave up when the laughter was forced. As she stood to clear the table, the children quickly disappeared, eager to escape the solemn setting. Greg and Sue offered to help, rising to scrape dishes. Exchanging a worried look with his wife, Stan took the stack of plates from her hands and followed Greg into the kitchen. The two women began gathering glasses, taking them into the kitchen to be washed.

"Pretty good, for a grandpa," Greg teased, holding the swinging door open for the large man.

"Grandpa, huh?" Stan challenged, setting the plates on the counter. "Wait till we finish up here. I'll take you down to the weight room and we'll just see who acts like an old man," he said, chuckling as he poked at Greg's distended stomach with a spoon.

"You're on," Greg said, patting Stan's slight tummy bulge. "Pretty soft," he commented with a grin.

"We'll see," Stan assured him, hurriedly loading the dishwasher.

"Those two never change," Sue commented, following Paige as she slipped back out to the dining room.

"I know," Paige agreed, relieved that things were finally lightening up. She reached for a pile of silverware and smiled at her sister-in-law.

"How did things go with Kate earlier?" Sue asked, picking up some stray paper napkins.

"She was really good about helping," Paige answered, not sure what the other woman was getting at. "She put the green salad together while I finished the spaghetti sauce."

"Oh," Sue replied, picking up another discarded napkin. "Did she talk much?" she asked, doing her best to appear calm.

"Sue," Paige said softly. She waited until her sister-in-law glanced up. "I'm not sure what's going on with you two, but it must be pretty serious. Kate broke down in the kitchen for a minute. I don't think I've ever seen her like this. So hurt and vulnerable . . ."

"She's hurt and vulnerable? It figures. She's probably playing the role of the wounded victim to the hilt! I suppose she gave you her version of what happened?"

"No. She just said you two were having some problems."

"Oh. I guess I shouldn't be surprised. You're the last person she'd ever tell." The words were out before she could stop herself. True, she was envious of the relationship Paige had with Kate. But that was no reason to lash out at her sister-in-law. It wasn't Paige's fault Kate was drawn to the petite blonde. How could she get out of this without hurting Paige?

Raising an eyebrow, Paige patiently waited for an explanation.

"I didn't mean that the way it sounded," Sue said apologetically. "It's just . . . Kate has always idolized you. It would crush her if you ever found out . . ."

Paige took a chance, asking the question that had nagged at her all evening. "She isn't . . . pregnant, is she?"

Startled, Sue violently shook her head. "No, at least, I don't think so. But, the way she's carrying on, I wouldn't be surprised if she ended up that way."

Paige dropped the silverware on the table and quickly walked around to Sue, sliding an arm around the other woman's shoulders. "I had a feeling it was something like this. The way you were both acting . . . I kept hoping it was something else . . ."

"You're not alone," Sue sniffed, pulling away from Paige to lean against the table. The pained look on her sister-in-law's face matched her own. "I'm sorry, Paige. I shouldn't have dumped this on you . . . or Stan."

"That's what family's for." Paige gripped the back of a wooden chair for support. "How is Greg handling this?"

"He doesn't know. I just found out two nights ago . . . in Jackson. I caught her with a boy . . . they were . . . I saw them. And then she said . . ." She paused, tears streaming down her face.

"Let's go upstairs where we can talk. We'll let these men finish cleaning up." Paige quietly guided Sue to the carpeted stairs, leading her to the guest room she'd prepared for their stay.

"Well, you've certainly been quiet tonight," Kyle commented, sitting in the wooden porch swing with Kate.

"So?" Kate countered, her head down, her shoulders slumped.

"I know I've been gone for two years, but people don't change that much," he teased. He bent down to pull up a feathery weed. Leaning close to his cousin, he tried tickling her face.

"Knock it off," she complained, straightening to glare at him.

"Finally, a response," he said with a smile. "Tyler said you were becoming a drag. That you've missed numerous insults. He's quite dejected over the whole thing."

"Good!" Kate snapped, staring angrily across the back yard.

"Well, you're a lot of fun to be around," he commented, dropping the weed.

"If you want fun, go bother Tyler, and while you're at it, give him one of these for me," she said, offering an obscene gesture.

"Katie Colleen, I am appalled! Aghast! Simply shocked!"

"Keep it up and I'll tell you what else you are!"

Kyle grinned at his cousin. "I'll just bet you would, too. So, to what do we owe your current good mood? Let me guess, you broke a nail? Nope, there hasn't been enough wailing."

"Kyle!" she threatened, glaring at her cousin, hating the way his hazel eyes laughed at her.

"I know, has it been a bad hair day?" he asked, patting his own head of thick brown hair.

"Kyle Mahoney!"

"Wait, I've got it, maybe your fall in the lake permanently dampened your spirits. Or, it's the after-shock of being hauled up onstage at the good old Bar-J!"

"I'm going to kill Tyler," Kate promised through clenched teeth.

"But he's the only brother you have."

"Good!"

"He really does care about you, you know. That's why he's worried. He thinks something major happened between you and your mother."

"Well, pin a gold star on his forehead!" she fumed, standing. She walked to the other side of the cement patio and kicked a soccer ball out into the middle of the backyard.

"Nice form," Kyle commented, moving to her side. "Although it did seem a little flat. Arch your foot next time, it'll make a big difference."

"Don't you ever let up?" she tersely asked, whirling around to glower at him. "Back off, all right! This doesn't concern you or Tyler! So, leave me alone! Both of you just leave me alone!"

Kyle frowned, uncomfortably aware of how close his cousin was to tears. "Sorry. I was just trying to cheer you up. You can't blame a guy for tryin'." He paused, waiting for his cousin to regain her composure. "C'mon," he gently encouraged, "let's go sit down and talk things over. Maybe it won't seem so bad then," he offered, guiding her back to the swing. He sat beside her, allowing several minutes to pass before breaking the silence between them. "You don't have to talk about it if you don't want to, but I'm here if you need me," he said quietly.

"You're just like your mother," Kate sniffed, wiping at her eyes.

"What?"

"I never realized it before. Maybe because you've always been such a jerk, but, just now, you sounded exactly like Aunt Paige."

"Oh, c'mon."

"No, really. Earlier, when I was helping her with supper, she said the same thing to me."

"Well, I'll take the comparison as a compliment. Mom's all right."

"I know," Kate agreed, looking down at her hands. "Sometimes I wish . . ." She frowned. "Forget it, it's silly."

"Wishes aren't silly. Tell me."

"It's just . . . sometimes I've wondered what it would've been like to have had Aunt Paige for a mother."

"Well," Kyle said, scratching behind one ear, "speaking from personal experience, I can testify that the woman is pretty terrific."

"I wish Mom was more like her."

Kyle gazed at his cousin. "Am I to understand that you think Aunt Sue is lacking in the mothering department?" Kate nodded, her eyes sparkling with defiance. "You've got it, mister," she said grimly.

"Kate, that's not true and you know it! Aunt Sue is a great lady, and from what I've seen, a wonderful mother."

"You couldn't prove it by me," Kate snapped, blowing at a piece of stray hair.

Kyle raised an eyebrow. Tyler hadn't exaggerated. Things weren't good between Aunt Sue and Kate. Praying for inspiration, he rubbed at the dark stubble that had appeared on his chin. *Mom was right*, he thought, *I should've shaved before supper*. As he reflected on the lecture she'd given him earlier concerning his personal grooming habits, an idea came to mind. "Kate, do you resent it when your mother gives you advice?"

"She doesn't just give advice, she rubs it in my face!"

"And you feel threatened by that?"

"Wouldn't you?"

He shrugged, then stood, turning to lean against the back of the house. "It depends. When I was about your age, I resented a lot of the things my parents said because I thought I had all of the answers."

"And now?"

"Now, I realize I'm not as smart as I thought I was, and I appreciate the counsel they give me."

"Yeah, but it's different with you. Your parents are cool. They never blow off steam."

⁻He chuckled, shaking his head.

"What's so funny?"

"You," he replied. "Look, I'm not sure why you think your parents are such ogres. Most parents get upset with their kids at one time or another."

"I've never seen Aunt Paige lose her temper with you guys, not that you didn't deserve it."

"You're not around enough. Mom can get riled, especially if she thinks we're heading for trouble. I remember her reaction a few years ago when I decided to let my hair grow past my shoulders. She came down on me pretty hard . . ."

"Aunt Paige?" Kate asked, her eyes widening.

"Aunt Paige," Kyle assured her. "She may be tiny, but boy can she put fear into a person when she gets upset."

"No way!"

"Yes, way!" he countered, meeting her expression of disbelief with one of certainty. "She threatened me with Dad's razor if I didn't get it cut."

"What?"

"Yep. It was either butch-city with the razor, or a trip to the hair stylist. I picked the stylist."

"Good choice." Kate shook her head. "I never would've believed that of Aunt Paige."

"Mom was looking out for me," he replied. "Just like she was for Tami when my sister started dating a total jerk."

"You're kidding?"

"Nope. Mom and Tami went the rounds like you wouldn't believe over a guy who drooled when his mouth was closed."

"You're making this up," Kate accused.

"Hardly," he said with disgust. "We're talkin' major dud. I'm still not sure what Tami ever saw in him. Mom and Dad both knew he would eventually hurt her. Only Tami couldn't see it. She thought he was Mr. Wonderful. Our parents caught on right away that in reality, he was Mr. Hormone. They knew he was only after one thing."

"Which was?" she asked, batting her eyes innocently at him.

"Guess," he said dryly, a light blush creeping across his face.

"I'll pass," she answered, enjoying his embarrassment. "But, do go on with your impressive fable."

"Okay, I will. Eventually, Tami realized Mom was right. She matured enough to see that our parents were only trying to protect her."

"My mom doesn't protect, she suffocates," Kate complained, pulling a face.

"Tami felt the same way."

"Well, Tami was right. I guess all parents are the same. I never would've believed it of Aunt Paige, but it sounds like she's just like the rest of them. They always interfere! They never give us any consideration or respect, and then turn around and demand we show them exactly that!"

"Kate, Tami was able to marry in the temple because of Mom's so-called interference. She's now happily married to a wonderful guy, and she'd be the first one to admit she was wrong about Mom."

"That's because she's sided with the enemy. She's a mother now herself."

"No wonder Aunt Sue is sprouting gray hair!" Kyle exclaimed, glaring at his cousin. "Trying to talk sense to you is like talking to a brick wall!"

Kate stood, glowering in return. "And do you know what I've decided, cousin dear? You're rapidly joining ranks with your sister!"

"You think so, huh? Well, I'd say I'm in pretty good company, then!"

"Temper, temper," Kate said wickedly. "Looks like smarty-pants has lost his sense of humor."

Kyle took a deep breath, then let it out slowly. "Okay, maybe I let you ruffle my feathers a bit. But before you get too cocky, let me ask you a question."

"Ask away," Kate said lightly, bowing in front of him.

"Only if you promise to answer me truthfully."

"I promise," Kate replied with a grin, deliberately crossing her fingers in front of him.

"I guess that'll have to do," he sighed. "I want you to think about why you're going the rounds with your mother right now. Is it because she's interfering, or because she's worried about something you're doing that might be harmful or dangerous?"

"Oh, c'mon, Kyle. Give me a break."

"No. You promised."

"My fingers were . . ."

"I know. But, if you're serious about figuring this mess out, you need to be honest with yourself. Is she interfering, or trying to help?" He watched as a myriad of conflicting emotions surfaced. "Well, Ms. I-Have-All-The-Answers, which is it?"

"That's not a fair question. In Mom's eyes, she probably thinks she's saving me from harm."

"How does it look through the eyes of Katie Colleen?"

"Quit calling me that! Has anyone ever told you that you have a talent for annoying people?"

"Yes, thank you. Now, quit changing the subject. I believe you were about to answer a question."

"If you think I'm going to tell you what Mom and I are fighting about . . ."

"I don't need to hear the sordid details. Just tell me, is she imposing on your precious space, or is she trying to save you from yourself?"

"She's . . . Kyle, you can't believe what she accused me of! I kept trying to tell her she was wrong, but would she listen to me? No!"

"Ah. I see. You're adding a new dimension to the question. You're claiming you have been falsely accused of something your mother thinks is harmful."

"I'm not claiming anything! It's the truth, only no one wants to believe me!"

"I'll believe you," Kyle said, sensing the pain behind her words.

"Really?"

"Really."

Kate leaned against the cool metal pole of the swing. Closing her eyes, she weighed the pros and cons of telling Kyle everything.

"It might help to talk about it," Kyle encouraged.

Kate opened her eyes and gazed at her cousin. "I'm not sure about this," she said softly. "But, I've got to tell someone before I explode. I couldn't tell your mother. Dad is out of the question." She stared intently at Kyle. "If I tell you, you've got to promise you won't breathe a word of this to anyone."

"Kate, this is silly."

"Promise me, Kyle, or you can forget the whole thing!"

Kyle sighed, realizing this might be the only chance he'd have to help his troubled cousin. "Okay, I promise."

"Good." She glanced at the returned missionary and wondered how he would react. "See, there was this boy from the Bar-J, Randy something. Anyway, he was helping me get some splinters out of my hand. Naturally my mother found us together and started accusing me of horrible things! And when I tried to defend myself, she wouldn't listen. She was having too much fun believing the worst. She all but called me a slut. It hurt, Kyle. I may be a lot of things, but I'm not a slut!" She ignored the burning sensation behind her eyes. She would not cry!

Kyle waited patiently. He pictured the scene that must have taken place between Aunt Sue and his cousin. Shaking his head, he quietly listened as Kate continued.

"It made me so mad when she kept pressuring me to confess to something I hadn't done, I snapped! I told her what she wanted to hear. What really hurt was the fact that she believed me. I've never done anything like that, and she believed the lie over the truth. I was so angry, I kept adding to the lie. I told her I'd been with more boys than she could count. And she believed it! She stared at me as though I'd just climbed out of the garbage can, and she slapped me. Something she's never done before. But it didn't hurt half as much as knowing she would actually think . . ." She buried her face in her hands and softly cried.

Kyle guided her back into the swing. As he waited for her to pull herself together, he mulled over the situation. No wonder everyone seemed so upset. After several minutes, he turned to gaze at his cousin. "Kate, have you told your mother it was all a lie?"

Kate lifted her face from her hands and shook her head. Sniffing, she wiped at her eyes.

"Why?"

"I tried! After things calmed down, I tried three times! Later that same night. Then early the next morning before we went to breakfast. I tried again later that afternoon when we stopped for lunch."

"And?"

"It's like I'm this non-person as far as she's concerned. She won't listen. I see the pain in her eyes . . . then she gives me one of those accusing stares, and part of me thinks it serves her right. How could she think that of me?"

"I don't suppose you've ever given her reason to worry?"

Kate frowned. "Kyle!"

"The truth, Kate," he said sternly.

"Okay, maybe I've done a few things she hasn't been very thrilled about."

"Like what?"

"I tried smoking last summer . . ."

Kyle stared at his cousin. "Smoking?"

"I didn't stick with it very long. It made me so sick, I can't even look at a cigarette now without turning green."

"Good," he weakly replied, wondering if this conversation had turned into a confessional.

"And, she did find the six-pack of beer I was hiding downstairs for Jace. It was supposed to be for Linda's birthday party last November. Jace had talked his older brother into buying it for us. I stuck it in with the Christmas decorations, thinking it was the perfect hiding place."

"And?"

"I forgot to bring it to the party. There was so much booze floating around, no one even missed it. Then I forgot it was downstairs. I guess Mom found it a few weeks later. But she didn't say anything about it until two nights ago."

"Nice," he commented, thinking about how his own mother would've reacted. It wouldn't have been good. "Why did she wait to lower the boom?"

"How should I know? I never have figured that lady out. I guess I never will."

"Kate, did it ever occur to you that maybe she was waiting for you to come to her? Maybe she was trying to give you the benefit of the doubt."

Kate shook her head. Her mother had just been saving it to throw in her face when the occasion presented itself.

"Aunt Sue has always seemed very fair-minded. I'm sure she was . . ."

"Fair-minded? Hah! That's a good one, Kyle!"

"Give me a chance to explain . . ."

"Explain what? Can you tell me why she always assumes the worst? Why she never lets me explain anything? Why she's always throwing the Church in my face? Like that's really going to change anything!"

"Kate, maybe if you'd give the Church a chance . . ."

"I've given it all the chances I'm going to give. I've read the scriptures. I've attended one boring meeting after another. I've even prayed once in awhile, and I've never once felt this wonderful glow Mom is always spouting off about!"

"The Lord's Spirit can't dwell in unholy temples," Kyle said softly, watching closely for her reaction.

"Now you sound like Mom! I haven't done anything that wrong."

"You're not exactly squeaky clean, Kate. You've broken the Word of Wisdom, and you're running around with a crowd of kids who thrive on breaking rules."

"And let's not forget my moral decline," Kate snapped.

"I thought you said you'd never . . ."

"I haven't! I did look through some magazines once though," she said, suddenly eager to shock Kyle. He was judging her just like everyone else. Well, let him! It was no skin off her nose!

"What kind of magazines?"

"Let's just say they weren't *Reader's Digest.*"

"Oh," Kyle said, trying to prevent the dismay he was feeling from showing in his face.

"Linda loaned them to me . . ."

"Who's this Linda you keep mentioning?"

"A very good friend. Someone who actually cares about me. Unlike other people I could mention! She thought I was a bit naive about certain aspects of life. So, like I was saying, she loaned me some educational literature."

"Let me guess," Kyle sighed, shaking his head. "Your mother found them?"

"Bingo! And, do you know what she did?"

"Burned them?"

"Besides that!"

Disgusted, Kyle shrugged.

"She sat me down and gave me a rehashed version of the talk we'd had when I was twelve. It was all I could do to keep from giggling. She was the color of your t-shirt the entire time," she said, pointing to Kyle's red shirt. "Then I got this prudish lecture on the evils of porn. Like I'm sure I was going to keep those magazines! I was going to throw them away myself. She just never gave me the chance. It's the same old story. She rushes in, interferes, and assumes the worst."

"Don't you think you're being unfair?"

"No!"

"Look, I'll admit that parents aren't perfect. They make mistakes. But, from what you've told me, it's no wonder Aunt Sue came unglued the other night. Maybe she accused you of some painful things, but think about what you've put her through, especially the past couple of days. She looks like walking death. Maybe you've had your feelings hurt, but she's had her heart shattered."

"Kyle, I don't need another lecture!

"I'm not lecturing! But it's time to end the pain. Tell your mother what really happened."

"I will when I'm good and ready," she retorted, rising. "And now, if you'll excuse me, Mr. Know-It-All, I'm going in to find some Tylenol. You've given me a headache."

"Kate . . ."

"Back off, Kyle. Oh, and in case you've forgotten, you've promised to keep silent about this. And returned missionaries never lie, right?" Refusing to look at him, she marched into the house, slamming the screen door behind her.

"Kate," he said, in total exasperation, helplessly watching as she disappeared into the house. He finally stood, walking out to the middle of the yard. Drawing his foot back, he kicked the soccer ball over the back fence.

CHAPTER TWELVE

Greg slowly lowered the weights Stan had assigned him into the metal rests at the head of the weight bench.

"Not bad, old man," Stan said, grinning.

"Thanks," Greg replied, sitting up. He took a deep breath and wiped the perspiration from his face with the bottom of his t-shirt.

"How about a soak in the hot tub?"

"Sounds good," Greg admitted, retrieving his glasses from Stan's extended hand. As he slid them into place, he thought about how wonderful he'd feel tomorrow. He'd probably be so stiff, he'd have to make Sue push him around in a stroller. "So, I gather you were able to talk with your little sister before supper."

Slowly nodding, Stan wondered how to handle this.

"Don't worry, I won't ask. I know something's up. And I think I even have a pretty good idea what it's about. I just wish Sue would level with me."

"She will," Stan replied, gazing down at the tiled floor.

"The way she's acting, I'd almost guess Kate was pregnant."

Stan quickly glanced up, staring at his brother-in-law.

"I know things have been too thick between Jace and Kate. The hours they keep. The way she sneaks off to meet him. It's not good, Stan. Sue must've stumbled onto something the other night. They were really having it out before I interrupted them." He gripped the back of his neck with one hand and tried to unkink his neck. "And, of course, I'm merely the father, so I'm not entitled to know why they both look like casualties of war."

"Greg, Sue wants to tell you, but she's afraid of ruining the rest of the trip for you . . ."

"It's already ruined! Kate has sabotaged us like you wouldn't believe."

"Talk to Sue, Greg. I think she'll open up. She really needs you right now."

"I know. I've been holding off, hoping she'd come to me with it. But, I think it's time I started putting the pieces of my family back together."

"If there's anything Paige and I can do to help . . ."

"Thanks for the offer. I may need some assistance patching."

"You've got it," Stan promised, handing Greg a soft towel.

Greg threw the towel around his neck. "Let's go have that soak first," he said, slowly rising to his feet. "It'll give me time to think of a strategy."

"Not to mention a chance to relax the stiffness," Stan teased.

"Who's stiff?" Greg asked, hobbling to the door. "I'll race you up the stairs."

"On your knees, maybe," Stan joked as the two men bolted for the door.

Kate cautiously wandered through the main level of the house. She didn't want to talk to anyone. Quietly moving up the stairs, she was anxious to find the room she'd been assigned to share with Sabrina. The way her head was pounding, she wanted to lie down. The Tylenol hadn't made a dent in the pain. Walking past a closed door, she heard someone sob. She took a step back and listened carefully. She scowled, realizing it was her mother. Great! Now who was the woman blubbering to? She'd already figured out that her mother had confided in Uncle Stan. The look he'd given her at dinner was a pretty good indication. Maybe now the tragic tale was being shared with her dad. Fine! Great! Let everyone think she was a tramp! Maybe she'd go home and prove them right. Maybe Jace would be in for a little homecoming surprise!

She muttered under her breath and moved away from the door. Then she stopped, recognizing Paige's soft voice. Aunt Paige knew? Her heart sagged with an intense heaviness. Would her aunt believe the lie? Pressing her ear against the door, she strained to hear what was being said. She only caught a muffled sentence, but it was enough to confirm the dread in her heart. ". . . young people sometimes make horrible mistakes. . ." Kate backed away, her eyes glistening with tears. She bolted to a darkened bedroom down the hall. Closing the door, she threw herself onto the bed and sobbed into a pillow.

Nearly an hour later, Paige left Sue alone with Greg. She closed the guest room door and walked down to the bedroom Kate would be sharing with Sabrina. She couldn't remember if she'd gathered the pile of dirty sheets from the double bed. Turning the knob, she walked in. As she reached for the light switch, she saw a still form lying on top of the bed. She impatiently waited for her eyes to adjust to the darkness. What was Kate doing in bed already? Quietly closing the door, she moved to the bed and saw that her niece was sound asleep. She shook her head, then moved to the closet for an extra blanket.

When she came back to the bed, she unfolded the yellow blanket and carefully covered the sleeping teen. She nearly jumped when Kate moaned, rolling onto her back. As Paige gazed down at her, a lump formed in her throat. It was obvious her niece had been crying. "Oh, Kate, what have you done to yourself?" she asked in a hushed voice.

". . . mmph . . . no . . . Mom . . ."

Paige blinked. Did her niece always talk in her sleep?

". . . nnmph . . . nomph . . . not true . . . nomph . . . mmmnnn . . ." Quieting, Kate rolled onto her side, the blanket settling around her hips.

Paige leaned across the bed to pull the blanket back over her niece. Smoothing the long hair away from the teenager's face, she then quietly left the room, puzzled by the mumbled words.

"Well, I still say they've let that girl get away with too much over the years," Stan growled as he slipped into his pajamas.

"Stan, don't be so judgmental. Look what we went through with Tami. We're very lucky that little scenario didn't blossom into this."

"Maybe," Stan admitted, turning down the covers on his side

of the king-sized bed. "But, if you ask me, Tami has always had more sense than Kate. Sorry, but I call 'em as I see 'em."

"Not that you're prejudiced or anything," she said dryly.

"That's entirely beside the point," he replied, smiling at his wife. "You always have had a soft spot for Kate," he added, sitting down on the bed.

"True," she admitted, wiggling out of her white robe.

"Why? She's about as obnoxious as they come! And that temper of hers!"

"Sounds like someone else I know and love," she teased, approaching her side of the bed.

"Do m'ears deceive me," he said with an Irish lilt, "or is it m'sainted wife is mockin' me again?"

"Been kissing the old blarney stone lately?" she asked, giving him a dirty look. "I know Kate has her problems. But beneath that tough exterior is a very sweet young lady."

"Now that's a lot of blarney!"

"I call 'em as I see 'em," she said, imitating her husband. "And right now, Sue isn't the only one who's hurting."

"True. There's Greg, Tyler, Sabrina, you, me . . ."

"And Kate."

Stan slipped between the sheets, rolling on his side to ignore his wife.

"I'm not so sure we have all of the pieces yet, either," she continued, sitting down on the bed.

"How much more do you need to know?" he asked, turning onto his back to glare at her. "I think the facts are pretty much in."

"I'm not so sure about that. I want to hear Kate's side of the story."

"That ought to be entertaining!"

Paige ignored him and reached to turn off the lamp on the nightstand.

"And what makes you think she'll talk to you? She didn't earlier. I think Sue's right. She's too ashamed to face you with what she's done."

"We'll see," Paige murmured, sliding into bed. "We'll see."

CHAPTER THIRTEEN

The next day was spent wandering around Salt Lake City. First, they went to see "Legacy" at the Joseph Smith Memorial Building. They then visited several landmarks, including the Beehive House, Brigham Young's former official residence, and the Lion House, the home constructed for twelve of his wives.

"The poor man," Stan quipped as they left the Lion House. "I can't even keep up with one!"

"I hear you," Greg agreed, both men ignoring the looks they were getting from their indignant spouses.

"After that cutting remark, I think our dear husbands owe us a trip to the mall," Paige said to Sue.

"I hear you," Sue replied, echoing her husband.

"All right," Stan answered, grinning at Greg. He was glad his in-laws were doing their best to keep a stiff upper lip today. All but Kate. The teenager kept to herself, giving frosty glares to anyone who attempted to speak to her, including Paige.

After supper, Stan talked everyone into gathering downstairs in the family room. "I've got something to show you," he bragged, moving to a large, covered object. He quietly removed the blanket he'd used to hide the treasure from the past.

"Grandma Colleen's trunk!" Sue exclaimed, quickly moving beside her brother.

"How . . . where . . ."

"It was hiding in Uncle David's attic," Stan replied, enjoying the look of surprised pleasure on his sister's face.

"We thought it was lost forever," she said, kneeling to run her hands over the weathered exterior.

"I know. We sort of lost track of it after Dad's parents passed away. Uncle David was hoarding it."

"Sounds like him," Sue muttered. "Have you opened it?"

"Yes."

"Well, let's see what's in here," Sue said excitedly. "May I?" she asked, glancing at Stan.

"Be my guest," he replied. He watched in amused silence as Sue slowly raised the metal lid encased in a wooden frame. She gasped, then lowered her hands into the trunk, pulling out a worn, red velvet-covered book. "Go ahead, try it, the music box still works," Stan encouraged.

Sue carefully wound the tiny music box neatly hidden in the back of the book.

"What exactly is it?" Greg asked, intrigued by the tinkling sounds emanating from the book.

"It's a combination photo album and music box. They were all the rage back in the late eighteen hundreds."

"It's beautiful," Sue sighed, reverently opening the cover to gaze at the small tintypes and faded black and white pictures. "That's Aunt Molly there, right?" she asked, pointing to an oval-shaped picture of a beautiful woman.

"Yep, that's who you get your looks from," Stan teased.

And where Kate gets her rebellious streak, Sue thought quietly, glancing at her brooding daughter.

"We're not sure, but we think that's a wedding picture of Grandma Colleen and Grandpa James," Stan said, kneeling to point out the tintype of a couple dressed in their finest attire.

Tyler had moved to peek over his mother's shoulder. "Well, they look real happy," he commented, pointing to the picture.

"Back then, people were discouraged from smiling in pictures. I guess they thought it looked more dignified to frown," Stan explained.

"Maybe I'll try that in our next family picture," Tyler joked.

"Don't you dare," Sue warned, setting the book on the carpeted floor. "What other family treasures are in here?" she asked, gazing into the trunk. As Stan helped her look through the other antique heirlooms, Paige retrieved the velvet-covered photo album. She walked to the couch and sat next to Kate, hoping to initiate a conversation.

"There's the woman you're named after," Paige said, pointing to a worn tintype. "Grandma Colleen."

Kate shrugged, barely glancing at the woman in the picture.

"Your Uncle Stan thinks Tami looks a lot like her," Paige continued, smiling warmly at her niece.

"Then why didn't you saddle her with the name?" Kate asked coldly.

Raising an eyebrow, Paige gazed at the defiant teenager. "Tami was named after my mother," she said quietly.

Kate ignored the expression on her aunt's face, and glanced at the pictures, one in particular drawing her attention. She stared at the beautiful woman with a haunted look, curiosity getting the best of her. "Who's that?" she asked, pointing to the picture.

"Your Aunt Molly," Paige replied.

"Why does she seem so . . . unhappy?"

"She made a lot of mistakes in her life."

"Oh, right! What did she do, forget to churn the butter?"

"She left the Church when she was not much older than you. According to your Uncle Stan, her mother, Grandma Colleen, died shortly after that. It was said she died of a broken heart."

Kate stiffened, receiving her aunt's message loud and clear. Giving Paige an intensely cold glare, she left the room.

CHAPTER FOURTEEN

I don't ever want to hear another lecture on the evils of sleeping in church," Greg quietly teased, draping his arm around his wife's shoulders.

Sue shifted uncomfortably on the padded bench, forcing her eyes open, fighting an intense battle to stay awake. Blinking rapidly, she straightened, stifling a yawn.

"You two are a real pair," Greg whispered, nodding his head at Paige, who was experiencing a similar struggle.

Sue glanced down the bench at her sister-in-law. Greg was right. Paige was frantically trying to keep her eyes open. "I can't believe this," Sue said, covering the yawn that wouldn't go away.

"I can. Look at the amount of sleep you've been getting lately."

"I know. Things are better now, though. At least I have someone to cry with me at night."

"You mean Paige?"

"I mean you, smart aleck," Sue replied, leaning against her husband. "I should've told you Wednesday night."

"True. But, it's water under the bridge. Hopefully we can finish sorting this mess out after we head home to Bozeman tomorrow."

"You're sure about this?" Sue asked quietly.

Greg slowly nodded. "I don't think any of us are in the mood to continue with our vacation plans. And we're not making much progress with Kate here."

Sue sadly smiled and reached to squeeze her husband's hand. Glancing around, she suddenly looked concerned. The sacrament hymn was nearly finished. She prayed Kate would have the decency to avoid partaking from the silver trays. She shuddered when she realized how many times her daughter had participated unworthily Sunday after Sunday.

"Are you cold?" Greg whispered.

Sue shook her head, then quickly closed her eyes for the prayer.

A few minutes later, a tall youth wearing a colorful tie with his crisp white shirt approached their bench. Tyler took the offered tray, holding it out for Rachel and Renae. He then handed it down to Kyle. The returned missionary balanced it for Johnny, then passed it to Kate. Sue sucked in sharply, staring at her daughter.

Kate reached into the tray, more out of habit than desire. Sensing someone was boring holes through her, she glanced up. She scowled as she read the expression on her mother's face. She rolled her eyes, dropped the piece of bread, and passed the tray to Sabrina.

Oh, that's right! I'm not good enough for the Church. How silly of me to forget, Kate fumed in silence.

"But, Kate, you didn't take one," Sabrina whispered.

Kate ignored her little sister and focused on the strangers sitting in front of them. She smirked, staring at a woman with blue-tinted hair.

"Mom," Sabrina said, turning to gaze at her mother, "Kate didn't . . ."

"I know, sweetie," Sue quickly whispered. "Don't worry about it. It's all right."

"Is she sick?"

"Something like that," Sue quietly replied, taking the tray from the five-year-old. She handed it to Greg, refusing to let tears form.

"This was a neat idea, Dad," Tyler said excitedly as the two families wandered down a sidewalk flanked by a tall, metal fence. "I wish I'd brought my camera, though," he added, gazing up at the towering spires of the Salt Lake Temple.

"Sorry, son, this was a spontaneous kind of thing," Greg

explained, tugging at his tie.

"I still don't know why we're here," Kate complained, annoyed that they'd come straight from church. The high heels she'd borrowed from her aunt were killing her feet. Not to mention how difficult it was to walk in the tight, black leather skirt she'd brought, just in case. She'd never dreamed she'd be wearing it to church in her uncle's ward. Stuffing a white blouse inside of the skirt, she'd unbuttoned it to the point of obscenity. Then, reluctantly giving in to her mother's disapproving glare, she'd refastened one button. She'd had to wear her aunt's dress shoes instead of the black boots she normally used as an accent. They'd been forgotten, left in Bozeman.

"I thought this would be a perfect Sunday afternoon activity," her father said, interrupting her train of thought.

"Well, if this little adventure is for my benefit, you can forget it. It's not going to change anything!" Kate snapped, hanging back as the others continued moving forward.

Sue gazed tiredly at her daughter. Why had Kate chosen today to find her voice? The sullen silent treatment had been better than this. She sighed, anticipating another shouting match with the feisty teen. But, when she saw that Paige was making her way to Kate's side, she decided to let someone else bear the brunt of her daughter's anger. Turning, she followed the rest of her family through the metal gate.

Paige moved directly in front of her glowering niece. "Give it a chance, Kate," she said quietly, her brown eyes pleading for cooperation. "I know you're going through a rough time right now, but . . ."

"Leave me alone," Kate warned, glaring at the woman who had betrayed her.

"Kate . . ." Paige said softly, "we all love you so much . . ."

"Then you have a funny way of showing it," Kate retorted. "None of you care! You're all so wrapped up in judging me none of you can see straight! And you're worse than the others! I've always known where I stood with everyone else. But I thought you were different. I really thought you cared . . ."

Paige silenced her niece by grabbing the young woman's shoulders and gazing directly into the bitter eyes. "I do care," she said. "We all care. And if you weren't so wrapped up in self-pity, maybe you'd see that!"

Kate pulled away from her aunt and marched off. Paige reluctantly let her go. She leaned against the dark metal fence and gazed up at the sky. "Please, Father, help her," she whispered. "Touch her heart. Help her see what she's doing to herself . . . to all of us."

"Mom?"

Startled, Paige focused on Kyle. "Yes?"

"I need some advice," he said, looking as miserable as she felt.

"About what?"

"Well . . . if a person knows something that would change the way everyone's feeling . . . but, they've promised not to tell . . . what should they do?"

Paige stared at her son. "What exactly are you trying to say?" she finally asked.

"That's just it, I can't. I've promised . . . given my word that I wouldn't say anything. But, I see what it's doing to you . . . to Dad . . . to Aunt Sue . . ."

"Kyle Mahoney, if you know something about this mess with Kate, tell me!"

"But I promised Kate I wouldn't."

"You've talked to her about what's going on?"

Kyle slowly nodded.

"And, what you're saying, or rather not saying, is that we don't know the whole story?"

Kyle nodded again.

"Look, in most instances, I would applaud your loyalty. But, to be honest, if you don't tell me what you know, I'm going to wring your neck!"

"Mom!"

"Kyle, you can see how everyone's hurting over this. If you know something that would help, I'm sure Heavenly Father would be very understanding if you shared it with me now. I promise I'll take full responsibility!"

"Well, I would like to get it off my chest. Kate can be so stubborn sometimes . . ."

"Cut to the chase. What's going on?"

"She lied to her mother." Kyle quickly explained what Kate had told him about the incident in Jackson.

"It was all a lie?" Paige said, sweet relief replacing the knot in her stomach. "Kyle, you may have just added years to your mother's life." She grabbed him, pulled his face down and gave him a big kiss on the cheek. Startled, Kyle rubbed at the lipstick she'd left on his face.

"So she's never actually . . . you know . . . been with a guy?" she asked, blushing.

Kyle shook his head, trying not to smile. His mother didn't embarrass easily. This was a side of her he didn't see very often.

"You're sure, Kyle?"

"Mom, you should've heard the things she admitted doing. She's made some mistakes, some of them pretty serious, but she was telling me the truth about that. You should've seen the look in her eyes. I've never seen her so upset."

"Then why doesn't she straighten this out with her mother?"

"She said she tried, but Aunt Sue wouldn't listen. I guess Kate finally gave up."

"Well, this certainly sheds a new light on the whole mess." Scowling, she glanced through the metal fence at the people walking around on the other side. "I'm almost tempted to turn that girl over my knee! Does she have any idea what she's put us through?"

"Go easy on her, Mom. She's suffered quite a bit herself. I think it really killed her when Aunt Sue believed everything she said. Then when you did . . . she's always admired you so much. It devastated her."

Paige slowly nodded. "Okay. But, if you think Kate's got a temper, wait until you see your Aunt Sue's reaction to this little revelation."

"Can I go wait in the mini-van?"

Shaking her head, Paige firmly gripped her son's arm, dragging him down the sidewalk. "I'm not facing this one alone," she said as they hurried through the gate.

Kate glanced around at the busy visitors' center. "Jace, I wish you were here," she said in a hushed voice. "You and Linda were right. You are the only ones who really care about me." She moved away from a group of excited Japanese tourists and wandered around with bored indifference, avoiding the missionaries who seemed to be everywhere answering questions. She knew they couldn't begin to answer the questions she longed to ask.

She retreated into a corner and ignored the painting of the Savior beside her. Leaning against the wall, she defiantly loosened a button on her blouse. She then closed her eyes and wondered when this nightmare of a vacation would end.

"Kate?"

Kate opened her eyes to return her mother's stare.

Sue's eyes shifted from her daughter's face to the blouse. Gritting her teeth, she decided not to push the issue. "Are you okay?" she asked, wondering if Paige had gotten anywhere.

"Just peachy! And you?"

"Do you honestly need to ask?"

Kate looked away, bothered by the expression on her mother's face. *It's her own fault,* she silently thought. *Why should I care what she's feeling?*

"Look, I know you're not exactly thrilled to be here, but would you at least give it a chance?"

"Why?"

"Because this should mean something to you. We're surrounded by our heritage. Didn't you gain anything from "Legacy" yesterday?"

"A little beauty rest," she replied. It was the truth. She hadn't slept well the night before. Once the lights had dimmed, she'd managed to doze in the soft, padded chair. There were times when thundering hoof beats and loud voices coming from the huge screen had jarred her awake, but she'd refused to watch the historical movie. None of it interested her. None of it at all.

Sue gazed down at her hands. The initial shock of her daughter's confession was wearing off. The anger was fading to sorrow. Kate was still her daughter, despite what she had done. "Honey, I don't think you understand what you're giving up."

"I see. You've already written me off."

"You know that's not true," Sue said softly, realizing she very nearly had. "But you do have a long, hard road ahead of you if you don't start turning things around now." She paused, gazing intently at her daughter. "There is a way back, Kate. But it won't happen if you close your heart to the good things life has to offer."

"Like this wonderful little tourist attraction?" Kate asked snidely.

"This place is more than just a tourist attraction. It contains a history of what our Heavenly Father has given us in love. He wants us to be able to return to him someday. By restoring the true church, he's provided a way back through his son, Jesus Christ. Surely you understand all of that?"

"Guess not."

Struggling with her temper, Sue decided to use a different approach. "Do you realize how much our ancestors sacrificed to belong to the Church?"

Kate shrugged.

"Do you know what they went through so that their posterity, of which you are a part, could be born into the Church, under the covenant?"

"Oh, so they're the ones I can blame."

Choosing to ignore her daughter's comment, Sue persisted. "The woman you're named after, Colleen Mahoney, was an example of tremendous courage."

"Go tell someone who cares, because I certainly don't!" Kate snapped.

"You should care, young lady, and care very much! It's because of her that you and I even exist! I've tried telling you this before, only you've never listened. Well, you're going to listen now! I want you to understand who you're going to have to face someday."

"Oh, honestly!" Kate rolled her eyes at the look on her mother's face. "All right, if it will make you feel better, go ahead. Tell me all about good old Grandma what's-'er-fanny!"

Frowning severely, Sue glared at her daughter. "Grandma Colleen came from Ireland with her husband, James, in 1835. Two of their children died during the long journey across the ocean. Their tiny bodies were wrapped in dirty blankets and buried at sea." She paused, but Kate's face revealed nothing. Sighing, she continued. "The Mahoneys joined the Church after hearing two

Mormon missionaries preach the gospel in New York. They later moved from New York to Missouri. There, they were driven from their home at Far West by an angry mob who burned it to the ground. Taking the few possessions left to them, they fled to Nauvoo, Illinois in the middle of winter.

"Grandpa James was a skilled carpenter, and after building a new home for his own family, he helped build several for the other Saints. We've been told that he also assisted in the construction of the Nauvoo temple. It nearly broke his heart when they were driven from Illinois in 1846, two years after Joseph Smith was killed. Gathering their meager belongings into a covered wagon, the Mahoneys began the long journey west.

"They made it to Winter Quarters, Nebraska, where Uncle James died of scurvy a few months later. Unwilling to give up, Grandma Colleen insisted on making the trip to Salt Lake Valley with her remaining children in the spring of 1848. Her youngest child became ill and died just before they reached the valley. Her oldest daughter, Molly, rebelled and left the Church after that."

"So?" Kate asked, blowing at a piece of stiff hair.

"So? After everything Colleen went through, she never lost faith in the gospel."

"That's not what I heard. Aunt Paige said she finally gave up and died when Molly left," Kate pointed out.

"We don't know that for sure. Her death happened to coincide with Molly's disappearance. Regardless, Grandma Colleen was a courageous, compassionate woman, and because of her example, her two remaining sons stayed active in the Church. We descended from the youngest one, Daniel," she said, studying her daughter's face. Disappointed, she realized Kate was tuning her out. Her daughter was staring off into the distance, disgust curving her lips into a pouting grimace. "Kate? Kate!"

"Oh, sorry. Have you finally finished?"

"Stop it! I don't know why I bother. None of what I've said has even fazed you!"

"I'm a lost cause, remember?" Kate asked smugly.

"I've just about had all I'm going to take from you, you miserable little . . ."

"Slut? Is that what you were going to say, Mother?" Kate

retorted. "Well, believe it or not, we seem to have a lot in common, because I'm not going to take any more of this, either! No more lectures, no more accusations, no more pretending that we care about each other when we don't, because I'm out of here! Out of this building, out of the Church, and out of your life!" Whirling around, she stomped back the way she'd come in.

"Kate, come back here, now!" Sue threatened, her face flushing with embarrassed rage. People were staring. But, suddenly, she didn't care. She didn't care about anything but catching up with her daughter and having this out once and for all.

Kate glanced over her shoulder and saw that her mother was coming after her. "Leave me alone!" she thundered, pushing people out of the way. She increased her speed and tripped up the carpeted steps.

Serves you right, Sue thought, as she paused to catch her breath. She hurried on, running up the same steps Kate had climbed. She failed to notice that Sabrina was tagging along behind.

"Okay, here's the plan. We'll tie Sue and Kate to chairs in separate corners. Then one of us will try to reason with them."

"One of us?" Kyle nervously asked.

"Yes. That's where you come in, dear. After all, we've had two extra days of suffering, thanks to you. You could've cleared this up Friday night. But no, you decided to sit back and watch everyone bask in misery."

"Mom!"

"What?"

"I've suffered too," he pointed out.

"Not as much as you're going to," she promised. "Just wait till Aunt Sue gets hold of you."

"Speaking of which, there she goes now after Kate."

"Oh, great," Paige muttered as she watched her sister-in-law chase her niece down the sidewalk on the other side of the temple grounds. "C'mon, son, it's time to save the day." Racing across the green lawn, she jumped over a flower bed.

More than surprised at his mother's agility, he followed, making the same leap himself.

Kate stumbled when the heel broke off one of her aunt's shoes. Swearing under her breath, she paused long enough to take them both off. She threw the shoes to the side and continued running, unwilling to let her mother catch up with her. She ignored the burning sensation of her nylon-clad feet as they pounded against the hot cement. Dashing out of the gate, she glanced at the busy street. If she hurried, she could probably beat the string of cars coming her direction.

"What . . . is . . . with . . . these . . . two?" Paige complained over her shoulder. She slowed down to catch her breath.

"Where'd they go?" Kyle asked as he caught up with his mother.

"Through that gate. C'mon," she said, picking up the pace.

"Hey, Mom, what's that?" Kyle asked, pointing to a flower bed.

"They look like shoes . . . my shoes." She hurried off the sidewalk and scooped them up, wincing over the broken heel.

A piercing scream shattered the air. Dropping the shoes, Paige tore out of the gate. Kyle was right behind her. They watched in stunned silence as a car sped towards Sabrina.

The scene laid out before their horrified eyes paralyzed them. Everyone seemed to be moving in slow motion. Kate stopped, whirling around at the sound of her mother's scream. Her eyes widened when she saw the car and little Sabrina, who was too scared to move. She raced back, picked up her little sister, and threw her in the direction of their mother. She then tried desperately to move out of the way. The car swerved the same direction Kate headed, throwing her into the air. She landed with a dull thump near the sidewalk.

Sue screamed in silence, clinging to Sabrina. Paige moved to her side. Sue tried to speak, but the words were lodged in her throat. Numbly handing Sabrina to Paige, she forced herself down to where a crowd had gathered. They parted as she approached, reverently giving her place beside the crumpled form. Kneeling, she reached a trembling hand to smooth the hair from the unsmiling face.

PART 2

. . . if thou be cast into the deep; if the billowing surge conspire against thee; if fierce winds become thine enemy; if the heavens gather blackness, and all the elements combine to hedge up the way; . . . know thou . . . that all these things shall give thee experience, and shall be for thy good.

D & C 122:7

CHAPTER FIFTEEN

The two families sat in stunned silence in the designated waiting room of the L.D.S. Hospital, their grim faces sharing common expressions. Sue hadn't spoken a word since they'd arrived. She sat quietly between Greg and Stan, clinging to the hands of comfort they offered. Paige was sitting nearby, holding Sabrina close, quieting the small girl's whimpers. Tyler stood near the door, keeping his back to the others as he occasionally wiped at eyes that were beyond his control.

Kyle sat in a corner staring at his hands. *My fault,* his mind silently taunted. *My fault.* He was unaware that each person in the room was shouldering similar blame. Tyler, for not watching Sabrina. Rachel and Renae, for distracting Tyler. Stan, for not noticing any of this. Greg, for being in the rest room when the whole thing had happened. Johnny, for pointing out to Sabrina that her mother was leaving the building. Paige, for arriving too late. Sabrina, for wandering out into the busy street. But, as miserable as they all felt, none carried the guilt-ridden weight of Sue.

Please, Father, don't take her from me now, she silently pleaded. *Give us another chance.* "She can't die now, Greg," she whispered, her voice cracking. "We can't lose her now! We'll lose her forever."

Shaking his head, Greg tightened his grip around her shoulders. "She'll live, Sue," he promised. "Remember the blessing?"

Nodding, she tried to focus on the words her husband had been inspired to utter. " . . . you will recover from these injuries, serious though they may be. The pain you will endure may be severe, but all things will serve a valiant purpose." As she remembered, an unexplained calm settled within. "She'll be all right," Sue said softly. "She has to be."

Paige glanced at Kyle. He looked up, his agonized stare tearing at her heart. A forceful prompting penetrated the overwhelming emotions clamoring for her attention. Sue needed to know. She needed to hear that her daughter's innocence was intact. Paige quietly handed Sabrina to Renae. Rising, she held her hand out to Kyle. She gripped his hand with loving tenderness and led him across the room, then released him to reach for her purse.

She removed her wallet and searched for a handful of loose change, giving it to Rachel. "Go get a snack for these kids," she said quietly to her daughter. "There are a couple of dispensing machines down the hall. We need some time alone with Aunt Sue," she whispered, indicating that the twins should take Tyler, Johnny and Sabrina and leave the room. Rachel obediently herded them out into the hall.

Puzzled, Stan gazed at his wife when she moved to close the door. "Paige, what is it?" he asked as she turned around.

"There's something you all need to be told," she said solemnly. "And I think it needs to be said now. Kyle?" Kyle moved in front of his aunt and uncle as his mother moved to sit near his father.

"I'm not sure how to say this. I made Kate a promise Friday night. I know I should've told Mom sooner. I'm so sorry . . ." His voice broke. Struggling for composure, he told them everything Kate had said. He then gazed at Sue, his eyes begging for forgiveness.

Stunned, Sue stared past her nephew, reliving the events of Wednesday night. Moaning, she buried her face in her hands.

"Son, you're sure about this?"

Kyle nodded at his father.

"Stan, I know it's the truth," Paige said softly. "I kept wondering if we had the whole story. The way Kate looked at us, like we'd done something to hurt her."

"She's right, Stan. The pieces all fit. Kate has acted like a wounded bear since Wednesday night. Now we know why," Greg said, tightening his grip around Sue's shoulders. "I appreciate how hard this has been for you, Kyle," he added, smiling grimly at his nephew. "Don't blame yourself for what's happened. Kate should've been the one to tell us."

"I really thought she would," Kyle stammered, sinking into a chair. "I should've said something earlier."

"It's not your fault," Sue said, lifting her face to gaze at Kyle. "If anyone's to blame, it's me," she added, slowly rising to her feet. She crossed the room and stared at the ceiling. "What have I done?" she asked, her voice fading to a whisper.

Standing, Paige quickly moved behind her sister-in-law, gently turning her around. "Sue, it's not your fault either. We all thought the same thing. And Kate didn't help matters. Don't blame yourself." She embraced her sister-in-law as Sue began to sob.

After what seemed like an eternity, a doctor entered the somber room. Uncomfortably aware of the questions in their eyes, he sighed.

"How is Kate?" Greg asked, standing.

"All things considered, she's lucky to still be with us."

"Then, she'll be all right?" Sue asked, rising to stand next to her husband.

"In time, I believe so. We just finished casting her left leg. It's fractured in two places. She has a broken rib, and one that's cracked, plus numerous scrapes and contusions. None of these are serious or life-threatening. It's amazing there were no internal injuries. But . . ."

"What?" Stan asked sharply.

"She hasn't regained consciousness yet. We're afraid she's slipping into a coma."

"No," Sue moaned, clinging to Greg.

"Her forehead hit against solid pavement. It took several stitches to close the gash. We haven't seen any signs of clots or swelling, but she has sustained a concussion. Hopefully, after a day or two of recovery, she'll snap out of this. Sometimes our bodies have a way of shutting down to heal. We'll just hope for the best."

Sue sank onto the couch, frightened by what the doctor was

saying and yet not saying. What if Kate never woke up? What if her daughter regained consciousness, but was unable to function as before? The others continued listening to the doctor. But for her, the world had stopped. The voices were incoherent buzzings that didn't make sense. Wrapping her arms around herself, she began to rock back and forth, unaware of the moaning that came from her lips. She couldn't feel it when Paige and Greg sat on either side of her, trying to offer comfort. Her daughter was in a coma, and it was all her fault.

CHAPTER SIXTEEN

K ate moaned. Her eyelids felt heavy. Her mouth was dry, and her head pounded with relentless fury. "What happened?" she asked, the sound of her own voice sending a splitting pain through the center of her skull.

She forced her eyes open and glanced around, waiting for her eyes to adjust to the darkness. But the blackness wouldn't fade. Panicking, she sat up. "Ow!" she exclaimed, holding her stomach. How could one person hurt so much? She took tinier breaths. The pain wasn't as bad, but the darkness refused to go away.

She slowly turned her head, but nothing was visible. "Oh, nice! What am I now, blind?" No one answered. A cooling breeze played with her hair. Confused, she felt around for a clue that would reveal where she was. She reached under one leg and pulled out what felt like a small, sharp pebble. Shivering, she threw it away and tried to remember what had happened. Things were so fuzzy. She had no idea where she was.

She tried to stand, but one leg collapsed beneath her. Moaning as her head collided with a hard surface, she sank into the depths of unconsciousness.

A loud shot rang out, jarring her awake. "What the . . ." Sitting up sharply, Kate swore. She blinked, her eyes slowly adjusting to the bright sunlight. At least she could see now. Shading her eyes, she turned, spotting a man on horseback. He was pointing a rifle at her. "Don't shoot . . . please," she stammered, slowly lifting her hands into the air.

David Miles lowered his rifle. Shaking his head, he pointed to the ground beside her. Kate turned to look and screamed.

"It's all right, it's dead," he assured her, replacing the Hawken .56 caliber rifle in the bedroll behind the saddle.

Kate was still gaping at the red-banded body beside her. "It's a . . . a snake," she whimpered.

"A copperhead," he added, smiling at her. "You're lucky I happened along. One bite from that pesky critter, and you'd be a very sick girl." As he glanced from the snake to the young woman, David raised an eyebrow. What was a girl doing out here alone, dressed like that? He gaped at the short, tight skirt and the blouse with the plunging neckline. Flushing, he concentrated on her face instead. He stared, stunned by how familiar she seemed. "Where's the rest of your train?" he asked, assuming she must have wandered away from a nearby wagon train.

"Train?" she asked, confused, wondering if Amtrak was nearby. Staring at the man in the dusty hat, she blinked.

"Your family . . . the people you came out here with . . . where are they?"

"I . . . I don't know," she stammered, trying to stand. Her head pounded furiously. Sharp pains cut through her chest as she took a step forward. Collapsing, she fell onto her stomach in the prairie grass.

David scowled, adjusting his tight-fitting hat down low over his black hair. "Miss?" When she didn't answer, he slid down from his horse, dropped the reins to the ground, and hurried to the young woman's side. Turning her over, he searched for signs of injury. Puzzled, he found nothing until he checked her strangely covered legs. A familiar swelling caught his eye. The copperhead had already done its mischief. He drew out a knife, wiping it on his soft, buckskin breeches. Holding it up to the sun, he peered at the sharp blade. He tore the flimsy stocking out of the way, then tried to brace her leg with one hand while he used the other to open the snake bite.

Kate moaned, but didn't open her eyes. David quickly forced blood from the cut. Replacing his knife in his belt, he knelt down to suck the poison from her leg. He spit out the bitter fluid, continuing until he was satisfied that he'd done his best. He walked back to his saddlebags to search for something that could be used as a bandage.

He found nothing but an extra shirt. The only one he had. It would have to do. He tucked it under his arm and walked back to the unconscious girl. He knelt down and prepared to rip the homespun garment. Scowling, he tried to forget that it had been made for him by his mother in Nauvoo. She was gone now. Like everyone else in his family. Reluctantly gripping the shirt, he glanced at the girl. He could see something white hanging down past her skirt. Relieved, he tucked his shirt inside of the buckskin jacket he was wearing. Grabbing hold of what looked like some form of a petticoat, he ripped it loose. The material was unlike anything he'd ever touched before. Smooth and silky, not coarse or stiff like most linens. He quickly dabbed at the oozing cut, then wrapped the white fabric around the leg, firmly tying it in place.

He picked the moaning girl up in his arms and carried her to the horse. Carefully balancing her body, he lifted the young woman up, setting her across the front of his saddle. He steadied her from behind, then climbed up and grabbed at the reins. Murmuring to his horse, he turned the animal around to head back the way he'd come.

"Come, Molly, take Shannon and settle her in the wagon. Captain Roberts wants to break camp as soon as possible."

An attractive redhead with flashing green eyes gripped her younger sister's hand, marching the girl to the wagon.

Colleen Mahoney walked up to examine one of their three oxen. Jamie had mentioned it was acting lame. Patting the animal's head sympathetically, she knew it had been pushed beyond endurance.

"Here, Mother, let me do it," Jamie offered, moving to his mother's side. Gently brushing her aside, he bent down to lift up the afflicted leg. "It's caught a stone," he said, reaching for his knife. "I'll make it right," he assured her, digging the culprit out of the hoof. "There now, good as new," the fifteen-year-old said with a smile, releasing the leg.

"Ah, Jamie, I can always depend on you. You are your father's son."

Jamie tried not to grin as he examined the wooden yoke. "We'd best be on our way," he said.

"True enough," she answered with a sad smile, moving to affectionately pat their cow's nose. She hated seeing it yoked up with the oxen, but they had no choice. Not since losing one of their sturdy oxen as they'd crossed the Elkhorn River. "On with the journey." She glanced up as excited voices clamored near the front of the wagon train. "Now what is the matter?" she wondered aloud, moving toward the commotion.

"It's David, Mother," nine-year-old Daniel said, running toward his mother. "He's found a girl on the trail. She's snakebit."

Colleen pursed her lips together, glancing up at the scout who had ridden back into camp. David Miles was a fine young man. If only Molly would give him a chance. Her thoughts were forced to the present crisis as she gazed at the girl David had brought with him. Her eyes widened at the sight of the stranger lying on the ground beside David's horse. Wild auburn hair and indecent, outlandish clothes. Glancing around, she could see that most were uncomfortable with how the young woman was dressed.

"She must be one of those . . . those sinful women," Bessie Porter sniffed, watching as Emily Gartner moved to examine the strangely-attired girl. "She was very likely on her way to the nearest den of iniquity!"

Colleen struggled with her temper. Bessie had no right to judge this poor girl.

"And we don't need any more mouths to feed," Bessie continued, whining to her husband.

"She does look near to death," Gus Porter muttered. He removed his hat to scratch the top of his head.

"Would you have us leave her here to die?" Colleen angrily sputtered. "She's a child of God, same as the rest of us. Who or whatever she is, it shouldn't matter!" she exclaimed in her thick Irish brogue.

"Are you willing to care for her, Sister Colleen?" Bessie asked, turning to glare at the woman.

"I am if no one else is offerin'!"

Bessie shifted her gaze to the ground where the girl was lying. As ashamed as most felt, none was eager to extend a similar offer. Food was already being rationed. Wagons were crowded. The only family with room for one more was the Mahoney clan. With James dead, that left only Colleen and her four children.

"Sister Colleen, you're carryin' burdens enough. Surely someone else has room till we reach Fort Laramie," Captain Roberts pleaded, unwilling to saddle the brave widow with another charge. He waited, but no one stepped forward. "Gus, you and Bessie do have a little extra room . . ." He paused, uncomfortably aware of the looks the grieving couple was sending his direction. He stared at the ground and wished again that he could've prevented four-year-old Nathan Porter from falling under a wagon wheel last week. Burying the tiny child on the open plain had made both parents bitter.

"We'll have no part of this," Bessie said tersely, whirling around to leave. Her long, brown skirt brushed the ground as she stormed back to her family's wagon.

Gus stared at the ground, ashamed to meet the captain's eyes. "I'm sorry as I can be, but she'll have to ride with someone else," he quietly murmured. He was all too aware that others had suffered as much or more during the turbulent years of persecution and hardship. Replacing his hat, he slowly followed his wife.

Colleen knelt down beside her friend. "How is the lass?"

Looking up, Emily shook her head. "See how she struggles for every breath."

Colleen nodded.

"I think we'll be buryin' this one by morning," Emily said sadly. She smoothed the auburn hair away from the young woman's face. "I wish I had the room to keep her with my brood," she added wistfully. "Perhaps I could . . ."

"You're carryin' extra passengers as it is," Colleen gently reminded her, thinking of the young couple, the Myers. They'd lost everything crossing the Elkhorn river. Emily and her husband Warren had taken them under their wing since that time.

Straightening, Colleen gazed at Captain Roberts. "I have the room. She'll ride with us." Looking for David, she motioned for him to come near. As he approached, she instructed him to help the captain carry the stranger to her wagon. "Is there anything that can be done for the girl?" she turned to ask Emily.

"Pray for her, Colleen, pray for her. Our skills and medicines are so lacking. I know of no other recourse now."

Nodding, Colleen lifted up the bottom of her skirt and walked back to her wagon.

CHAPTER SEVENTEEN

H as there been any change?"

Slowly tearing her eyes from Kate's still form, Sue shook her head at Paige.

Paige stepped close to Sue's chair, placing an arm around her sister-in-law's shoulders. "Sue, you haven't eaten enough to keep a bird alive for the past two days. Let me sit with her for a while. Greg and Stan are out in the hall talking to Dr. Webster. They'll go with you down to the cafeteria."

Sue shook her head again, reaching to hold Kate's hand.

"If you don't start taking care of yourself, you're not going to be able to take care of Kate."

Reluctantly admitting Paige was right, Sue finally stood. She turned to gaze at the other woman.

"Here's a change of clothes. The nurse said there's a shower available near the waiting room down the hall." She handed Sue the duffel bag she'd brought from home. "I stuck in some shampoo, makeup, toothpaste . . . that kind of thing."

Numb with exhaustion, Sue silently nodded.

Deciding to push the issue, Paige smiled warmly at her sister-in-law. "After you eat, why don't you go home with Stan? Greg and I can stay here with Kate."

"No!" Sue said defiantly, setting the bag in the chair.

"Sue, I want you to take a good look at yourself," Paige said firmly, guiding her sister-in-law to the mirror above the tiny sink in the intensive care unit. "Does this look like someone who can go one more hour without sleep?"

Sue stared at her reflection. Who was this gray-faced stranger with the haunted eyes?

"Even if you just rest for a few hours, anything's better than what you're getting now."

Turning away from the mirror, Sue glanced at her daughter. "I . . . can't," she mumbled, leaning against the sink for support. "If she wakes up and I'm not . . . I've got to be here," she insisted, moving back to the bed.

"If you keep pushing yourself, you're not going to be here," Paige said, moving beside the stubborn woman. "They'll be setting you up in a unit just like this one down the hall."

"But . . . you don't understand. I have to be here."

"Sue . . ."

"She needs me. I talk to her. Sometimes . . . I think she can hear me. And, I've been doing her bed bath every morning. I . . ."

"Sue, you're exhausted! Let Greg and I take over for the day. The last thing Kate would want is for you to make yourself sick."

"I'm not so sure about that," Sue replied, trembling. "If you could've seen the way she looked at me . . ."

"Don't do this to yourself," Paige pleaded. "Go home with Stan. Get some rest. We don't need another casualty on our hands."

Sue finally nodded. Stepping close to the hospital bed, she leaned down to kiss Kate's forehead. "I love you, sweetheart," she said in a strained voice. "I won't be gone long," she promised, slowly straightening. She grabbed the bag and quietly left the room.

Kate groaned, sensing her mother's soft kiss.

"Did y'hear that?" Colleen asked, wiping Kate's forehead with a damp rag. "This lass may surprise us all and recover," she added, smiling up at Molly.

"That would be a blessing!" Molly snapped. "Another mouth to feed when we can barely feed our own!"

"Molly Mahoney, I'll not be hearin' another word about it,"

Colleen warned. "Now, bring me the nightgown I've asked for."

Her eyes blazing with stubborn fury, the seventeen-year-old moved across the wagon, kneeling beside her mother's trunk. She opened the lid, reached inside, and pulled out a white cotton gown. Angrily closing the lid, she straightened, moving back to her mother's side. Wordlessly, she handed the nightgown to her mother.

"Thank you, dear," Colleen murmured, all too aware of her daughter's attitude toward the strange girl lying helplessly on the wooden pallet. Sighing, she pulled back the quilt she'd used to cover the young woman. "Here, Molly, help me slide this o'er her body."

Molly grudgingly moved to assist, taking a certain amount of satisfaction in remembering what she'd done with this intruder's black lace underwear. The small black bloomers were unlike anything she'd ever seen before, covering only the barest of essentials. An indecent black support device had been removed from the young woman's small breasts. Repulsed, Molly had tied the offending garments to a stone, throwing them out into the middle of Platte River. Convinced they were caring for a young woman of ill repute, she was eager to be rid of the wanton female.

"There, now, that's better," Colleen said, smoothing the quilt back into place around the unconscious girl.

"I'd like to know what's better about it," Molly challenged.

"Molly, we have no way of knowin' what this poor creature's been through . . ."

"Creature is right!"

"She is our sister, a daughter of God," Colleen chided, gazing at her daughter.

"I hope you'll be feelin' so generous when she wakes and starts leading the young men astray, Jamie included," Molly retorted, moving to the front of the wagon. Lifting the canvas flap, she quickly climbed through, disappearing from sight.

Frowning, Colleen realized Molly had a point. She shifted her gaze to the freshly scrubbed young woman and wondered what kind of girl would wander off, dressed in the manner they'd found her. Was she opening a door to temptation for the young males of the camp? But, on the other hand, the girl was so sick and alone.

She rinsed the rag in the small metal basin, squeezing out most of the water. Turning, she wiped at the young woman's face, carefully cleaning around the scrapes and bruises. "For some reason, God has led you to us. We'll not be doubting his good works," she muttered, determined to help this girl no matter what anyone else thought.

Kate felt something damp brush her face. She moaned and struggled to open her eyes. The blackness was overwhelming. It beckoned her away from the pain. Reaching for its comforting relief, she drifted down a darkened tunnel of unconsciousness.

"Kate," Paige said softly, sensing her niece was slipping further away. "Please come back to us." She set the sponge she was holding into a plastic container of warm water. Leaning down, she tenderly kissed Kate's cheek. "Don't leave us, honey," she pleaded.

"Paige . . ." Kate mumbled. She couldn't tell who it was anymore. Shadowed images surrounded her. She felt the concern, the love. But she couldn't focus. The pain discouraged her from surfacing into coherence. Seeking relief in the blackness, she slipped from the edge of consciousness.

"See how she calls out," Colleen commented, glancing at Emily.

"Who is this Paige?" the other woman questioned, replacing the quilt around the young woman's shoulders.

"I'm not sure. Could it be a sister?"

"Perhaps," Emily replied. "She is looking better than last night," she commented. "Her breathing isn't as labored."

"True. Do y'think she'll be makin' a full recovery?"

"It's too early to tell. She's still very ill. But, I would say her chances are better. Keep her covered today. She is cool to the touch. That brisk breeze this morning will only chill her more."

Colleen smoothed a wrinkle from the heavy, block quilt. "Molly and I will take turns sitting with her," she promised, moving a stray strand of hair from the young woman's face.

"I'll check with you later when we stop to set up camp for the night. If you need me before then, wave a flag for the train to come to a halt." With that, the tall woman moved out of the wagon.

Colleen watched her friend leave, wishing she had the medical training Emily Gartner had learned from her father, a distinguished doctor in New York. A father who had disowned Emily for joining the Mormon Church. Sighing, Colleen knew that a majority of the Saints had paid a price for membership in the true church of Christ. Sacrifice seemed to be a requirement to become one of the Lord's people. Most accepted the trials, knowing the blessings far outweighed the suffering. She wished she could somehow get Molly to understand that concept. With each additional struggle, her daughter grew more bitter. If only Molly would realize the gift that had been given to them. Hope in a world filled with sorrow and fear.

Captain Roberts rode his horse past each wagon, tipping his hat to those who happened to glance in his direction. Everyone seemed ready to begin the day's journey. Satisfied, he approached the Mahoney wagon. Molly and Jamie were sitting together, arguing over who would drive the team. "Good morning," he said, smiling brightly. "And how is our sick guest faring this day?"

"As well as can be expected," Molly answered, the expression on her face showing her distaste for the strange girl.

"Sister Emily said she was improving," Jamie offered, grinning at the captain.

"Glad to hear it," Captain Roberts replied. "We'll be pulling out soon," he added, nudging his horse forward.

"Glad to hear it," Molly mimicked. "Little does he care. We're responsible for her now. That's all that matters to him."

Jamie ignored his sister and gripped the reins, waiting for the signal to move forward.

After following the rutted trail for nearly sixteen miles, the call to halt was passed from wagon to wagon. Within ten minutes, a night ring had been formed, the wagons drawn together in a tight circle. Oxen, mules, horses, and cows were unharnessed and driven in a herd to the rich wild pasture to feed. Children were sent scampering after buffalo chips and sagebrush to start a campfire that would offer warmth and cook the evening meal. Three buffalo had been shot earlier in the day, so meat would be plentiful for the entire camp. Women, young and old, hurriedly prepared rounded loaves of bread to go with the buffalo meat. They baked the loaves on flat pans in the coals, keeping a close watch to prevent it from burning. When it was done, the bread was set on rocks to cool.

While preparations for supper were underway, the older boys and men hurriedly milked the cows that had been brought on the journey. Setting aside the milk needed for the evening meal, they stored the surplus in containers which were placed in the Platte River. Families were soon gathered for the evening prayer and blessing on the food.

Famished after a hard day's drive, the meal was devoured with relish. A few noses wrinkled at the wild flavor of the buffalo meat, but there were no complaints. Episodes of near starvation had taught them to be grateful for the food that was available.

Molly dished up a plate for her mother, carrying it and a tin cup of warm milk back to the wagon. It annoyed her how the woman insisted on caring for the deviant sick girl. Muttering under her breath, she glanced up, nearly bumping into David Miles.

"Good evening, Sister Molly," David said, his blue eyes teasing. Removing his hat, he grinned. "How kind of you to bring me my supper."

"This isn't for you. It's for my mother."

"I'll let you pass then," he replied, offering an exaggerated bow. "A good meal may bring her the cheer she needs. I've just come from speakin' with her myself."

"And why were you doin' that, might I ask?" she questioned, immediately suspicious. She knew her mother had already given her blessing to the impending union between herself and David. The entire wagon train was convinced there would be a wedding in the near future.

David's smile quickly faded. "We made a discovery up ahead."

"That's your duty as our scout, is it not?" she taunted.

"I found the remains of a charred wagon."

"Indians?" Molly asked, dismayed by the news.

He slowly nodded. "Captain Roberts feels certain our mysterious stranger was with whoever was riding in that wagon. She somehow escaped the attack and ran off." Shaking his head, he stared at the ground. "She must've wandered for days before I discovered her. We're still tryin' to figure out why a wagon was out there in the middle of nowhere by itself."

"Perhaps they couldn't continue with their train. It could've been they were waiting for another to come along," Molly answered thoughtfully, surprised by the pity she felt for the strange girl. "Were there signs of other survivors?"

"No," David answered, replacing his hat. "The rest of her family must've been killed or taken by the Indians."

"We could send word to her living relatives when we reach Fort Laramie," she said hopefully, still anxious to get the young woman out of their wagon.

"She may have no one," he softly replied. "What then?"

"She's old enough to be on her own," Molly said, suddenly wondering who the girl had been traveling with. Had she been with a family, as David thought, or a group of unscrupulous women on their way to entertain men in a western town? Shuddering, she guessed the latter. If that was the case, perhaps they'd deserved the attack. Forcing a grim smile at David, she hurried on her way to the wagon.

CHAPTER EIGHTEEN

Kate groaned, rolling her head from side to side.

"It's all right, lass," Colleen soothed, patting the young woman's shoulder. "You're among friends now. No need to fear."

Reluctantly opening her eyes, Kate blinked. Who was this strangely-dressed woman leaning over her? A nurse? Gazing intently, she felt sure she'd seen that kind face with the piercing green eyes somewhere before. "Where am I?" she finally asked, her uncooperative tongue feeling strangely thick.

"There'll be time for answers later," Colleen replied, forcing a smile.

Kate tried to sit up. Everything seemed to spin, a sharp pain through her head causing her to groan. Too sick to protest, she allowed the woman to help her lie down. Shivering, she gratefully snuggled beneath the heavy quilt that was tucked around her shoulders. Quilt? What kind of hospital was this, anyway? "Where am I?" she repeated.

"You're safe, and that's all that matters. You've been very ill, thanks to the bite of a vile snake, but you're on the mend. Here now, I want you to take a sip of this tea."

"Snake bite? Tea?" Puzzled, she struggled through the fuzzy cobwebs clouding her memory. "There was a man with a gun . . . he shot at me," she said, frowning.

"The man you saw was Brother David Miles. He's a scout for our train. He did indeed shoot the copperhead, but not in time to stop it from biting you. Now, be a good lass and down this tea. You haven't had a thing for nigh onto three days." Dipping a spoon into the tin cup, she carefully captured a small portion of the dark liquid, bringing it to Kate's lips.

Kate thought of the reaction her mother would have to this infraction of the Word of Wisdom and cooperated, opening her mouth. She pulled a face as she swallowed. "What is that stuff?" she asked, gagging over the bitterness.

"It's made from boiled herbs. Sister Emily said it would help."

Cursing, Kate stopped mid-sentence when she saw the look on the woman's face. "Who is this Emily person?" she asked, rephrasing her original question. "Is she a doctor or what?"

"Sister Emily Gartner is the closest thing we have to a doctor, and I'll thank you to keep a civilized tongue in that head of yours," Colleen chided, looking from Kate to the small girl sitting near the front of the wagon. "Perhaps you've used language of that nature around your own people, but you'll not be using it around me or mine. Do we have an understandin', girl?"

Kate slowly nodded. She was too weak to argue. And for the moment, it seemed she was dependent on this person with the strange Irish accent, whoever she was. Wincing as her bed shifted hard against another surface, she stared around her. Just where had she been taken? "What was that?" she demanded as another bump rattled her bed.

"The trail's been a bit rough this afternoon."

"Trail?" Kate asked, her voice wavering as she glanced around. If she didn't know better, she'd think she was inside of a covered wagon. But of course she knew better, so this was obviously just an illusion. She must be sicker than she thought. She closed her eyes, attempting to shut out the nightmare she'd stumbled into. "Where am I?"

"Hush, now," Colleen said, trying to comfort the girl. "We'll stop soon. When you're stronger, we'll talk. Rest, and we'll try the tea later."

Kate pulled a face and silently swore.

As Jamie unyoked the oxen and cow, he winced, overhearing the argument his mother and sister were having on the other side of the wagon.

"I want that trouble-making snip of a girl out of our wagon now!"

"Molly, she's stayin' with us and that's the end of it!"

"Did you hear what she called me?" Molly angrily demanded.

"And a good thing it was I was there to stop you from slapping her! She's ill, girl, talking out of her head. She can't be held accountable for what she says or does, and you'd do well to remember that!"

"She was well enough to try tossing your quilt out of the wagon! If I hadn't been there to grab it . . ."

"I could've sent Daniel back after it," Colleen replied, her eyes flashing dangerously at her daughter. "Enough of this! We have a meal to prepare and chores to attend to."

"And that's the end of it?"

"It is for now," Colleen warned. "This girl is our responsibility, and we will treat her as such! Do I make m'self clear?"

Molly walked away, raising a cloud of dust in her fury.

Inside the wagon, Kate tearfully scowled. She'd heard every word that had passed between Molly and her mother. Why couldn't she wake up from this horrid dream? "Where am I?" she moaned, tears sliding down her face. "Please . . . somebody . . . help me."

Lowering the wooden tailgate, Colleen peered inside the wagon. Her stern expression softened when she saw the young woman's tears. She smiled warmly as the girl turned her head to look at her. "Here, now, what's the matter?" she asked, climbing inside the wagon.

"I want . . . I want to go home now. Or, at least back to Aunt Paige's house."

"Paige was an aunt," Colleen muttered to herself. "This girl was with her family then, as I thought."

"What?" Kate stammered.

"'Tis nothing, lass. Nothing at all. Now, calm yourself. All will be well," she soothed, patting Kate's shoulder. She smiled kindly and pulled a soft white handkerchief from a hidden pocket, gently using a corner to dry the silvery tears. "I'll have Daniel fetch you a good, cool drink of water. That'll soon put your spirits to right."

She moved to the back of the wagon, raising a hand to shield her eyes from the brightness. "Daniel, lad, come fetch your mother a cup of water from the barrel."

Water isn't going to solve anything, Kate sullenly thought. *What's going on? Why can't I wake up?*

"I spoke with Jamie. He said your patient has improved," Emily remarked, walking up to the fire Colleen was laboring over.

Colleen turned to gaze at her friend.

"Have you tried the tea?"

Grimacing, Colleen nodded. "Aye. I'm wearing part of it."

Emily glanced at the stained dress. "Jamie said she was a bit of a spit-fire. Why don't you try a little broth tonight? I have some dried pork . . ."

"Keep it, dear. You may need it before this journey's end. I'm boiling a bit of what we have. Perhaps she'll like it better than the tea."

"Has she told you who she is or what's happened to her family?"

Shaking her head, Colleen stirred the bubbling liquid in the cast iron pan. "It near breaks y'r heart to hear the girl call for her family."

"She doesn't know?"

Colleen glanced up at the other woman and sighed. "Either she doesn't remember or she's trying her best not to."

"She'll have to be told," Emily said.

Colleen carefully removed the pan from the fire, pouring a portion of the broth into a tin cup. Setting the cup on a flat rock to cool, she replaced the pan on the fire. "I'll make a hearty stew from this," she commented, motioning for Daniel. "Bring me a couple of potatoes from the wagon, Danny-boy," she said, smiling at her son. He glanced up from where he was playing with his younger sister, then hurried to comply with his mother's wishes. As he moved from view, Colleen's eyes wandered to where five-year-old Shannon was playing in the tall grass.

"Would you like me to tell her?" Emily offered.

"No," Colleen softly answered, afraid of the filthy language the young beauty might choose to throw in her friend's face. "I appreciate your willingness, but I'll be the one to tell her. Not tonight, though. She'll need her strength to bear it."

"There is wisdom in that. Perhaps tomorrow . . ."

"Perhaps," Colleen answered, taking the potatoes from Daniel.

"Soon, Colleen. I know you wish to spare her pain, but the sooner she knows, the quicker she'll heal." Smiling sadly at the woman who was intent on peeling potatoes, she finally turned and walked away.

Colleen looked up as Emily moved from view. "I know you're right, dear friend. But I can't do this alone," she said softly, closing her eyes. "Help me Father, when the time comes, to have the strength to break that girl's heart."

Later that evening, Molly helped Kate sit up, steadying her from behind as Colleen patiently held the cup near the young woman's mouth.

"There now, lass, it isn't so bad, is it?" Colleen asked, smiling at the girl.

Shaking her head, Kate continued to sip at the warm liquid. It was quite good, actually. Much better than that horrible tea. She drank most of the broth, then began to tremble with the strain of sitting. She was relieved when Molly and her mother finally lowered her back on the hard bed. "I, uh . . . thanks," she mumbled, watching as the older woman smoothed the quilt around her shivering body.

"Y'are indeed welcome," Colleen replied, glad for the improvement in the girl's mood. The illness had no doubt been responsible for the outburst earlier, although she shuddered to think where the young woman might've learned such language. Perhaps Molly was right, thinking this stranger had come from an undesirable lot. It was even possible that the young woman's mother had been a lady of ill repute. Regardless, she couldn't bring herself to think that of this girl. She was so young, her face revealing a certain innocence. And the way she'd blushed earlier when they'd dressed her in a fresh nightgown. She had been dreadfully embarrassed; it hadn't helped learning it wasn't the first time they'd cared for her needs. Ashamed anger had caused her to lash out at them, screaming vulgar obscenities that had enraged Molly.

Colleen smiled at the mysterious young woman, struck by how

familiar she seemed. Now that the dirt had been carefully scrubbed away, her long auburn hair properly brushed, she bore an uncanny resemblance to . . . Molly. Sure her eyes were deceiving her, she blinked, staring at her daughter, then at the stranger lying on the pallet.

"What is it, Mother, what's wrong?" Molly asked, alarmed by the look on her mother's face.

"It's this girl . . . I . . ."

Convinced this had something to do with the way she'd acted earlier, Kate frowned. "I'm . . . sorry about what I said before. I know you were just trying to help," she stammered, focusing on the canvas ceiling. If she had to depend on these people, she might as well make an effort to be courteous. She certainly wasn't making any strides being difficult. Besides, this was only a dream. Nothing to take too seriously. Might as well make the best of what her imagination had chosen to entertain her with.

"Consider it forgotten," Colleen said, gazing intently at the young woman. "Forgive me for starin'," she added, glancing back again at Molly, "but, have we met somewhere before?"

Annoyed by the question, Kate shook her head.

"We haven't had a chance to get properly acquainted yet. If you don't mind me askin', what is your name, girl?" Colleen ventured, suddenly very curious.

"Kate."

"Kate. What a lovely name. This of course is Molly," Colleen said, pointing to her daughter. "And I am Colleen. Colleen Mahoney. You can call me Sister Colleen if you'd like."

Kate blinked, then swallowed nervously. "What?" she asked, paling considerably.

"I'm not sure what you're meanin'?"

"I . . . it's just . . . no . . . there's no way. This is just a dream." Closing her eyes, she tried to wake herself up. This couldn't be happening.

"Kate, what is it? What's wrong?"

Fearfully opening her eyes, Kate stared at the woman who was calling herself Colleen Mahoney.

"What ails you, child?" Colleen pressed.

"You're Colleen Mahoney?" Kate weakly asked.

Nodding, Colleen glanced at her daughter. Molly looked as confused as she felt.

"What year is this?" Kate asked, the alarm in her eyes penetrating Colleen's heart.

"Why, it's 1848, in the latter part of the month of June. Don't you remember, lass? Is that what's frightening you?"

Kate choked back a scream. This was just a dream! None of it was real. It was merely her subconscious reviving the tales of her ancestors. Nothing more!

"Kate?"

Calming, Kate focused on the figures her mind had somehow conjured. "I . . . my full name is Katherine Colleen Erickson. My mother . . . she is . . . was . . . she's an Erickson now . . . but before she married . . . she was a Mahoney.

Colleen turned as white as Kate. "But . . . but how can this be?"

"It's a lie!" Molly exclaimed, storming to the front of the wagon. "Along with everything else, the girl is a bold-faced liar! She's full of blather! She doesn't belong to us! She's overheard we're Mahoneys!"

Stunned, Colleen glanced from her daughter to Kate. Then, as confusion threatened to overpower her, a logical explanation presented itself. "Your mother's father, what was his name?"

"Steven," Kate answered, wondering what Great-Great-Great-Great Grandma Colleen was getting at.

"Praise be to God, you are a Mahoney!" Bending, Colleen kissed Kate's cheek with a fierce intensity. Surprised by the affectionate gesture, Kate stared at the woman. "Steven is my husband's oldest brother, gone these long years from Ireland," Colleen revealed.

"That doesn't prove a thing!" Molly exclaimed, whirling around to climb out of the wagon.

Colleen sighed and watched her go. She turned to gaze at Kate. "You'll have to excuse my Molly. It hasn't been an easy time for her. Losing her father has filled her heart with bitter gall."

"No problem," Kate murmured, concentrating on her current predicament. Was she dreaming this because of her mother's lecture? And why did everything seem so real? The pain was much too intense to ignore, and her ability to taste, more than adequate. Had all of her dreams been like this? Just that one nightmare . . . the one with the women who wore bonnets. Her eyes widened as she stared at Colleen. Colleen had been in those nightmares. She recognized her now. Was this a variation of that dream?

". . . but, I won't give up hope. Hidden beneath Molly's bitterness beats a heart of pure gold. I'm thinking the same could be said of you," Colleen added, smiling kindly at the girl she now thought of as her niece.

Eager to change the subject, Kate hesitantly asked about the man called Steven, a man her grandfather was named after.

"My James told me years ago that his brother, Steven Mahoney, had been the first in his family to leave Ireland. He came to America seeking his fortune when James was but a lad. We'd all feared he was lost forever. There's never been a word from him. And now, here you are, guided by God's own hand to the family bosom." Lending action to her meaning, a teary-eyed Colleen gathered Kate in her arms, pressing the young woman against her ample breast.

Startled, Kate tried to pull back, but her weak resistance was effectively thwarted by the red-haired woman she was named after. Finally giving in, she was surprised by the comfort the embrace offered. She leaned against her grandmother, and lulled by the consoling softness, cried tears of pain and fear.

"There now, let it go, Katie. I can scarce imagine what you've been through. But you're safe enough now, and you'll always have place with this family," Colleen promised, gently rocking the young woman in her arms. "You're part of the Mahoney clan, dear girl, a stranger no more." Holding her close, she softly crooned an ancient Gaelic lullaby, determined to instill a sense of secure love within the trembling girl.

CHAPTER NINETEEN

Molly ran from the circle of wagons toward the river, nearly shrieking when a hand reached out to stop her.

"Molly," David Miles said quietly, "I didn't mean to frighten you," he added, stepping out of a small group of willows.

"Well, what are you doin' jumpin' out at a person then?" Molly angrily accused.

"It's my turn to watch," he replied, shouldering his half-stock rifle. "We've been a little nervous since spotting the charred wagon." His eyes narrowed as he gazed at his intended bride. "And what are you doing outside of camp this time of night?"

"That, sir, is none of your concern," she retorted, glaring back at him.

"You're distressed. And for that reason alone, it concerns me. What is it, Molly, what's wrong?"

"It's the beastly girl you and Captain Roberts have forced upon us! The lyin' little tramp. She'd have us believe she has Mahoney blood flowin' through her corrupted veins! Why didn't you burden someone else with her care? Then she could try to pass herself off as a Gartner, or a Porter!"

"Simmer down. You're letting that fine Irish temper get the best of you. Perhaps there's truth to her words," he said, remembering the mysterious girl's face. He hadn't thought of it before, but there was a resemblance. The flashing green eyes of the bedraggled stranger were identical to Molly's. "We are living in the midst of latter-day miracles."

"Oooooh, you fiendish brute! You're as bad as my mother! She's convinced God has led Kate to us."

"Kate?" he asked, turning the name over in his mind. "It fits. And, I might point out that your sweet mother, out of the goodness of her saintly heart, offered to take the poor girl in. The way things are, it's not like we have a choice. No one else has room. What were we supposed to do, leave her for dead?" He waited, uncomfortably aware of the silence growing between them. "Well?"

"I'm thinkin'," she said crossly.

"Molly Mahoney, you wouldn't have left her behind. I know you too well to believe that."

"Oh? And just how well do you think you know me, Brother Miles?"

"Well enough to do this," he replied, leaning his rifle against a willow.

"David Miles," Molly protested, stepping back. "You just keep your distance," she threatened.

"And why would I want to do that?" he teased, taking a step forward.

"I'm warnin' you . . ."

Stepping close, David tilted her chin.

"I'll scream!"

"And when the entire camp comes running down here, what then?"

"I'll tell them . . . I'll say . . ."

"That you just happened to wander away from the wagons and found yourself in my clutches?"

"It's the truth," she snapped, all too aware of how his nearness was affecting her.

"Something they'll all believe," he said sarcastically, caressing the side of her soft face. "Why, everyone knows how we despise each other," he continued, his fingers straying to her hair.

Molly closed her eyes and tried to ignore the gentle touch that was sending shivers up her spine. "Please . . ." she pleaded, stepping back.

"How can I resist when you ask so politely," he replied, leaning forward to kiss her. She struggled, then gradually relaxed, responding to his passionate kiss. Breathless, they pulled apart.

"We must marry soon," he finally said, breaking the silence.

"I . . . we can't . . . not yet."

"But, Molly, we love each other. We already have your mother's blessing. And we'll have the opportunity to be sealed someday. Why Brother Brigham has promised we'll build new temples. Maybe even an endowment house. You'll see. Our family will be eternal, just as we've planned."

"I need time, David. I have questions . . . about the gospel . . . this Church. I once thought it all made sense. But now . . . I'm not sure. Please, be patient. You don't know what you're askin' of me."

"Madam, I can assure you it's the other way around. I'm trying to be patient. But, do you know how difficult it is, seeing you day after day, wondering if you'll ever be mine? Have you ever wondered why I volunteered to be a scout on this train?" He paused, but Molly remained silent. "When I'm in camp, you're all I think about. I've loved you since the first day I saw you at Winter Quarters. Perhaps I was mistaken, but I thought that feeling of love was shared."

"David, you need someone who can share not only your love, but your faith. After everything that's happened . . . my testimony is nothing more than dyin' embers! I'm not sure I ever possessed one!"

Thoughtfully considering her words, he turned to face her. Filled with intense longing, he tried to ignore the way the moonlight was illuminating her fiery beauty. "You have a testimony, Molly," he said softly. "It's just a matter of getting past that stubborn pride of yours!" He tenderly kissed her, hoping to convey the depth of his love. As he drew back, he gazed into her glistening eyes. "Think on this moment when you feel plagued with doubts," he said, touching her cheek with his hand. "And now, to preserve my moral integrity, you'd best head back to the wagons. I'd rather face Indians on the warpath than your mother if she ever thought I'd sullied your reputation."

"Meaning my purity would be challenged if I stayed?" she asked, smiling at his attempt to be gallant.

"Meaning a man, Mormon or Gentile, can only stand so much

temptation. Off with you, maiden," he said, gently pushing her back up the sloping hill. "We'll speak of our impending nuptials another time when you're not so enchanting." He gave her a quick peck on the cheek, then returned to his post, picking up his rifle.

Glancing in his direction, Molly smiled, then walked up to the ring of wagons. The anger she'd felt only moments before was gone, dissipated by David's humor and reasoning. His ability to calm her was one of the things she loved most about him. But was it enough? Could love alone sustain them through life's journey? Unanswered questions haunted her, renewing the pain within her heart, opening wounds that wouldn't heal. If only she could be as sure about the Church as her mother was. Sighing, she made her way through the camp, heading for the wagon she now called home.

Colleen reached for the small lantern hanging from the ceiling of white canvas and carefully removed the glass chimney, preparing to blow out the flickering flame. Shannon and Kate were both asleep. Jamie and Daniel had bedded down under the wagon for the night. That left Molly. She'd go search for her high-strung daughter after plunging the wagon into darkness. Startled by a noise, she let the lantern flicker a moment longer. "Molly?" she called out, sighing with relief as her red-haired daughter opened a flap to step into the wagon. "I was about to come after you, lass," she scolded, replacing the lamp's chimney.

"I'm sorry if I caused you worry," Molly quietly replied.

"I'm not the only one in need of an apology," Colleen answered, pointing toward Kate's still form. "Whether you want to admit it or not, Kate Erickson is family. A Mahoney. Your cousin. I've no doubts about it. And you'll treat her accordingly. Do y' hear me, girl?"

"Aye," Molly responded, offering a timid smile. "I still have my doubts. But if you think she's family, I'll try to accept her as such."

"Well, now. We've had a bit of a change of heart," Colleen said softly, returning her daughter's smile. "Would I be wrong thinkin' Brother Miles has had anything to do with it?" she asked, studying Molly's face.

Blushing, Molly glanced down at Shannon, then at Kate, making sure they were both asleep.

"It's as I thought. When are you going to give that man his peace of mind and become his wife?"

"When I'm ready, Mother, and not one day before," Molly replied, meeting her mother's questioning stare with one of her own. "Why are you so anxious to be rid of me?"

"You know that's not true, Molly. No one will shed more tears than your mother when you move on to start your own life. I only want your happiness . . ."

"And you think I need David to be happy?"

"Look at yourself, girl. You're all atwitter. You always are after being with that boy. That ought to tell you something."

"I'll marry David when the time is right."

"We'll hope he's still moonin' around by then," Colleen answered, gazing at her daughter. "He's not the only one seekin' your hand, you know."

"What are you saying, Mother?" Molly asked, suddenly looking concerned.

"Just what I said. Brother Wicker came to talk to me the other day."

Molly pulled a face, thinking of the solemn man.

"Aye, I feel the same, dear," Colleen admitted, her expression matching Molly's.

"But he's ancient, and he already has two wives."

"He's asked to make you his third . . . provided things don't work out between you and David."

Flushing with indignant rage, Molly clenched her fists. "I won't marry that old goat! I won't!"

"Listen to me, my dear girl, I haven't given my consent, nor will I have to if . . ."

"If I'll marry David," Molly said, finishing the sentence for her mother.

"Would it be so bad, lass? He loves you dearly, treats you like a queen. And you . . . you have feelings for him as well, don't deny it. I've seen your face often enough after you've been with him. It fairly glows as it does tonight."

"Mother," Molly protested, turning red. As her current

predicament registered, she slowly sank to her knees, leaning against the rough interior of the wagon.

Stepping over Shannon, Colleen knelt in front of her oldest daughter, cupping the girl's troubled face in her hands. "I promise I won't be marryin' you off to anyone like Brother Wicker. All I'm sayin' is you need to start taking David seriously, or one of these days, he'll look around and find someone else, leavin' you with a less desirable suitor."

"Don't you think that haunts me, Mother? But I'm not a hypocrite. I can't marry David and pretend to be one thing when I'm really another."

Colleen pursed her lips together as tears gathered in Molly's eyes. She drew her daughter close, making sympathetic clicking sounds with her tongue. "My poor confused Molly, someday you'll forget the pain you're carryin' inside," she quietly soothed. "'Tis true, we've had our share of trials, but one thing we've never lacked is love. Love for each other, and love from our Father in Heaven. He does exist, you know."

"Then why does he let such horrible things happen?" Molly tearfully asked, pulling back to gaze at her mother.

"Are you still blamin' God for our troubles?" she asked, brushing a wandering tear from her daughter's face. "God didn't stir those heathen hearts against us. And he's guided us to safety, time and again. You've seen miracles that can be explained no other way. God is with us. We have only to pray to feel his loving protection."

"But, when I pray for peace . . . for comfort . . . this empty pain, it doesn't fade."

"Have you prayed with sincerity? He is there, and he does listen, but he can only help us when we open the door to our hearts. How d'you think I've stood it, losing Brian and Maureen, every home we've ever had, and finally your father, a man I loved more than life itself?"

Molly sniffed and stared at the small pile of wooden crates stacked in one corner of the wagon. The contents were wrapped in rags. Worn pots and pans, what was left of their dishes, a few of her father's books. The meager possessions left to them.

"My testimony, Molly, it's held me together. That, and

knowing someday we'll be reunited, a family forever in the eternities . . . it's made endless burdens seem light. To have the comfort of being sealed to your father in the Nauvoo temple. To know you children will always be mine. To know death cannot separate us. Can you understand, Molly?"

Molly slowly nodded.

"And when you first read the inspired pages of the Book of Mormon, how did it make you feel?"

"I know what you're meanin', Mother. But the burnin' within, I haven't felt it since Papa died. Why did God take him when he knew how much we needed him? Why did God take Papa?" she asked, tears streaming down her face.

"I'm not sure, Molly. He must've had need of your father, more so in heaven than we did here on earth."

"How is that possible?"

"I don't know, Molly. 'Tis true, the road we've traveled has been a hard one to follow. And it will be difficult at best, starting new in the Salt Lake Valley. But when discouragement threatens, I like to think of your father with Brian and Maureen. Perhaps he's takin' care of them as I'm tryin' to do with the rest of you."

Molly wiped at her eyes, pondering her mother's words. "You truly believe that?"

"Aye, darlin'. And with those skilled hands of his, no doubt he's laborin' to prepare a place on high for the rest of us when we leave this mortal test of our endurance. Think of your father, Molly. Did you ever know a more noble, kind-hearted soul?"

Molly shook her head.

"Your father's tests are over now. We should be celebratin', not mournin' his passing. He's beyond suffering, Molly, beyond the misery and pain that go with living. And someday, if we live our lives patterned after his, we'll join him." Colleen sadly smiled, then leaned to kiss her daughter's forehead. "This blackness you feel, it comes from hate and anger. You must forgive those who've done us wrong. It will all be made right in the end. Until then, we must allow faith to guide us on our journey through life." Squeezing Molly's shoulder, she straightened, and moved to extinguish the lantern. Lifting the glass chimney, she smiled at her daughter. "Think on what I've said tonight when you say your prayers. The answers you seek will come, but you must be patient, dear girl. Don't turn away from the only road that offers happiness in this life." She quietly snuffed the flame, carefully replacing the chimney. Moving silently, she settled down next to Shannon, wrapping herself inside of a blanket.

"Goodnight, Mother," Molly softly whispered.

"Goodnight, Molly."

"I love you."

"As I do you, dear. Now, try to get some rest. Tomorrow will be here before we know it."

Molly arranged her bedroll, then knelt quietly in prayer.

At the other end of the wagon, Kate brushed silently at the tears as they flowed. Tears that she couldn't explain. She breathed out slowly and struggled for control, mentally lecturing herself for being so weak.

CHAPTER TWENTY

I can't believe an entire week's already gone by," Greg said, gazing down at Kate.

"I know," Sue replied, leaning against his shoulder.

"I could arrange to take more time off," he offered, squeezing her against him. "I called the office, Gary said I could have as much time as I needed."

"Without pay, right?"

Greg slowly nodded.

"I don't know, Greg, we have no idea how long she'll be like this. Dr. Webster said she could regain consciousness anytime, but the coma could drag on for weeks . . . even months."

"Sometimes it's a guessing game, even for the medical profession," Greg said, trying to make sense of the nightmare they were living. "She will recover, Sue. Every blessing she's had since the accident has reassured us of that. But we have no way of knowing when."

Sue nodded, reaching down to grip Kate's hand. As she held it in her own, she willed her daughter to open her eyes. "Sometimes she feels so close. Then, she slips further away. It's so frustrating! I want to help her . . . but I don't know how."

"You are helping her, Sue. Somehow, she senses we're here."

"Sometimes, I think it's just my imagination getting the best of me. I want so desperately for her to come back to us that every time she flinches or moans, I feel certain she's trying to communicate."

"Maybe she is," Greg replied, reaching a decision. "I'll stick around for a few more days," he said brightly, trying to cheer his wife. "I would like to be here when she does finally decide to wake up."

"Do you think it could happen that soon?" she asked hopefully, turning to gaze at her husband.

"Could be," he replied, unwilling to puncture her fragile balloon of hope. He pulled her close, hugging her with a fierce intensity.

Sue relaxed against him, drawing strength from his comforting presence. It helped to have others here with her. When she was alone, she relived the horrible scene that had taken place at Temple Square, continuously berating herself for not listening when Kate had tried to talk to her. For once, her daughter had been reaching out, and she'd slammed the door in her face. If she'd listened, none of this would've happened.

Greg stayed for a few hours, then left to spend time with Tyler and Sabrina. Sue remained with Kate. Standing beside the bed, she tenderly brushed the hair from her daughter's face. "Kate," she said softly. "I am so very . . . Please, come back to us. Give me the chance to make things right. Don't shut me out forever. If you could only know what this is doing to me." She leaned over the bed and gently kissed her daughter's bruised cheek.

"Mom?" Kate moaned, forcing her eyes open. Her mother was near. She could feel the woman's sorrowing pain. "Mom?"

"Katie, dear, you're awake," Colleen said, gazing down at the puzzled girl. "How are you feelin' this morning?"

"Okay, I guess," Kate stammered with confusion. Why was she continually waking up to this dream? "Where's my mother?" she asked, suddenly needing to see her. She'd never thought she'd actually miss her mother, but now, she'd give anything to see the woman, to have her assurance that everything would be all right. Nothing made sense anymore.

"Katie, I'm afraid the time has come for you to know the truth."

"What truth? What are you trying to say?" Kate asked, searching her grandmother's face for answers.

"Your mother, dear girl, she's . . . she's gone."

"Gone?" Perplexed, Kate blinked. "Gone where?"

Colleen gripped Kate's trembling hand, squeezing it tightly in her own. "Do you remember the raid on your wagon?"

Frightened, Kate shook her head.

"What do you remember, lass?"

"I . . . I told you about that man . . . the one with the gun?"

"David," Colleen said, nodding. "Before David found you, Katie, what took place?"

Glancing around at the wagon, Kate nearly choked on the fear thickening in her throat.

"It's all right, you're safe now. Don't be frightened by memories. You must face them. You're a Mahoney, strength flows in your veins. Be strong, Katie girl. You must face your past to preserve your future. Now, tell me what you remember."

Kate closed her eyes, trying to cooperate. "It was dark . . . and cold. There was a breeze and . . . I was lying on a bunch of rocks."

Colleen smiled warmly. "Not a very comfortable bed, to my way of thinkin'."

Silently agreeing, Kate opened her eyes.

"When David first saw you, you were alone on the trail . . . dressed in clothes I would never choose for my own daughters. But, perhaps there was a reason for it."

"I was wearing my black leather skirt and a white blouse."

"Aye, Molly disposed of them . . . as well as the black lacy undergarments you were wearin'."

Blushing, Kate stared at her fourth great grandmother. "But . . . it's the way we dress . . . everyone wears clothes like that."

"Not everyone, Kate," Colleen corrected. "We'll not hold it against you, dear, you can't help the way you were taught." Kate frowned, remembering her mother's reaction to the outfit. Sue Erickson had hated it as much as Grandma Colleen. "What else do you recall?"

"Well . . ." Things were still a bit fuzzy. "I had been . . . talking to my mother," she said, remembering the intense argument that had actually taken place. "My little sister ran out into the street. A car was coming . . ."

"A car? A railway car?" Colleen asked, puzzled. There were no railroads across this prairie.

Kate rolled her eyes. Great, how was she supposed to explain what had happened?

"Think, Kate. If it wasn't important, I wouldn't press. Captain Roberts wishes to know if Indians were responsible for the attack. It might mean we'll have trouble with them as well."

"Indians?" Kate asked, stunned. "You mean those naked guys with the feathers?"

"Well, that is indeed one way of putting it," Colleen sputtered, staring at her niece.

"There weren't any Indians, I . . . look, I had an argument with my mother, okay? I ran off . . ."

"Well, now, that explains it," Molly interrupted, lifting Shannon up into the wagon. "She ran off from her family . . . she has no idea what happened to them. Now we know why she alone survived," she said, climbing in behind Shannon.

Kate stared at Molly, then turned her head to gape at Colleen. What was going on? She was the one who'd been hit by the car. She was sure of it. What were these people talking about?

"Molly!" Colleen warned. "That's enough!"

Angered, Molly clamped her mouth shut, whirling around to leave the wagon.

"What did Molly mean?" Kate stammered, frantically searching her grandmother's face.

"Your family's gone, Katie," Colleen sadly answered. "I wish it were not so, but it's true. We found the wagon . . . it had been burned. There were no signs of survivors."

"Wagon? What wagon?"

"The one belonging to your family," Colleen said quietly.

"No way! I'm not even from this century! And my family doesn't own a wagon. We have a Ford Explorer."

"You were traveling with an explorer named Ford?"

Frustrated, Kate covered her face with her hands and groaned.

Thinking her niece was overcome with grief, Colleen tried to comfort her, alternating between squeezing and gently patting the girl's trembling shoulders.

Thoroughly disgusted, Kate dropped her hands, glaring up at her grandmother. "This isn't happening, you know," she said quietly. "None of this is real. Very soon now, I'm going to wake up, and all of this will be gone," she said, trying to reassure herself.

"Wishin' won't make it true, dear," Colleen said, fearing for her niece's sanity. "Your family's gone, and they're not comin' back."

"I'm the one who's gone!" Kate shrieked. "Only I'm not sure where it is I've gone to! My family is out there, somewhere on the other side of this dream. And once I've discovered how to wake up from this nightmare, I am out of here! Do you hear me? Gone!"

"Oh, this is lovely. Now we have a looney for a cousin," Molly remarked, poking her head back inside of the wagon.

"I thought you'd gone off to sulk somewhere, Molly-kins. Why don't you go cozy up to David for awhile! That always seems to put you in a better mood!" Kate snapped, glowering at the young woman who was in reality an aunt, not a cousin.

"Ooooooh, you little . . ."

"Molly!" Colleen warned. "Go bring me the broth coolin' near the fire."

Muttering under her breath, Molly shot a scathing look in Kate's direction, then disappeared through the canvas flap.

"And as for you, Katie, ill or no, I'll not hold with you provokin' my daughter!"

"Me? But she . . ."

"Hush now. You've had a shock. I can see it will take time for you to accept what's happened. I'm sorry it's come as such a blow, but, in time, the pain will fade."

"I want to see my mother, now!" Kate said, through clenched teeth. "And don't give me that crap about how the Indians hauled her off somewhere! It's not true! It's not!" she said, sitting up to glare at her grandmother. Just then, the wagon lurched forward, causing her to hit her head against the wooden tailgate. She pitched to one side, unaware that Colleen had grabbed her.

"Just what we needed!" Colleen angrily exclaimed, gently laying Kate down on the pallet. Quickly covering the young woman with the quilt, she hurried to the front of the wagon. "Here, now, what's the cause of this?"

"I'm sorry, Mother. It's these stubborn beasts. They're eager to be off this morning," Jamie apologized, holding tight to the ear of the culprit.

"Was anyone hurt?"

Leaning out, Colleen gazed down at Emily. "Kate's bumped her noggin. The rest of us are fine."

"I'll come around behind," Emily said, moving from sight.

Colleen sighed and pulled back inside of the wagon.

"Mama," Shannon called. "Kate's sleepin'."

"I know, dear, I know," Colleen muttered, making her way to the back of the wagon. Kneeling beside the unconscious girl, she frowned at the bump developing on the side of Kate's head. She helped Emily unfasten the tailgate, offering a hand as the other woman climbed up inside the wagon.

"She'll have a nasty bruise," Emily commented.

"Aye. Perhaps it'll knock sense into that stubborn head."

"I heard heated words coming from this direction," Emily said, examining the swollen bump.

"The girl's a Mahoney, all right," Colleen replied. "Feisty to the core."

"She's the spitting image of your Molly," Emily added. "Her hair is darker, but the two could pass for sisters."

"That's for certain," Colleen said, thinking of the temper the two girls had inherited. "Will she be all right?"

"I believe so. It doesn't appear to be serious. I'll warn you, though, when she wakes, she'll be in a bit of pain."

"That ought to improve her mood." Colleen gazed somberly at her friend. "I tried to tell Kate about her family this mornin'."

"How did she take the news?"

Shaking her head, Colleen stared out of the wagon. "She won't believe a word of it."

"Give her time, Colleen. She's been through so much."

Colleen nodded in agreement. "We know now why she survived the raid . . . why she knows nothing about it. She'd had words with her mother and had run off from the others."

"That's why Brother David Miles found her so far from the wagon."

"Aye. And I can't say I blame the girl for leaving that so-called family. I'd like to fairly shake the mother of this child. The way they had her dressed, the language she's been taught. It would destroy her Grandmother Mahoney, may she rest in peace, to see how her granddaughter has been raised. This Susan Mahoney Erickson will have a day of reckoning, of that there is no doubt. I shudder to think what the woman very likely was."

Kate moaned and opened her eyes. "Don't say that about my mother," she pleaded.

"Hush, now, Katie. We'll speak of this another time," Colleen soothed, reaching for the cup of broth Molly had handed up to Emily. "Drink this, child, we'll be pullin' out soon." She waited until Emily had propped Kate up from behind, then held the tin cup to the young woman's lips. "You need your strength, dear, drink it down."

Kate reluctantly opened her mouth, shakily draining the broth from the cup. She'd just thought she'd had a headache before. Wincing as her head pounded unmercifully, she allowed the women to lower her on the pallet. "Colleen . . ."

"Aunt Colleen to you," Colleen scolded, determined to teach this girl proper etiquette.

"Aunt Colleen," Kate said, closing her eyes as the pain in her head increased. "What you were saying about my mother . . . it's not true."

"Hush, Katie. Rest now. We'll speak of these things later." Patting the young woman's shoulder, she quickly replaced the quilt. She waited until Emily had climbed down to the ground, then motioned for Molly to help latch the tailgate into place. Soon the wagon train was again in motion, weaving through the waving prairie grass.

CHAPTER TWENTY-ONE

As the days progressed, Kate slowly regained her strength. After a week of lying on her back inside the wagon, she was able to sit next to Jamie as he skillfully drove the oxen. Staring at the vast emptiness of the plains, she tried to accept the fact that she was somehow caught in this never-ending dream.

To pass the time, she asked questions, often annoying the source of her information. She'd learned that this wagon train was made up of 35 wagons. It had started out with 36, but the wagon belonging to the young couple now traveling with Emily Gartner's family had been destroyed while crossing the Elkhorn River.

The man in charge was named Captain Roberts. Three other men worked under Captain Roberts to lead the group of Saints. Her grandmother had informed her that all wagon trains were organized into groups of ten. This had been done according to the wishes of the prophet, Brigham Young. Ordinary problems and decisions were to be handled by the captains of ten. This allowed Captain Roberts to focus on the major issues faced by the group of pioneers.

The three groups of ten in this particular wagon train actually consisted of two groups of ten and one of fifteen, but Kate resisted the temptation to point that out to the pioneers. Each day, the order in which they traveled rotated so that each group had the chance to lead and follow in the dust left behind by the others. This kept contention to a minimum.

David Miles had traveled to Salt Lake Valley the year before, so it was only natural that he act as a scout for the train. He was familiar with the best camping locations and had been able to guide them to sites with fresh water and feed for the animals. He often rode ahead to search for potential dangers or challenges that would have to be faced or avoided.

When Kate was told this journey would cover a little over one thousand miles, she'd retorted that she had flown that far in a matter of hours. The looks she'd been given had convinced her to keep quiet about modern technology. The pioneers simply had no appreciation for the finer things life would eventually have to offer.

Her current existence wasn't all bad. She was actually becoming rather fond of the woman who insisted on being called Aunt Colleen. Her mother had been right. Grandma Colleen was a courageous, compassionate woman. The only widow traveling alone with her children on this wagon train. Her grandmother often took a turn at driving the mangy oxen, the sight of which filled Kate with a strange sense of pride. How many other teenagers could say that a distant grandmother had actually driven a wagon across what would eventually become the state of Nebraska?

The prairie itself was a little on the boring side. Nothing but tall grass and sagebrush for endless miles. Unless you counted the large herds of buffalo roaming nearby—a convenient source of meat for the monotonous meals she'd been subjected to night after dreary night. She'd nearly had her fill of the wild-flavored steaks, not to mention the dull scripture readings that usually took place after dinner. Tuning out the impromptu sermons, she spent the time daydreaming about Jace and the parties she would attend when she returned to consciousness.

Kate had been slightly shocked the night Molly had been asked to read from the Book of Mormon. Grudgingly admitting her aunt did have talent in that department, she was surprised that Molly actually read better than most of the men she'd heard so far. Kate had assumed that only men were allowed to read, the way they seemed to dominate over everything else, like they were supreme beings, entitled to special treatment! She'd managed to put a few in their place. All it took was a withering look, or a teasing grin. A well-timed insult or two that went right over their heads while she smiled sweetly, feigning innocence. There was one man in particular that Kate enjoyed getting the best of. A man named Truman Wicker. A confused man who seemed to think he was a gift to women. An ornery man who obviously had his eye on Molly.

Kate shifted on the wooden seat of the wagon, reliving the events that had taken place two nights ago. Benjamin Whitney had been talked into providing music for a series of reels after yet another scrumptious meal of buffalo meat. Smirking while Brother Whitney frantically fiddled tune after ridiculous tune, Kate had watched, amused, as the pioneers had danced around a large campfire. Bored, she'd finally decided to head back to the wagon. Making her way through the gathered saints, she'd noticed Truman Wicker was up to his favorite pastime, drooling over Molly as her aunt whirled around in David's strong arms. Limping quietly to Truman's side, Kate had given him a dirty look, telling him to get real. Puzzled, the deluded man had turned to her, eagerly asking if she was requesting a dance. Rolling her eyes, Kate had assured him it would be a cold day in the satanic realm before she'd ever request such a thing. Walking away, she'd enjoyed the look on his face. Stunned fury.

"Do not speak to me in this manner, child of the devil!" he'd angrily sputtered.

"Sit on it, Gramps," Kate had retorted, pulling a face.

"Sit on what, pray tell?" Truman had indignantly asked.

Grinning, Kate had enjoyed her reply.

Later, as Kate had tried to explain to her grandmother that she had merely answered the man's question, she was informed that if she ever used such words again, a willow switch would be taken to her behind. Convinced this was a bluff on Colleen's part, Kate had amazed herself by agreeing to her grandmother's demands.

Kate yawned and stretched, wondering how much longer today's journey would drag on. This company, as the pioneers liked to call themselves, moved at a snail's pace! No wonder those who walked could keep up. She silently wondered how these people would react to the luxurious cars of the future. The fifteen to twenty miles they slowly plodded each day could be reached in a matter of minutes. This journey that was taking forever could be wrapped up in two or three days, instead of months.

She often giggled to herself, comparing real life with the one these poor pioneers were leading. They were so sadly behind the times. Their clothing, beyond salvation. She glanced down at the dress they were making her wear. A faded calico that belonged to Molly. She hated it, detesting the way it covered her body from her neck to her feet. The long sleeves even hid her arms. Sighing, she realized she didn't have much choice. Molly had thrown her clothes in the river. In fact, her aunt had actually seemed to take delight in it. Well, two could play at that game. She'd be sure to remodel this dress as soon as she had the chance!

A nervous laugh captured her attention. She glanced at the wagon ahead. A teenage boy had ridden his horse up to speak to a girl Jamie had fallen for. Amy Olsen. A shy blonde who had more manners than sense. Sneaking a glance at Jamie, she was amused by the outraged expression on his face.

"What's wrong, Jamie?" she asked, enjoying his sudden blush.

"It's none of your concern," he stammered.

"I see. It doesn't bother you when a studly dude makes time with your girl?"

Turning sharply, he glared at Kate. Molly was right. Kate didn't possess a shred of decency. Why couldn't their mother see that? He gritted his teeth and focused on the oxen.

Kate laughed and shifted her gaze to Amy, who was walking beside her family's wagon. The girls her age were so silly. Acting like embarrassed prudes every time a boy came near them. She wondered what they'd think if she tried to kiss one of the lanky males. It would be fun just to see the reaction she'd get, especially from Molly. Her aunt would turn inside out. The only thing stopping her was Colleen. Her grandmother seemed to have a strange hold on her. As time went on, she was reluctant to do anything that would upset the woman. Surprised by this, she decided not to worry about it, concentrating instead on irritating Molly or Jamie.

Nearly two hours later, the call to halt sounded. The wagons were quickly pulled together in a close-fitting ring. As Jamie and Molly moved to unyoke the oxen and cow, Kate climbed down from the wagon. Shaking the trail dust from the calico dress, she straightened, breathing deeply. Her head didn't even hurt today.

Aside from a slight case of tired buns, compliments of the lengthy wagon ride, she actually felt pretty good.

"How are y'feelin', Katie?" her grandmother worriedly asked, coming up from behind.

Kate experienced a twinge of guilt. Her grandmother had walked every step of the eighteen miles today. Molly had informed Kate two days ago that she had taken Colleen's place sitting next to Jamie. Shannon was being allowed to ride most of the time, but, to spare the oxen added weight, the rest of them walked. "Fine," she stammered, turning to smile at the woman.

"And glad I am to hear it," Colleen replied. "Your color's better today."

"I'd say she's well enough to gather chips for this evening's fire, Jamie, wouldn't you?" Molly snidely asked, leading the cow away from the wagon to be milked.

"Aye," Jamie responded, remembering the way Kate had embarrassed him earlier. "Unless of course she's too frail to lend a hand."

"That's enough, Jamie. Kate will help in good time. Let the girl get her strength back," Colleen said, clearing a place for a small fire.

"I can help," Kate said, angered by Jamie's insinuation that she was fragile. "What can I do?" she asked, watching as Shannon and Daniel scampered off.

"Well, if you're sure," Colleen said, straightening to gaze at Kate. "Go help Daniel gather chips and sagebrush if you'd like. Just don't overdo."

"I can handle it," Kate responded, hurrying after Daniel. She quickly caught up with the nine-year-old and watched as her third great-grandfather bent down to gather dusty brown circles from the ground.

Daniel looked up at Kate. "What do you want?" he asked sharply. He'd heard Jamie and Molly say that Kate was a bad person. They'd warned him to stay away from her. Wrinkling his nose, he stared at her now. She was as pretty as Molly. Puzzled, he wondered what she had done that was so wrong.

"I just want to help," she offered, smiling. "I came to gather chips."

"Oh," he replied, confused. Kate couldn't be all bad if she was willing to help.

"These are chips?" she asked, kneeling to gather one in her hand.

"Yep. We'll need a whole pile of 'em, too. There's not much sagebrush around here."

Kate quickly gathered an armful, proudly walking back with Daniel to where Colleen wanted the fire.

"Well, now, would you look at that, our grand lady has stooped to carryin' buffalo chips," Molly said, smugly grinning at Jamie.

"What?" Kate asked, glancing at the brown circles she'd collected. As the realization of what she'd gathered descended upon her, she shrieked, throwing the chips in every direction. Furious, she glowered at everyone, expressing in a loud voice what she thought about the entire situation.

Colleen winced. Turning, she scowled at Kate, who was furiously wiping her hands on the calico dress. Jamie and Molly laughed uncontrollably as a disgusted Daniel scurried to pick up what Kate had dropped. "Katie, surely you realized what we were using. We don't have a lot of choice out here on the prairie," Colleen patiently explained.

"And it's not like we asked you to gather the fresh ones," Jamie added, biting his lip in an attempt to appear serious. As Molly continued to laugh, he joined her, his eyes twinkling with avenged delight.

Enraged, Kate stormed off, heading down to the river to wash her hands. Ignoring her grandmother's calls to come back, she continued moving away.

"Your family seems to be in high spirits this afternoon," Captain Roberts commented, walking toward the Mahoney wagon. "Is everything well here?"

"Aye," Colleen said, barely stifling a grin. "We're slowly breaking Kate into the wonders of camp life."

"Good," he replied, lifting an eyebrow as Kate moved close to the river. "Don't let the girl wander off too far," he warned. "Brother Miles found Indian tracks by the river not far from here."

Colleen nodded. "Jamie, go fetch your cousin. I'll not have the red-skinned heathen drag her off."

Sobering quickly, Jamie replaced his hat, hurrying after Kate.

"I suppose I get the privilege of milking the cow alone tonight then," Molly grumbled, walking away.

Colleen sighed and focused on building a fire. There was bread to bake and buffalo meat to cook. And daylight only lasted so long.

CHAPTER TWENTY-TWO

The next day passed slowly, the sun beating down with relentless fury. After enduring seventeen miles of uncomfortable heat, the signal was finally given to set up camp. David had promised the river was deep enough at this location to permit bathing. Welcoming the chance to cool off, the women hurriedly prepared for a quick session in the river while the men took care of the livestock.

Colleen led her daughters and Kate to the river's sandy edge. She waded into the water and beckoned the girls to join her. Kate stuck one toe in the river and shook her head. Gasping as a shove from Molly forced her into the cold water, Kate came up sputtering obscenities.

"Katie Colleen, that will do," Colleen chided as she took Shannon from Molly. "Hurry now, lasses," she continued, scrubbing her young daughter with a tiny bar of lye soap. "There's still much to do before dark. We've a meal to prepare, clothes to mend, and a lunch to make up for tomorrow's noon stop." Colleen rinsed the soapy film from Shannon's body, then handed the soap to Molly.

Molly quickly washed herself, plunging in the water to rinse. She came up gasping for air, shaking the water from her hair. Looking around, she had the uneasy feeling that they were being watched. Puzzled, she glanced around at the other pioneer women. No one else seemed alarmed. Still, something didn't feel right.

"What's wrong, Molly?" Kate sneered. "The shock of being clean too much for you?"

"I could ask you the same," Molly retorted. "And if you insist on using such filthy language, I may just use this soap to clean that mouth of yours," she threatened.

"I'd like to see you try," Kate countered, splashing water on the other girl.

"Oooooh, now you've done it," Molly responded, moving through the water to Kate's side. She gripped Kate and shoved the soap into her mouth.

"Molly! Kate! Cease this fighting at once!" Colleen scolded, moving to the teenagers, dragging Shannon with her.

As Kate tried to spit the bitter taste out of her mouth, she was caught by surprise from behind. Molly knocked her off balance, forcing her head beneath the water.

"There, now, we'll just cool you off for a bit," Molly said through clenched teeth.

"Girls! What'll these dear sisters think?"

Somewhat ashamed, Molly pulled away from Kate, painfully aware of the disapproving stares.

"You're dead meat!" Kate gasped at Molly, trying to catch her breath.

"Katie," Colleen warned, touching the girl's shoulder. "That will do."

Kate muttered under her breath and sent a scathing look in Molly's direction. Molly sent one in return, then slowly made her way to the river bank. As Molly climbed out of the water, she was again accosted by a sense of wrongness. Drying off with a blanket, she quickly dressed, nervously glancing around. No one was visible, but the feeling persisted. She turned as her mother called to her and bent to lift Shannon from the river. "Mother, I can't explain it, but . . . something's not right. I feel as though someone is watching us."

"It's probably the looks you're getting from Kate. And if you don't cease this fighting, I'll take a willow switch to you both," Colleen warned, glaring up at her daughter. She moved out of the water and reached for a blanket to dry herself. Then, slowly turning, she gazed toward a group of willows not far from where they were standing. "Molly, take Shannon back to the wagon. I'll bring Kate," she said in a low voice.

Following her mother's alarmed gaze, Molly stared at the group of willows. "Someone's hiding in there," she whispered, the color draining from her face.

"Aye, dear, that would be my guess," Colleen replied, suddenly afraid for her daughters and Kate. "Take your sister. I'll warn the others." Tucking the blanket around her slightly rounded body, Colleen moved down the river bank.

Shortly after the women had dressed and hurried back to camp, Captain Roberts, David Miles, and the other three captains searched the group of willows. Fearful they would find Indian tracks, they were alarmed by the evidence discovered.

"It's tobacco juice all right," David said, the disgust he was feeling apparent by the expression on his face.

"It weren't Indians?" Amos Grant nervously asked, his grip tightening on the old percussion rifle in his hands.

David pointed to the bootprints. "Indian tracks are different."

Captain Roberts removed his hat to scratch the top of his head. "Brother David, were there signs of trappers or another company near this area?"

Shaking his head, David shifted his gaze from the ground to the captain's face as he realized what that meant. These tracks were made by one of their own. Anger silently surfaced with the knowledge that his sweet Molly had been a victim of sinful lust.

Later that evening, after a tension-filled supper, Captain Roberts called for a special meeting of the brethren. He stood a slight distance from the wagons and waited until all of the men, young and old alike, had gathered around the fire he'd built. "Brothers in Zion," he began, "we have a difficult matter to discuss. There is among us a man unworthy of the priesthood he is holdin'. Someone guilty of a most heinous sin."

As the chastising call to repentance continued, Truman Wicker took out his knife, idly whittling on a piece of willow he'd collected earlier in the afternoon.

Chapter Twenty-Three

The next morning dawned bright and clear. But the usual good-natured camp banter was replaced by hushed whisperings. Neighbor nodded politely at neighbor, but the stiff smiles didn't extend to the cold eyes of mistrust. The unity of the camp was disintegrating, the mystery of yesterday's transgression hanging heavily over their heads as the guilty party refused to step forward.

"I don't like the looks of this," David remarked, lifting himself up into his saddle. Gripping his buckskin's reins, he glanced around at the wagon train.

"It isn't good," Captain Roberts replied. "Brother Miles, I propose we keep alert. Report to me if you discover anything out of the ordinary."

David nodded, clicked to his horse, and moved out of camp to examine the trail ahead.

"What is the big deal?" Kate asked Molly. "I mean, okay, so the camp has a peeping Tom. It's not like anyone was hurt!"

"Knowing you, you probably enjoyed being seen improperly!"

Kate glared at the other girl. "And you didn't? The way you were parading up there on the bank . . ."

Her eyes blazing with indignant rage, Molly slapped Kate hard across the face. Slowly lowering her hand, she blinked. "Kate . . . I . . ." she stammered, her smoldering eyes cooling with regret. Kate glowered at her aunt, raising a hand to her reddening cheek.

"Come, girls, we're ready for the day's journey. Kate, put on your bonnet and let's boost you up on the wagon by Jamie," Colleen said, tying the bonnet strings beneath her own chin.

"I'd rather walk," Kate said through clenched teeth, moving away from the wagon. "And I'm not wearing a stupid bonnet!" she added, still holding a hand against her throbbing face.

"Katie?" Colleen called. When Kate refused to answer, she turned to look at Molly, raising an eyebrow at her daughter's panicked expression. "What's the trouble now, daughter?"

"I . . . she . . ." Molly sputtered.

"It's nothing, Aunt Colleen," Kate said, facing her grandmother. "I'd just rather walk. You ride today." She gave Molly a livid look. She wasn't about to provide her aunt with ammunition today!

"Are you sure, Katie?" Colleen asked, wondering at the way Kate was covering one side of her face. Kate silently nodded, then walked away. Colleen turned to gaze at her daughter. "Did you upset her again about riding?" she quietly probed.

"No," Molly said, avoiding her mother's eyes. "You heard her, though, you'll be riding today," she added, moving to help her mother up onto the wagon.

"Well, I'm not sure about this. It will indeed be good to give these feet of mine a rest. But if Kate looks at all unwell, I want to know about it." Molly nodded, then walked away.

The wagon train stopped at noon for a hurried cold lunch. Tempers were short, and patience nonexistent. It had been a trying day at best, the sagging spirits of the company persisting as time progressed. Continuing with the day's journey, they reached a landmark known as Lone Tree, a small group of cedars that had somehow managed to thrive along the prairie trail. The entire train halted briefly to examine the initials carved in one of the three trees. Captain Roberts pointed out Brother Brigham's initials, hoping to spark renewed interest and faith in the journey they were making. A half-hearted cheer started by David met with subtle resistance; the pioneers were not in a festive mood.

Admitting defeat, Captain Roberts signaled for the train to continue. As the company moved forward, several head of buffalo ran among the wagons, tipping over the one belonging to Truman Wicker. Working together, the pioneers soon set things right, restoring Truman's wagon to a semblance of order and calming the livestock that had been spooked. David managed to bring down two of the wild beasts, offering the promise of fresh buffalo for supper. Enthusiasm was restrained. Most were tiring of the wild-flavored steaks.

They traveled for nearly five miles before suffering another mishap. This time, the wagon belonging to the Spencer family lost its right front wheel. As the wheel worked loose, the axle ground into the dirt, throwing John Spencer into some sagebrush. The brush succeeded in breaking the man's fall, limiting his injuries to minor scrapes and bruises. The company again halted, impatiently waiting while Brother Levi Lott, a blacksmith by trade, assessed the damage. When Levi determined that it would be morning before the wagon could be repaired, Captain Roberts instructed the other captains to ride down the line of wagons to announce that camp would be set up at this location. "Be wary of the creek branching off from the river," he advised. "According to the guide book by Brother William Clayton, Castle Creek is plagued with quicksand. It will be a difficult crossing on the morrow."

"We'll never reach Salt Lake Valley," Molly complained, glaring around at the makeshift camp.

"Tell someone who cares," Kate grumbled, wiping beads of sweat from her forehead.

Molly turned to give Kate a dirty look. She was relieved to see that the reddened bruise she'd raised earlier was hidden by a glaring sunburn. Kate had refused to wear a bonnet, claiming it would mess up her hair. Molly thought the sunburn served Kate right. Turning from the younger girl, she moved to help Jamie with the oxen and cow.

"So, Katie, how are you farin' this day?" Colleen asked, moving beside the girl. "Did you survive the walk?" She frowned at the sight of Kate's sunburn. "Oh, my stubborn girl, why would you not wear a bonnet? Look at that face of yours," she quietly scolded, shaking her head. "Come with me," she beckoned, motioning to the shallow river.

Kate lifted up the bottom of her dress and moved to follow her grandmother.

Colleen walked down to the river bank, glancing around until she'd found what she was looking for. She turned and motioned for Kate to move to her side.

"No way!" Kate said, refusing to get near the mud.

"It'll ease the burnin', Katie," Colleen persisted. "First, bathe your face in the water," she instructed, leading the young woman to the edge of the river.

Kneeling down, Kate reluctantly stuck her hand in the lazy, silt-laced water. It wasn't very cold, but it did feel wonderful after the long, hot march in the sun. She hurriedly splashed water on her face, gasping as it penetrated her sensitive skin.

"There, now, that should help draw the heat out a bit. Splash on more water, then I'll dab some of this damp earth over the worst of the burn."

"Colleen," Kate whined, straightening to gaze at the woman.

Frowning severely, Colleen cleared her throat.

"Oh, honestly! Okay, all right, Aunt Colleen!"

"Thank you, child. Now, quit squirmin' about. This'll take the fight right out of that burn." Scooping up a handful of mud, Colleen skillfully applied a layer to Kate's face.

"This is so gross!"

"Aye, but it works," Colleen said, smiling. "If you'd like, you can hide in the wagon for a time. No one need see you."

"Promise?"

"Aye," Colleen replied, rinsing her hands in the river.

Kate was amazed. The stinging pain was fading. Maybe Grandma Colleen knew what she was doing. She grinned, wondering if this was how facial masks had originated.

"Let's head back to camp," Colleen said, putting a protective arm around Kate. "Until they discover last night's culprit, I want you girls to stick close to the wagon."

Kate woke with a start. Blinking rapidly, she sat up, staring around at the wagon. As she stretched, she wondered how long she'd slept. She touched the hardened mud-pack and shuddered. This had to come off. She moved cautiously to the back of the wagon, hoping no one was in sight. She was in luck; the voices were all coming from the other direction.

"Molly? Molly Mahoney! Now where did that girl wander off

to?" Colleen complained in a loud voice.

Smiling, Kate realized what had startled her out of the nap—Grandma Colleen hollering for Molly. Secretly hoping her aunt was in for an overdue tongue-lashing, Kate quietly climbed out of the wagon. There was no need to bother Colleen. She'd just sneak down to the river and wash this mess off herself before anyone saw her.

She hurried down to the Platte River. Luck was with her. She'd escaped unseen. Kneeling by the river's edge, she began splashing water on her face. At first, the dried mud had to be pried off. Then it gradually released its hold, the tiny chunks of moist dirt falling into the river. Rinsing until she was convinced the mud was gone, she lifted her head, allowing the droplets of water to slide down the neck of her dress. She closed her eyes and enjoyed the relaxing coolness, startled by the sound of angry voices.

She nervously glanced around. It was obvious the argument was coming from a small group of willows down by the creek. Why hadn't she listened to Colleen? Suppose there were Indians running around, or a pioneer pervert? She slowly stood and searched for a weapon.

Molly stared at the man who had followed her to Castle Creek. She had wanted to be alone with her thoughts, and this unwelcome distraction filled her with angry revulsion.

"Sister Molly, thou art in danger. I felt prompted to seek after thy safety."

Meeting the man's disturbing gaze, Molly shuddered. "Thank you for your concern, but I'm perfectly capable of takin' care of myself . . ."

"Thou art possessed by the spirit of pride," Truman Wicker said, his narrow eyes wandering from her face to assess her slender body. "Pride is of the devil. It must be driven out."

"Brother Wicker, I must protest your words . . ."

"It will take the firm hand of the priesthood to lead thee to the path of righteousness. Brother Miles is not for thee."

"Leave me be . . ."

Truman grabbed Molly by the shoulders. "I must stop thee from cultivating sinful desires in the hearts of men!" he snarled, shaking her.

"Release me," she stammered. "I'll . . . I'll scream!"

"Last eve, I was granted a vision. Thou art to be mine, Molly Mahoney. Mine to tame into submissiveness!" Leaning down, he forced his lips on hers.

Molly frantically pulled away from the nauseating smell of tobacco. Averting her face, she was caught off-guard by the sharp sting of Truman's hand. She cried out as she fell to the ground, praying fervently in her mind. *Help me, Father! Bring someone to my aid!* She struggled to her feet and backed away, her eyes darting up the bank. Surely someone would hear the struggle. As he came toward her, she dodged his hands, running past him with all her might. In her haste, she tripped over a willow branch, lost her balance, and fell onto the hard-baked earth.

"Cease this contention! Thou art mine, given by divine revelation. I will bring salvation to thy troubled soul!"

Molly shakily stood and faced her opponent.

"I claim thee for my own," he growled, gripping her trembling shoulders. As he pulled her close, he reached a hand to her hair, yanking it until the pain brought tears to her eyes. She tried to scream for help, but the sound was immediately muffled as he forced another kiss on her unwilling lips.

"Take that, you dirty rotten . . ."

For once, Molly was relieved to hear Kate's vulgar language. A blow across Truman's shoulders caught him by surprise. The sputtering man released Molly and turned to glower at the younger girl.

"Thou art full of the devil!" he accused, reaching to strike Kate.

"And thou art full of yourself!" Kate returned, dodging his intended blow. Unaware of Molly's pained smile, she swung the heavy piece of driftwood she'd brought with her, hitting the man in the stomach. "Run, Molly!" she hollered as Truman crumpled to his knees. "Go get help!"

Frozen in place, Molly couldn't respond.

"Molly, would you snap out of it! Move those buns of yours and hustle back to camp!"

Breathing deeply, Molly whirled around, running through the willows.

Kate scowled, brandishing the heavy piece of driftwood as a furious Truman ran towards her. She quickly stepped to the side, allowing the man to plunge headlong into the creek. When she heard him cry out in pain, she turned, staring at the large rock responsible for the bloody gash in his forehead. Her heart pounding, she dropped the piece of soggy wood and watched as Truman stumbled, dropping to his knees in the swift current. She stared in stunned silence and considered diving in after him. As she hurried to the water's edge, David Miles pushed her aside, throwing off his boots to splash into the shallow water. Behind him, Captain Roberts removed his own boots, plunging in after David. Blinking, she glanced up the bank. Colleen and several of the men from camp had found them. Molly was clinging to her mother, her gasping sobs revealing Truman's intent.

Startled by a shout from David, all eyes were riveted on the creek. Truman was nowhere to be seen. David gulped air, then disappeared into the swift current. Captain Roberts followed his example. Minutes passed like hours. David and the captain finally broke the surface of the water, filling their lungs with air.

Kate's eyes widened when David drew out his knife. As he plunged back into the water, she imagined what the scout must be doing to poor Truman. Poor Truman? After what he tried to do to Molly? Surprised by the feelings she had for the other girl, Kate glanced back at her aunt. Her grandmother had locked Molly in a fierce embrace. Meeting Kate's gaze, Colleen motioned for her to join them. Kate shook her head and turned to watch the drama unfolding before her eyes.

Captain Roberts and David finally reappeared, dragging Truman between them. Coughing up water, they waded back to the bank, pulling Truman's limp body to shore.

Kate moved toward them. "Is he . . . did you kill him?"

David frowned and dropped Truman's body on the ground, glancing up at the girl. "As much as I would've liked to . . . no. He was caught in some weeds."

"We tried to save him. It's the first time I've ever heard tell of a man drowning in two feet of water. He'd landed in a mess of quicksand and weeds. By the time Brother Miles was able to cut him loose, he was gone," Captain Roberts explained.

"He'll have his just reward," David said quietly, looking at Kate. "I thank you for helping Molly," he added, gripping her shoulder.

Kate stared at the soaked scout. "I . . . I guess we're even, now," she stammered, remembering how he'd tried to save her from the snake. Because of his efforts, she was still alive. If you could call this living. Frowning, she wondered if any of this had actually happened. Or was it all part of some crazy dream? She turned and slowly walked back to camp.

"There you are, Katie. If you girls don't cease this wandering off, I'm going to tie you both to the wagon," Colleen chided, sliding an arm around Kate's trembling shoulders. "You're cold, lass. Come back to camp. We've got a nice fire goin'. It'll warm your tremblin' bones. Brother Benjamin Whitney is playin' a few hymns on his fiddle. His sweet music is a balm to us all. Especially after the misdeeds of this afternoon."

"Why am I still here?" Kate asked, looking up at Colleen.

"Well, now, you never have been one to ask an easy question." Colleen drew back to face the young woman. "It's Truman's passing that has upset you, am I right, girl?"

Kate shrugged, sure she wouldn't hear the answer she was seeking.

"What Truman tried to do to my Molly . . . it was wrong, Katie. Don't blame yourself for his death. His fate was in God's hands. He was a twisted, cruel man. I shudder to think what those two wives of his have endured." She smoothed a stray strand of hair from Kate's face and sadly smiled. "He was the one peeking at us yesterday from the bushes."

"I kind of figured that one out already," Kate replied.

"Molly has told us . . . if it wasn't for you . . ." She paused, her sight blurring with tearful moisture. "I'll be forever grateful to you, Katie Colleen."

"What I did was no big deal!" Kate said gruffly, turning from the river to walk back to camp.

Puzzled, Colleen watched as the young woman struggled up the sloping bank. Shaking her head, she slowly moved to follow.

CHAPTER TWENTY-FOUR

It was a somber crowd that gathered the next morning around a shallow grave topped by rocks. A piece of driftwood had been shoved into the dirt at the head to provide a marker. Kate stared at the driftwood, then at the two widows who were focusing on the grave, too humiliated to meet the sympathetic looks being sent their direction by the entire camp. Kate saw there was a vast age difference between the two women. The one they called Sister Lovina was much older than the pretty young woman named Caroline. Caroline wasn't much older than Molly. Kate wondered why Truman had been allowed to have even one wife. From what she'd overheard, he'd treated both women abominably. And if he'd had his way, Molly would've been next. Shuddering, she shifted her gaze to the wooden marker, still trying to comprehend that Truman Wicker was gone.

Captain Roberts took charge of the simple graveside service. After uttering a few words over the grave, he offered a quiet prayer, ending with a request for safety on the day's journey. Hats and bonnets were then quickly replaced as families moved to prepare for the day ahead.

"Brother David," Captain Roberts called, catching up with the tall scout. "Have you reconsidered my proposition?"

David slowly nodded. "I'll drive the team for the widows. But it's for them, not that sorry excuse for a man we buried!"

"Hatred has no place in the Lord's gospel," the captain replied, gazing intently at the young man.

"But, Captain, after what he tried to do to Molly . . . I mean Sister Molly," he stammered, turning red.

"I know, lad. But despise the sin, not the sinner. Brother Wicker will be dealt with in heaven."

"You speak truly, but it puzzles me how a man . . . a latter-day priesthood holder, can become so twisted."

"Brother Brigham has said that when men turn from truth, they invite evil into their lives. Brother Truman abused a sacred trust, using it to gain power over those in his stewardship. One indiscretion always leads to another down the pathway of sin. And, once you fall prey to the power of Satan, it is astounding the travesties that are committed in the name of religion."

"If he'd hurt Molly . . ."

"God was with her. Of that there is no doubt. Sister Kate was an instrument in his hands."

"I'll be eternally grateful to Kate," David said, his eyes straying to where Molly was helping Jamie yoke up the oxen to their wagon.

"When are you going to take that young woman to wife?" the captain asked, following David's gaze.

"As soon as she'll have me," David answered, staring wistfully at the young woman who had captured his heart.

"Perhaps now she'll soften . . ."

"This ordeal with Truman has shaken her. But, I don't dare to hope . . . since her father's death . . ."

"Trials stretch us to our limits. We either grow or wither. If only Sister Molly would adhere to her sweet mother's example."

"I keep praying time will heal the heartache she bears."

"Dwelling on past grievances will only produce a caustic soul. Pray for inspiration, Brother Miles. It may be that marriage and a family will shift Molly's focus from the angry bile of bitterness."

Lifting an eyebrow, David watched as the captain walked away. He adjusted his hat and headed in the opposite direction, moving toward the newly-widowed Wickers.

Kate eased out from behind a nearby wagon. She hadn't meant to eavesdrop, but, on the other hand, the conversation between Captain Roberts and David had been rather interesting. She looked up when she heard Colleen call her name and reluctantly trudged toward the Mahoney wagon.

"Are y'sure about driving the team today, Mother?" Jamie asked, frowning with concern.

"Aye. It'll give your poor blistered hands a rest," Colleen replied, pulling herself up onto the wagon.

"My hands have nearly healed," Jamie protested.

"Quit arguin' and hand me Shannon."

Jamie muttered under his breath and searched for the five-year-old. "Shannon!" he impatiently called.

"Here she is," Kate mumbled, dragging the small red-haired girl along with her. "Cut her some slack. She was heeding Mother Nature's call."

"Bring 'er here! We're leavin' now," Jamie said, scowling at Kate.

"Well, you're in a mood!" she replied, pushing Shannon toward him. "What's wrong, not enough fiber in your diet lately?" she asked with a smirk.

"I don't know why I listen to a word you say, Kate Erickson. You never make any sense!" Jamie guided Shannon to the wagon and lifted her up to their mother.

"Kate, would you care to ride today?" Colleen asked, helping Shannon into the covered protection of the wagon.

"Contrary to popular belief, I am not a wuss!" Kate snapped, walking off.

"Wuss?" Colleen repeated, looking puzzled.

"Kate says it's the same as a wimp," Daniel offered, gazing up at his mother.

"And just what is a wimp, pray tell?"

Daniel shrugged. "I think it's a name. It's what she called Molly yesterday."

"I see," Colleen said, shifting her gaze to the two feuding females. Molly was moving close to Kate. Grimacing, Colleen prayed for guidance. How would they ever survive two stubborn, Irish-willed beauties?

"Kate . . . wait please. I wish to speak with you."

Kate reluctantly stopped to face her aunt.

"About last eve . . . I never had the chance to thank . . ."

"Don't bother!" Kate warned.

"But, you risked yourself to help me. Even after . . ."

"You belted me across the chops? Look, forget it, okay? Eventually, none of this will matter anyway. One of these days, I'll wake up. You'll see." As far as she was concerned, the conversation was over. Turning, she began to walk away.

"Kate . . . I'm tryin' my best to make things right with you! Will you kindly give me a chance?"

"Like the one you gave me?" Kate demanded, whirling around to glare at Molly. "You've treated me like dirt since this whole mess began!"

"I'm sorry. I was wrong to do so. I'd like to start again. I've come to believe you are a Mahoney. It's only right that we act like kin. What do you say to that, Kate?"

The rest of the day, Molly pondered the obscenities that had rolled off Kate's tongue, trying to make sense of the insult. By the time the train had stopped to make camp, both girls were in a foul mood. Even Colleen couldn't reason with the feisty young women. She silently prayed for the inspiration and strength to cope with this added challenge.

During the next afternoon, a small group of Indians approached the wagon train. Captain Roberts called everyone to a halt, then rode out with David to meet them.

"I think they're Sioux," David said in a hushed voice as they drew near. The Indians were dressed in fringed and beaded leather breeches, their bronzed arms and chests left bare, their black hair defiantly hanging down to their muscular shoulders.

"Can you understand their language?" Captain Roberts worriedly asked as he reined in his horse.

"I speak some Sioux. I picked it up on my return from the Battalion."

Nodding, the captain offered a silent prayer.

A brave with shoulder-length braids grunted a greeting and moved forward to meet them. He spoke haltingly, gazing boldly at the white men.

"They are Sioux," David said, returning a greeting in the Sioux tongue.

Somewhat startled, the brave glanced back at the others in his party. A handsome young chief with long black hair nudged his horse forward. Coming within a few inches of David's buckskin, he stared at the scout, then spit out a few terse words in his native language.

"What do they want?" the captain asked, trying his best to appear calm. It was said Indians respected bravery. He hoped that was the case.

"They're a hunting party. They wish to trade buffalo meat for grain."

Realizing they had little choice in the matter, the captain reluctantly agreed. "It's a poor trade, considering we've managed to supply ourselves with an overabundance of that particular meat, but, it's worth the price to avoid bloodshed. Tell them I will return to the wagons and bring back a sack of meal."

David nodded and gave the Sioux the captain's answer. The young chief frowned, uttering a string of harsh-sounding words.

"What's wrong now?"

"They want four sacks of meal."

"Four? Why . . . that's thievery!"

"They'll accept four sacks of meal, or two women. We decide."

Captain Roberts scowled. "Quite a choice they've given us," he muttered. He turned his horse around to head back to the wagons. "Tell them I'll bring two sacks of meal. That's all we can spare."

David used gestures and his limited Sioux vocabulary to convey the captain's message. Agreeing to the exchange, the chief rode back to his hunting party to retrieve the buffalo slain earlier that morning. He grinned at his braves, knowing they'd made a better trade than the pioneers.

It wasn't long before Captain Roberts returned, two sacks of meal tied on behind his saddle.

"Who gave up their rations?"

"One sack came from the Wickers . . . They're hoping to atone for Truman's deeds."

"But the blame for his actions doesn't rest with the family. We bear them no ill will."

"True enough, but if it makes those dear sisters feel better, we'll oblige them, under the circumstances."

"And the other sack?"

"From the Mahoneys."

Remaining silent, David frowned.

"Sister Colleen said we'd not be denyin' her the blessing," the captain said, imitating the thick Irish brogue.

"She's a saint to the core," David murmured, moving down from his horse to untie one of the sacks of meal. "But, she can't spare this," he added, gripping the sack in his hands.

"True. I intend to replace her donation when we reach Fort Laramie," the captain replied, sliding down from his horse.

"Count on me to pay for a share of that," David offered, glancing at the captain.

Nodding at David, the captain untied the other sack, toting it to where the Indians waited.

"David, tell us again about the Sioux chief," Daniel begged, his eyes bright with excitement.

David shook his head, stirring the fire with a small stick. "It's late, Daniel. And we have a long day's travel ahead of us tomorrow."

"Brother David is right," Colleen agreed, shooing her younger children off to bed. Taking pleasure from the sight of David sitting next to Molly, she followed the children to the wagon, dragging Kate with her.

"I'm not tired," Kate snapped, trying to pull away from her grandmother.

"Tired or no, we'll be leavin' those two alone now," Colleen said, giving Kate a strange look.

Kate rolled her eyes and climbed up into the wagon behind Shannon. Who wanted to watch Aunt Molly make out anyway? She pulled a face and crawled off into a corner to sulk.

Curiosity eventually got the best of her, and after convincing Colleen that a trip to the bushes was a necessity, she quietly climbed out of the back of the wagon. Creeping alongside the wagon bed, she peered around the corner at the fire. She frowned at the couple. They were just talking! True excitement! She was about to turn away when David timidly leaned close to Molly. Grinning, Kate watched as the scout planted a firm kiss on Molly's receptive lips. As the enraptured couple pulled away from each other, Kate felt a sharp inner twinge. Jace had never looked at her the way David was gazing at Molly. The respectful adoration David felt for her aunt was plainly visible. As a rush of painful longing tugged at her heart, Kate leaned against the wagon and closed her eyes.

CHAPTER TWENTY-FIVE

C olleen," Emily puffed, hurrying to catch up with the other woman. "Is it true? Has Molly finally agreed to marry young David?"

"Aye," Colleen responded, her eyes twinkling with elated joy.

"What changed her mind?" Emily probed, falling in step with her friend as the wagons slowly lumbered over the trail.

"You should've seen her face when David rode out to face those red-skinned heathen! White as a ghost, she was, thinkin' they might harm him."

Emily chuckled. "Whatever the reason, it will be good to have a reason to celebrate. We've had enough cause to mourn on this journey."

"Aye," Colleen agreed.

"When are they to be wed?"

"After we reach Fort Laramie. David wants to trade his horse off for a wagon and supplies."

"Your Molly will never find a finer man."

"Truer words have ne'er been spoken, dear friend." Smiling, Colleen confided her plans for the wedding.

Much to Colleen's delight, Molly's mood improved drastically. But to her dismay, Kate's took a turn for the worse. Sullen, Kate avoided conversation, using terse sentences when speech was necessary.

"Katie girl, what ails you?" Colleen finally asked after two days of gloom on the young woman's part. Shrugging, Kate walked off, heading down to the river.

"Let me try to reason with her," Molly offered, moving to follow the other girl.

"Be careful with your words, daughter. The wounds of her heart, they are festering."

"I know her pain, Mother. Let me speak with her."

Colleen agreed to her daughter's request and returned her attention to the meal she was preparing for supper.

"Kate?"

Kate continued staring across the river at a sandstone formation the company called Chimney Rock.

"Kate," Molly persisted, moving until she was standing next to the other girl. "Are you well? The truth of it is, we're worried about you."

Kate sighed. "Look, just leave me alone, okay? None of you understand what I'm going through, so just leave me alone!"

"I see. You alone have endured loss of family and home. How sad that you must carry the weight of the world on those puny shoulders. Could it be you're a wimp, or wuss, was it now?"

Kate turned to glower at Molly. "I am not a wimp or a wuss!"

"Then prove it. Show us Mahoney blood courses through your veins! Pull yourself together, girl. You're not the only one who's ever lost someone," Molly said, her expression softening. "I know your pain, Kate. I'll always carry within the loss of my father, not to mention Brian and Maureen. But life goes on, with or without us."

"You just don't get it, do you? My life isn't going on! I'm trapped in this ridiculous nightmare!"

"I'm not sure what luxuries you were acquainted with before, but we've given you the best we have to offer!"

"Oh, right! I get to parade around in a stupid dress, walk for miles every day in the broiling heat, eat the same thing night after miserable night, and sleep on a mattress of boards. Yeah, boy, you guys really know how to live!"

"Stop it, Kate!" Molly warned, an angry fire flickering in her eyes. "You know nothing of suffering!"

"Oh, and I suppose you do," Kate retorted.

Struggling with her temper, Molly took a deep breath. When she finally spoke, her voice was low and strained. "Do you know what it is, Kate, to live for weeks at a time in the cargohold of a ship with hundreds of other immigrants, so crowded that you near faint for want of fresh air? To desperately crave a sip of cool water to relieve a parched throat that feels as though it's swollen shut? Do you know how it feels to watch helplessly as a younger brother and sister slowly succumb to the rages of yellow fever, to witness their tiny bodies being wrapped in a torn, dirty blanket to be thrown overboard into the sea because there isn't the means for a proper burial? To have nightmares that the same will happen to you, that your body with someday feed the fish?" She paused, forcing the bitter memory from her mind. Her eyes held Kate's in a locked stare.

"Do you know the fear, Kate, of being driven from place to place in this so-called land of promise because of who and what you are? The anguish of watching as a home built by your father lies in ashes from the torches of hate? Do you know the pain of walking barefoot through the snow, your feet cracked and bleeding, day after miserable day until you reach the Mississippi River? A river that couldn't be crossed with a ferry because of the ice. We were taken, a family at a time, in canoes and skiffs across that frigid water, praying we wouldn't capsize and sink before reaching the soil of Illinois. There, we spent five years building a city from swampland no one else wanted. Fighting Nauvoo flies and mosquitoes that plagued us night and day! And always there was death. Friends and neighbors. The losses were all around us as illness and fatigue took their toll."

"I was there, cousin, the day they brought the slain body of the Prophet Joseph Smith home to Nauvoo. I heard the anguished cries of his wife and mother as they laid his body to rest next to Brother Hyrum's. And still the mobocrats were not satisfied! Persecution of the vilest nature persisted until we were forced in the middle of winter to leave our homes once again!

"That first ill-fated night we made camp at Sugar Creek, on the west bank of the Mississippi River, clearing away snow to set up tents for those fortunate enough to have them. The rest made do with wagons or blankets. On that same eve, I helped my mother bring an infant into this world of cruelty and pain. He was delivered in the crudest of circumstances, under a blanket, during a storm of rain and snow. Sisters stood, holding dishes to catch the frigid water as it dripped into the makeshift tent.

"Then, a few days later, with rationed supplies, to Chariton River—wagons, livestock, and those of us who were strong enough to walk, wading through icy mud. We journeyed for days till we reached a place called Garden Grove in the latter part of April. Men were left behind to till the earth, to plant grain, and build houses for those who would come behind. On the rest of us went to establish the next permanent camp, a place called Mount Pisgah. Again, men were left behind to build and to plant, leaving several women in sole charge of their families.

"After journeying to Council Bluffs, a third camp was wrought from the barren plain. We continued on to cross the Missouri River, where several lost what little they had left. Wagons and livestock were swept away in the fierce current. Completely destitute, we gathered what remained in our possession to build homes at a place called Winter Quarters.

"By that first winter, 538 log homes and 83 sod houses had been constructed. The numbers doubled by spring. But before winter came, we had dug graves for nearly three hundred souls. People who perished needlessly from scurvy, my father among them. Too late for him, we discovered that horseradish and potatoes worked to cure the disease."

Winded, Molly stopped, the haunting memories threatening to dissolve her composure. Stunned, Kate remained silent.

"So, Kate Erickson, be wary of telling this company that they have no understanding when it comes to suffering! We all bear wounds that heal slowly." She turned and began walking away. Stopping, she glanced over her shoulder. "We were never promised it would be a world of comfort. As my mother is fond of saying, we're here to prove our worth." She waited, but there was no response. "When you decide you're ready to join the living, we'll be waiting to show you how it's done," she finally sighed. Molly walked back to the wagon train, convinced that Kate was a lost cause. Burying her face in her hands, Kate cried tears that Molly would never see.

CHAPTER TWENTY-SIX

Certain everyone was asleep, Kate quietly slipped out of her bedroll. She reached for the pair of ugly leather shoes she'd inherited from Molly. Gripping them tightly in one hand, she crept to the back of the wagon. As she straddled the tailgate, she was startled by a scraping sound. She looked up, staring in the moonlit darkness at Molly.

"And where are you off to, might I ask?" Molly demanded in a hushed voice, slowly sitting up.

"Just heeding nature's call," Kate whispered back.

Molly stifled a yawn, turned on her side, and snuggled down beneath her warm blankets.

Breathing out slowly, Kate quickly lowered herself to the ground. So far so good. She hurriedly laced on the awkward shoes and moved in silence away from camp. Shivering, she wished she'd thought to grab Aunt . . . Grandma Colleen's shawl. She ignored the cold and slipped through the ring of wagons, pausing every few minutes to listen. She was fairly confident no one was following. She took a few more steps, her heart leaping into her throat when she stumbled over a pair of legs.

"Halt!" a sleepy voice demanded.

Kate suddenly found herself face to face with a man who had quickly scrambled to his feet. A man named Isaac Kimble. She mentally kicked herself for forgetting about the guards who were posted at night. "It's just me," she said timidly.

"Me, who?"

"Kate Erickson."

"Oh. Well, what are you doing out this far from camp?" Isaac asked, rubbing at his tired eyes.

"I . . . uh . . . have to . . . you know," she stammered, wondering how to politely explain the excuse she'd given Molly.

"Oh. Well, a person can't help that. Be quick about your business, though, young lady. And next time, don't come alone."

"Okay," Kate lied, moving down closer to the river. When she reached the sandy bank, she ran for all she was worth, back the way they'd come, slowing only after tripping over a rock. She rubbed her twisted ankle, then limped off, unaware that the posted guard had fallen back asleep.

Early the next morning, Molly gently shook her mother awake. Colleen glanced up into Molly's worried face and patted the trembling hand resting on her shoulder. "What is it, dear?"

"Kate's missing," Molly replied.

"What is it you're sayin'? Kate's gone?"

Molly nodded. "I thought at first she'd risen before me. But there's no sign of her. She slipped out late last night . . . I didn't think anything of it. I should've gone with her! The fool girl's gone and gotten herself lost!"

"Are you sure, lass?" Colleen asked, moving out of the warm quilt she'd slept in.

"Aye," Molly responded. "Brother Kimble was guarding in the night. He talked to her. That's the last anyone's seen of her."

Dressing quickly, Colleen followed her daughter out of the wagon. "Jamie, look after Shannon," she ordered, hurrying behind Molly. "Didn't Brother Kimble search for her?"

"Brother Kimble?"

Colleen realized Molly had a point. Isaac Kimble was known for his ability to sleep through just about anything. She glanced up and saw that David and Captain Roberts were coming their way.

"'Mornin' sisters," the captain greeted. "Brother Isaac tells me we have a stray."

"Aye," Colleen said worriedly. "I can't imagine what could've happened to that girl."

"We'll find her," David said, smiling at both women. "Luckily it's the Sabbath, so we won't be pulling out from camp this morning. We'll spread out and search the area. She can't be far."

Hoping he was right, Colleen smoothed the hair away from her face. She hadn't taken the time to make herself presentable. It seemed rather trivial at the moment.

"We'll gather the company together for a prayer on her behalf," Captain Roberts said. "With the Lord's guidance, we'll find Sister Kate."

"I'm still not fond of the idea," Colleen protested later as David boosted Molly up into a horse's saddle.

"I'm as good as any man when it comes to handlin' a horse," Molly insisted, reaching for the reins. "And Sister Lovina said I was welcome to take Truman's mare."

Colleen flinched at the disrespect intended by her daughter toward Brother Wicker. The young woman staunchly refused to call him a brother in the gospel.

"Don't worry, Sister Colleen, we'll look after this girl. If she didn't have the eyes of a hawk, we'd insist on her staying behind," Captain Roberts said, reaching down to pat his brown gelding.

Frowning, Colleen moved close to the captain's horse. "I've stood many hardships. But, this . . . I can't bear it. Bring both of my girls back to me," she said in a low voice.

Silently nodding, the captain gazed down at the woman. "It's in the Lord's hands," he said softly. "But I feel certain we'll find your niece."

Colleen offered a worried smile and stepped out of the way as the five riders prepared to leave. Staring as they rode out of camp, she was unaware that Emily had moved to her side.

"They'll find Kate," Emily said quietly, slipping an arm around Colleen's waist. "They'll find her."

"We found her tracks down here by the river. She's heading back the way we've come." David shouted to be heard above the wind stirring in a small group of willows.

"It's not good riding along this bank," Captain Roberts pointed out. "There's quicksand, and as fate would have it, the one place where this blasted river decides to sprout a few willows is the one place we need to search."

"If we ride on the other side, we may miss her," David replied. "She might be asleep, curled up somewhere in these bushes. She may not hear us."

Molly frowned, a tiny stab of fear creeping into her thoughts. A dead girl wouldn't hear them pass either. Closing her eyes, she offered a silent prayer. If anything had happened to Kate, her mother wouldn't take it well.

"What do you suggest?"

David walked his horse over to the captain. "I'll search this side on foot," he said, handing the buckskin's reins to Captain Roberts. "I'll fire off two shots if I discover her."

Nodding, the captain secured the horse's reins to the back of his saddle. "Brother Lott . . ."

"Glad to, Captain," the burly blacksmith answered, guessing the request. He slid down from the black mare and handed the reins of his horse to Brother Kimble.

"I'll be stayin' with them," Molly added, preparing to dismount.

"No, Molly," David said firmly. If Kate had met with peril, he didn't want his future bride to discover the body.

"Brother David is right," Captain Roberts said, meeting Molly's annoyed glare. "You'll be of more help to us out in the open with your sharp vision." Nudging his horse, he led the mounted search party away from the river.

Molly gave David a worried glance, then tugged at the mare's reins, reluctantly following the captain.

Dragging herself to the clear stream a few feet ahead, Kate groaned. The pain from her swollen ankle was unbearable. The numerous scrapes and bruises she'd suffered during her fight with the willows were stinging with a fierce intensity. By the position of the sun, she guessed it was close to noon. Her stomach growled loudly, reminding her that she hadn't eaten since supper last night.

This was ridiculous! Determined to walk out of this living nightmare, she was trying to reach the place where David had first found her, hoping she could somehow slip back into reality.

She dropped to her knees at the stream and drank greedily from the gurgling water. After splashing the refreshing coldness onto her face, she stared at her reflection. Cursing at the wild hair and dirt-smudged expression, she turned away.

She shakily stood and forced herself forward, wading across the small stream. As she reached the other side, she stumbled, a dizzying weakness causing her to collapse.

NO! This couldn't happen now! She had to go back . . . find the way she'd entered this bizarre world. "Mom!" she called out before the blackness descended.

Sue lifted her head from the metal railing of Kate's hospital bed. "Kate?" she said, sure she'd heard her daughter cry out. Quickly rising, she gripped Kate's hand. "Sweetheart, I'm here. Please, honey, try. Try . . ." Silence enveloped the room. "Kate?" Sue pleaded. "Please, Father, help her."

CHAPTER TWENTY-SEVEN

So help me, Kate, if you don't turn up soon . . ." Molly stopped and stared. Directly ahead, a body was slumped on the ground near a small stream. "Kate?" She paused, shading her eyes for a better look. Lowering her hand, she frowned. It was Kate; she recognized the calico dress. A strange tightness afflicted her throat. Images of Indians or lawless white men flashed through her mind. Which had it been? No matter the trouble this girl had caused, Kate hadn't deserved to end like this. Shuddering, she prayed her cousin hadn't suffered.

She moved forward, staring at the still form of the girl she'd grudgingly come to love as a sister. A lone, beautiful girl, stranded on the open plain, totally at the mercy of whoever found her. Molly shook her head and tried to dispel the haunting images of the tortuous death Kate must've endured. "At least it's over now," she said in a hushed voice, choking back tears.

Reluctantly approaching the body, Molly knelt beside it, reaching out to touch Kate's shoulder. She gasped when the other girl moaned. "You live?" Molly asked, bringing a trembling hand to her mouth.

"Sorry to disappoint you," Kate murmured, rolling onto her back. She struggled to sit up, but she felt as though she'd just ridden on the Tilt-a-Whirl at the fair. It was the same feeling she usually got whenever she tried one of Linda's alcoholic creations. She felt like she'd been pulled through a knothole backwards. That was one of Linda's favorite sayings. Linda had probably made it up when she made up the ingredients for the potent punch she always served at Jace's parties. Kate started to lean sideways. Molly quickly grabbed her, pulling her close, hugging the sister she'd thought was lost.

"It's over, Katie," she soothed. "No matter what . . ." Molly paused, trying to keep the quiver out of her voice. "We'll make it right," she finally said, repeating the line her mother used on a regular basis.

"Right!" Kate mumbled, pulling back to glare at Molly. "How can anything be right again?" She staggered to her feet and wrapped trembling arms around herself.

Rising, Molly wiped at her eyes. "Katie . . . was it the Indians?" she asked softly.

"Indians?" Kate whirled around, her eyes wide with fear. "Indians? Here? Oh, great! Just what we need!"

"Then, it wasn't the Indians?" Molly asked, gazing at Kate. The signs of a struggle were evident. Kate's dress was torn, ripped in several places. There were scratches on her face. Her hair was matted, sticking out wildly in every direction. "You needn't say what's happened," she said quietly, stepping closer. "But let's get you back to camp," she added. "Mother's waitin' . . . she's been so worried. We've all been lookin' for you . . . myself, Captain Roberts, even David. Come, now, Katie, let's go." She tried to take hold of Kate's arm, to lead her to where the others were waiting, but Kate refused to budge.

"Leave me alone," she wailed, pulling away from Molly. She moved forward, tripping over a small rock. She cried out with rage and pain as she fell onto her stomach.

Molly moved quickly to her side, kneeling on the clay-like soil. "Oh, Katie, was it as bad as all that?"

Kate slowly sat up and rubbed her ankle. "I was trying to find my way back. I got lost. I've walked all day in this . . ." she paused, curbing her language for Molly's benefit. "In this rotten heat. I have blisters on one foot, I twisted my other ankle on a . . . a lousy rock. I'm starving. All I've had today is water," she gestured to the stream. "And then . . . and then . . ."

Molly put an arm around Kate's shoulders. "It's all right, Kate, whatever happened, it's over now. You're safe," she promised.

Tears rolled down Kate's face. "But it's not over. It won't ever go away!"

"Hush, Kate," Molly said, squeezing the other girl. "Whatever took place, it wasn't your shame. Many girls . . . younger than yourself, have endured much worse at the hands of the mobocrats."

"How could it be worse?" Kate sobbed, turning to bury her face against Molly. "I'm so filthy . . . I'll never be clean again . . ."

"It just feels that way now," Molly said quietly, gently patting Kate's back.

"I mean, look at this dress . . ."

"It's all right," Molly said, trying to comfort Kate. "I've got another you can wear."

"No, you don't understand. I hate it! I want my own clothes. I want my t-shirts and jeans. Not this uncomfortable . . ."

"Kate Erickson!" Molly quickly interrupted, guessing what the other girl was about to say. "No matter the circumstances, I'll not be hearin' that kind of language from you."

Kate drew back from Molly. "You'll hear worse than that!" she exclaimed, rattling off a line of obscenities.

Rising, Molly held her hands over her ears, shaking her head. She reminded herself that Kate had been traumatized, and waited impatiently for the angry tirade to end. Finally, she dropped her hands to her sides.

"And do you want to hear the worst part?" Kate asked, waving a fist in the air. "I . . . I . . ."

"If it'll make you feel better, say it and be done with it," Molly reluctantly encouraged. Bracing herself, she gazed at the trembling girl.

"I'm having the most horrible bad hair day of my life!" Kate finally said with a sob, realizing Molly wouldn't understand the desperation she felt to escape this dream.

Molly raised an eyebrow. "And?" she finally asked, wondering if the girl had gone daft.

"Isn't that bad enough?" Kate stammered, wiping at her face.

"Kate Erickson, do you mean to tell me this is all because your hair looks bad?"

Glaring at Molly, Kate nodded.

"You weren't . . . attacked . . . molested, as it were?"

Kate pulled a face and shook her head.

"But your dress, it's torn, and the scratches on your face . . ."

"It was those dirty rotten no-good willows," Kate snapped, angered by the look of contempt on Molly's face. "You're the first person I've seen since . . . since last night . . ." she paused, wincing under Molly's icy glare.

Molly stared hard at the whimpering girl, empathy and tenderness replaced by anger and disgust. "We've ridden a full day's journey to find you. Do you understand? And for what? To find a sniveling idiot!" Molly whirled around and stomped off.

Stunned, Kate watched as her aunt marched angrily away. Regaining her senses, she began to run after the other girl. "Molly, wait . . . Molly . . ." She tripped, falling hard against the ground.

"Do that a few more times," Molly encouraged, glowering at Kate. "Perhaps it'll knock some sense into that addled head of yours." She continued moving away, too angry to offer help.

"Molly?"

Molly glanced up. Captain Roberts and Isaac Kimble were heading in their direction. The looks on their faces sent an obvious message. They were both furious. She'd slipped off alone when they'd stopped to rest the horses.

"Praise the good Lord, you've found her!" was the excited shout, their worried anger over Molly's disappearance dissolving. Urging the horses forward, the men eagerly approached the two girls, congratulating Molly on her success.

"The Lord was with you this day," Captain Roberts said, slipping down from his horse, shifting his gaze from Molly to the bedraggled girl behind her. "We'd near given up hope of finding you, Sister Kate."

"Yeah, yeah, yeah! I suppose now you're going to drag me back to camp," Kate mumbled, sending a scathing look in Molly's direction.

"Forgive her, Captain, she's been having a bad hair day!" Molly countered, glaring at Kate.

The captain sighed, exchanging a pained look with Isaac Kimble. "Mount up, sisters. We'll be riding hard to make camp by dark."

Moving to the mare she'd been riding, Molly took the reins from Brother Kimble.

"Miss Erickson, you can ride Brother Lott's mare."

Kate stared at the captain. "But, but I've never ridden a horse before."

Captain Roberts gently patted his horse's neck. "Molly, I'll boost your cousin up behind you. We'll have to double up eventually when we find David and Brother Lott."

Molly frowned her displeasure, but nudged her horse forward, extending a hand down to Kate. After a great deal of effort and persuasion, Kate was finally seated behind her aunt. "Quit sniveling," Molly said in a biting tone, forcing Kate's trembling arms around her waist. "And hold tight. I'll not be stopping to pick you up if you fall."

Gritting her teeth, Kate pulled her hands in sharply against Molly's stomach. She smiled briefly at Molly's soft gasp. Molly shot an elbow into Kate's ribs. Breathing out slowly, Kate relaxed her grip, vowing to get even with her aunt.

Nervously pacing, Colleen peered anxiously into the darkness. "Bring them back to me, Father, don't take my girls from me now," she softly pleaded.

Emily moved up behind her trembling friend. "Here, Colleen, you're shivering," she said, draping a worn shawl around Colleen's shoulders.

"Thank you, dear friend," Colleen said softly. "If only they'd come . . ."

"Standing in the cold won't bring them any faster," Emily gently chided. "Come next to the fire. Catching a chill won't help anyone."

Reluctantly agreeing, Colleen turned to follow her friend back to camp. Just then, a familiar shout rang out. "It's David!" she eagerly cried. "They're comin'!" She impatiently waited as the riders drew close, searching eagerly for signs of Molly and Kate. "Saints be praised, they found her!" she exclaimed, hurrying to the horse bearing the two girls. She waited as David jumped down from his horse to help the girls down from the mare, gratitude and pride shining from her eyes. "I knew you'd find her," she said, patting David's shoulder.

"Your Molly is the one who found her," he murmured, gazing up with admiration at his fiancee.

"Is my dear niece all right?" Colleen asked, staring intently at Kate as David lifted the young woman to the ground.

"That's a matter of opinion!" Molly snapped, climbing down with David's assistance.

Puzzled, Colleen glanced at her daughter before moving to greet Kate. As Kate hobbled forward, Colleen reached for her, gathering the young woman close. Squeezing the quivering shoulders, she cried quiet tears of relief. Several moments passed before she drew Kate back to survey the damage. Shaking her head, she clicked her tongue in concern.

"I . . . I'm sorry," Kate stammered, suddenly feeling ashamed. She hadn't thought about the grief she'd caused her grandmother.

"Katie, let's not be hearin' apologies for what couldn't be helped. Come, dear, we'll clean you up a bit. Then there'll be time for talkin'." Shifting her gaze to Molly, Colleen smiled. "I'm proud of you, lass," she said softly, moving to embrace her daughter. "My prayers have been with you since you left."

Molly returned the hug, kissing her mother's soft cheek. She then pulled away, moving to walk with David as he led the horses to a nearby creek.

Sighing contentedly, Colleen slipped an arm around Kate's shoulders, guiding the limping girl to a warm fire.

As Kate stumbled along, she wasn't sure which hurt more, her pride, her ankle, or her backside from the long ride back to camp. Regardless, it looked as though there would be no escape from this dream tonight. Depressed, she offered little resistance as her grandmother forced her to eat a dish of buffalo stew. After a day of fasting, it tasted good. Washing it down with a cup of fresh milk, she obediently retired to the wagon, allowing Colleen to clean and treat her numerous scratches and scrapes. Wiggling into a soft, white nightgown, exhaustion overtook her and she fell asleep soon after being tucked into a bedroll.

CHAPTER TWENTY-EIGHT

All during the next day, Kate shifted uncomfortably on the hard wooden seat of the wagon. After yesterday's riding adventure, certain portions of her anatomy were still extremely tender. Colleen had insisted that she ride beside her while the others walked. Hot shame flushed Kate's cheeks. Insisting it was because the young woman was exhausted from her ordeal, Colleen's kind face revealed the truth. The sprained ankle would have slowed them down. Discouraged, tears burned for release, but Kate forced them back, determined to show what little strength remained at her disposal.

Late in the afternoon, Kate limped near the fire Jamie was building. Trying to make up for the trouble she'd caused, she handed him tiny pieces of sage brush, and the infamous buffalo chips gathered by Shannon and Daniel. After supper, she kept to herself, confusion weighing heavily upon shoulders that were already burdened. Why was she still here? And just where was here? Was she dead? Was this her eternal reward? Something, somewhere had to start making sense before she lost her mind. As she approached the Mahoney wagon, she leaned against one of the wooden wheels, sliding down to her knees. "Mom?" she called quietly, tears racing down her face. "Where are you? I need you." She heard someone approach and hurriedly wiped at her eyes.

"Katie," Colleen murmured, kneeling beside the grieving girl. Sighing, she held out her arms. "There's no shame in tears."

Leaning into the soft comfort Colleen offered, Kate clung to the one person who had shown her kindness and sobbed without restraint.

"There, now," Colleen said after several minutes. "Is it better?" Kate shook her head, burying her face against her grandmother. "I know, lass, I know," Colleen soothed. "Sometimes our hearts seem nigh to breaking. A good cry helps."

"But . . . you don't understand. I want to go home. I want . . . I want to see my family . . . my mother," Kate stammered, fresh tears spilling down each cheek.

"I understand more than you think, dear girl. Whatever else the woman was, she was indeed your mother."

Kate pulled back from her grandmother. "Why do you keep saying things like that about my mother? She was . . . is a good lady!"

"What kind of lady, might I be so bold as to ask, would allow her own daughter to dress in the manner you were clothed? And the language you've been taught, your Grandmother Mahoney, God rest her soul, is surely beside herself in heaven!"

"My mom didn't teach me those words . . . she was always on my case about them. And I picked out my own clothes! My mother hated them."

"Then why is it she allowed you to wear them?"

"She asked me not to. I wore them anyway."

"I see," Colleen said, scowling.

"You've got it all wrong Grandma . . . I mean, Aunt Colleen," Kate stammered, hurrying past the slip she'd just made. "My mother was . . . is a wonderful person. I just never listened to her. She always seemed so . . . so stuffy and old-fashioned. I guess I was wrong . . . and I never had a chance to tell her . . ." her throat tightened with the memory of her how she'd left things with her mother. "I'd give anything to see her again."

"There'll be a time for that later, lass."

Sniffing, Kate gazed up into the concerned eyes of her grandmother. "I'll . . . I'll see her again?" she asked.

"Why o'course you will. It's part of the plan."

"What plan?"

"The plan of salvation taught by our church. I can see that I'll have to tell you what it means to be a Mormon, as we're called. Perhaps someday you'll wish to join our faith."

"But, I am a Mormon," Kate said, staring at the ground. "I was baptized by my father when I was eight."

Colleen blinked in stunned surprise. When she finally spoke, it was with a great deal of effort. "Katie, speak true, now girl. Are you indeed a Mormon?"

Kate nodded, gazing sorrowfully at her grandmother. Shame filled her heart as she realized how little she'd cared about that membership the past few years.

"You speak truly," Colleen said in a hushed voice. "I can see it in your eyes. But, Katie, if you've had the gospel in your life, why would you choose the path you've followed?"

Continuing to stare at the ground, Kate remained silent.

"Did your parents try to teach you right from wrong?" she persisted.

"Yes," Kate answered, slowly lifting her face to meet her grandmother's intense gaze. "I thought it was all a bunch of . . . of hooey," she said in an attempt to control her language. "I guess I've never really had much of a testimony."

"That would explain a lot of it," Colleen murmured, shaking her head. "Katie-girl, there's still time for your testimony to grow."

"But, I've never felt anything inside. My mother kept telling me it would happen someday. I even prayed, but nothing ever happened. My prayers were never answered."

"Perhaps they were answered in ways you couldn't see," Colleen replied. "We don't always get the answer we want, dear girl."

"Yeah, well, maybe. I don't think Grandma Erickson dying was an answer. I prayed for her to get better and she still died."

"Death is not an easy thing," Colleen began, "but we're not left without comfort. The Holy Spirit can calm the shattered heart. The scriptures can give us relief when times are hard."

"Look, I tried to read some of the Book of Mormon, but it was boring . . . and most of it didn't make sense."

"Katie, you have to open your heart. God's holy spirit can't dwell within us unless we invite it into our lives. Pray with sincerity. Search the sacred scriptures with reverent fervor. Soon a warming glow will bring you the peace you're seeking."

"It's too late for me now," Kate said quietly. "I'm being punished . . . and I'll never see my family again."

Colleen frowned as she gently wiped the tears from Kate's face. "Were your parents sealed in the sacred temple?"

Kate silently nodded.

"Put your life in order, and you'll be with them someday," Colleen promised.

Kate said nothing, her expression revealing confusion.

"Surely you remember the teachings of the Prophet Joseph Smith?" Colleen softly asked. "It's why we're here. Why so many of us have given up so much."

Kate decided it was too complicated to understand and leaned against Colleen, trying to block out the inner pain.

"Death isn't the end of it," Colleen continued, gently rocking the young woman in her arms. "If it was, I wouldn't have survived. Two children . . . my darling Maureen . . . and little Brian . . . both buried at sea."

Opening her eyes, Kate drew back to stare at Colleen.

"Aye. They were not strong . . . an illness claimed their lives. I wanted to join them. But God had other plans. He wouldn't let me die. He took my James at Winter Quarters, and left me once again behind," she said softly, reaching to brush the hair from Kate's face.

"What do you mean, death isn't the end of it?" Kate asked, grasping at the new hope being offered.

"Didn't your good parents tell you about heaven?"

Kate shook her head. "They tried. I didn't listen."

"Stubborn to the core, aren't you, my Katie?"

Hanging her head, Kate slowly nodded.

"Well now, where to begin?" Colleen said, glancing around. She shifted into a more comfortable position and leaned against the wagon wheel, motioning for Kate to sit beside her. "This will take some tellin'," she began. "The way I understand it, there are three kingdoms in heaven."

"That's right," Kate said, snapping her fingers. "I remember that part. The celestial, the terr-something, and . . . and," she paused, trying to think.

Colleen chuckled. "Well, I'm glad t'see you have the gist of it," she said with a grin. "The Prophet Joseph, God rest his soul, has said we will be judged for the lives we've led. We'll be awarded kingdoms accordingly. If we prove ourselves worthy in this life, great will be our reward in the next."

Kate gasped as a horrible thought came to mind. Had she died? When that car had hit, and everything had gone black, had her spirit left her body? Was she now in one of those kingdoms? She shivered. If that was true, she was obviously in the lowest. It was supposed to be earth-like. A place of misery in comparison to celestial grandeur. Was this the reward she had earned? A strange sound gurgled from her throat.

Colleen raised an eyebrow. "Katie, what is it? What's wrong?"

"Am I . . . is this . . ." she couldn't put her fear into words. "Where am I?" she finally stammered.

"Out in the middle of the great nowhere," Colleen said, perplexed by the look on the young woman's face.

Concentrating, Kate struggled to remember. Who went to the . . . the telestial, that was it, the telestial kingdom? Who was supposed to end up there? Her forehead wrinkled as she searched her memory for the answer. Murderers, thieves, liars. Liars? She groaned as she remembered the pain she'd caused her mother. Those expressive green eyes had been filled with heartache and sorrow. And for what? Nothing! Choking sobs broke free as remorse consumed her. "I didn't mean it, Mom, I didn't mean it," she wailed.

"Didn't mean what?" Colleen gently urged.

"I told her . . . she thinks . . . oh, please, let me have another chance. I promise I'll do better, I promise, Col . . . Aunt Colleen. If they'll let me go back, I'll make it up to her. I have to settle things between us. She'll always think . . . oh, Mom, what have I done?" Trembling, she reflected on the most horrible thought of all. Would she spend eternity sorrowing for what she'd put her mother through?

Overwhelmed, Kate collapsed in a heap and lay trembling on the ground until Colleen and Molly gently lifted her up into the back of the wagon. Paralyzed by a form of catatonic shock, she lay staring, unaware of her surroundings.

Colleen remained by Kate's side until the young woman slipped into a fitful slumber. Worried, unsure of what had befallen her niece, Colleen slept next to Kate, instructing Molly to sleep with Shannon near the front of the wagon.

It was dark. Reaching above her head, Kate pushed, puzzled by the confinement. She felt around, wondering at the silk lining that surrounded her. Panic gripped her with the realization of where she was. "No!" she cried out as a shovelful of dirt hit the top of the casket. "NO! MOM, MAKE THEM STOP! MOM!" Kate sat up, perspiration beading on her forehead and upper lip.

"Katie-girl, it's all right, lass," Colleen said, gathering Kate against her. She gently rocked the sobbing girl. "It was naught but a dream. A silly nightmare."

Kate shivered. It was the worst nightmare she'd ever had! More terrible than the one that had haunted her in Bozeman. And more horrible than the one she lived now. But, she couldn't tell her grandmotherabout it; Colleen would never understand.

"Here, now, Katie, calm yourself," Colleen murmured, alarmed by the intensity of the young woman's grief. She had decided this was all a result of the shock Kate had suffered. Her niece was finally coming to terms with the loss of her family. "It will pass. The pain will pass," she crooned. "Y're not alone, dear Katie. Y're not alone."

Kate shuddered and wished she could believe that. Sniffing, she finally pulled away.

"Are you feelin' better?" Colleen asked, offering a handkerchief.

"Yeah," Kate answered weakly, wiping at her nose.

"It's never an easy thing to lose those you love," Colleen replied, leaning to kiss the young woman's forehead. "But, y'don't bear that burden alone."

"I know," Kate lied. She'd never felt more alone in her entire life—death.

CHAPTER TWENTY-NINE

During the next two days, Kate rode on the wagon beside Colleen. She decided to take advantage of the chance for private conversation and bombarded her grandmother with numerous questions about the gospel. Chuckling at Kate's sudden interest, Colleen did her best to answer.

"So . . . if a person repents, then everything's square?"

"I'm not sure of your meanin', Kate," Colleen replied, glancing briefly at the young woman.

"I mean . . . like . . . you're forgiven for what you've done?"

"Aye. But, only after confessing and making things right."

"What?" Kate asked, scowling.

"Say you stole Brother Lott's horse . . ."

"I did not. I don't even like horses!"

"Katie, I'm not meanin' that you did. I'm tryin' to give you a sample of how this works."

"Oh. Okay. Just so we have that straight. I'm not a thief. I've never . . . well, there was that one time when Linda dared me to take some makeup from a drugstore . . . but that was only one time, and it wasn't like anybody ever found out about it."

"That's where you're wrong, Kate," Colleen said, trying to understand the young woman's strange confession. "If you took somethin' that didn't belong to you, it's stealin', Katie Colleen. You've broken a commandment."

"But . . . it was just a little shoplifting. Everyone does it."

"Does that make it right, girl? Does it say in the scriptures, Thou shalt not steal, but it's the proper thing to do if everyone else is doin' it?"

"Well, no. But . . ."

"There are no exceptions to God's commandments. They were given to us out of love. And no matter how you try to reason with yourself, when you break one, it's a sin."

Kate mentally went down the list of commandments she could remember. She winced, realizing she'd slightly bent a few.

Colleen glanced at Kate and sighed. Helping this young woman put her life in order would take some doing. She hoped she was up to the challenge.

"So, how do I make things right?"

"It depends on what you've done. If you've stolen an item, it should be replaced or paid for. The person you've taken it from is entitled to an apology. That would be a good start."

"What do you mean that's just a start? Isn't that enough?"

"After you've settled with the party who's been wronged, then you must make peace with God. Pray in the name of Christ, our elder brother who died to atone for our sins. It's because of his sacrifice that we can regain the presence of our Father. But, we must repent with sincerity, begging for forgiveness, promising to never commit the sin again."

"Whoa! This is heavy!"

"What are you meanin', girl? These oxen are doing their best to pull this wagon . . ."

"No. That's not what I meant. I was trying to say this repentance thing is more complicated than I thought."

"Aye. But it's possible. None of us are perfect. We all have need of righting our lives. Don't give up on yourself, Katie. If you'll truly repent, you'll be reunited with your loved ones someday."

Kate stared in silence at the plodding oxen. Was that the answer she was looking for? The key to returning to her family? Could she progress from where she was to where they would be if she repented? As she pondered her grandmother's words, she closed her eyes, offering a silent prayer.

Heavenly Father, it's me. I know it's been a long time, but I'm really in a mess here. Please . . . help me. I know I have no right to ask . . . not after everything I've done . . . but if you could help me know I'm on the right track . . . please . . .

"Katie, are you all right?" Colleen asked, fearing the girl was about to faint.

Kate opened her eyes and looked at her grandmother. "Yeah, I guess. I was trying to pray. But nothing happened. I didn't feel anything."

"It takes time, Kate. Prayers aren't always answered immediately. It's very often a test of faith."

"Well, I'm in trouble then, because I don't have any."

"Any what, dear?"

"Faith," Kate said, trying not to sound as disappointed as she felt.

"Well, now, aren't you giving up a bit quick?"

Discouraged, Kate shrugged.

"Tell me, lass, what exactly does it mean to have faith?"

"I don't know. I guess it means having the courage to get up and blubber in the microphone during fast and testimony meeting."

Colleen gave Kate a very long, hard stare. "The micro-what?"

"Nothing. Look, don't worry about it, this isn't going to work. I'm a lost cause."

Colleen was about to lecture Kate, then saw the look on the young woman's face. It was a look that said, *I'm not worth the effort.* Colleen knew better. Kate was a Mahoney. A beloved daughter of God. Someone who needed help remembering that fact. And Colleen was just the person to jog Kate's memory. *When I'm through with you, lass, you'll be singin' a different tune,* Colleen silently promised. *You'll never doubt again.*

After supper, Colleen cornered Kate near their wagon. "Katie, I'd like you to come sit by the fire with me for a time," she said, smiling brightly.

"Why?" Kate asked sullenly.

"Are you indeed serious about this quest of yours?"

"What quest?"

"The one to find peace within that troubled heart of yours?"

Kate slowly nodded.

"Then come with me." She led Kate to the fire and held out a worn copy of the Book of Mormon.

"Aunt Colleen . . ."

"Now, we'll have none of that whining. Take it."

Kate rolled her eyes, but took the book, sitting next to her grandmother.

"Just so you know, we'll be doin' this every night. It's high time you were learnin' what the Lord's gospel is all about." She prodded with her finger until Kate began to read.

"'I, Nephi, having been born of goodly parents . . .'"

"Good, lass. Now, read that part again, only replace Nephi with your own name."

Kate gave her grandmother an extremely dirty look.

"Kate," Colleen said firmly.

"Oh, honestly! Okay, all right. I, Kate, having been born of goodly parents . . ."

"There's truth in those words, Kate. Do y'believe it?"

Kate thought about her parents. Greg and Sue Erickson. She may not have always seen eye to eye with them, but, they were good people. It was the parent part she was having trouble with.

"Come, now, Kate, I saw the other night the feelings you have for your mother and father. Y'do indeed love them, though y'may not admit it to y'rself."

"I didn't say I didn't love them."

"Well then?"

"It's just . . . they were always trying to change me. They were always on my case."

Colleen gazed at Kate. Then, taking the book of scripture from her hand, thumbed through the pages. "Here, read this."

Annoyed, Kate took the book back from her grandmother and stared at the page. "Read what?"

"There, Mosiah, chapter four, verse 14."

"All of it?"

"Katie . . ."

"Okay, okay. 'And ye will not suffer your children that they go hungry, or naked . . .'" Kate looked up. "Well, they did feed me, and they tried to keep me from running around naked," she said, smirking.

Colleen frowned sternly and pointed to the page.

Kate sighed and continued to read. "'Neither will ye suffer that they transgress the laws of God . . .'" She paused, a strange tingling sensation moving along her spine.

"What is it, Katie?"

"Nothing. That breeze is a little chilly."

"Well, move closer to the fire, then." Colleen peered down at the page Kate was staring at. "Read down here, now," she said. "Verse fifteen."

"'But ye will teach them to walk in the ways of truth and soberness; ye will teach them to love one another, and to serve one another.'" Kate stared at the fire.

"Your parents loved you enough to try to teach you the truths of the gospel. Perhaps they went about it a bit strongly; but the important thing is they tried, Kate. That's all any parent can ever do."

A single tear slid down Kate's cheek. She remained there, staring into the fire, long after Colleen left to tuck Shannon into bed.

In the days that followed, Colleen guided Kate through other sections of the Book of Mormon. As Kate began to see that the scriptures actually made sense and could be applied to her life, she became a dedicated student, reading near the fire each night after the chores were attended to. With Colleen's encouragement, she also began saying personal prayers on a regular basis. She still didn't feel anything, but the nightmares had stopped.

One night, after reading about Alma the younger and the process of repentance, Kate turned to gaze at her grandmother.

"Aunt Colleen, how do I ever make things right with my parents? They're not here."

"I've no doubt they're closer than you think. Speak what's in your heart, Kate. Tell them you were wrong, that you're sorry. Then, beg our Heavenly Father's forgiveness. Make the most of every day you're given on this earth. That will help atone for your mistakes."

Kate gazed up at the star-filled sky. "Mom . . . Dad . . . I'm sorry . . . for everything . . . for not listening . . . for being such a pain in the . . . the neck," she said, determined to clean up her vocabulary. "I'm sorry for smoking . . . and drinking . . . for sneaking around with Jace." As she continued with her list, her grandmother frowned, glancing at her in alarm over several of the transgressions. ". . . and most of all, Mom . . . I'm sorry for the pain I've caused you . . . for telling you those horrible lies . . . I've never been with a boy . . . not the way you were thinking . . . I'm sorry . . . please forgive me." Sobbing into her hands, she silently vowed to change her life. *I'll do better, Mom, you'll see. And someday, maybe I can tell you face to face.*

CHAPTER THIRTY

Greg gave his wife a final squeeze. "I hate leaving like this."

"I know," Sue answered softly.

Paige and Stan turned away, staring uncomfortably down the hall.

"I could take more time off . . ."

"No. You already took an extra week. This could drag on for months."

"If it goes on much longer, Dr. Webster said we might want to consider transferring her to Montana."

Sue nodded. "Sometimes she feels so close. I could've sworn she called out for me two nights ago."

"Well, we'll give her a couple of weeks. Then we'll look into making other arrangements. In the meantime, Tyler and I will be fine."

"Okay."

"And remember, you've promised to let Paige spell you off. It won't do anyone any good if you make yourself sick."

Sue forced a smile. "Don't worry, Sabrina and I and . . . Kate . . ." She paused and gazed at the carpeted floor. "We'll be all right."

Greg leaned forward to kiss her, then turned to hurry out of the hospital. "I'll call you tonight. We'll probably stop in Rexburg," he called over his shoulder, offering a weak wave.

Her shoulders sagging, Sue returned the wave, watching as

Tyler and Greg moved down the cement steps. She was grateful Paige and Stan were there. Numb with exhaustion and inner pain, she let them guide her down to the cafeteria.

The next afternoon, as Sue stepped from Kate's room to stretch the kinks out of her legs, she bumped into a young man who was hurrying down the hall.

"Sorry," they both murmured, then froze as recognition settled in. "Randy?" Sue stammered.

Flushing with embarrassment, Randy nodded. "Mrs., uh . . ."

"Erickson," Sue supplied.

"Oh, yes. Mrs. Erickson. How are you?" he nervously asked, the expression on her face answering his question.

"I've been better."

"Is someone in your family . . . here?" he ventured, trying to be polite.

Sue's eyes wandered to Kate's room. Grimacing, she debated with herself. "Randy, Kate was in an accident . . ."

"An accident? A car accident? Is she okay?"

Touched by his concern, Sue motioned to the chairs that were against the wall. They each selected a chair, then she told him about Kate.

Frowning, his eyes reflecting worried concern, he stood, nervously pacing the floor. "I can't believe this. She was . . . is so full of life. I'm . . . I'm really sorry."

Rising, Sue sadly smiled. "We all are. Now, we're just waiting for her to come back to us."

"How long has she been in the coma?"

"Two weeks."

"But the doctors think she'll snap out of it?"

"They're optimistic she will. But the longer it drags on, the slimmer the chances are . . ." The words caught in her throat. She took a deep breath and gazed at the handsome young man. His western attire had been replaced by a green t-shirt and a pair of worn jeans. Instead of boots, he was wearing an old pair of Reeboks. A blue baseball cap had taken the place of his cowboy hat. Puzzled, she wondered why he was in Salt Lake. "If you don't mind me asking, why are you here?"

"It's my grandfather . . . he had a heart attack. I came down from Jackson as soon as I heard."

"How is he doing?"

Randy slowly shook his head.

"I'm sorry, Randy."

He nodded. "Could I see Kate?" he timidly asked, a light blush creeping across his face. "Just for a minute? I wouldn't stay long."

Agreeing to his request, Sue led him into Kate's room. It was slightly smaller than the one her daughter had occupied in intensive care. Only one I.V. remained hooked into Kate's arm; a single heart monitor tracked her steady heartbeat. Randy shook his head sympathetically as he gazed down at the beautiful girl. He'd had a difficult time forcing her memory from his heart before. Now, it would never leave. Smiling sadly at Sue, he quietly left the room.

Sighing, Sue watched him go. She was stunned when two hours later a bouquet of pink roses was brought to the room. Removing the attached card, her eyes blurred.

Dear Kate,

Get well soon. I'll need a pen pal while I'm off tracting in Ireland.

Sincerely,
Elder Randy Miles

CHAPTER THIRTY-ONE

Here you are, Bessie," Gus Porter exclaimed, panting as he moved down to the river beside his wife.

"I told you I would be washing the few changes of clothes left to our possession," Bessie returned, furiously scrubbing the neck of her husband's shirt with a powdered substance she'd found along the bank. She shoved the shirt in the water to rinse the foaming bubbles into the Platte River.

"I was concerned. You've been gone from camp for nigh onto two hours."

"And what of it? These clothes don't wash themselves. I have no one to help me now."

Frowning, Gus forced Sarah's face from his mind. Their thirteen-year-old daughter had died before reaching Winter Quarters of what they called the fever-and-ague. First Sarah, then Nathan—two children sacrificed to Zion's cause. Shaking his head, he gazed down at his wife's back as she continued to scrub at his shirt. "Let me help."

"And be the laughing stock of the camp? Off with you, Brother Porter. Attend to the stock."

"They've been seen to," he replied, rubbing at the stiff stubble on his chin. "Jacob and Eli caught a mess of fish," he said brightly, proud of their two remaining sons. "We'll feast tonight."

"As soon as I cook the meal," she replied, wiping at her forehead.

"Eli's roasting them. We'll eat soon."

Tempted by the inviting prospect of fish instead of buffalo, she quickly wrung the water from the shirt. "That's the last of it. If you want to help, bring your boys' clothes and we'll hang them in these sorry-looking willows to dry."

Gus scooped up the damp garments, obediently following his wife. As she reached to take the clothes one at a time from his arms, she glanced up. The Wicker widows passed by, offering smiles and timid waves. Gus politely nodded while Bessie scowled. "I suppose that'll be the next blessing to come into our lives," she snapped, reaching for another shirt.

"What are you meanin'?"

"Those Wicker women. I've heard they're looking for a husband to replace Truman."

"Now, Bessie . . . I've not got intentions towards those two. A man must receive a sacred call from the priesthood brethren . . ."

"I'm beginning to believe this is a gospel of convenience, not inspiration. We have extra room. They nearly made us take on the little tramp Brother David Miles rescued. Why he didn't just leave that girl for dead I'll never know . . . she's been nothing but trouble!"

Down by the river on the other side of the thin group of willows, Molly tried to restrain her mother.

"Let me be," Colleen said sharply. "I'll soon set that woman's mind to rest concernin' Kate!"

"Mother, let it pass. Sister Bessie's not herself these days. Not since little Nathan died."

Pursing her lips together, Colleen finally nodded, forcing Shannon's small dress into the river to be rinsed.

"Bessie!" Gus exclaimed. "That poor child is Sister Colleen's lost niece, led to us by God's own hand."

"Another Mahoney miracle!" she answered sharply. "Well, why haven't we been granted one? Tell me, dear husband, are they more worthy of the extra blessings?"

Colleen wrung the water from the dress, squeezing it with added force. She felt Molly's hand on her shoulder. "Don't worry, m'girl," she said in a hushed voice. "I'll not say a thing."

Shifting his tired gaze to the ground, Gus decided to approach the subject responsible for his wife's current mood. "There's only one man in camp who could possibly take on the Wicker widows, and that would be Brother David. I believe that's why the good captain has given the young man the responsibility of driving their team."

Now it was Colleen's turn to restrain Molly. "Remember your words, child, they've come back to haunt you," she whispered, curbing a smile.

"But, Mother, this is different! If you don't let me respond, I'll . . ."

"You'll sit here and take it, same as your mother," Colleen warned.

A gleam came to Bessie's eye. "Perhaps this wedding Sister Colleen has taken such delight in planning will give Brother David three brides, not one."

Colleen kept a firm hand on Molly's shoulder. Gesturing for silence, she finally released the young woman when she was convinced the Porters were out of earshot.

"Mother!" Molly sputtered angrily, glaring at Colleen. "So help me . . ."

"It wouldn't have changed that woman's mind nor eased yours. Contention is . . ."

"If you say 'of the devil,' I'll scream!" she said, thinking of Truman.

"I was going to say, 'best avoided,' dear," Colleen said with a smile. "Don't give heed to Bessie. As you said, she's not been right since the loss of her son."

"And what about Brother Porter? He said the same thing!" Molly retorted indignantly.

"Molly, don't go lookin' for trouble. David's asked for your hand in marriage, not that of the Wicker widows."

"But . . . what if Brother Porter's right? What if that's what they want David to do?"

"Molly . . ."

"Oh, Mother, I couldn't stand it! I'll not be sharin' my husband with another woman!" Rising, Molly trembled.

Colleen quickly stood, placing her hands on her daughter's shoulders. "My dear girl, Captain Roberts has given me his word that David will halt driving for the widows after we reach Fort Laramie. Cease this needless worry!"

"Is it needless?" Molly asked, searching her mother's green eyes.

"Aye, lass. Sister Lovina Wicker has a sister already livin' in the valley. They'll be stayin' with her when we finally arrive in blessed Zion."

"What about the time between now and then?"

"Between now and then, you'll give me a fine son-in-law and make an effort at supplying me with grandchildren to love."

Molly blushed and stared at the ground, refusing to meet her mother's amused gaze.

"And if they look anything at all like their parents, they'll be the loveliest children this earth has ever seen."

Continuing to blush, Molly glanced up, forcing an embarrassed smile at her mother.

"That's my girl. Now, let's finish with these clothes. Kate'll have dinner burned by now."

Molly knelt by the river to collect the dampened clothes. Despite her mother's assurance, the tiny seeds of doubt were firmly planted. Vowing to speak to David as soon as the occasion presented itself, she carried the clothes, helping her mother hang them on the willows to dry.

"This is good, huh, Daniel?" Shannon bubbled, taking another bite of the meal Kate had prepared.

Daniel nodded and continued to chew, savoring the unique flavor. Glancing at his older brother, he was delighted to see that Jamie was enjoying the supper. Maybe Jamie wouldn't be so quick to criticize their newfound cousin after this.

"Well, now, by the looks on your faces, a body'd think you were in heaven."

Shannon and Daniel eagerly grinned at their mother.

"Kate fixed us an . . . amulet," Shannon lisped.

"That's omelet," Kate corrected with a smile. "Daniel found a nest full of eggs down by the river. I think they're duck eggs. Anyway, I thought I'd make up some of these. I've watched my mother do it enough times." She paused, carefully flipping one side of a large omelet over top of the other in the cast iron pan.

Colleen beamed with pride. "There may be hope for you yet, Katie girl. After this morning's breakfast attempt . . ."

Kate silently acknowledged her failure with the morning meal. She'd managed to burn everything over the fire, blackening the buffalo steaks beyond recognition, scorching what was left of the bread made up the night before in an effort to make toast, campfire style.

"So, you've created omelets for us this evening?"

"Yeah," Kate replied. "I hope it was okay, I used some of the butter that was churned earlier to grease the pan. The first one stuck pretty bad . . ."

"It was black," Shannon helpfully added.

"Yeah, well . . . first tries don't count. I got it right the second time around," Kate countered, carefully sliding the large omelet onto a waiting plate. Picking up the knife she'd borrowed from Jamie, she cut it into two pieces, pushing half of it onto another plate. "Here you go," she said, offering a fork and extending one of the plates to Colleen. She then handed the other plate to Molly. Turning, she began making another omelet for herself.

Colleen exchanged a curious glance with Molly, then timidly nibbled at a small portion she'd cut away with her fork. "Why, this is glorious! Try it, Molly."

Molly hesitantly cut into the egg mass on her plate, sampling a small bite. She smiled with relief. It was good.

Colleen moved next to Kate to watch what the girl was adding to the egg mixture. "What are you puttin' in it?" she asked.

"Pieces of this dried jerky stuff. And some dried onion I found in the wagon. Plus a little bit of salt," she answered, sprinkling the salt over the egg mixture. "Cheese would be wonderful, or mushrooms, maybe even green peppers . . . but, I made do with what we had."

Colleen nodded. "You did well, lass. Creating a veritable feast from a little bit of nothing."

"Something smells good," David commented, as he moved toward their small fire. He sniffed the air appreciatively.

"Our Katie's made us omelets," Colleen said proudly.

"There's enough here for another person," Kate offered.

"Would you like to try it?" she asked, smiling up at the young man.

"I never turn down a free meal," he replied. Soon he was wolfing down half of Kate's omelet, adding his compliments to the others she'd already received. Shaking his head, he patted his stomach. "That was honestly some of the best campfire grub I've eaten in a while."

"Brother David's right, Katie. I'll not hesitate again to let you cook supper," Colleen said proudly.

"Aw, c'mon, guys, it wasn't that great."

"Sure now, it was," Colleen insisted,

Blushing with delight, Kate quietly sat next to Daniel to eat her portion of the meal. After savoring the final bite, she stood and gathered the plates to clean them in the water that had been boiling over the fire.

Colleen moved to help her. "Don't burn yourself," she cautioned, wincing as Kate stuck her hands into the steaming water.

"OW! Da . . . ang it!" Kate said, trying to control herself.

"We usually let it cool a bit first," Molly said, trying not to laugh.

Kate pulled a face and backed away from the fire, tripping over a gopher hole. Falling onto her back, she shrieked, but didn't swear.

Colleen helped her up, smiling warmly at the young woman. "You're makin' great strides, dear girl," she said quietly, proud that Kate had refrained from using vulgar language.

"Then why is everything going to crap?" Kate snapped.

"Katie," Colleen interrupted with a frown. "I'm not certain of the meanin', but I don't like the sound of that. Come with me to the river, and we'll ease the burnin' of those hands." She firmly guided Kate away from camp.

"Look," Kate said, "I wasn't swearing. Crap isn't a . . ."

"It sounded crude enough to me."

"It just seems like the more I try to do the right thing, the harder everything gets."

"You're being tested to see if you're truly sincere about changing your life."

"Really?" Kate asked, pulling a face.

"Aye. It'll get easier. You'll see. Now, kneel down and let's soak those poor hands of yours."

Kate obeyed, welcoming the relief the cool river provided.

"The thing to remember, dear, is that no matter how difficult the road ahead may seem, there is always a way to succeed. Remember the story of Nephi and the brass plates?"

"Sort of."

"He was able to accomplish the impossible with the Lord's help. The same can be true for any one of us. We have but to ask for his guidance."

"You mean I'm not in this alone?"

"No. If that were true, I'd've given up long ago. Each time I've felt as though my heart was shattered . . . each time fear or despair has threatened my peace of mind, the Comforter has been there to remind me of our Father's presence."

"Like when the mob burned your home?"

"Aye. There in Missouri. Your Uncle James had built that house with his own hands. Watching it burn was one of the hardest things I've had to do. But I could bear it, knowing God would provide a way for us to abide it. How I wish I'd had that comforting knowledge when the bodies of my dear babies were thrown into the cold depths of the ocean." She paused, her eyes misting at the memory. "I never thought I'd survive it. Then, in New York, when the Mormon missionaries came preaching, telling us we'd again be with our loved ones lost to death, it was as though heaven itself had opened the door to my heart. Bitter grief was replaced with loving hope. I knew then life had a purpose, that every trial, every mortal pain was worth the reward awaiting us in the eternities." She wiped at her eyes, staring off across the river. "To be sealed together as an eternal family in the sacred temple . . . it means everything, Katie. To know that no matter what we suffer here, if we're faithful to the end, we'll be reunited with those who have gone before."

Kate was touched by her grandmother's firm testimony. She silently vowed to endure her own tests with the same courage her grandmother possessed, determined to someday be worthy of the covenants her parents had made years ago in the Idaho Falls temple. *Please, Heavenly Father, don't give up on me. And if it's not too much trouble, give me the strength to face what lies ahead.* She bowed her head, oblivious to the silvery tears as they fell into the river.

"You'll make it, Katie," Colleen said softly, slipping a comforting arm around the young woman's shoulders. "We'll help each other to be strong. And when that's not enough, the good Lord will provide what's lacking."

Hoping her grandmother was right, Kate lifted her head to smile at Colleen. *I won't let you down,* she silently promised. *You'll see. Someday you'll be proud we share the same name.*

On the way back, Colleen stopped to check the clothes that were drying. Leaving those that were still damp, she handed the few that were dry to Kate. "Let's head for the wagon," she said, glancing around at the darkening sky. "I don't like being out from camp in the dark," she added, quickening her stride.

Kate agreed with her grandmother and hurried to keep up, carefully carrying the clothes Colleen had handed to her. As they approached the campfire, loud voices drifted toward them on the cooling breeze.

"I can't believe you'd think that of me!" David said angrily.

Colleen shook her head. "Oh, Molly," she sighed.

"Well, am I wrong? Is that what you and the good captain have planned?" Molly persisted.

"I was asked to drive their team, nothing more!" David returned sharply.

"And if you were asked to do more, what then?"

Colleen frowned and muttered something under her breath. Kate glanced at her grandmother, confused by the argument they were overhearing.

"Well? Answer me, David! I'm entitled to know! Is my husband-to-be thinking of taking more than one wife?"

"Polygamy," Kate murmured.

"Aye," Colleen answered softly.

"Would David . . . I mean, Brother David, really do that to Molly?"

"It's for God and the priesthood brethren to decide," Colleen replied. "There are those who have heeded the call. Most out of righteousness," she added, thinking of Truman Wicker. "For some, it's a blessing. There are indeed more women than men in the camp of Zion."

Kate gazed toward the campfire and wondered how she would react in Molly's place.

"Go now to the wagon, lass. I'll try to talk sense to these two."

Silently nodding, Kate took a few steps, then paused, curious to see how her grandmother would handle this mess.

"Molly, I love you," David said in his defense. "I would never do anything to hurt you."

"Then I have your word you'd never take another bride?"

Kate watched as David shifted uncomfortably beneath Molly's caustic stare.

"David?"

"Molly, how can I make such a promise? If I was called . . ."

Turning her back to him, Molly hugged herself tightly. "It's as I thought, then."

"Molly," David said softly, "it may be that the call would never come. I know of only a few who are . . ."

"Leave me be!" Molly said bitterly. "I can't marry a man who needs more than one wife!"

"Molly . . ."

"There'll be no wedding! Not now, not ever! I'll not be some cow to be added to your herd!" Running, she fled into the shadows with her pain.

"Molly!" he exclaimed, starting after her.

"Let her go," Colleen advised, stepping near the fire.

"But . . . I . . . I do love her," David said, looking miserable.

"I know, lad. If I thought it otherwise, I would not have consented to your request for her hand."

"Then you'll talk to her?"

"Aye. When her temper cools. Till then, not even the patience of Job could hope to reason with her."

David turned to leave. "I should've married her the moment she agreed! I had a feeling she'd . . ."

"David, she'll come around. She loves you dearly. Give her time. She'll soon return to her senses."

Hoping Colleen was right, he slowly trudged off. Colleen

watched him go, her heart as heavy as his steps. "Dear Father, is it patience thou art tryin' to teach me?" she asked softly, thinking she was alone. "Giving me charge of two fiery young women filled with consuming pride? Grant me the strength and inspiration to guide them both from destruction." Turning around, she left to find her stubborn daughter.

Kate stared at the ground. Her grandmother's plea had slipped inside of her heart. "I'm sorry, Grandma. I know I've been nothing but trouble. I'll make it up to you, I promise," she whispered. She walked to the wagon and set the dry clothes inside. Then, retrieving the Book of Mormon, she moved back to the fire and began to read.

"Molly," Colleen called as she approached the weeping girl near the river. "Did I not warn that you were lookin' for trouble?" she asked, sitting beside her daughter. Patting the young woman's back, she frowned. "Hush, now, you're makin' more of this than needs be."

"Am I, Mother?" Molly returned.

"Aye. He loves naught but you."

"But he . . ."

"Don't waste your life seekin' after what might be. Live each day as it comes, being grateful for the blessings you're given."

"Would you be feeling so blessed if Papa had decided to take another wife?" Molly countered.

Colleen returned her daughter's angry glare with a look of compassion. "It would've been a monstrous challenge, but if it had been the good Lord's will, we would've found a way to make a go of it. Now, let me ask you a question. Have you prayed concerning this matter?"

Molly slowly shook her head.

"Then I suggest you do just that. Pray long and hard, lass, if you seek the answer to your heart's question. Forget your stubborn pride. I'll not watch you turn your back to the man you profess to love. This was a marriage meant to be. I've felt it all along. Now, dry those tears and be quick about it!"

"But, if he ever looked at another woman the way he looks at me, I couldn't bear it!"

Colleen's expression softened. "With God's help, all things are possible." She tenderly wiped at the tears rolling down her daughter's face. "It may be you're the only woman destined to be his wife."

"Do you truly believe that?" Molly asked, searching her mother's face.

"Molly-girl, I don't have all the answers. Pray to the One who does. Seek comfort from his loving guidance. If it will help, I'll pray with you."

Slowly nodding, Molly took the hand her mother offered, rising to kneel in the cooling earth. Bowing her head, she stared at the ground.

"Dear Father in Heaven," Colleen began, "hear now the prayer of our hearts."

Molly closed her eyes and forced herself to listen to the prayer her mother was offering on her behalf.

CHAPTER THIRTY-TWO

C aptain Roberts says we'll make Fort Laramie by tomorrow," Jamie said excitedly, unyoking the oxen.

Kate smiled. "Fort Laramie, huh?" she probed.

"Aye. We'll buy the supplies needed to finish the journey. It means we're halfway to the valley!" He turned to herd the oxen to feed with the rest of the camp's livestock.

Kate sighed and moved to help Daniel gather buffalo chips. Silently she wondered if her own journey would ever reach an end. Ignoring the discouragement that came with that thought, she entertained Shannon and Daniel with stories as they gathered fuel for the fire. When they returned to the place Colleen had cleared, she dropped the chips in a tidy pile. She rinsed her hands in a pail of cool river water and smiled at the grandmother she'd grown to love. She then moved to the wagon to retrieve the dough that had been rising since early that morning.

"Mama," Shannon bubbled, "Kate told us funny stories."

"Did she now?" Colleen replied, shielding the tiny blaze from the wind stirring across the plains.

"She told us 'bout Superman."

"He flies in the air," Daniel added, holding out his young arms as he ran around the fire.

"He has to stay away from crypts that are tight," Shannon said somberly.

"That's kryptonite, it's a green rock," Kate corrected, setting the bowl of dough near her grandmother. She watched as Shannon giggled and ran off to play in the tall grass.

"You've quite the imagination," Colleen observed, her eyes twinkling with amused pride.

"I was just telling them some stories I grew up with," Kate replied.

"Thank you for bringing such joy into their lives. Shannon dearly loves a good story."

"She reminds me so much of Sabrina," Kate started, sobering with the memory of how she'd often treated her younger sister. "Oh, Breeny," she said softly, staring across the windy plain.

Colleen glanced up and saw Kate's pain. "Katie-girl, would you be so good as to see if Molly's finished milking the cow?"

Kate nodded and moved off to find Molly, unaware of the thoughtful eyes that followed her.

"Someday your heart will heal," Colleen said softly. "Till then, we'll keep you busy. Idle hands lend to troubling thoughts." Frowning, she pictured Molly's sad face. "Oh, child, if you'd only try to make peace with yourself." Rising, she walked to the wagon, seeking the flat pan that would be used to bake the bread.

Kate moved down to the river and found the metal container Molly had already stashed in the cooling water. She removed the lid and saw that it was filled with warm milk. Tamping the lid back into place, she stood for a several minutes, staring at the murky water. Finally walking up the bank, she overheard a pair of familiar voices arguing.

"I'll marry you when I'm good and ready, and not a moment before!" Molly exclaimed.

"The day has already been set," David insisted. "And I mean to claim my bride."

Trying her best to be inconspicuous, Kate flushed as David gripped Molly in a tight embrace, kissing her aunt with a fierce intensity. Molly tried to pull away, but as the kiss continued, grudgingly gave in. When he finally released her, she gasped for air, giving him a dirty look.

"You try that again, Brother David, and . . ."

"Molly, whether you admit it to yourself or not, we have feelings for each other. Nothing will ever change the love shared between us." He took her in his arms, holding her rebelling body against his, and kissed her with tenderness and longing. Reluctantly pulling away, he gazed into her troubled eyes. "I won't force it, Molly. If you want more time, I'll grant it. Though each day that passes seems an eternity without you." Turning, he began to walk away.

"David . . . it won't be an eternity," Molly said softly, her eyes glistening. "We'll marry in one week's time."

Throwing his hat in the air, David whooped loudly, running back to the river bank to swing Molly around.

"Here, now, what's the commotion?" Colleen asked with a knowing grin as she hurried down to the river's edge. Glancing at Kate, she smiled brightly. "Come, lass, it looks as though we have a wedding to plan."

After a supper of dried pork gravy served over fresh bread, Colleen slowly made her way back to the wagon. Puzzled by the look on her face, Kate followed, climbing up into the wagon behind her grandmother.

"Aunt Colleen, what's wrong?" she timidly asked, blinking as her eyes adjusted to the flickering light of the lantern.

Colleen replaced the glass chimney and forced a smile. "I'm afraid you've caught me, lass. I'm having a moment of weakness."

"But you were so happy earlier, about the wedding . . ."

"Aye. It's not the wedding, Kate."

"Then what? Have I done something . . ."

"No, dear girl. You've made the load lighter for us all. I'm so very proud of how hard you're tryin' to put your life in order."

"Then why are you so sad?"

Colleen moved to the large steamer trunk and sighed. "It's pride girl, nothing more. I've come to a road I'd hoped I'd not have to travel." Lifting the heavy lid, she gazed at the contents. Kate moved beside her, staring into the trunk. A few changes of clothes. The Book of Mormon they'd been sharing. A few ribbons. The sampler Molly had been working on in her spare time. Several tiny skeins of colored embroidery floss. Molly's autograph book from her days in Nauvoo. Kate had thumbed through it before, gasping over the signatures, poems, and messages her aunt had collected from Eliza R. Snow, Joseph Smith, Mary Fielding Smith, John Taylor, Emma Smith, and several other prominent members of the Church. Her favorite was a poem by Brigham Young.

To live with Saints in Heaven is bliss and glory,
To live with Saints on Earth is another story.

Molly had explained that seeking autographs had been a popular pastime of women, old and young alike, before Nauvoo had met with disaster.

Colleen began removing articles from the trunk. Kate helped, wondering what had upset her grandmother. Confused, she watched as Colleen slid a finger along the wooden base, forcing a fingernail between the side and the bottom. A tiny click startled Kate. She stared in amazement as her grandmother unlatched a second catch hidden on the opposite side.

"I didn't know that was there," Kate said in a hushed voice, staring as Colleen removed a thin square of wood, revealing a false bottom.

"My James built this to store our valuables," Colleen said reverently, setting the square piece of wood on top of the pile of clothes. She reached into the hidden compartment and carefully lifted out two portraits. Holding them out for Kate to see, she sadly smiled. "We had these taken in Nauvoo. Brother Lucian Foster had a studio there. James insisted we set an appointment. When the time came, we had one done of the family, and one of him and me alone."

Kate stared at the tintypes. She'd seen the one of Colleen and James before. It had been in the old photo album Paige had shown her.

"This was your Uncle James," Colleen said, pointing to the bearded man. She closed her eyes and clutched the pictures to her breast. "Forgive me, dear husband, for being so weak. I'm not sure I can part with any more of you." Opening her eyes, she gazed sadly at Kate. "When James knew he wouldn't live, he gave me his gold watch, making me promise I would use it to keep starvation from our door. We've managed without selling it, but tomorrow, I'll not have a choice." Fighting tears, she set the portraits on top of the square piece of wood. She then reached back into the trunk and pulled out a beautiful gold pocket watch and chain.

"No, Mother. You can't sell it! It's all we have left of Papa!" Molly said, poking her head through the canvas flap.

Colleen glanced up at her daughter's indignant face. "We have no choice, dear girl. We're down to scrapin' the barrel as it is. We must have flour, meal, salt pork, powder and lead for Jamie's gun . . ."

"I'll not listen to this! There has to be another way!"

"And what do you suggest, Molly? We have nothing else but our lives to offer. Do you think your father would be proud if we spare his watch at the sacrifice of our family welfare?"

"You can't sell it," Molly repeated, her bottom lip trembling.

"Remember the promise he forced from my lips before he died?" Colleen asked. "This watch was to be used to provide for our needs. I'd hoped myself to never part with it. But now . . . it'll be all right, you'll see," she said. "We'll always cherish his memory. Nothing can take that from us. And we still have the mirror and brush he made me with his own hands." She pulled out the set, made from blonde ash. Kate saw that her grandmother's initials had been engraved on the back of the set. "Someday, these will be yours," Colleen promised, extending them to Molly.

Tears streaking down her face, Molly shook her head, moving out of the wagon. Ignoring her mother's pleas to come back, she fled into the night.

CHAPTER THIRTY-THREE

Early the next morning, the pioneers bustled about, eager to start the day's journey. Colleen insisted on driving the wagon to keep from dwelling on the sacrifice she would soon be making. Shannon rode beside her, the others walking nearby. Kate walked with Jamie, preferring his company to Molly's sour mood.

"Last night, your mother showed me those pictures you guys had taken in Nauvoo," she said, trying to start a conversation.

"Did she now?" Jamie asked, less than enthusiastic. He was as upset as Molly, but was trying to hide it.

"Yeah. She said Lucy something had a studio there."

"That's Lucian Foster, a gifted man if I ever saw one. I worked with him for a time. I thought perhaps it would become my trade."

"Trade? Trade for what?"

"My apprenticeship. I was thinking of someday opening my own studio."

"Oh," Kate responded, surprised. Jamie wanted to be a photographer? It was difficult to remember that at one time, these pioneers had led an entirely different life. Her grandmother had told her of their lives in Nauvoo.

"Why, Katie-girl, in five years' time, we had built a city to rival the others in Illinois. There were loving homes, and delightful shops. Our children attended schools. And the temple, Kate, the glorious temple of our Lord . . ." Colleen had started to cry, ending the conversation.

Kate sighed and glanced at the pioneers around her. These people were destitute, most wearing rags, barely living from day to day. She felt a sudden empathy for her uncle whose dreams had been shattered. She listened attentively as he eagerly told her all he'd learned from Lucian Foster.

". . . it's a sheet of silver-coated copper that's been exposed. Then the image is developed with mercury vapor and fixed permanently with salt."

"I see," Kate murmured, trying to appear impressed. "And they're called what again?"

"Daguerreotypes."

"Dagger-types?"

"Daguerreotypes," Jamie said with a small smile. "Brother Lucian had taken several of Nauvoo and the temple. I wish you could've seen them, Kate. What a glorious thing, to preserve images for later viewing." He sighed and kicked at a small rock.

"You know, Jamie, you could start a studio of your own in Salt Lake Valley," Kate ventured, trying to cheer him up.

"No. It isn't possible."

"Ah, c'mon, where's that famous Mahoney spirit I keep hearing so much about? You could do it. Someday, you guys will build a city in Salt Lake, a bigger one than you had in Nauvoo. And you can just bet they're gonna want someone to take pictures of it. Not to mention all of the people who'll want to ham it up in front of a camera. Somebody's got to be there to take their picture. It might as well be you."

Jamie pondered Kate's advice. "You know, you may have something there," he said eagerly. "Perhaps someday I will have my own studio."

"Go for it, Jamie," Kate said ardently.

"Go for what?" he asked, confused.

"I meant, you should follow your dreams."

"Aye," Jamie agreed, smiling at the young woman. "Do you have dreams, Kate?"

A shadow passed through Kate's heart. "Just one, Jamie," she said, thinking of her family. "Just one."

It was early afternoon when the wagon train pulled into Fort

Laramie, an area named for Jacques LaRamie, a French-Canadian fur trapper. Excitement rippled through the company as they drove in past Indians offering skins, furs, and blankets for trade. Most sighed with relief. They had survived the trek through what would later be known as the Nebraska Plains. Five hundred and twenty-two miles had been successfully traveled. Ahead lay another five hundred miles with rivers to cross, mountains to climb and descend. But for now, for this one glorious afternoon, they would bask in the achievement of the trail already conquered. It was a time for relaxing, a time for trading for those items sorely needed, a time to forget the dangers that had been endured. Childike enthusiasm glowed from eager faces. With the exception of one family. For the Mahoneys, it was a sharpened remembrance of what had been lost.

Jamie quietly calmed the oxen as his mother gathered the shreds of her dignity. Quite willing to bear this burden alone, she was touched by Kate's offer to accompany her to the trading post.

"Ah, sweet girl," Colleen said quietly, caressing Kate's cheek, "I'll not forget this." Linking arms with the young woman, they crossed the fort, following the others who were seeking supplies.

David led his horse to the Mahoney wagon, saddened by Molly's tears. Silently, he handed the reins to Jamie and gathered the grieving young woman into his arms.

"I don't know how I'll bear it," she sobbed, unaware of a large man who was observing the emotional scene. "How can she sell Papa's watch?"

"She's doing the only thing that can be done for the sake of the family," David said, trying to comfort her. "We're all making sacrifices," he added, glancing at his buckskin stallion. Drawing back, he smiled. "We'll be blessed for it all someday," he promised, kissing her forehead. Taking the buckskin's reins, he walked off to sell his best friend.

Jedediah Taylor leaned against a wooden pole and spat out the wad of tobacco he'd held against one cheek. Wiping his mouth on the beaded buckskin shirt he was wearing, he grinned. He'd come to Fort Laramie to trade off the beaver fur he'd trapped along the North Platte River. He was also toying with the idea of seeking out a wife. The winters were long and cold in the Rocky Mountains. A little female companionship would go a long way toward making it tolerable. And he wasn't getting any younger. He was nearly thirty, as close as he could figure. It was time to pass on the Taylor name. Time to produce a legacy of sons to share in the work of survival in the mountains.

He'd almost reconciled himself to taking an Indian bride. A proud Sioux father had offered him a skinny, buck-toothed daughter in exchange for a pile of furs. He'd been tempted, but had held off, wanting to scout out his options. His eyes narrowed as he stared at the young women near the wagon train that had just arrived. His options had just been given new boundaries. Excited by one young lady in particular, he mingled with the newcomers to the fort, quickly gathering the information he would need to set a trap for the finest specimen he would ever try to capture.

The sun was moving low in the western sky as the wagon train finally halted to set up camp for the night near the North Platte River, a few miles outside of Fort Laramie. Scattered wood was plentiful for the fires that were soon built. After a hurried supper meal, the company gathered around a large campfire built in the center of the wagon ring. Benjamin Whitney had brought out his fiddle, playing loud, joyous reels for his companions to dance to.

David walked across the camp searching for Molly. Finding her alone by the river, he sighed. "Brother Benjamin's making his fiddle sing tonight," he said brightly. "Care to join me in a reel?"

Shaking her head, Molly continued to stare into the darkness.

"Molly, dwelling on your loss won't make it easier to bear . . ."

"If you want to dance, go ask the Wicker widows. I'm sure they'll oblige you!" Molly snapped. "Leave me be! I want to be left alone this night!"

Angry, David turned, tempted to do just that. Common sense prevailed. He knew how Molly would react if he had anything to do with the widows. Instead, he moved off to examine the new wagon he'd purchased earlier, wondering if his bride-to-be would ever learn tolerance, patience, or at the very least, to keep her temper under control. He peered into the black interior of the

wagon that would be their first home. Cursing, he kicked at one of
the wooden wheels, then hopped around on one foot as the other
throbbed with pain.

CHAPTER THIRTY-FOUR

As the company prepared for another day's journey, a lone rider was seen approaching from the east. Curious, Captain Roberts nudged his horse forward to meet the stranger. When the captain came within sight of the man riding a black stallion, he halted.

"Friend," the large man said, raising a hand in salute. "I heard tell you was headed toward Fort Bridger. Thought I might ride along with you folks. Got myself a cabin in the hills southeast of Bridger's place."

As he gazed at the man, the captain remembered seeing him at Fort Laramie the day before. "Why were you tradin' at Laramie if you live near Fort Bridger?" he finally asked.

The other man grinned. "Jim Bridger likes a good price for his wares. You'll pay near double for supplies buyin' from that rogue. If I got the time, I make a trip to Laramie when I got furs to trade."

The captain considered the stranger's words. He'd heard similar reports about Jim Bridger. Brother Brigham was encouraging the migrating Saints to bypass both forts, stopping for supplies at Laramie only if it was deemed absolutely necessary.

"Think I could ride with you folks?" the stranger persisted.

The captain gazed at the large man, tempted to deny his request. "I'm not sure this would be in our best interest . . ."

"Hold on, now, 'afore you say no, hear me out. I'm a trapper in these parts. Name's Jedediah Taylor." Pausing, he spat out the wad of tobacco in his cheek. "I know this trail like the back of my hand. I'd be a great help guidin' you to Bridger."

Weighing the added information against a nagging twinge of apprehension, Captain Roberts put the welfare of the company ahead of his own misgivings, silently promising to keep an eye on this trapper. "Truth of it is, we could use a good guide," he finally answered, gazing at the bearded man. David would be busy driving his own team now, he silently reasoned, certain that an upcoming wedding would distract the former scout. This trapper might be a godsend. But, on the other hand, if he proved to be more trouble than he was worth, what then? Fixing the trapper with a piercing gaze, he voiced his concerns. "We won't hold with any tomfoolery," he warned. "We have certain ways, customs that must be honored by those who ride with us."

"Amen to that. It gets a mite lonely on the trail. I would purely appreciate ridin' along with you good folks. And if I don't earn my keep, you c'n send me on my way," he added with a stained grin.

Nodding in agreement, the captain turned his horse around, leading the trapper to the wagon train. He paused by the Wicker wagon, driven now by Jamie Mahoney. Curbing a smile, he knew it was Sister Colleen's way of keeping peace between her daughter and David. "Have you seen Brother David?" he asked the young man.

"Aye. He's moved his wagon up behind ours."

The captain tipped his hat to the youth and motioned for Jedediah to follow. As they rode up to David's wagon, the captain grinned. David and his bride-to-be were exchanging a kiss near the team of oxen. Hearing the horses, a blushing David pulled back from Molly, urging her on her way. Molly offered an embarrassed smile at the captain, then glanced briefly at the large man who was staring at her. She quickly disappeared, hurrying to her family's wagon.

"'Mornin'," Captain Roberts greeted, enjoying the discomfiture of his former scout. "The wedding is still on, I gather," he added, his brown eyes laughing.

"For the time being," David responded, adjusting his hat.

The captain grinned. "We'd best proceed with the nuptials

before the young lady sees fit to change her mind again."

Jedediah shifted in his saddle. This wouldn't do at all! He'd learned at the fort that the wedding was to take place in one week. His plans to win Molly's favor would require the full seven days.

Coughing to remind the captain of his presence, he stared hard at the young man called David. Not much competition, to his way of thinking. The youth was handsome enough, but scrawny in comparison to himself.

Captain Roberts glanced at the trapper, then nodded his head at David. "Brother David Miles, I'd like to introduce Mr. Jedediah Taylor . . ."

"I go by Jedediah," the trapper responded, spitting a stream of tobacco near David's worn leather boot. He watched in amusement as David moved his foot, repulsed.

"Jedediah it is, then," the captain said, continuing with the introduction. "He's a trapper . . . he's offered to show us the way to Fort Bridger."

David forced a smile and reached up to shake the trapper's hand, wincing at the intensity of the other man's grip. Pulling his hand away, he scowled at the stranger. He hadn't liked the way the man had stared at Molly. Inviting this trapper along was just asking for trouble. "I'm familiar with this territory. And, we have maps and the book by Brother William Clayton in our possession," he added. "What do we need with a guide?"

"Bah! Maps don't tell you what you need to know," Jedediah said loudly. "I've lived in this territory for nigh onto eight years. Nothin' can take the place of experience," he added, glaring at David. "'Course, you're barely wet behind the ears, you'd hardly know that."

"Brother David's been our scout on this journey," the captain quickly explained, hoping to ease the tension building between the two men. "He was with the Mormon Battalion on their journey to California," he added proudly. He'd come to look on the orphaned young man as a son; not that anyone could ever replace Thomas, his lanky boy who'd fallen prey to scurvy at Winter Quarters. He'd lost his wife, son, and a daughter during the first winter in the makeshift camp. His two remaining daughters looked after him now, but they were both nearly of the marrying age. He knew the time would soon come when they would both leave him to start families of their own. Sighing, he forced his mind to the present situation. Dwelling on the past only served to open old wounds.

"Mormon Battalion?" Jedediah said, offering a mock salute to David. "Got us a soldier boy in camp. Don't that beat all! You jest might come in handy, sonny boy," he said with a grin. "Tell you what, you can handle the Indians if we come across any of those red-skinned varmints," he said with a wink. Tipping his hat, he nudged his horse off toward the head of the wagon train.

Eyes blazing, David focused on the captain. "Do you think this is wise?" he asked indignantly.

"Time will tell. I'll admit, he's a bit rough. But the Lord works in mysterious ways. If he can guide us to Fort Bridger without mishap, it may be worth tolerating the man."

Muttering under his breath, David turned to examine his team of oxen.

"We'll be pulling out soon," the captain continued. "Give thought to my advice," he added.

"Advice?"

"Marry up with that young woman of yours while she's receptive to your intent. I feel haste might be expedient in this matter."

David shook his head. "If I suggest it, she'll put me off even longer. We're set now for one week from this day. She's promised, and I intend to make the date binding."

"See that you do," the captain said with a nod. Urging his horse forward, he caught up with his new scout.

It proved to be a long and trying day at best. A particularly steep hill in the morning challenged those driving the teams of oxen, mules, and horses. Fortunately, most made it without mishap. Jedediah Taylor took the reins from Jamie to guide the Wicker wagon to safety while Jamie went to help his mother with their own wagon. Levi Lott's wagon, loaded down with scrap metal for repairs, nearly turned over when one of the wooden wheels worked loose, snapping the axle. Hurrying back up the hill, Jedediah did his best to steady the oxen while several other men came to the blacksmith's aid. Easing the wagon to the bottom, they halted for repairs.

It was late afternoon when they approached a rocky hill. Assuring the company it could be traveled with great care, Jedediah again tied his horse to the back of the wagon belonging to the Wicker widows, expertly urging the mule team up the steep climb. David watched with grim admiration, grudgingly admitting to Captain Roberts that the trapper was proving to be an asset. All too soon, it was his turn at the hill. David carefully drove his wagon up the sharp ascent, determined to show the trapper his own expertise. He grinned with relief as he guided his team of oxen to the bottom of the hill in safety. Leaping down from the wagon, he congratulated his future brother-in-law on achieving a similar success with the Mahoney wagon.

"Well done, Jamie," David said brightly, gratefully accepting a cup of water from Colleen.

"Aye, it was a test a grown man couldn't have passed any better," Colleen said proudly, scooping another cup of water from the barrel on the side of their wagon. Handing the tin cup to her son, she smiled. "Your father would be so very proud, lad."

"That he would, Sister Colleen," Captain Roberts added, moving his horse near David. "We'll be setting up camp two and a half miles from here. According to the guide book, we'll be leaving the Platte River behind us for nearly eighty miles."

"Would it be wiser to camp near the river?" David asked, glancing up at the captain.

"Well, if our new scout is accurate, a clear spring of warm water lies at the end of two and a half miles. After today's journey, I'm thinking the company would enjoy a good soaking in that spring." Kicking his horse, he headed off to check with one of the other captains.

"Did someone say warm water?" Kate asked, moving beside her grandmother. She'd hated the icy river baths they'd endured on the trail. "I say wagons-ho!" she exclaimed, motioning forward with her hands.

"Ditto!" Daniel said with enthusiasm.

"Ditto?" Colleen asked, raising an eyebrow.

"Kate says it means 'same here,'" the nine-year-old explained before hurrying off to chase Shannon.

"I see," Colleen said, turning to gaze at Kate.

"It's not a bad word," Kate whispered softly.

Smiling, Colleen slipped an arm around the young woman's waist. "Then, come, lass, it would appear this day's journey is not yet over." Kate fell in step with her grandmother, eager to relax in the natural spring.

Gasping as she plunged into the tepid water, Kate bit back the obscenity that came to mind. Molly laughed at Kate's reaction, and moved further into the spring.

"Who said this was warm?" Kate persisted, glancing at her grandmother.

"It is compared to the river," Colleen pointed out, keeping a firm grip on Shannon. Quickly bathing, they slipped out of the spring, hurrying to start supper while the men had their turn in the clear water.

"I have to admit, that spring felt wonderful," Kate said, helping her grandmother prepare ash cakes from a sack of cornmeal that had been purchased in Laramie. Mixing the meal with a dash of salt, the cakes were set in a pan near the fire and covered with hot wood ashes. Later, after baking, the cakes would be removed from the ashes. Washed and dried, they would be served with milk and a piece of dried jerky for supper.

"Aye. Bein' clean makes a body feel like a new person," Colleen observed, hinting at something deeper than Kate had implied. "But, I'm thinkin' you already know that," she continued, smiling warmly at the young woman. "You're doin' so well, Kate."

"Am I?" Kate asked, glancing at her grandmother.

"Aye. That you are, and proud I am of it."

"Proud you are of what, Mother?" Molly asked, flipping a strand of wet hair over one shoulder. She shivered, moving closer to the fire.

"Proud I am of all my children," Colleen replied, rising to meet her daughter's curious gaze with a look of concern. "And happy I'll be when your wedding day finally arrives."

"Now, Mother . . ."

"Don't argue with me, Molly. We must speak later this night. We have plans to make . . ."

"Mama," Daniel yelled excitedly, rushing across the camp. "We found some berries! The whole camp's goin' to pick 'em."

"Berries?" Colleen asked, taking the orange berry from Daniel's hand. "He's right enough, they're currants. Kate, can you mind the cakes if the rest of us pick?"

Kate nodded, watching as the Mahoneys hurried off with buckets and bowls to gather a harvest of promised sweetness.

Nearly an hour later, Kate had managed to clean the last of the ashes from the rounded cornmeal cakes, setting them inside of a pan on a smooth rock to cool.

"Smells good," a deep voice commented.

Startled, she stared up at the trapper everyone was calling Jedediah. "Uh . . . thanks," she said.

"You must be Molly's sister," Jedediah said, turning his head to spit a stream of tobacco juice.

"No, I'm her . . . cousin, Kate."

Jedediah grinned at the young beauty sitting near the fire and wondered if he was limiting his possibilities. This young woman was as pretty as the girl named Molly. Her hair wasn't as red, but those green eyes flickered with the same intensity. Chuckling to himself, he rubbed at his beard, his eyes wandering from the girl's face to her slender body.

"You know Molly?" Kate asked. Staring with dismay at the dirty guide, she wondered why he hadn't joined the other men for a bath. As he stepped closer, she held her breath. This guy was ripe! "Uh . . . I guess you didn't hear about the spring," she hinted.

Slapping his thigh, Jedediah laughed. "I like a woman who speaks her mind plainly."

"Then you won't mind me askin' what you're doin' here with my niece?" Colleen countered, stepping protectively between the trapper and Kate.

"I see where these fine young women git their beauty," he replied, taking off his dusty hat to bow. "I meant no harm, ma'am. I saw this li'l gal sittin' here alone and thought I'd keep her company." He replaced his hat and grinned. "Jedediah Taylor at your service," he added, his eyes wandering to Molly. Kate was tempting, but it was Molly he desired. With renewed determination, he smiled at the beautiful redhead, then turned to leave.

"Would you be in need of some supper?" Molly asked politely, puzzled that her mother hadn't offered. After all, this man had done much to help the wagon train over the rocky hills today. True, he was a bit unkempt, but underneath all that grime, the brown-haired man was quite handsome. And he seemed nice enough.

"Much as I'd like to oblige you . . . uh . . . Miss?" he paused, waiting for an invitation to use her name.

"Molly," she answered shyly, wondering at the look her mother was giving her.

"Molly. My, but that's a perty name. Well, as I was sayin', those dear Wicker widows have already promised me a meal. I'd hate to disappoint them. Maybe another time." Whistling, he turned and walked away.

"Are you all right, Katie?" Colleen asked, frowning.

Rising, Kate nodded. "But that overgrown B.O. factory is lying through his teeth. He already knew Molly's name."

"B.O. factory?" Colleen asked in confusion.

"B.O. is short for body odor. And that man stinks to high heaven!"

Molly ignored the laughter from the rest of the family and glared at Kate. "And how would you know he was lyin'?" she demanded, annoyed by the way everyone was treating the strange man. After all, he'd only tried to help. It wasn't like he'd been a burden to anyone.

"Because before you guys showed up, he asked me if I was Molly's sister," Kate retorted, gazing intently at her aunt. "Didn't it bother you, the way he was looking at us . . . like we were the centerfold for . . ."

"He was trying to be polite, which is more than I can say for the lot of you!" Molly snapped, grabbing Daniel's berries to dump in with her own. She handed him back the empty tin bucket and stormed to the wagon.

"Gran . . . Aunt Colleen . . . I'm telling the truth about that man . . . and I didn't like the way he was looking at Molly."

Meeting Kate's worried stare, Colleen sighed. "I know, lass. I can't say that I cared for how he was lookin' at you, either. From now on, neither of you are to go anywhere alone. And I'm not so

sure you'll be safe together. Jamie or I will have to be with you."
Lowering her voice so only Kate could hear, she stepped close. "I
had a feelin' there was trouble here," she whispered. "That's why
we came back before the others. There's something about that man
I don't like. The look on his face as I approached did nothing to
ease my heart's concern." Squeezing the young woman's shoulder,
she handed Kate the container of berries she'd gathered. "Take
these to the wagon. We'll use them tomorrow. Jamie, keep a sharp
eye till I return. I believe I'll have a word with the good captain
about this newfound scout of ours."

"Mind if I join you?" David asked, moving into view.

Colleen shook her head and took the arm David extended to
her. Together they moved off to search for Captain Roberts.

CHAPTER THIRTY-FIVE

Three days passed. During that time, Jedediah kept the promise he'd been forced to make to the captain and steered clear of the Mahoneys. He'd learned from Kate that females didn't appreciate the pungent smell of his body. Deciding it was worth the sacrifice, he bathed and began taking great pains with his appearance. As a result, the available females in camp began paying a great deal of attention to the handsome trapper. He'd received several invitations to supper, and felt as though his salvation was in peril. People kept saying things like he was a golden contact, whatever that was. One thing was for certain, he wasn't about to become a Mormon, wife or no. These Mormons made him nervous, but he'd bide his time and make nice until he caught Molly's eye. His heart was set on the beautiful redhead. Silently, the trapper plotted against her wedding plans, confident he could gain her favor. Much to his surprised delight, fate played into his hands. Little Shannon Mahoney became ill, her small body fighting a desperate battle against a disease the pioneers called mountain fever.

"You're certain that's what it is?" the captain asked, his concerned gaze flickering to Jedediah.

"Yeah, it's the fever, all right," Jedediah replied, stepping back as Colleen hovered protectively over her tiny daughter. "I seen this more than I'd care to. It always starts the same. Chills till your teeth near rattle out of your head, then a fever sets in that makes you feel as though y're in hell itself."

"Mr. Taylor, I'll be thankin' you to control your language," Colleen snapped, turning to glare at the trapper.

"Sorry," he mumbled, making a mental note to clean up his vocabulary. If he wanted the chance to impress Molly, he had to start with the girl's mother.

"Is it contagious?" the captain probed, fearing they'd be facing an epidemic.

"Well now, I been around it often enough. Can't say as I ever come down with it."

"And those who've had it, are they quick to recover?" the captain continued.

Jedediah slowly shook his head. Motioning for the trapper to join him outside of the wagon, Captain Roberts offered a grim smile in Colleen's direction. "We'll return to give her a blessing," he said quietly.

Tiredly nodding, Colleen took a damp cloth from Emily and wiped at Shannon's fevered forehead. Outside the wagon, the captain glanced around and gestured for David to approach.

"How is she?" David asked somberly.

"It don't look good, boy," Jedediah said slowly.

"Jedediah thinks it may be mountain fever," the captain added.

"Will she recover?" Molly asked, anxiously stepping forward.

The captain smiled sadly at the young woman and struggled for an answer.

"She'll be fine, right guys?" Kate pressed, moving beside Molly. A strange lump swelled in her throat. "I mean, it's just a little fever. She'll be okay," she said, doing her best to block out what her mother had told her at Temple Square. Shannon couldn't die! It wasn't fair! Not after everything else that had already happened to this family!

"Brother David and I will give your sister a blessing. Her fate is in God's hands." Turning to David, the captain smiled sympathetically. "I'll return to my wagon for a bottle of the sacred oil consecrated in the Nauvoo Temple."

David nodded and slipped a comforting arm around Molly's waist.

The family gathered around the back of the wagon as Captain

Roberts and David laid their hands on Shannon's head. Closing their eyes, each silently prayed for a miracle. When the blessing was finished, moist eyes gazed at the ground. There were no promises for health returned, only the assurance that Shannon would soon be at peace, and a promise that the family would find comfort in the Lord. Turning, Molly walked, then ran away from camp. Kate hurried after her. David leaped down from the wagon to follow, but stopped when Colleen called out to him.

"Let them have this time together," Colleen pleaded, hoping her firstborn would turn to Kate. *Dear Lord, let Kate fill the hole in Molly's heart if Shannon dies,* she silently prayed. She adjusted the rag on her small daughter's forehead and tried to make Shannon as comfortable as possible.

Out of breath, Kate paused, still reeling from the blessing Shannon had received. *Please, Heavenly Father, don't let Shannon die,* she silently pleaded, glancing up to see which direction Molly was heading. It was as she thought, her aunt was running toward the river Captain Roberts had called the La Bonte. The river of benevolence. David had explained that the shallow river had been named by the explorer, John Fremont.

As Molly threw herself onto the soggy bank, Kate moved forward and knelt next to her aunt. Timidly extending a hand, she rested it on Molly's quivering shoulder.

"If she dies . . . I'll not bear it!" Molly wailed, shifting her face from her hands to Kate's lap.

Unable to answer, Kate gently stroked Molly's back, trying to comfort the other girl. Several minutes passed. Then Molly sat up and stared across the river, an occasional sniff from herself and Kate the only sounds marring the peaceful gurgling of the water as it hurried on its way.

"Would it help if we prayed?" Kate finally asked, feeling unsure of the offer. Her prayers didn't seem to meet with the best results. Buddy had never returned, and Grandma Erickson had still died. Not to mention the fact that she was still stuck in this dream world.

"Aye," Molly said softly, turning to gaze at Kate. "But, let me say it," she murmured, shifting to her knees. She gripped Kate's hand in her own, squeezing it for support.

Kate returned Molly's squeeze, then quickly closed her eyes.

"Dear Father in Heaven, we kneel before thee this day to plead for the life of our sister, Shannon. Please let her live. She's so young . . ." Her voice breaking, Molly paused. "We know miracles are possible. Please grant us one now. Forgive our numerous faults, knowing we will ever strive to serve thee. Let our dear sister live, and we'll promise to walk uprightly before thee in all things. Amen."

"Amen," Kate echoed in a choked voice. Molly shakily stood and moved down to the river's edge. She wrapped her arms around herself, staring up into the darkening sky. Kate moved beside her aunt, wishing the feeling of unease would fade from her heart. Shared misery brought them together and they reached for each other, hugging tightly against the fear of what the future would bring.

Three days passed. The hours blurred together as Kate, Molly, and Colleen took turns fighting the fever raging in Shannon's small body. Molly tended to her sister's needs during the day, cradling Shannon's head in her lap as the wagon shifted and bumped over the rocky trail. Kate kept watch over her tiny aunt in the late afternoon while the others concentrated on the evening chores. Colleen tearfully cared for her daughter at night, trying her best to comfort her youngest child as a persistent throbbing settled in Shannon's legs and joints.

"Mama!" Shannon cried out during the third night. "It hurts . . . my legs . . ." she moaned, hot tears streaking down her young face.

"I know, child, I wish I could take it away," Colleen answered, glancing at Molly, who had risen from her bedroll to kneel at her sister's side.

"Let me sit with her for a while," Molly offered. "You've not had sleep for three nights, Mother."

"I'll be fine," Colleen insisted, taking Shannon's small hand in her own.

"Sleep, Mother, please," Molly begged, fearing for her mother's health.

"I can sit with Shannon," Kate said, smiling in the moonlight at her grandmother. "Would you like to hear a story, Shannon?" she added hastily, before Molly or Colleen could argue.

Weakly nodding, Shannon focused on Kate.

Kate leaned close to Molly's ear. "The story will take Shannon's mind off the pain," she whispered. "Besides, I think your mother needs you. She's making herself sick. Make her lie down and get some rest." Then, moving close to Shannon, Kate began one of her small aunt's favorite stories. "Once upon a time there were three bears . . ."

Shifting her gaze to her mother's face, Molly winced at the pained exhaustion she saw there. She firmly guided Colleen to Kate's bedroll. "Sleep now, Mother. Kate and I will watch over Shannon," she said softly, urging her mother to lie down.

"I can't bear this," Colleen whispered, lying on the quilt Molly had smoothed out. "If only she didn't have to suffer . . ."

Molly glanced at Kate, then sat, leaning against the side of the wagon, holding her mother's hand.

". . . but it was too hot. So Goldilocks tried the middle-sized bowl, but it was too cold. She tried the smallest bowl and it was just right, so she ate it all up. Boy, that Goldilocks was some kind of pig, huh, Shannon?"

Shannon weakly nodded.

Kate continued with the story, unaware that her soothing voice would eventually lull both Colleen and Molly to sleep.

Early the next morning, Kate awoke with a start. She rubbed at her kinked neck and gazed at Shannon. Her small aunt was sleeping peacefully. As she smoothed the blankets in place, she brushed Shannon's hand. It was so cold. Concerned, she tried to place Shannon's hand under the blanket. Surprised by the stiffness, Kate suddenly blinked and covered her horrified mouth with a trembling hand. "Oh, no," she said in a hushed voice.

"What is it?" Colleen sleepily murmured. Her eyes widened with alarm at the expression on Kate's face. Hurrying to the back of the wagon, she examined Shannon. Quivering, she bowed her head and pulled the blanket over her daughter's face.

"No, Mother!" Molly exclaimed, pulling the blanket away from her sister. Shannon couldn't be gone. Not Shannon too! She buried her face against her sister's lifeless body and silently screamed.

CHAPTER THIRTY-SIX

It took the combined efforts of David, Kate, and Jamie to force Molly to the tiny grave lying in the shadow of a small bush. Colleen was kneeling beside her youngest daughter's final resting place, planting a peony bulb.

"These flowers are your favorite color, Shannon. Their blooms will be lovely," she promised, ignoring the tears as they ran freely down her face.

A brief service was conducted by Captain Roberts. As he offered a prayer at the close, a feeling of calming warmth invaded Kate's torn heart. She glanced around. Her grandmother, Jamie, and Daniel seemed to be experiencing the same sweet sensation. Shifting her gaze to Molly, she blinked. Why couldn't Molly feel the peace that was being granted to everyone else? She stepped close to her aunt and reached out to the suffering girl.

Molly pulled away from Kate, turned her back to the family, and stared down at her sister's grave. Falling to her knees, she lay across the tiny mound, refusing to leave Shannon alone in the wilderness. Colleen sadly shook her head and motioned for the others to head back to camp.

"But, Mother, do you think it wise to leave her here alone?" Jamie protested, his dark eyes shifting to Molly.

"She'll not be alone," Colleen assured him. "I'll stay with her. Go now and see to the livestock. Keep track of Daniel and Kate."

Jamie obediently walked away, his shoulders sagging under the added weight of losing Shannon.

"Molly," Colleen called quietly, kneeling beside her daughter. "Come, my dear girl. Shannon isn't there. She's in heaven with your father. And happier now, I'll grant you, than she ever was with us. We'll miss her, of that there is no doubt. But we must go on."

Lifting her head, Molly glared at her mother. "If you must go, then leave. I'll not abandon Shannon . . . I'll not leave her for the wild animals to molest!"

"They'll not touch our Shannon. We'll drive the wagons over the grave in the morning. The earth will be packed tight. Her body's resting place will not be disturbed."

"I'm not leaving her here alone," Molly repeated.

Anticipating hysterical sobs, Colleen was alarmed. Molly had turned inward since the discovery of Shannon's death, refusing to give in to the healing power of tears. "If it will help, we can spend the day here, Molly. Captain Roberts has graciously called off today's journey. It will give Brother Levi a chance to make the repairs that are needed," she added, caressing Molly's cheek. She frowned when her daughter pulled away from her touch.

"Aunt Colleen," Kate timidly called, hating to interrupt. She quietly waited until her grandmother had moved to where she was standing. "Captain Roberts and David want to talk to you," she said in a hushed voice. "I'll stay with her," she quietly offered, gazing at her aunt. Molly was sitting at the base of the tiny grave, staring into the distance.

Glancing from Molly to Kate, Colleen reluctantly agreed. "Keep a sharp eye," she cautioned. "We don't need further cause to mourn. If that trapper fellow comes near, you have but to call and we'll come runnin'."

Flushing slightly, Kate nodded. She walked down to where Molly was keeping a bitter vigil. Sitting quietly beside her aunt, she felt as troubled as Molly looked. *What's going on?* she silently questioned. *If we're already dead, then how is Shannon's death possible? And why are these pioneers in the telestial kingdom anyway? Most of them are really good people. It just doesn't make sense. Unless . . .* She remembered the stern lecture her mother had given her in the visitors' center. Was this her punishment? Did she have to experience the same trials her ancestors had endured? Was that it? Confused, she wrapped her arms around herself, so caught up in troubling thoughts that she didn't hear Jedediah approach.

"Miss Molly, Miss Kate," he began, politely removing his hat. "It's a mighty da . . . darn shame," he said, trying his best to control his language. He was out to impress Molly, not drive her away by his foul mouth. "Sometimes life just don't seem fair a'tall."

Molly slowly lifted her face, staring at the large man.

"And, I can't say as I blame you for feelin' poorly. Why, these folks just up and expect you to go on livin' as though nothin' had happened," he said sympathetically.

Kate jumped up. "Look, Mr. Taylor . . ."

"Call me, Jedediah," he invited, replacing his hat.

"I'll call you worse if you don't leave us alone!" she threatened, her eyes glittering with an emerald sheen. She wasn't in the mood to put up with this guy.

Molly stood and placed a firm hand on Kate's arm. "Cousin," she warned, "keep a civil tongue in that head of yours. This man's done no harm."

Smiling at Molly, Jedediah stole at look at Kate's enraged face. It was a real tossup between these two. Kate's spunk excited him, but Molly's red hair filled him with an intense longing. Why, it was almost tempting to become a Mormon just to take both girls to wife! Forcing himself to remain calm, he remembered the reason he'd come out to talk to Molly. "I thought you ought to know what your mama and the good captain's got planned for you this day."

Frowning, Molly stared at the trapper. "And what would that be, pray tell?"

"I hear there's to be a weddin' later on," he started, waiting for the desired reaction. Molly didn't disappoint him. Her eyes blazing with raging fury, she violently shook her head.

"They're wrong if they think I'm going to marry David on this day!"

"Well, now, that's kinda how I looked at it. Here ya are, mournin' for your sister, and they're plannin' to make a celebration out of it." Shaking his head, he frowned. "If ya ask me, I'd say that's a mite unkind."

"No one asked you!" Kate snapped.

"Oh, I see. You're in on the plannin' as well," Molly accused, turning to glower at Kate.

"Molly, this is the first I've heard about it. And coming from him, I'd take it with a grain of salt! The man's about as smart as a fence post."

Jedediah glared at Kate. She was making him look bad, and that wouldn't do at all, now that he'd put a wedge between Molly and David.

Molly whirled around and stormed back to camp. "We'll soon see about this," she fumed.

Kate returned Jedediah's scathing glare. "I have a pretty good idea of what you're up to, Mr. Jedediah Taylor, and you can just forget it! Keep your distance from Molly or you'll regret it, I promise!" she threatened.

He shook his head and spit a mouthful of tobacco away from the grave. "You done put the fear into me, li'l gal," he countered, stepping close. "Best watch your step, missy," he warned. "Accidents happen on the trail," he added. He pushed her, laughing when she fell near Shannon's grave. "We might be diggin' one of those for you, if you catch my meanin', 'though it'd be a terrible waste of female companionship," he added, leering at her.

Kate quickly scrambled to her feet. As he stepped close, she utilized a well-placed kick she'd learned in a self-defense class a year ago. Crying out in pain, Jedediah folded over.

"Why, you little . . ." He stopped, hearing someone approach from behind. Straightening, he stared at Colleen Mahoney. He forced a strained smile, tipped his hat, then hobbled off, silently promising to settle the score with Kate. He'd fix her good, one way or another!

"Katie, are you all right?"

Kate nodded and brushed the dust from her dress.

"Did he hurt you, lass?" Colleen pressed, not exactly sure what had taken place between the trapper and her niece. She stared hard at Kate as the girl silently nodded again. "It was an ill wind that brought that lout to camp," she muttered, placing an arm around Kate's shoulders. "Come with me, now, dear girl. This day is proving to be one of sorrow and vexation for us all."

As they walked back to camp, Kate revealed what had taken place at Shannon's grave, intentionally leaving out the shove and threat she'd received from the trapper. It would only upset Colleen more than she already was.

"He had no business pushing himself into our affair," Colleen muttered, looking up as David chased Molly down the sloping bank. "Oh, Molly, why won't you listen to reason? We want nothing but your happiness."

"Then it's true, you want her to go through with the wedding today?"

Colleen slowly turned to meet Kate's outraged stare. "Katie, I'm well aware of the trial of this day. My heart feels nigh to breaking." Pausing, she wiped at her eyes. "But, we must go on. Shannon is in a far better place, though it's hard for us to see that now. If only Molly wouldn't dwell on the pain of her sister's death, I would encourage David to wait. But as it stands, that girl is on the brink of despair. I feel it's best if she marries right away. Today was to be her wedding day . . . they'd settled on it a week ago. David could do much to comfort her. And the way that beast of a gentile looks at my Molly, I'll not rest until she's safely wed to David."

"I guess I can see your point. That trapper jerk upset Molly on purpose. I think he wants her for himself."

"He'll not have her! I'd sooner see her in the grave than in the clutches of that heathen!" Straightening, Colleen possessed a look of determination Kate had seen several times in her own mother. "We'll soon put an end to this mischief once and for all! Come, Kate, we'll be payin' a visit to Captain Roberts! Guide or no, this Jedediah Taylor will soon be on his way!" She marched off, confident Kate would follow.

Kate obediently trudged along behind her grandmother, wondering if this would do any good. Shannon had still died, despite their efforts to save her. Would her Aunt Molly still leave the Church? Was this something else she'd be forced to witness first-hand? And what then? Would her grandmother die as well? Her shoulders drooping as she continued to follow Colleen, she wished for a way to change the destiny of these people she'd grown to love. For once, it didn't matter what happened to her; she cared more about those around her. Filled with sorrowing compassion, she extended a silent plea to heaven. *Heavenly Father, it's me again. I hope I'm not being a pain, but I need some help here. Please . . . I'll do anything. I'd even be willing to stay in this . . . this fantasy world forever, if you could just help me make things right for everyone. Please . . .* She waited, but the comforting peace she'd come to expect was missing. "Don't make me go through this," she tearfully pleaded out loud. "I'm sorry for not ever caring about what my ancestors went through, for taking the Church and everything else for granted," she whispered. "Please don't do this to me, I can't stand it," she said in a louder voice.

"Katie, darlin', I'm sorry. You don't have to come with me to see Captain Roberts. Go on back to the wagon and wait for me there. I won't be long."

Kate glanced at her grandmother. Wiping at her eyes, she slowly shook her head. "I didn't mean . . . I . . . I'll come with you," she said, hurrying to catch up with Colleen.

"You're sure now?" Colleen asked, her grieving eyes searching Kate's.

Nodding, Kate walked beside her grandmother, fearing what the days ahead would bring.

Chapter Thirty-Seven

Shivering in the cool morning breeze, Colleen knelt beside her daughter's grave, arranging the wildflowers she'd brought with her. "Ah, Shannon, much as it grieves me, I must be leavin' you this day. But I'll always hold your memory in my heart." She bowed her head and quietly cried. Then, realizing the wagon train would soon be pulling out, she wiped at her eyes and struggled for composure, unaware that Kate was standing behind her.

"You were always such a sweet girl, Shannon," Colleen said, breaking the silence. "If only Molly had your patience." Shaking her head, she rearranged a couple of wild daisies. "She'll not have anything to do with David now, the stubborn lass. I talked until I was near blue in the face last eve, but the wedding is off, and who knows if it'll ever be on again. Captain Roberts says to give her till we reach the valley. He may be right. It may be that she'll come to her senses by then. But, I've not seen her take a death quite so hard. She was bitter before, after her father's passing, but now . . ." Sighing, she shifted her gaze to the sky. "James, if you can hear me, take care of our sweet Shannon. And if you can find a way, help me now with Molly." She looked down at the grave. "Goodbye, dear child," she said softly. As she began to rise, Kate moved to help her. "Thank you, dear," Colleen said, linking arms with Kate. "You've been such a comfort, lass. Glad I am that you came into our lives."

Blinking back hot tears, Kate remained silent, the words she longed to say sticking in her throat.

The hours slowly dragged into days. Captain Roberts had decided to let Jedediah Taylor travel with them to Fort Bridger, at which time the trapper was to permanently leave the company of the wagon train—unless, of course, he decided to get baptized and permanently join their ranks. But while he remained with the pioneers, he was to steer clear of the Mahoneys, the threat of abandonment hanging over his head if he so much as glanced at Molly or Kate.

The trapper seemed to take it all in stride and even conveyed an attitude of repentance. As near as Jedediah could figure, he had a little over two weeks to come up with a plan; and, if it came right down to it, he still held the trump card. Fingering the object in his jacket pocket, he grinned. Molly would be his sooner or later. He'd learned patience as a trapper. If the prize was worth the effort, he could wait an eternity if he had to.

As the days progressed, Colleen grew weary of trying to reach Molly. The young woman had turned her grief into a bitter wall that she kept between herself those around her. One afternoon, after another heated exchange, Colleen retired to the wagon, finding Kate already there.

"Oh, Katie, if only Molly were more like you," she sighed with exasperation.

"You don't mean that," Kate said uncomfortably. "I'm really not . . ."

"You've made a few mistakes, dear girl. But, you're tryin'. You've changed your life . . . you're reachin' to embrace the gospel. The light of a testimony fairly glows in your eyes. In you, I see everything Molly could be if she'd only try." Closing her eyes, Colleen shook her head. "Oh, Molly, you'll be the death of me yet," she murmured.

"I . . . uh . . . promised Daniel I'd help him gather sagebrush for the fire," Kate stammered, escaping from the wagon. Mumbling under her breath, she set out in search of Molly. She found her aunt near Sweetwater River and stomped determinedly toward the other girl. But when she reached Molly, she came to an abrupt halt. Her aunt was crying. The Iron Maiden, as Kate called her, was finally letting go of the bottled emotions. Her own anger fading, Kate began to move away.

"How can you stand it, Kate?" Molly softly asked, turning to gaze at the other girl.

"What do you mean?"

"Losing all of your family as you did. How do you keep going?"

Kate nervously swallowed. She was in no position to start handing out advice.

"I was wrong to judge you," Molly continued. "I've been wrong about a lot of things." Turning from the river, she stared at the granite formation known as Independence Rock. A large, turtle-shaped mound covered with carved and painted emigrant signatures. Jamie had climbed up earlier to add his own carved initials to the assortment of pioneer names. It was said that if a wagon train reached this landmark by Independence Day, it would arrive in Salt Lake Valley before the winter snows threatened the mountain area.

Kate followed her aunt's solemn gaze and wondered what Molly was implying. "Molly, those things you told me, down by the Platte, the night before I ran away . . ."

Molly stared at Kate. "You ran away? You weren't lost?"

Shaking her head, Kate blushed. "I was upset . . . I thought if I headed back, I'd find my family."

Molly gave her a funny look, then stared at the ground.

"I'm sorry, Molly. I shouldn't have run off . . . I mean, you guys risked your lives and everything to find me. Which reminds me, I don't think I ever thanked you . . ."

"Kate, I don't care . . ."

"What?" Kate asked sharply, staring at her aunt.

"I don't care about what happened. It doesn't matter anymore. Nothing does." Turning her back to Kate, she gazed at the churning river water.

Kate scowled. Grandma Colleen was wrong! Molly was just like Kate Erickson! Stubborn, filled with pride, prone to self-pity, blind to the things that really mattered. Taking a deep breath, she searched for the words to reach her aunt before it was too late. "You're wrong, Molly, a lot of things matter. Gran . . . Aunt Colleen matters! Daniel matters! Jamie matters! And David matters! He loves you, Molly! Guys have never looked at me the way he looks at you! That ought to count for something! Not to mention the gospel . . ."

Molly spun around to glower at Kate. "They're duping you into believing all of this nonsense, aren't they now?" she countered.

"It's not nonsense, Molly. I used to think so, I used to feel just like you do now . . ."

"Then what's happened to your common sense? You were right, cousin, there's nothing special about this church! It's brought nothing but misery into our lives!"

"It's given me a reason to go on, to have hope. Lately, I've felt things inside I never dreamed existed! It's real, Molly. Everything your mother has tried to tell you."

Molly brushed past Kate, angrily making her way into a group of willows to sulk.

Admitting defeat, Kate slowly wandered up the river bank.

"Have you seen Molly?"

Kate gazed at David. She didn't know who looked more miserable, David or Molly. The poor guy looked like he was losing weight. "Yeah, she's pouting down in that willow patch."

"Were you able to speak with her?"

"I tried," she said in a tired voice. "I don't know, David, she's really messed up this time. But I'll keep trying. They didn't give up on me . . ." Lowering her gaze, she frowned.

David leaned forward to kiss her cheek. "Thank you for your patience with her. You may be my last hope." He then slowly walked away, fearing another confrontation with Molly would only force her further away.

Holding her cheek, Kate watched him leave.

Down in the willows, Molly covered her mouth to keep from screaming.

"That cousin of yours is a shameless girl," a low voice drawled.

Startled, Molly whirled around, finding herself face to face with Jedediah Taylor.

"It's not the first time they've been seen together," he said, gesturing to where Molly had seen David kiss Kate.

Breathing hard, Molly clenched her fists.

"Ya ask me, ya done the right thing, puttin' him off thatta way. Talk in the camp is he'll soon be takin' the Wicker widows to wife as well. 'Course, that'd be after marryin' you. Now, if it was me, I'd be right honored to settle for one fine bride. 'Course, I ain't cultured like some of these dandies. Reckon it'll take a while to find a good woman willin' to put up with a cantankerous fellow like me." Doing his best to look pitiful, he slowly replaced his hat. "Well, I'll be leavin' now. It wouldn't be good, you and me bein' seen together."

Finally finding her voice, Molly began to sputter with angry pain. "Why would it matter?"

"Well, your ma, no disrespect intended, saw fit to speak to Captain Roberts 'bout me. Seems I let loose a bee in Miss Kate's bonnet. When I caught her with David a few nights ago, she made up a whoppin' story to cover her own tracks, told your ma I had ideas concernin' you. Nearly lost the privilege of travelin' with your fine company over it. I've been told to steer clear of the Mahoneys." Chuckling, he slapped at his leg. "Ya ever heard tell of such a thing?" he asked, studying her reaction.

Enraged, Molly gripped a willow branch for support. "If what you're sayin' is true, then my cousin is no better than a . . . a . . ."

"Hold on, now, miss, don't go sayin' things you'll regret later. It might be Miss Kate is jest searchin' to find herself a husband. She's of the marryin' age, ain't she?"

Refusing to answer, Molly stormed back to camp. Jedediah watched until she had disappeared from sight. Things had gone better than he'd ever dared imagine. He began to whistle as he took his time cutting down a few willows. *Kate Erickson is about to be cut down to size herself*, he thought gleefully.

"Kate Erickson!" Molly exclaimed loudly.

Kate looked up from the small fire she'd help Jamie build and blinked.

Molly stomped close to the fire and slapped Kate, knocking the other girl off balance. Falling to the ground on her back, Kate stared up in disbelief at her aunt. "You shameless harlot!" Molly accused, reaching back as if she wanted to hit Kate again.

Colleen ran from the wagon to stand between the two girls, the fire in Colleen's eyes more than matching the fury blazing in her daughter's. "Strike her again and you'll wish you hadn't," she warned. Nodding for Jamie to help Kate to her feet, Colleen stared at her daughter. "Now tell me what this is about—and be quick before I give you a taste of what you just gave Katie!"

Molly glared at her mother, a woman who had never lifted a hand to strike anyone in her life.

"What is it, girl? Why are you striking the only sister left to you in this world?"

Kate stood beside Jamie and raised a hand to her throbbing cheek.

"She's no sister of mine!" Molly snapped. "Not after what I've seen and heard this day!"

"What?" Kate asked, the shock she felt quickly replaced by indignant anger. "Just what did I do that was so terrible, Miss P.M.S. Syndrome?"

"Enough with the name-callin'," Colleen demanded. Gripping Molly's arm, she led her daughter over to the wagon for an explanation. Several tense minutes passed while angry words were traded back and forth. Colleen finally beckoned for Kate to join them.

Confused, Kate approached the two women. "Would somebody tell me what's going on?" she demanded, her own temper flaring.

"Kate, Molly claims she saw you kissin' David down by the river. Is she right? Answer me truly, girl. I'll not tolerate a lie."

Stunned, Kate looked from her grandmother to her aunt.

"Well?" Colleen persisted, anxious to settle the matter.

"I didn't kiss David . . ." Kate started.

"Liar!" Molly accused.

"He kissed me!" Kate returned, glaring at her aunt. "And it was just a quick peck on the cheek. He was thanking me for trying to help you! Although why I bothered, I don't know, if this is the thanks I get!"

"It's as I thought," Colleen said with relief. "Now, Molly, I believe you have something to say to your cousin."

"Indeed I do! What about the other times you've been seen with David? Was he thanking you then, too?"

"What other times?" Kate asked, incensed by the accusation.

"Molly, make plain what you're sayin'," Colleen warned.

"I'm sayin' what I've known all along. Kate is a lyin' tramp!"

Stung by the allegation, Kate remained mute, gaping at her aunt.

"Molly, I'll not hear this kind of talk about our Katie! If you have proof of your claims, you'd best be making it known!"

Kate turned to stare at her grandmother. "Aunt Colleen . . . I don't know what she's talking about. I haven't been with David . . . not like she's saying. I swear it!"

Colleen gazed at Kate, praying silently for inspiration. Glancing from one girl to the other, she felt certain Kate was speaking the truth. "Molly, who told you these things concernin' your cousin?"

Unwilling to reveal her source, Molly shifted her gaze to the ground.

"I've no doubts it was the trapper who put you up to this." She saw the answer in her daughter's face. "Molly, it's time you and I had a wee bit of a chat." Her grip tightening on her daughter's arm, she smiled kindly at Kate. "Katie, we're sorry indeed for what's transpired here. Please forgive us both."

Silently nodding, Kate slowly moved back to the fire, Molly's angry words burning a hole through her heart. It wasn't the first time she'd been falsely accused.

The next morning, the pioneer company moved past another landmark, a cleft in the mountains known as Devil's Gate. It lay to the right of the trail, the two towering ridges running perpendicular to each other. Sweetwater River separated the four-hundred-foot cliffs, carving a narrow slit in the rock. Averting her eyes, Molly refused to gaze at the curious sight. She ignored the excited babble around her, dwelling bitterly on the harsh words spoken the night before by her mother.

Why is it you can think of no one but yourself? The way you just treated Kate, I've never been so ashamed. Taking a stranger's

word over that of your cousin. What's gotten into you, girl? I know
you're hurtin' . . . we're all sufferin' the same pain. But life, it
must go on. Instead of risin' to the challenge with the rest of us,
you've done naught but sulk about like a wounded buffalo, lashin'
out at loved ones who want nothing more than to ease your heart.
And I'll tell you somethin', lass, if you don't cease this endless
brooding, you'll lose the chance for happiness David offers. Is that
what you want?

The question echoed silently in her heart and mind. Didn't
anyone understand her pain? Why were they all acting as though
everything was as it should be? Hadn't they lost everything? Time
and again? Was there a promise things would be better in the Salt
Lake Valley? Somehow she doubted her life would ever be
anything but heartache and misery, especially if she remained true
and faithful to this church that demanded sacrifice at every turn.
Consumed with hopeless despair, she trudged forward in the
broiling heat, wishing death would claim her. If that was how this
would eventually end for all of them, she longed for the release it
would bring.

A week later, Jedediah saw his next opportunity to speak
unobserved to Molly. She had wandered away from camp to be
alone with her troubled thoughts. Selecting a large rock to sit on,
she stared unseeing at the cloudy sky.

"It jest might surprise us all and rain," the trapper drawled,
walking down to the rock Molly was sitting on.

Molly slowly turned her head, her eyes glinting dangerously.

"Might be more than one storm comin' my way," he said,
reading her expression. "I purely hope that look on yer face is
intended for someone else."

"Indeed? And what would you say if it was intended for you,"
she snapped.

"Ain't sure. Have I wronged you in some way?"

"A few days ago . . . the things you said about my
cousin . . . were you speaking the truth concerning Kate and
David?"

"Yep. But, don't let that fret you none. Yer much too perty to
be frownin' all the time." He reached into his pocket, concealing

an object in his large hand. "Bet I know somethin' that'll cheer yer tender heart." Holding his hand out in plain view, he revealed a gold watch.

Her eyes widening in surprise, Molly stared at his hand. "But, how is it possible? Where did you get this?"

"I traded for it, back in Laramie. I had no idee it belonged to your family till the other night. I pulled it out to take a gander at the time. Captain Roberts up and said it looked jest like the one yer ma traded off at the fort."

Molly gazed at the handsome trapper. Every warning her mother had given concerning this man faded to the background. He had been sweeter and more understanding than anyone since Shannon's death.

"I'd like you to have it," he said, solemnly placing it in her hand. "It don't belong to me, and I don't feel right keepin' it." Tipping his hat to her, he turned to leave.

"Wait," she said, moving down from the rock. "I can't . . ."

"Keep it. It's yers, as it rightfully should be. I'd not tell yer ma 'bout this, though. She might not be understandin'."

"But, how can I ever thank you?"

"Jest keep a smile on that perty face of yers. It's all the thanks I need." He walked away, certain the tide of her affection was heading his way.

CHAPTER THIRTY-EIGHT

By the next day, the clouds of the previous afternoon had disappeared, and the sun was shining with merciless splendor. The company passed through the South Pass, a dividing ridge of the Continental Divide. Excitement rippled throughout the wagon train. They were within two hundred miles of Salt Lake Valley. A celebration was held that night. Benjamin Whitney fiddled one joyous reel after another as couples gathered around him to dance.

David drifted off to find Molly, hoping the music and excitement would alter her depressed state of mind. He walked down to the springs near the camp and spied her sitting on a rock next to Jedediah Taylor. Frowning, he moved closer, freezing in place when Molly leaned into the trapper's bold kiss. Stunned, he turned away, his features contorting with wounded rage. He discovered Kate on his way back to camp, and gripping her arm, steered her to the circle of wagons.

"David . . . wait . . . I know you're upset. I saw it too. But I'm sure Jedediah forced the kiss on her . . . Molly wouldn't . . ."

David refused to answer and dragged her inside the wagon ring to dance.

"David . . . I can't dance. I don't know how. I mean, I know how, but not this stuff. Give me a little rock and roll, and I'd boogie this place down. But . . ."

"I don't care how many rocks you've rolled, we're going to dance," he snarled.

Sensing she had little choice in the matter, Kate reluctantly gave in, worrying over what Colleen and Molly would think. "This isn't a good idea, David," she whispered as he put his hands around her slender waist. "If Molly sees us . . ."

"Let her!" he snapped.

Kate stared into his pained blue eyes. "Don't turn away from Molly now," she pleaded.

"I'm not the one turning away," David replied, whirling her around in time to the music.

"But, Jedediah is making her . . ."

"She didn't look forced to me," he countered, dragging her with him around the large campfire.

Down by the springs, Molly pulled away from the trapper. What had she been thinking? She didn't really know this man. He was a stranger to her. And yet, he'd given her something she'd thought had been taken away forever. A part of her father. Facing the springs, she shivered, imagining what her mother would say if she ever found out about the pocket watch. Or about the secret meetings with Jedediah.

"I'm right sorry 'bout this, Miss Molly. I don't know what came over me. Yer so darn perty, I purely lost my mind."

Molly gazed at the man who had just kissed her. He was so unlike David. And yet, those differences attracted her. Excited her in ways she couldn't begin to explain. As surprising as it was, she had feelings for Jedediah. Feelings that conflicted with those she had for David.

David was gentle and kind. He would never intentionally hurt her. And yet, he had, by admitting he would consider taking another bride if the call for plural marriage came. David would always put the needs of the Church above himself. He would expect her to do the same. She wasn't sure she could live up to his expectations. But she loved him—loved him so much it kept her awake at nights when she thought she might lose him.

Jedediah was a coarser man. But he was honest and thoughtful. He alone had cheered her in these black days of sorrowing despair. For that, she would always be grateful. His kiss just now had caught her off guard. She hadn't expected it, and yet the excited stirring he had awakened was with her still.

Confusion descended. It was too early to be certain with Jedediah, but she feared she loved both men. Only one, however, could have her. Only one truly held her heart in his hands—David. And he was the one who had the power to hurt her the most.

"Molly, I have need of speakin' what's in my heart. I love you. I would be right proud if you would be my wife." Jedediah held his breath. He'd seen the look in her eyes, and had decided this was as good a time as any to make his intentions known.

Molly felt as though the wind had just been knocked out of her. One kiss, and the man was asking her to marry him? What had she been thinking? What had he been thinking? This couldn't be. The confusion cleared. David was only man she'd ever marry. "Jedediah . . . I . . ."

Sensing what was coming, Jedediah tried to sway her with another kiss. She struggled at first; then, as his lips grew bolder and more demanding, hers became more receptive. Just as he thought she was coming around to his point of view, she surprised him by pulling away. She slipped down from the rock and stared at him.

"No. This can't be. David and I are to be married when we reach the valley. I have no wish to hurt you, but, this . . ." she gestured between herself and the trapper, "it cannot be."

Jedediah scowled. Why had he rushed things? She'd been coming around. A little more time, and she would've bent easily to his will. "I see," he said quietly, wondering if she'd struggle much if he carried her off. "Young David has a way with you women folk."

"What you thought you saw with David and Kate—I've talked to them both. It was a misunderstanding. David's kiss was a gesture of gratitude."

"Call it what you will, I know what these eyes have seen, and it weren't gratitude!" he replied.

"I'm going back to camp now," she said. "It would be better if we weren't seen together." Holding her breath, she moved past him and headed toward the wagon train. A few minutes later, she slipped into the sanctuary of the circle and blinked. David was holding Kate close, whirling her around in time to a festive reel. David glanced up, looking in her direction. She frowned, then gasped as Jedediah's arm went around her waist. She tried to pull away, then froze in place when David bent his head to kiss Kate.

"Tell me, Miss Molly, is yer sweet David thankin' Miss Kate for the dance?"

Angrily jerking away from the trapper, Molly stormed off to the wagon, unaware that her mother had moved to follow. She climbed inside their canvas home and crawled into a corner to cry.

"Molly," Colleen softly called, moving to light the small lantern. "What am I going to do with you, lass?" she asked, replacing the glass chimney as the flame flickered into life. She gazed down at her daughter and sadly shook her head. A moth flew inside the wagon, beating itself frantically against the glass chimney of the lantern. "Dear girl, see how this moth is? Drawn to the destruction of itself?" she asked quietly, kneeling in front of Molly.

"I'm not a moth, Mother," Molly angrily sputtered. "I'm not the one out there, in the arms of a man who belongs to someone else!"

"No. You're the one who turned that fine young man away, seeking the company of a vile, uncouth creature who will bring you nothin' but misery!"

Flushing, Molly looked away.

"Answer me this, daughter. What did David see when he came to find you?"

Her eyes widening, Molly stared at her mother.

"Aye. He asked where you were. Then went off to search. Kate followed. When he returned with your cousin, the look on his face, it's the first time I've seen anyone put the fear into Kate. She danced with him, true enough, but it was against her will."

Remaining silent, Molly closed her eyes, sure of what David had seen.

"What kind of hold does that heathen gentile have on you? Why would you turn David away for the likes of Jedediah Taylor?"

Molly opened her eyes, but refused to look at her mother. "He . . . he's been so sweet," she tried to explain. "So understandin' since Shannon . . . and we're just friends. That's all."

"Is it, Molly-girl? The way he was holdin' you to himself, it looked like more than friends to me!"

"I'm . . . I'm not going to see him anymore," Molly stammered. "And I'll give him back Papa's watch."

Now it was Colleen's turn to stare. "Your father's watch?"

Molly hid her face in her hands. What had possessed her to admit she had the watch?

"Tell me about the watch, Molly," Colleen angrily demanded.

"Jedediah . . . Mr. Taylor traded for it in Laramie. He gave it to me yesterday afternoon. Captain Roberts told him it was Papa's. He said . . . he just wanted to make me smile again . . ."

Colleen moved close to her daughter. "Look at me daughter. Look at me now."

Molly hesitantly lifted her face to look her mother in the eye.

"Answer me true. Do you have feelings for this man?"

Miserable, Molly shut her eyes. She'd never lied to her mother and couldn't start now.

"Molly. How could you even think of . . ."

"I don't love him, Mother, not like David. Feelings are there, but they're not as strong."

"I'd dare bet that man has had his eye on you since we stopped at the fort!" Colleen muttered. "Give me the watch, Molly. From this time forward, you'll not have anything more to do with the trapper. Do y'hear me, girl?"

Shakily nodding, Molly moved to the trunk. Lifting the lid, she reached for the small tin container that held thread and embroidery floss. She reluctantly opened it and pulled out the watch, setting it in her mother's outstretched hand.

"I'll set this heathen straight!" Colleen promised, making her way out of the wagon. "We'll soon be done with that man! Until then, you'll be stayin' in this wagon unless I'm with you!" Closing the canvas flap behind her, she climbed down from the wagon, bumping into Kate as she turned around.

"Aunt Colleen . . . about that kiss. I . . . uh . . . David . . . well . . ."

Colleen gazed sadly at Kate. "All is well, Katie Colleen. You're not to blame for what's happened this eve."

Relieved, Kate stared at the watch her grandmother was holding. "Where did that come from?" she asked.

"It was a gift from Mr. Taylor to Molly. One that's about to be returned! Do me a favor, dear girl, and stay here with your cousin." Patting Kate's shoulder, she hurried off. As she made her way across camp, she ran into Bessie Porter.

"Oh, Sister Colleen, I can scarce imagine how you must feel after tonight. The influence your niece is having on Molly and poor David."

"Sister Bessie, I'll thank you to keep your nose from our affairs! What my girls are doin' is no business of yours, and if Molly would allow Kate to influence her, I'd be happy indeed!" She moved past the gaping woman to find Jedediah. Her eyes narrowed as she spied him talking to Captain Roberts. "Mr. Jedediah Taylor," she said loudly, not caring who overheard. "I'll thank you to keep what's yours and to stay away from what isn't!" Shoving the watch into his calloused hand, she gave him a scathing glare before whirling around to leave.

Jedediah scowled, gripping the watch tightly in his hand. Ignoring the curious stares, he quickly devised an alternate plan. *I'll keep what's mine*, he promised himself. *One way or t'other, that gal will belong to me!*

CHAPTER THIRTY-NINE

After this latest transgression, Captain Roberts kept his promise, sending Jedediah on his way. The company then proceeded to Fort Bridger without further incident, arriving at their destination six days later.

Avoiding the fort, the train halted to set up camp in the nearby mountain valley. Two days were spent in this location, giving the Saints a chance to rest and prepare for the journey ahead. They reset wheels, caught trout in clear mountain streams, washed the trail dust from their ragged clothes, and contemplated the fact that they were one hundred and thirteen miles from Zion. Their exodus of over a thousand miles was nearly at an end. Rumor had it that the trail ahead would be the roughest yet encountered. They would be challenged by canyons, sharp inclines, and willows that reportedly grew thicker than porcupine needles. Reflecting on this and the sacrifices already made, a spiritual happiness unique to these courageous pioneers softened the suffering that had and would be endured. They were nearly home.

Kate sat on a rock near a bubbling crystal creek and breathed in deeply. The fresh mountain air tingled. Glancing around, she saw that most were savoring the same experience. By the looks on their faces, she knew they were excited to be so close to the valley. With a sigh, she wondered if her own journey was nearly over.

"Here you are," Colleen softly chided, making her way to the young woman. "Picked quite a spot for daydreamin', I'll grant you that."

Kate smiled sheepishly at her grandmother. "Sorry. Is there something you need me to do?"

"Aye, lass," Colleen said, using a hand to shield her eyes from the bright sun. "Would you try reasoning with that willful cousin of yours? It might be she'll listen to you."

Kate frowned. Molly had hardly spoken a word to anyone since Jedediah had been forced to leave.

"She'll not hear what I try to say. I spoke harshly with her the night she was with that cursed trapper. Banished her to the wagon. Now she'll do nothing but sulk there. I've told her to cease acting like a child. To join us out here in this fine valley. She'll have no part of it."

"I'll try," Kate said, standing. "But, I'm not sure she'll listen to me, either. I'm kind of on her black list."

"What are you meanin', girl?"

"Well, it's just . . . since David kissed me, I'm not exactly her favorite person."

"She knows well enough why David did such a thing. It was no fault of your own. If that girl was younger, I swear I'd take a willow switch to her stubborn behind! We should be plannin' a wedding now. Indeed, this would've been a lovely place for such a thing. If only those two would cease filling their hearts with angry pride!"

Kate silently agreed, knowing how upset David had been since the dance. He wouldn't even consider talking things out with Molly, exclaiming he had washed his hands of the temperamental redhead. "Maybe I'd have better luck talking to David," she ventured.

"No, lass. I think it's best if you keep your distance from that young man. He might decide to up and marry you out of spite. Not that you wouldn't make him a wonderful wife, but it's Molly he loves. You'd only be hurt."

"Well, here goes nothin'," Kate said, walking back to camp.

"I'll be prayin' for you, Katie," Colleen promised. "But I'm afraid it will take a miracle to soften that girl's heart now."

"Leave me be!" Molly exclaimed, glaring at Kate when the

younger girl entered the wagon.

"Has anyone mentioned that you have a slight attitude problem?" Kate retorted, crawling forward. "Come on, Molly, snap out of it!"

"Leave me alone!"

"You know, I used to think you had a lot of spunk, the way you've stood up for yourself in the past. Now, you're in here hiding, acting like a spineless wimp, and for what? A total jerk!"

"If you're speakin' of David, then you speak true. He's as you say, a total jerk!"

"He isn't either!"

"Well, then, if you like him so much, why don't you marry him? You've both made it clear how you feel toward each other!"

"Look, you dweeb, you're the one he loves! And you love him, only you're too stubborn to admit it!"

"Oooooh, what I'd love do to you," Molly threatened, clenching her fists.

"Molly, I didn't come in here to fight with you."

"Then why did you come?" she snapped.

"Your mother is worried sick about you. She wanted me to try to pound some sense into that thick head of yours."

"I'd like to see you try," Molly challenged, shoving Kate away from her. Losing her balance, Kate fell over backwards, landing against a wooden crate.

"Molly, knock it off!" Kate angrily sputtered.

"I was trying," Molly returned, forming a fist. "Come close again, and I'll finish what I've started.

Kate smoothed her dress down into place and glared at her aunt. "You're really something, you know that? I've never seen anyone hold a grudge like you do." *Except for me*, she added silently. Shivering, she gazed at Molly. "Let's get something straight here. I'm not interested in David. David loves you, not me. He's a little mad right now because of how you carried on with that trapper creep, but he'll get over it. In the meantime, you have got to pull yourself together! If not for your own sake, then for your mother's!"

"And what does my mother have to do with any of this, pray tell?"

"Plenty! Try this one on for size. Don't you think that lady's been through enough? Or are you determined to put her into an early grave?"

Molly's face grew dark with fury. "Explain yourself and be quick about it, before I knock you across this wagon!"

"Your mother has already lost a husband and three children. Not to mention every home she's ever had. You, Daniel, and Jamie, you're all she has left. Don't fill what's left of her life with pain." Her own eyes softening, she reached out to touch her aunt's hand. "Please, Molly, I don't think she can handle much more. And believe it or not, I don't want to see you hurt either. Go make up with David, please."

Molly opened her mouth to speak, but the words wouldn't come. In silence, she reflected on what Kate had said, searching the green eyes so like her own for the answers no one had been able to give her.

"Trust me on this one, Molly. I can't possibly make you understand how your decisions will affect the future, but I do know your life will be very bleak if you don't marry David."

Frightened by the look in Kate's eyes, Molly turned away.

Deciding she'd said enough, Kate quietly left the wagon. As she climbed out of the canvas opening, she glanced over her shoulder. Molly was staring at Colleen's trunk, tears threatening to spill. "Yes!" Kate said quietly, hurrying down to the ground. She had to find David. If the couple talked now, maybe there would be a wedding after all. She lifted up the bottom of her skirt and ran to David's wagon.

"Afternoon, Sister Kate," Captain Roberts greeted, stepping down from David's wagon.

"Hi," she panted. "Is David around here?"

"Yes."

"Good! I need to talk to him. It's about Molly."

"Well, I'm not sure that's possible. Brother David's come down with the mountain fever."

Her eager smile fading, Kate stared at the captain.

During the next two weeks, Molly hovered over David, mopping his fevered brow, her softened eyes consumed with anguish. He had been moved into the Mahoney wagon, Jamie driving David's wagon while Colleen and Kate took turns managing their own team of oxen. As Molly struggled to control his fever, David began to suffer from blinding headaches, the pain in his joints causing him to writhe in misery. Calling out in his delirium, he mumbled nonsensical phrases that were ignored until late one afternoon.

As Molly gently wiped at his face with a cool rag, David gazed up at her, reaching out to pat her cheek. "Oh, sweet Kate, if only Molly were more like you."

Furious, Molly drew back, shoving the rag into her mother's hand. "Here, Mother. If it's Kate he wants, he's welcome to her!"

"Molly, he's out of his mind with fever! Molly . . . come back here, lass!" Her words falling on deaf ears, she groaned as her daughter stormed from the wagon.

Late that night, after everyone was asleep, Molly crept out of the wagon, seeking time alone with the troubling thoughts that had plagued her since Shannon's death. Quietly moving past the sleeping guard, Isaac Kimble, she wandered nearly a mile from camp, pausing near a ridge known simply as Mountain Summit. Here, she gazed down into the darkened Salt Lake Valley. They would enter that valley tomorrow, embracing the new life promised them by Brother Brigham. She sat near the edge of the ridge, reliving the sacrifices and suffering that had led them here.

"Not much t' look at, t'my way a' thinkin'," a familiar voice calmly stated.

Startled, Molly jumped, turning to stare at the man behind her. "Jedediah? What are you doing here?"

"All in good time, Miss Molly. Give this poor soul a chance to explain hisself." Grinning, he sat down on a rock near the young woman. "Truth of it is, I couldn't forgit you, gal," he said earnestly, raising his hands to the heavens. "Why, only the good Lord knows. I've had my pick of Indian squaws, but I couldn't forgit yer face. I've traveled by night, slept in the day to keep up with this train of wagons. I'd near given up hope of bein' able to talk to you. Yer ma's kept you under wraps but good."

"But you shouldn't be here . . . you shouldn't have come."

"Hold on now, let me speak my piece. Then if you truly want me gone, I'll leave."

Breathing rapidly, Molly moved to lean against a rock a few feet from where Jedediah was smiling at her in the moonlight.

"Now, I been studyin' this out, and it looks to me that yer not happy with this folk."

"I've never said that."

"Maybe not with that perty mouth of yers, but it shows in yer eyes. I cain't say I ever seen a' look a joy in that face, 'cept maybe for the time when I gave you this." He held out the gold watch. "Take it, gal. It'll remind you of me when yer a proper Mormon wife, sharin' yer man with twenty other gals."

"I won't," she snapped, glaring at him.

"Won't take the watch, or won't share yer man?"

"I'll do neither! Now, please, leave me be."

"I don't mean no harm, Molly. Like I said, I jest want t' know for myself how it stands 'tween us. I guess it'd give me peace of mind to know you'd truly be happy, slavin' here on this desert, raisin' a herd of children, some of them yers, married to Brother David."

"David's got the fever. He may not live," Molly said, lowering her eyes to stare at the ground, wishing Jedediah would stop talking. She could conjure up enough unpleasant mental pictures of her future without his help.

"Well, that poses a differnt picture, don't it now? But, if Brother David dies, I'm sure some good-hearted soul, say, Brother Levi Lott, or Isaac Kimble, or maybe some old codger down there in that valley, will take you on as one of his concubines."

"I will not marry into a concubine!"

"Yeah, well, too bad you won't have a say in the matter. Yer ma'll see to it. Although I can't for the life of me understand why a good woman like that would want her daughter to live a life of misery."

"You don't know what you're talkin' about!" Molly returned.

"True enough. Why, I've never seen a people more blessed than you Mormons. How the good Lord must love you to chastise you the way he does."

"What are you sayin'?"

"Jest what I've observed. Answer me this, Miss Molly. Iffen you Mormons are chosen people as you claim, why are you bein' driven from place to place? To my way of thinkin' that's a punishment, not a reward."

Covering her ears, Molly turned away from him. "Stop it! Leave me alone!" She gasped as he spun her around, squeezing her arms with his large hands.

"Come with me, Molly. This life, it ain't for you. I'll take you up to the mountains where you'll see what Zion really is." Leaning down, he kissed her.

Molly knew she should resist. But his closeness confused her, made her question things as never before.

Jedediah pulled back and gazed at her. "Marry me, Molly," he said breathlessly. "Marry me! All I have is yers. It ain't much, but it's all I got."

"Marry you? I . . ."

"We kin be married at Fort Bridger. 'Till then, I promise t' treat' you with respect a proper lady like yerself is entitled to."

"But . . . my mother . . . my family . . ."

"After the weddin', I'll bring you back here t' see 'em. If we tell 'em now, they'll stop us. You know I speak true." He handed her the gold watch, closing her hand over the smooth surface. "I brought an extra horse. We can ride this night. They'll never find us 'till it's too late."

"I need time . . ."

"That's one thing we don't have, gal. Tomorrow, you reach the valley. Why, I wouldn't be surprised one bit if they made you marry David on his deathbed."

"I'm not the one he wants. It was Kate's name he called . . ."

"Then, come with me." He held out his hand. As she timidly reached to take it, they were both startled by a snapped twig.

"Over my dead body!" Kate exclaimed.

"Missy, that could be arranged," Jedediah replied, drawing his pistol.

"No, Jedediah," Molly said, quickly stepping between Kate and the gun.

Kate moved forward, too enraged to care for her own safety. After all, she was already dead. What could he do, kill her again?

"Molly, get back to the wagon!"

"I will do no such thing!" Molly returned, glaring at the younger girl. "This is none of your affair. You already have David; isn't he enough?"

"I don't want David!" Kate scowled, stepping close to Molly. "You know he didn't mean what he said earlier. He loves you and no one else!"

"Then he's got a peculiar way a' showin' it!" Jedediah growled, pushing Molly aside with the barrel of his gun. Aiming it at Kate's heart, he cocked the hammer.

"No!" Molly exclaimed, shoving Kate out of the way.

Struggling with his temper, Jedediah nodded, easing the tiny metal hammer back into place. "I wouldn't've hurt her none," he said, forcing a smile. "Jest wanted to scare her a bit. She's done her share of hurtin' you."

"Molly, what I have or haven't done is nothing compared to what this idiot will do to you! Don't leave with him, please!" She turned to plead with her aunt and didn't see the blow as it came, knocking her senseless.

"Kate!" Molly exclaimed, catching the young woman as she crumpled to the ground.

"Hush, now, someone'll hear. She'd've never let us leave," Jedediah said quickly, replacing the pistol in his holster. "She'd've gone back to warn the others. This way, she'll sleep 'till mornin', no harm done."

"You didn't have to hurt her," Molly accused.

"Didn't have no rope to tie her up with," he answered. "C'mon, I've got horses stashed in those trees over there."

Looking up from where she was cradling Kate's head in her lap, Molly shook her head.

"I see. You've decided you'll be right content bein' a good Mormon wife."

Confused, Molly offered a silent prayer. A feeling of unease settled in her chest.

"It's now or never," he said impatiently, hoping to sway her without using force.

"You promise to bring me back to see my mother?" she asked softly, picturing her mother's reaction to what she was considering.

She knew this marriage would cut through her mother's heart. But, maybe after time had passed, the woman would come to accept her decision. Regardless, she wasn't about to become a good Mormon wife. And Jedediah's offer seemed the only way out of becoming just that.

"Ya got my word of honor," he said brightly.

"All right," she said hesitantly. "But first, help me carry Kate back to camp. I won't be leavin' her out here alone at the mercy of who or whatever finds her."

The trapper obediently picked Kate's limp body up off the ground. Gritting his teeth, he heaved her over his shoulder. "We'll be found," he said, tempted to throw the troublesome girl over the cliff.

"No. Brother Kimble is guardin' this end of the camp. He's sound asleep. He'll not find her till morning."

Jedediah began making his way to the wagon train, carefully balancing Kate's body. Several minutes passed in silence as they quietly approached the camp. Setting Kate on the ground near a group of bushes, Jedediah glanced fearfully at the slumbering camp. "This is close enough," he whispered, straightening.

Nodding, Molly knelt beside Kate, leaning to kiss the other girl's forehead. "Goodbye, Kate," she said softly. Rising, she silently moved to follow her future husband.

CHAPTER FORTY

Early the next morning, a cry rang out in camp as Kate was discovered by Colleen. Hastening to Colleen's side, Captain Roberts glanced down at the girl.

"She's a gash in the back of her head," Colleen said, squeezing the unconscious girl against her.

"Does she live?" he asked, glancing around for evidence of what had happened.

"Aye. But there's no sign of my Molly."

"We'll search the area," he promised, barking orders to several men.

"Oh, man, have I got a hangover! What were we drinking last night, anyway?" Kate moaned, forcing her eyes open. Waiting until she could focus, she gazed up into her grandmother's worried face. "Gran . . . Aunt Colleen?"

"Aye, Katie. Lie still now, you've suffered a nasty blow."

"What happened?" Kate asked, trying to sit up. Wincing, she allowed her grandmother to ease her back on the bedroll.

"We were hoping you could tell us," Emily said quietly, replacing the cool rag on Kate's forehead.

"Ooooh, man . . . everything's so fuzzy," Kate complained.

"Where's Molly, Kate? Was she with you?"

It all came back in a rush. Groaning, Kate realized she'd witnessed another fun-filled moment of family history. "Oh,

Molly," she said softly. "I tried, Grandma. I really tried."

"Grandma?" Colleen repeated, glancing at Emily.

"She's confused from the injury," Emily said, smiling sadly at her friend.

"Listen to me," Kate insisted. "Maybe it's not too late. It's that trapper jerk, Jedediah. He talked Molly into going with him last night. I tried to stop them and got this nifty headache for my trouble. Hoooh, baby! Does anyone have any Tylenol? Advil?"

"She's delirious, Colleen. Same as David. Don't take what she says seriously," Emily counseled.

"You'd better take it seriously," Kate sputtered, trying to sit up again. "Molly ran off with that creep, which makes me wonder about her taste in men, but anyway . . . where was I . . . Ooooh, boy, I don't feel so good," she stammered, reaching for the metal basin Emily was holding.

Colleen flinched as the young woman quickly lost the contents of her stomach.

"Is there any sign of her?" Colleen asked, moving quickly to Captain Roberts.

"I'm afraid what your niece is saying is true. We found their tracks, and discovered this lying where Kate was found this morning." He held out a gold pocket watch and gave it to the distraught mother. "I'm inclined to think Molly left this behind as a sign that she went of her own accord."

Clutching the watch in her hand, Colleen sank to her knees, grief wedging its sharp blade within her heart.

In two days' time, Kate had recovered, the throbbing in her head subsiding to a dull ache. They were staying in a small, one-room log cabin at the edge of Salt Lake Valley. After hearing of the many hardships the Mahoneys had endured, the Saints in the valley had seen to it that their needs were provided for.

Sitting now beside the crudely-fashioned bed, Kate pleaded with her grandmother to drink the beef broth she'd fixed. "Please, Aunt Colleen, I made it just like you said. Drink it; you haven't eaten anything for two days."

Colleen closed her eyes. "I've never known such pain," she

moaned.

"Where does it hurt? Should I get Sister Emily?"

Opening her eyes, Colleen gazed at Kate. She raised a hand and pointed to her heart. "It hurts in here, Katie girl, where naught but God can heal. There's no sharper pain than a child lost forever. I'll not have the comfort of seeing her again in heaven. Oh, Molly, if only they'd bring you back."

"Captain Roberts and Jamie will find her. If David had been a little stronger, he would've gone with them. In the meantime, you need to get well, so that when they do bring Molly back, you can switch her backside good with a willow. I'll even cut it for you."

Smiling weakly, Colleen reached up to caress Kate's face. "I've no doubt you would," she said. "Help me with the broth, lass, I'll try it now," she added. Taking a small sip from the tin cup, she sank back against the rag-stuffed pillow.

"More?" Kate offered.

"No, dear girl. I believe I'll rest a bit. Wake me if they come."

Kate nodded and stood, setting the cup on the wooden table. She moved quietly to the fire, stirring it with a large stick. Noticing Daniel's sad face, she forced a smile.

"Tell me a story, Kate," he begged, gazing at her with large, somber eyes.

Kate sat in the chair beside her third-great-grandfather and tried to think of a story he hadn't already heard. "Well, Daniel, once there was a rabbit named Roger . . ."

Two and a half weeks dragged by, and still there was no sign of Captain Roberts or Jamie. Each day, Colleen grew weaker, a raging fever keeping Kate and Emily at her side. Kate prayed aloud and in her heart for Colleen's recovery. *Please, Heavenly Father, I've seen enough . . . I can't handle this. Please let her get well. Let her live. I need her so much . . . Don't take her away.* Her heart ached each time she thought about what could happen.

David recovered fully from his bout with the illness and was anxious to ride to Fort Bridger to find the answers they were all seeking. "If they don't return tomorrow, I'll set out after them," he promised Kate when she walked outside of the cabin to join him in the evening air. "I still can't believe Molly would do such a thing."

"I know, David. I really thought I'd talked her out of it."

"Perhaps that's why the fiend, Jedediah, struck you. I can't believe she'd go willingly."

"If he took her by force, then why did they bother bringing me back to camp, and why did she leave the watch?"

"I don't know, Kate. I don't know what to think anymore. I always believed she and I . . ."

"David . . . look, is that them?"

David squinted and saw two riders approach from the east. Hope turning to dread, he watched in silence as they drew near. It was Captain Roberts and Jamie, but Molly was nowhere to be seen.

Running to the horses, Kate stopped. "Jamie . . . did you find her? Where's Molly?" Unseen, Emily had moved to her side, slipping a comforting arm around her trembling shoulders.

Jamie seemed to slump in his saddle. Frowning, Captain Roberts slowly slid down from his horse. "Where's Sister Colleen?" the captain asked tiredly.

"Inside. She's not well, Captain. If it's bad news you bring, you'd best tell us out here," Emily replied.

Nodding, the captain waited until Jamie had dismounted. Seeing that the boy hadn't the heart to tell them, he took the responsibility upon himself. "She rode off with Jedediah to Fort Bridger. We talked to the man who married them there."

"Only it wasn't a real wedding!" Jamie said with disgust. "That rogue paid a man to pose as a preacher!" Walking off, he led his horse to a shed near the house.

Stunned, Kate stared at the captain.

"I'm sorry as I can be, David . . . Kate," the captain said, glancing from one to the other. "The way we heard it, Jedediah couldn't find a preacher. He was in such an all-fire hurry to claim her as a bride, he . . . well, Jamie already told you what we discovered," he said, realizing he was only making the pain worse for both of them.

"Where is she now?" David asked in a low voice.

"He'd promised to bring her back here. Instead, he forced her to ride up into the hills. He's got a cabin up in there somewhere. We tracked them for a ways. They rode their horses into a stream;

from there . . . we had no way of telling where they'd gone. It was as though he'd anticipated we would follow. We could organize a search party and try again, but I doubt we'll ever find her."

Kate closed her eyes and choked back a sob. *Molly . . . what have you done*? she silently asked.

"Come, Kate, we'd best attend to Colleen."

Kate was too numb to argue as Emily guided her back to the cabin. When they walked through the door, Colleen called out to them.

"Daniel says they've come. Where's my Molly?"

Kate pulled away from Emily and crossed the room to the bed.

"Molly! You're finally here. You've come back to us. I knew you'd not stay away and break your mother's heart." Colleen weakly reached out, beckoning to the young woman. "Come, child, come to me. Whatever you've done, all is well."

Frightened, Kate looked to Emily for help.

"It's all right, Molly, do as your mother says," Emily said, tearfully motioning for Kate to comply with Colleen's request.

Kate reluctantly forced herself to sit on the straw-stuffed mattress. Leaning down, she rested her head against her grandmother's chest, her own tears mingling with Colleen's.

"Oh, my sweet lass, promise you'll never leave us again," Colleen said softly, weakly squeezing Kate against her.

"I promise," Kate answered in a muffled voice.

"That's my girl," Colleen said softly. After several minutes, she relaxed her grip. "I'm so very tired. I must rest now. When I wake, we'll talk. I love you, dear girl," she sighed, closing her eyes. She shuddered briefly, then lay still, her raspy breath becoming strangely silent.

"I love you, too," Kate stammered, sitting up. "Aunt . . . I mean, Mother," she said, trying to imitate Molly's soft brogue. "Mother?" she repeated, frowning.

"She's gone, Kate," Emily said softly, moving close to the bed. "Take comfort in the peace you gave to her in these final moments."

"Nooooo!" Kate sobbed, falling to her knees beside the bed. "Nooooo! Grandma . . . don't leave me . . . please . . . I can't do this alone!" Burying her face in the bed next to Colleen's still body, Kate cried as she'd never cried before.

PART 3

And he shall plant in the hearts of the children the promises made to the fathers, and the hearts of the children shall turn to their fathers.

D & C 2:2

CHAPTER FORTY-ONE

Startled by a strange sound, Sue lifted her head from Kate's bed. Blinking, she straightened in the chair and stared at her daughter. She stood and moved closer for a better look. The tiny droplets were tears! Kate was crying! "Kate, can you hear me?" she asked, holding her breath.

". . . andma . . ." Kate moaned.

"Mama's here," Sue said softly, leaning down to kiss her daughter's forehead. "I'm right here, sweetheart."

Forcing her heavy eyelids open, Kate blinked rapidly. It was so bright. Everything seemed hazy . . . blurred out of proportion.

"Honey, can you hear me?" Sue asked, reaching to buzz for a nurse.

That voice was so familiar. Squinting to bring things into focus, Kate stared. She tried to speak, but could only manage a shrill-sounding squeak.

"It's all right, Kate," Sue said, ignoring the tears as they streaked down her face. "You're going to be fine."

Kate tried again, but her tongue felt swollen, thick. The words wouldn't come. "Mmmmm," she managed as everything started to spin. "Mom!" she called out as the blackness descended.

CHAPTER FORTY-TWO

Y ou're sure she'll snap out of this?" Greg questioned, gazing down at his daughter.

"Positive. She's come around twice in the past twenty-four hours. Both times she recognized your wife. That's a very good sign."

"But why can't she stay conscious?" Sue asked worriedly.

"She's weak. Your daughter's been in a coma for over a month. She needs time to regain her strength. Once that happens, I think this young lady will amaze us all."

"What about the other injuries?" Greg asked, glancing at the doctor.

"Her ribs have nearly healed. She'll be sore for a while, but that's to be expected."

"What about her leg?" Sue ventured, reaching down to smooth the hair from Kate's face.

"I'm sure we'll be looking at several therapy sessions, but she should regain full use of it."

Sue sighed with relief and settled back in her chair, anxiously waiting for Kate to rejoin the family.

As she drifted in and out of consciousness, Kate seemed increasingly aware of her parents' presence. Determined to keep a constant vigil, Greg finally gave in to Paige's pleadings to get some rest. Bleary-eyed, he reluctantly followed Paige from Kate's room. He knew his wife was in the same shape, but Sue refused to leave their daughter's side. Sensing it was pointless to argue, the others left after securing a promise from Sue that she would trade Greg places the next day.

Sue was rewarded for her stubbornness around one o'clock that morning. As she dozed in the chair beside Kate's bed, a low moan startled her. Her eyes snapped open. Clinging to hope, she quickly stood, leaning over the bed, watching as her daughter fought her way to consciousness. "C'mon, Kate . . . you can do this," she encouraged, gripping her daughter's hand.

Breathing rapidly, Kate forced her eyes open. She squinted. Things weren't as fuzzy, and she recognized her mother immediately. "Mom?" she softly moaned.

Sue nodded. Sitting on the edge of the bed, she continued to hold Kate's hand in her own.

". . . didn't think . . . see . . . again," Kate rasped. She tried to lift her head, but collapsed weakly against the pillow. "I . . . Mom . . ." she said hoarsely, frustration showing in her face.

"Relax, honey," Sue said, caressing Kate's face. "You're going to be just fine."

"Love you . . . Mom," the teenager croaked. Attempting a swallow, she winced.

"I love you too, sweetheart," Sue said tearfully, pouring a cup of water from a nearby pitcher. Turning, she helped Kate take a tiny sip from the plastic cup. "Don't overdo it, Kate. Just a little swallow. Dr. Webster said we'll have to take things slowly for a while. There, that should help," she added, setting the plastic cup on the stand next to the bed.

"Need to talk . . ." Kate insisted, her voice sounding clearer.

"We'll talk later. Right now, I'd better buzz for your nurse. They wanted to know if there was a change . . ."

"Mom . . . have to tell you . . ."

"Kate . . ."

"Please," Kate begged, struggling to sit up.

"We'll have plenty of time to talk," Sue answered, turning to press the nurse's call button on the handrail.

"But . . . I . . . need to tell you . . ." Closing her eyes, she ignored the buzzing sensation in her head and gripped the handrail tightly for support.

Sue reached to steady her daughter, pressing another button on the hospital bed to raise the head to a sloping angle. "Better?" she asked, easing Kate back against the pillow.

Kate nodded, gazing intently at her mother. "Mom . . . not sure this is real . . . but . . . Jackson . . . those lies . . ."

"I know, honey. Kyle told us," Sue responded, shaking her head. "I can't tell you how sorry I am . . ."

"My fault," Kate stammered, reaching out to her mother.

Sue carefully gathered Kate in her arms and held her daughter close, both of them crying. Unobserved, a nurse stepped into the room. Quietly moving out into the hall, she silently pulled the door shut. Taking her time, she walked back down to the nurses' station to call the numbers posted in Kate Erickson's chart.

In the days that followed, Kate endured numerous examinations and therapy sessions. In between, she revealed the strange dream she'd had to her parents. Smiling sympathetically, Sue and Greg both agreed that their daughter had been through quite an ordeal. It took constant reassurance from both parents to convince the teenager that she was no longer drifting in an unconscious realm. Finally accepting that she had returned to reality, Kate concentrated on regaining her strength.

Weakened from the coma, several days passed before she dared stand by herself. Proudly waving her mother back, Kate hesitantly took a step forward, using crutches for support. As she continued to push herself forward, a familiar face appeared in the doorway, a small vase of pink carnations in his hand.

"David?" Kate asked, staring at the handsome young man.

"David?" Sue asked, suddenly concerned. Turning from Randy to gaze at her daughter, she frowned. "Sweetheart, are you feeling all right?"

Kate continued to stare.

"Kate . . . it's me, Randy . . . from Jackson."

"Oh," she stammered. "That's right. Mom said you'd been by a few times."

"Yeah, well, Heber isn't that far from here. Besides, I had to do some shopping in Salt Lake anyway for my mission. I leave for the M.T.C. next month."

"Oh," Kate replied, confused by the resemblance between

Randy and the David she'd met in the dream.

"Here, these are for you," he said, a pink blush creeping across his face. Moving into the room, he extended the flowers to Kate. When he realized she couldn't let go of the crutches, he blushed again and handed the carnations to Sue.

She set the glass vase on the small table, then, sensing some privacy might be in order, smiled at her daughter. "I think I'll go get some water for this bouquet," she said brightly. Moving across the room, she helped Kate maneuver back into bed. Satisfied that her daughter was comfortable, she took the crutches and handed Kate the card from the flowers. She leaned the crutches against the wall by the head of the bed and quietly left the room.

"She's quite a lady," Randy observed.

"I know," Kate agreed. "Mom said your grandpa had been in here," she added nervously, trying to make conversation.

Nodding, Randy moved a chair close to the bed, then sat down. "It must've been hard to lose him like that."

"I guess it was his time to go," Randy replied, glancing down at his hands. Looking up, he gazed solemnly at the beautiful girl. "I'm just glad it wasn't yours."

Kate silently agreed. She gazed at the card in her hand and shyly opened the small envelope. Blinking, she gaped at the message and glanced from the card to Randy. "Your last name is Miles?"

"Uh . . . yeah," Randy responded, puzzled by the look on her face.

"This is too weird. Don't think I've lost my mind here, but are you related to a David Miles? You look just like him. He lived back in the 1800s . . . he was a scout for a wagon train."

"The name sounds familiar. He's like a third or fourth grandfather, I think. Why?"

"Who did he marry?"

"Well, he married twice, if I remember correctly. Mom has really been into genealogy lately. She's always telling us stories about our ancestors."

"Do you remember the names of his wives?"

"No, I don't. Sorry." He raised an eyebrow at the expression on her face. "I could ask Mom later. She'd know."

"Thanks. It's just . . . I had this crazy dream while I was in the coma. It was so real. I was on that wagon train . . ."

Randy quietly listened as Kate related a brief summary of the dream. When she finished, he shook his head. "Wow! Your imagination was really working overtime!"

"I know. But according to my mother, most of what I saw actually happened." Shrugging, she sighed. "I'm not sure if any of it was real . . . but I know I'll never take things for granted again."

"Like what?"

"My family . . . and the Church. Actually, I've been wrong about a lot of things. Which reminds me . . . I'm sorry for the way I acted in Jackson."

Rising, Randy grinned. "No problem," he said, his blue eyes twinkling. "You just keep getting better. I still need a musical number for my farewell."

"Musical number?" Kate asked with a puzzled frown.

"Your mother tells me you can sing like an angel. Can I count on you?"

Lifting an eyebrow, Kate continued to frown.

"Well?"

"Randy," she said finally, "I haven't sung in church for years!?"

"Then I'd say it's about time you started again," he replied, moving to the door. "I'll call you tonight," he promised as he left the room.

Kate watched him go, a pleasant warmth invading her overwhelmed heart. Jace had never made her feel this way.

Sue entered the room a few minutes later, smiling at the look on her daughter's face. She sat in the chair beside the bed and listened as Kate excitedly told her about Randy's visit.

It was nearly eight-thirty when Randy finally called. Sue answered, then handed the phone to her impatient daughter.

"Hi, Randy. What did you find out? Did your mother know?"

"Settle down. Don't you want to hear about the nifty socks I found on sale this afternoon?"

"Randy!"

"Okay, okay. Sorry it took so long, but Mom had to dig out Dad's genealogy book. And now . . . the drum roll please . . ."

"Randy!"

"Patience is definitely one of your virtues. Okay, here goes. Grandpa David's first wife was named *Caroline Morris Wicker.*"

Kate gasped. David married one of the Wicker widows! The youngest one. The pretty woman who hadn't been much older than Molly.

"And his second wife?" she asked, fearing the answer.

"Well, Grandma Caroline died after giving birth to a son, her second child with David. It says here she had two daughters from a previous marriage. Caroline's first marriage was to some guy named Truman Wicker. He died the year they came to Salt Lake."

"Yeah, I know," Kate interrupted. "Get to the good stuff."

"There's something here about David adopting Caroline's daughters, and then they had a little girl, and four years later, a little boy named Jacob. That's where we come from—Jacob, I mean."

"Okay. But . . ."

"I know. You want me to quit rambling and give you the scoop. First, I have a question for you."

"What?"

"Was your aunt's name Molly?"

"Yes. Molly Mahoney . . . Oh what was that jerk's name . . . uh . . . Taylor! Molly Mahoney Taylor . . . Only she wasn't really married to Jedediah, so I guess Taylor doesn't count."

Randy laughed, enjoying her excitement.

"What's so funny?" Kate demanded.

"You," he replied.

"Randy!"

"Sorry. Now, where were we? Oh, yes. I was about to tell you the name of Grandpa David's second wife."

"Well? Who was she? Tell me, Randy; I have to know!"

"According to this record, it would appear that we're related. David's second wife was none other than Molly Mahoney Taylor."

"No way! Really? Molly finally married David?"

"Uh-huh. Nearly a year after Caroline died."

"Did they have any children?" Kate asked in a choked voice.

"No. Anyway there aren't any listed. Just the names of two boys that were from Molly's first . . . marriage, I guess you'd say.

They were sealed to David and Molly."

"Two boys?"

"Yeah. James and Daniel. They evidently died before she married David. The date of death for both boys is about a year before she became Mrs. David Miles."

Kate closed her eyes, holding her breath.

"So, about our deal. I came through for you. Will you do the same for me? How about that song for my farewell?" He waited, but there was no reply. "Kate?"

Sensing Kate was in no shape to continue the conversation, Sue took the phone from her daughter's trembling hand.

"Kate?"

"Randy . . . I'm sorry," Sue said, handing her daughter a box of tissue. "Kate will have to call you back later. She's . . . had it for today."

"She has been through a lot. It's amazing how that dream's affected her."

"I know. I gather our Aunt Molly married your grandfather."

"Yeah. I hope it didn't upset Kate. I mean . . . it's not like we're related or anything . . . just by marriage," he stammered, suddenly embarrassed.

"I'm sure that wasn't it," Sue said, trying not to smile. "Why don't you call tomorrow . . . give her a chance to absorb this."

"Okay."

"And, Randy, thanks for finding this out. I think it was something Kate needed to hear."

"No problem. Tell her goodbye for me and that I'll call her in the morning."

"Okay." After hanging up the phone, Sue sat and contemplated the drastic change in her daughter. Whatever the reason for it, she would be eternally grateful that they both had been given another chance.

CHAPTER FORTY-THREE

I t's so good to finally get out of the hospital," Kate said brightly, trying to keep her balance as she stood between her mother and Paige.

"I'll bet!" Paige exclaimed, doing her best to help her niece down the stairs to the family room. "And the service you'll get here will have you spoiled in no time."

Kate turned to grin at her aunt. "I can hardly wait."

"She was spoiled enough in that hospital," Sue teased. "Honestly, the way those interns and male nurses doted on you . . . I thought Randy was going to go crazy trying to keep up with the competition."

"What's a girl to do?" Kate quipped, wincing as her cast bumped against a stair. She held her breath until the pain subsided, missing the look exchanged between her mother and aunt. The two women couldn't get over how much Kate had changed. They hadn't heard one obscenity uttered since the young woman had regained consciousness. Smiling at each other, they carefully maneuvered the teenager down the rest of the carpeted stairs. They guided Kate to the couch and eased her into a sitting position, propping her cast on top of a fluffy pillow.

Kate glanced around at the large room, "Grandma Colleen's trunk!" she exclaimed, pointing excitedly to the old steamer trunk.

"Uh-huh," Paige said, glancing at Sue. "You wouldn't like to take a look at that now, would you?" she teased, winking at her sister-in-law.

"Oh, yeah!" was the enthusiastic response.

"We kind of thought you might," Sue replied, smiling at her daughter. "Unless you'd rather watch these videos we rented for you."

"No way! Bring that trunk over here!"

The two women carefully slid the trunk across the room and placed it in front of Kate. Paige lifted the lid, reaching inside for the velvet-covered photo album. Handing it to her niece, she watched as Kate reverently opened it, smiling as the young woman gasped over the pictures.

"Grandma Colleen," Kate said softly, as she picked up a tintype, gazing tenderly at Colleen and James Mahoney.

"Is that how she looked in your dream?" Sue asked, touched by the look on her daughter's face.

Nodding, Kate wiped at her eyes. "This wasn't her wedding picture, though. It was taken in Nauvoo before they had to leave. There was another picture taken at the same time, one of the whole family. Grandma always kept them in the trunk. These were the only pictures that they had of Grandpa James." She handed the tintype to her mother, then gazed at the one of Molly. "You were so beautiful." she said quietly. "Why did you ever go with that trapper?" Shaking her head, she closed the album, handing it to her mother. "It all seemed so real," she stammered, closing her eyes.

Paige knelt beside the couch, reaching to squeeze Kate's hand. "We're glad you came back to us," she said, smiling at her niece. "You'll never know how glad."

After making sure Kate was comfortable, Sue went upstairs to help Paige fix lunch. Kate continued to look through the velvet-colored album, coming back to the pictures of Colleen and Molly. Something kept nagging at her. "The false bottom!" she finally exclaimed, staring at the trunk.

The trunk had been left beside the couch. Carefully swinging her leg off the pillow, Kate moved until she could reach the contents of the old steamer trunk. She removed several items, setting them on the couch beside her. Then, pushing the trunk back, she cautiously slipped to the floor in front of it.

It didn't take long to finish unloading the trunk. Eagerly, she pushed her finger down between the side and bottom of the trunk. Nothing. She tried again. Still nothing. Frowning, she was about to give up. Then her fingernail brushed a tiny metal clasp. Stunned, she pushed it, hearing a soft click. Thrilled, she searched for the other clasp. Finding it, she pushed and was rewarded with another soft click.

"I knew it!" Kate exclaimed, her eyes sparkling with excitement. Leaning, she lifted out the square piece of wood and gaped at the contents. "MOM! AUNT PAIGE!"

Later, they accused Kate of taking ten years off their lives. Hearing the yells and assuming she was in trouble, they had nearly broken their necks getting down the stairs. They had feared she'd rolled off the couch when they saw her sitting on the floor. Gradually, Kate calmed down enough to convince them she wasn't hurt and excitedly explained what she had discovered.

"Oh, Kate . . ." Paige said, covering her mouth with a trembling hand.

Sue reached into the hidden compartment and pulled out a gold pocket watch.

"Grandpa's watch," Kate said in a hushed voice.

Setting the watch in Kate's hand, Sue reached in a second time and pulled out a hand-carved mirror and brush set. The mirror had a tiny crack across the center, splitting the reflected image of her surprised face. She handed the set to Paige.

"Grandpa James made the set for Grandma Colleen. Those are her initials on the back."

Paige carefully turned the mirror over and blinked. Colleen's initials were there, just as Kate had said.

Sue pulled out a faded photograph of a family. Blinking, she held it up for Kate to see.

"That's the other picture! The one of the whole family." Reaching for the tintype, she took it from her mother's hands. "There's Daniel, Jamie, Molly . . . and Shannon." Kate stared at the tiny girl in the daguerreotype. "Oh, Shannon," she said softly.

Exchanging a bewildered look with Paige, Sue glanced into the trunk again. Only a small, worn book remained in the compartment. Pulling it out, she saw that it was a journal. "That's it," she said, feeling around inside the trunk to make sure. "Just this journal."

"Whose journal?" Kate asked.

Sue opened the small book and gasped. "It belonged to Molly," she said, her eyes widening.

"I can't believe this," Kate said softly, ignoring the tears trickling down her face.

"Join the crowd," Paige answered, staring in disbelief at her niece.

"It's for you, Kate," Sue announced, stepping down into the family room. She moved to the couch and handed the cordless phone to her daughter. "It's your dad," she added, smiling down at Sabrina. "Still keeping your sister entertained?" she asked the five-year-old.

"Uh-huh," Sabrina replied, gazing up at her mother. "She's cryin', though. That old book keeps makin' her cry."

Glancing at Kate, Sue saw that Sabrina was right. "Send the phone back up with Sabrina when you're through," she said quietly, squeezing the teenager's shoulder.

Silently nodding, Kate set the journal down on the couch, placing the phone to her ear as her mother left the room.

". . . anyway. I'm sure you don't want to hear about Tyler's adventures in the kitchen," Greg said, chuckling into the phone.

"Oh, yeah," Kate countered. "Somehow, I can't picture him playing chef."

"Well, he tries."

Kate grinned as she overheard her brother protesting in the background.

"Your mother tells me you've stumbled onto some family treasures."

"Yeah. I still don't know what to think about all of this."

"I don't think any of us do, now," Greg returned, shaking his head. "Guess it's one of those mysteries life seems to be full of. Anyway, like I was telling your mother, we'll start down Friday afternoon when we both get off work. It'll be late when we hit Salt Lake so don't wait up."

"You guys are driving straight through?"

"Yep."

"Dad, do you realize how far it is from Bozeman to Salt Lake?"

"Now you sound like your mother. We'll be fine. Tyler's already offered to serenade me on the way down. There's no way a person can sleep through that."

Kate silently agreed.

"Keep your chin up, sweetheart, and prepare yourself for a monster hug from me on Saturday."

"I can hardly wait."

"Same here," Greg said quietly, his glasses steaming from the mist gathering in his blue eyes. "Well, hang in there and we'll see you in couple of days," he said softly. "I love you, Kate."

"I love you too, Dad. 'Bye." Clicking off the phone, Kate handed it to her sister. "Here, Breeny, can you take this back up to Mom or Aunt Paige?"

"Uh-huh. I'll be right back."

Smiling at Sabrina, Kate watched as her sister quickly scrambled from sight. The five-year-old had been sticking to her like a shadow since her release from the hospital. Shaking her head, she hoped she could live up to the expectation glowing from Sabrina's eyes. "I'll make things up to you, Breeny," she quietly promised. "I'll be the best big sister you've ever seen."

CHAPTER FORTY-FOUR

Kate leaned against a plump pillow and rubbed at her tired eyes. She knew it was getting late, but couldn't resist Molly's journal. Ignoring the signals her body was sending, she stretched, then reached for the small book. Carefully opening the treasured record, she gazed at the first entry.

August 20, 1848

With a heavy heart I begin this record of my life. Thinking I'd already endured trials of a vile and cruel nature, I was unprepared for the hardships awaiting me at the hands of my new husband. Hoping these pages might someday reach my family, I now make use of this journal and pen. I wish for them to know of the fate that has befallen me through my own foolishness.

It was but two weeks ago that I became the wife of Jedediah Taylor. If I had known the atrocities that act of rashness would inspire, I would have never left with this creature I now call husband.

True to his word, Jedediah treated me with great respect until we reached Fort Bridger. We were united by the bonds of holy matrimony on that day, August 6, 1848. This journal and the quill pen I use are gifts, bought by my husband at the fort's trading post. Laughing when he saw how I admired the set, he added it to the supplies purchased for our journey ahead. Elated by this act of generosity, I felt sure I had chosen well, convinced my family would surely become reconciled to Jedediah. All was well until

*that ill-fated night when it was shown me the nature of the man I
had married. Securing a small cabin for the evening, I was
claimed as his bride in that unholy setting. The details of which I
shall not reveal, but will say I have never before known such
humiliation or callous treatment, though it is my lot to endure such
now.*

*The next morning dawned cold and dreary, matching the ache
in my heart. Jedediah lifted me up into the saddle of the mare he'd
purchased for me to ride. Holding tight to the reins of my mare, he
mounted his own horse, forcing me to follow him in a southeastern
direction. He laughed when I reminded him of his promise to take
me to Salt Lake Valley, and assured me I would never again
associate with the vile Mormons. I tried to reason with this man,
pleading with him to make good his word to allow me to see my
family. Striking me a harsh blow, he silenced my pleas with the
threat of further harm.*

*Bringing me to his filthy cabin in the depths of these Rocky
Mountains, he has kept me a prisoner. This journal I keep hidden,
knowing he would destroy it, for he delights in causing me pain.
He often compares me to the horses he has trained, promising to
break my willful spirit. It will take more than the likes of him to
bring me to my knees! He may control my mortal being, but he'll
not conquer my spirit! Though a way has yet to present itself, I
will not remain here, trapped by this heathen. I will escape, God
willing. Though why God has let this happen, I am perplexed, at
times wondering if such a being exists. How could a loving Father
in Heaven watch as his children suffer, refusing to ease the pain of
their existence?*

*Jedediah is gone at present, trapping near some unknown
river. I do not know which is better, to have his protection and
endure his crude behavior, or to be left alone, at the mercy of wild
beasts and Indians. Jedediah laughs at my fears, claiming that
only his closest associates know of this place, but it is of no
comfort to me. Friends or no, if they be like my husband, I shudder
to think of a visit from them.*

*Thinking I might try to escape, Jedediah has taken my horse
and shoes. If I could find rags, I'd tie them 'round my feet and
leave, but I must first discover the way to Fort Bridger. Having*

been blindfolded for the last portion of the journey here, I am not sure which direction would lead me to safety. Until then, I must bide my time, waiting for the chance to leave this place.

Dwelling on my current condition brings me such sorrow, I can scarce abide it. To occupy my mind, I will record the journey made from Winter Quarters to Salt Lake Valley.

Frowning, Kate flipped ahead, trying to find her place in the journal. She'd already read through Molly's brief description of the pioneer trek to Salt Lake. Everything she'd witnessed in her dream had taken place, with one exception. Caroline Wicker had been the one to save Molly from Truman. The two young women had then become close friends, until Bessie Porter had stirred things up with the rumor about David marrying the Wicker widows. Furious, Molly had misinterpreted innocent scenes between David and Caroline, eventually turning to Jedediah in defiance.

Molly's account of Shannon's death had touched a tender spot in Kate's heart. Remembering the tiny grave, she vowed to spend as much time as possible with Sabrina.

She'd read where David had danced with Caroline on that fateful night outside of Fort Bridger, and it reminded her of David's soft kiss. But it was Caroline he had kissed to repay Molly for being with Jedediah. It was Caroline's name David had called out in his delirium. And Caroline who had tried to stop Molly from leaving with Jedediah.

"I guess it was just a dream," Kate said slowly, finally finding her place. "She's never mentioned my name." Concentrating on the journal, she began to read.

November 26, 1848

Today is Thanksgiving Day. For those who have been blessed, it is indeed a day of gratitude. But, for me, it is a dismal reminder of what has been lost.

I have spent the day roasting venison. Flat biscuits are cooling on the hearth. I even managed to fashion a pie of sorts from wild berries I gathered early this morning.

My husband has yet to arrive, scoffing this morning that I was mistaken. According to his calculations, Thanksgiving Day had already come and gone. It isn't true. I've kept track of the time spent in this desolate prison, carving a tiny mark in a small tree near the cabin for each day that passes. Holiday or no, it will never seem as such until I am reunited with my family.

I am with child. As near as I can figure, my time will come in May. I am so very frightened, not knowing what to expect. I have not told my husband, fearing his response.

I cannot raise a child—my child—in these barbaric conditions. If it is a girl, I fear her fate. Jedediah wants naught but boys.

December 10, 1848

It is with sorrowing despair that I record what has transpired by my husband's brutal hand. At present, he is hunting. A part of me prays he will meet with disaster. The crude, barbaric beast! Murderer of my child! My sweet Colleen, for the tiny body was that of a girl. Zachariah Brown, a trapper and associate of my husband's, had chosen to pay us a visit a few days after Thanksgiving. Drunken with Jedediah's whiskey, Zachariah stared at me in a way no decent man would dare. Enraged, Jedediah struck me, calling me names of such vulgarity, that even his crude friend beseeched him to stop. It was in the night that the cramping began. I lost the baby soon after. Perhaps it is a blessing. I would not choose to bring a child into this world of cruelty and pain.

March 14, 1849

Again I find that I carry Jedediah's child, though I cannot rejoice in the news. I told my husband seven days ago. Whooping in his loud, crass way, he immediately set to drinking. Fearing for the child, I reminded him of our first, and the fate she'd met at his hand. Sobering, he promised to show gentleness in place of such behavior. He further promised if I gave him a son, he would reward me by taking the two of us with him to Fort Bridger this fall when he leaves to trade furs for supplies. Perhaps my prayers will be answered and a chance for escape will be granted. Surely some sympathetic soul would take pity at the fort, putting an end to the misery I now endure.

May 22, 1849

Spring has finally banished the cold months of winter. With it comes the renewed hope that I may yet be reunited with my family. I can scarce abide the days till September, when my baby will be born and sweet freedom will at last be mine

Little James stirs within, his movements bringing a strange comfort to my troubled heart. I feel certain this infant is a son. He'll be named after his grandfather, James Mahoney. Come soon, sweet child. My empty arms long to hold you.

August 12, 1849

My time is close at hand. Bloated as I am, I long for the ordeal of childbirth. Having witnessed several births, I have an idea of what is in store for me. How I wish my mother were here with me now. Jedediah claims he will fetch an Indian squaw to help when the time arrives, the wife of a Cheyenne chief who has befriended my husband. I shudder to think of my child being brought into this world by a red-skinned heathen. But, having no apparent choice in the matter, I will endure it, knowing the birth of my child will bring me closer to freedom.

Keeping his word, Jedediah has not touched me during these months. He is determined that our son will come into this world unscathed. I am just as determined to take my child away from this barbaric man to insure he will be raised in a family of love, within the protecting arms of the Mahoney clan. The family that once was mine. I can only hope they will welcome me when the time arrives. Their love is the strength I cling to now. Their memory, the only light in this dismal world of darkness in which I now dwell.

September 27, 1849

Oh, sweet Mother, how I've longed for you! Such pain as I've endured cannot be conveyed with mere words. I now have a son, but it is only by the will of God that I've survived to raise him. On the eve of his birth, such barbaric treatment was rendered by the Indian squaw, that I thought sure I was destined to leave this mortal existence. Tying me to the bed as I cried out in pain, my hands and legs were restrained by Jedediah at the Indian's request. A stick was wedged between my teeth. I near bit it in two

*as the pain intensified. Still, they were not finished with me.
Pushing on my stomach with harsh roughness, the woman laughed
at the increase in misery she was causing.*

*Convinced I was about to expire, I saw your face, dear Mother,
hovering near my own. Sure it was an illusion, I closed my eyes
and thought I felt your gentle touch. Quieting, I found comfort,
thinking you were near. I opened my eyes only when a baby's
sharp cry pierced the air. The squaw took him from me, claiming I
wasn't woman enough to raise a son. Jedediah laughed, and
removed the stick from my mouth. He then approached the chief-
tain's wife and argued in her language, leaving me tied to the bed
as my baby cried in her heathen arms. Finally taking him from her,
Jedediah escorted the Indian woman to the door. Upon closing it,
he held his squalling son up for inspection. Laughing at the tears
of our child, he announced his son would be called Zachariah,
after his fellow trapper. Sickened by the thought, I had not the
strength to argue, though I silently added a second name, James,
for my father.*

*Jedediah saw fit to untie me at last and set the distressed baby
into my waiting arms. Crying as I held him to my aching breast,
my husband misunderstood my tears, berating me for being so
weak. How could he know that an inner love deeper than anything
he'd ever known had possessed me as I nursed my infant son? I
promise, dear child, that we will soon leave this misery behind us.
I will not raise you here in the savage wilderness where men
become as the animals they trap.*

October 10, 1849

*Jedediah has left for Fort Bridger. Breaking his promise, I have
been left behind with our son, Zachariah. When I pleaded with my
husband to honor his word, he laughed, asking if I thought him a
fool. He would not take me to the fort, guessing rightly that I
would try to escape. He would not hear otherwise, though I
beseeched him with tearful pleas. He struck me until I was beaten
into submission, then mounted his horse, taking along the mule my
own horse was traded for last spring.*

*I've spent much of the day sorrowing for the chance at freedom
that has been denied. There is no hope, for how can I take so small*

an infant as Zachariah and flee on my own into the wilderness? My young son would surely die, and my strength has not been as it was since his birth. If there is a God, take pity on my soul and release me from this earthly prison.

Kate sniffed and glanced up at the clock. One thirty-five a.m. Wiping at her eyes, she closed the journal, replacing it on the nightstand. Troubled by Molly's plight, she was too exhausted to continue reading. She flipped off the lamp and settled down in the covers, finally drifting off to sleep.

CHAPTER FORTY-FIVE

After breakfast, Sue helped Kate back downstairs. She settled her daughter on the couch, then walked over to the TV. "I'll put a movie on for you to watch," she offered.

"I'd rather finish Aunt Molly's journal. Will you please get it for me? It's sitting on the nightstand in the bedroom."

Sue gazed at her daughter, concerned by how the journal had upset Kate. And yet, she sensed how important this was to her daughter. "It's on the nightstand, huh?"

"Yeah. I left it there last night."

"Okay. I'll be back in a minute." Sue hurried upstairs, returning with the journal a few minutes later. "Here you go."

"Thanks, Mom."

Nodding, Sue quietly left the room. Kate eagerly thumbed to where she had left off and began to read.

January 1, 1850

It has been too long since I've written in this journal, my only friend. My heart has been so burdened, the desire to record my thoughts has been snuffed into nonexistence. But today marks the start of a new year. At once fearing and longing for the events it will bring, the bitterness once held in my heart is dissipating. Caring for my son, I am possessed by such a feeling of love, that even the hatred I bear for my husband is lessened. As the long days progress, I feel the need to pray to the God I've all but turned from. How I long for little Zachariah to know his family. I see now that God is the only one who can help me. I've received a comforting peace within; it reminds me of the many times my dear mother knelt to pray with me. How I wish it was possible to kneel with her now.

I am with child again. Jedediah is impatient for the baby's arrival, claiming it will be another strong son. I am not so sure. It feels different this time. I've been quite ill. Having little patience with me, my husband often forgets himself, striking blows before I can remind him of the death of our first child. I pray he will not injure my baby as I do my best to stay out of his reach when it is at all possible.

April 7, 1850

How Zachariah has grown. He sits by himself, perfectly content to play with whatever is at hand. He is a strong, fine lad with a mischievous twinkle in his eye. Jedediah often frightens me, throwing our child into the air, catching him roughly beneath his little arms. Setting him on the horse or mule, taking pleasure in the fear this causes me. Zachariah laughs at it all, thinking it great sport. I worry that my son will grow up as rough as his father. I turn to my one solace at this time, prayer. I've come to know God is there. The angry pride I once adhered to has been replaced by humbling grief for those things that could've been mine. My own foolishness has led me to where I am now; God has but permitted me to choose my own way. I have not but myself to blame for all that has transpired. How I wish I had the comforting words of the Holy Bible to read or the Book of Mormon translated by Brother Joseph. There is truth in those sacred books that Jedediah has forbidden in our home. If only I'd swallowed my pride and married David. Our children would have been raised in the gospel, growing up with a father worthy of the sacred priesthood. I shudder to think what will become of my children now.

July 20, 1850

I have lived to see a second son born. This time, the Cheyenne chief's wife was not called upon for assistance. I made Jedediah promise beforehand, assuring him the baby and I would both die if that horrid woman touched either of us. But, as the hours of agony progressed, fearing more for the baby's life than my own, he sought the aid of Zachariah Brown's new wife, a soft-spoken Sioux the trapper had met at Fort Laramie some time ago. Bringing her to my side, Jedediah left the cabin, claiming he could not abide to hear my pain.

I could not speak her language, nor she mine, but a depth of understanding was reached between us as she discerned my plight. Making gestures with her hands, I was given to understand that the baby had need of turning. Gritting my teeth, I allowed her to do what needed to be done to spare my baby's life.

After several hours of excruciating pain, soaked with sweat and blood, I drew near to death. Anticipating a sweet release from this horrid existence, the faint cry of my infant son held me back. As I hovered between this life and the next, I thought I saw my mother, who spoke to me on several matters I cannot now recall. Only the look on her face, one of sadness and longing. I promised I would someday return to her, then drifted into the blackness that beckoned.

Jedediah later told me I was in this condition for three days. During that time, the Sioux woman cared for the lot of us, nursing my infant son with her own tiny girl. When I finally regained myself, it was she who gently laid my baby in my arms for the first time. As I gazed up into her sweet, lovely face, I was touched by the compassion and aid rendered by this woman. Lacking the words to thank her, I reached for her hand, weakly squeezing it in my own. She smiled quietly and returned the squeeze, lifting my hand to press against her heart.

Straightening, she moved across the cabin to strap her infant daughter to her back. She glanced at the wooden table where my drunken husband was sleeping and frowned, then gazed at me. Whispering words I could not hear or understand, she left, returning to the cabin she shared with her husband, several miles from our own. As she disappeared from sight, I felt as though I'd finally made a friend in this untamed wilderness.

When Jedediah woke from his drunken stupor, he crossed to the bed, kneeling beside me on the earthen floor. He gazed intently into my eyes and tearfully implored me to forgive him for the treatment I've endured at his hand. Fearing I would indeed die, he had promised God he would repent of his ways. Telling me this, he then allowed me to name our new son. As such, I've chosen to name our second son Daniel, for my dear little brother.

My life is at present tolerable. I have seen a great change in my husband. Now that he reaches out to me with renewed tenderness, I see the man I thought I'd wed. Perhaps there is hope for this union.

November 15, 1850

How soon joy slips from my fingers. His heart hardened once more, Jedediah has reverted to his former self. Renaming our second son Jedediah, he has turned his back on the promises made. He refused to take the boys and me with him to Fort Bridger to trade, thinking it would appease me if he promised to bring back cloth for a new dress. The one I've worn since our wedding is little more than rags.

Upon his return, he took great pleasure in handing me cloth of scarlet red, won in a game of cards. When I claimed I would never wear a dress from the garish fabric, he struck me, saying it was a color befitting my nature. I vowed again that I would never wear a dress from the shameful color, and he proceeded to rip what was left of the one I was wearing. Head bowed, I had no choice but to comply, sewing together a dress from the outlandish cloth. The final blow came a few days later. Calling me names of a vulgar nature, Jedediah taunted me for wearing the new dress. Speaking sharply, I informed him he had no business treating his wife in this manner. Striking me to the ground, he laughed, claiming I was never his wife. Shocked, I implored him to give me answer to this puzzlement. He then told me how he'd paid a man to perform a false ceremony at Fort Bridger, proudly stating he'd had no intentions of marrying me in the way religious men consider proper. What no other person has ever done, Jedediah did with that final blow. My spirit crushed beyond revival, I sank to my knees with the realization that I had been living in mortal sin.

With a heart as heavy as it's ever been, I remained silent for several days, reflecting on my plight. Repentant, Jedediah approached me, begging for forgiveness, blaming the ill-spoken words and deeds on the whiskey he is wont to drink. Well acquainted with his usual drunken behavior, I was nevertheless painfully aware he had indeed spoken the truth concerning our marriage, the Holy Spirit whispering this to me. Sure now of my eternal destruction, I could do naught but stare at him with sorrowing hate.

He disappeared for a month's time, leaving me to my misery. I pleaded for divine forgiveness concerning the mistakes I have made in my life, and found the strength to go on. Giving Jedediah up for dead, I made plans in that event. With no visible means of transportation, and the welfare of my children to consider, I stayed in the cabin, determined to leave in the spring. Zachariah's wife came to see me several times, cheering me with thoughtful acts of compassion. How I wished to unburden my soul to her, but knowing she would never understand, kept my sorrows to myself, the only comfort coming from the care of my two small sons.

Then one dark day, my husband returned from his wanderings. Filled with despair, I stared at the tall man he'd brought with him. Introducing the stranger as a Jesuit Priest, a man who had been proselyting among the Indians, Jedediah grinned, proud of himself, thinking he would now make right the wrongs committed. Giving in to his wish, I felt no joy in the hasty ceremony. Only the desire to take shame from our sons kept me from turning my back to the vile creature who had fathered them.

So, now I am truly joined in wedlock with this much despised man. Closing my eyes, I shudder at his touch, wishing for death, the only escape from this living nightmare.

Kate sadly stared at the paneled wall of the family room. Closing her eyes, her vivid imagination presented a colorful panorama of what she'd just read.

"You okay?"

Kate opened her eyes and gazed at her sister. "I'm all right, Breeny." She was touched by the worried adoration shining from her sister's eyes. "Maybe later I'll play you a game of somethin', okay?"

"Really?" Sabrina asked, her eyes widening.

"Uh-huh. You choose."

"Uncle Wiggily?"

Grimacing, Kate slowly nodded. "If that's what you want."

"'Kay!" the younger girl answered excitedly. "Wait till I tell Mommy." Dashing off, she reached the stairs, then retreated back to the couch. "When are we gonna play Uncle Wiggily?"

"As soon as I finish this book," Kate promised.

Sabrina ran off, tickled by the attention she was receiving from Kate.

Kate smiled, then returned to the yellowed pages of the journal. Alarmed, she noticed that the next entry was in January of 1852. Thumbing through the pages, she saw that none of them had been torn out. Confused, she began reading.

January 3, 1852

It has been a year since last I wrote. I used the ink I had sparingly, but it didn't last forever. Knowing Jedediah would refuse to purchase more from the trading post, that indeed, he would destroy this journal if it was ever found, I made a secret deal with Hannah, Zachariah Brown's wife. The trapper has renamed her, giving his Sioux bride a Christian name. Together, we have taught her some of the English language, which makes it easier to communicate with the beautiful woman. I gave Hannah the few coins I'd managed to glean from my husband's fat leather pouch, and she agreed to purchase the ink. True to her word, she brought me the ink in October. It has taken me this long to face the task of recording the contents of my heart.

Never have I known such despair. Daily I watch as my sons, Zachariah James, and Daniel, called Jedediah, grow up without the influence of God in our home. Zachariah, now two years and four months, emulates his father in every way possible. Little Daniel, for in my heart he will always be so, is of a gentler nature, crying easily when his brother knocks him about. When I come to his defense, for his father often rails at the tot for being weak, I take the blows intended for my youngest son. Perhaps it is best that I remain barren. I'll not bring more spirits into this home of contention and pain. I pray daily, begging for our deliverance. What's to become of us, only God knows.

April 18, 1852

Spring is nearly here. Something about the earth's rebirth sparks hope within even the most despairing heart. Jedediah is anxious to be out working with his traps, and I am just as anxious to see him go. It has been a long winter. One of violence and cruel accusations. He demands to know why I am not with child, refusing to hear that I will never bear another. Hannah has pleaded with her own husband, beseeching him to reason with Jedediah, all to no avail. Convinced I am purposely denying him the sons he desires, Jedediah has threatened to cast me off for another. My only fear is for my sons. Who will protect them when I am gone?

June 10, 1852

This day weighs heavy on my heart. Jedediah insisted on taking both boys with him to place his traps, claiming he will make men of them despite me. I pleaded with him, reminding him of their tender age, ceasing my barrage when he struck me into silence. Tearfully watching as he placed little Daniel on the mule behind Zachariah James, I felt as though my heart would shatter. Babies, both of them, being robbed of their childhood. True to his nature, Zachariah grinned with excitement. Too scared to cry, Daniel buried his face in his brother's back, lifting his head once to glance fearfully in my direction. Helpless, I watched them leave, possessed by a feeling of supreme sorrow.

July 15, 1852

It has been a month now. Still no sign of my sons or Jedediah. I pray constantly for their safety. Troubled, I fell into a fitful sleep last eve. I dreamt I saw my mother. She came to me, dressed in brilliant white. Bearing an expression of deep sadness, she told me to leave this place. To make my way to Salt Lake Valley. I pleaded with her to stay with me. Smiling, she did her best to soothe my aching heart, promising to never be far away. When I awoke this morning, the feeling of comfort lingered. Praying for guidance, I felt prompted to gather my few possessions and leave. I make this entry, not knowing what the days ahead will bring. I will put my trust in the Lord and abide by the counsel received.

August 6, 1852

I can scarce bear to record the events of the past few weeks. Never have I known such sorrow.

Upon leaving the cabin, I walked for three days, led by the Holy Spirit. I slept at night upon the cold ground, and it was a wonder I didn't freeze, for I had but one blanket with me. The biscuits I'd brought didn't last long, but I found a few berries along the way to sustain me.

Coming at last to a clearing, I saw the remains of a camp. I moved to the ashes of the fire and glanced around, gasping at the sight of Jedediah's horse as it walked to where I stood. The bridle had somehow been ripped from its head, the saddle gone as well. Briars clung to its mane and tail. Fear clutching at my heart, a feeling within prompted that the horse would lead me to my family.

I covered its back with my blanket and mounted, letting him have his head as I held fast to the stallion's tangled mane. He sauntered out of the camp, taking a trail that led to the river. The sight that met my eyes there will haunt me forever. My sons, my dear babies, dead. Murdered by Indians or thieves, I'll not know in this life. Screaming, I fell from the horse, my hand brushing something hard and cold. I scrambled to my feet and gazed in horror at my dead husband, his vacant eyes staring at the heavens he continuously berated.

After a time, I found a strength beyond my own. Placing myself in the Lord's hands, I buried my family in mounds of rocks. As I covered my tiny sons, I wept, promising that someday they would be mine forever.

I mounted Jedediah's stallion and arrived at Hannah's cabin in two days' time. Telling both Zachariah and Hannah of my family's fate, they offered such sympathy as could be rendered. Reluctantly, they agreed to escort me to Fort Bridger.

On the way to the fort, we learned of a marauding band of Indians who had been responsible for the deaths of several in the area. Having no way of proving their guilt in the murder of my own family, I focused on keeping the promise made to my small sons, intent on reaching the Salt Lake Valley.

Three days later, we reached the fort and discovered a small company of Mormons was camped nearby. The captain of this company happened to be trading for supplies when we rode in. He agreed to let me travel with them to the valley. I assured him I would pay for my own supplies.

It wasn't difficult finding a buyer for Jedediah's horse. With the money, I purchased a modest brown dress of coarse linen, discarding forever the red-colored rag I'd been wearing. As I bartered for a fair price on the much-needed supplies, the merchant took pity on my plight, selling cheaper to me than he had at any other time to any other traveler. Promising to keep silent about the bargains made, it was time to bid farewell to Hannah and Zachariah. Tearfully embracing Hannah, I left with Captain Richards, leaving behind the only friends I'd known in four years of misery.

I felt somewhat anxious as we approached the camp of Mormon emigrants. I expected to be treated with scorn, but was welcomed as a daughter lost to Zion. I told them a brief account of what had transpired, and asked to be taken to Salt Lake Valley. An older couple stepped forward, claiming they had extra room in their wagon before hearing I had acquired enough supplies to adequately provide for my needs. Touched by the act of kindness, I wept for a time, wondering how I could have ever scorned these people and their gentle ways.

It is now the evening of the third day of my journey with this wagon train. Eagerly I wait for the time when I'll be reunited with my family.

Kate quickly scanned the entries that followed, noting that most contained brief descriptions of the land and campsites she had already witnessed in her dream. Hurrying through these pages, she stopped at an entry written the day before Molly had finally entered Salt Lake Valley.

August 20, 1852

I'm sitting near the same ridge I left four years ago. It all seems as a horrible dream. Closing my eyes, I expect to hear my mother call for me. Opening them, I gaze into the valley below. A small city now lies among the dry desert. Four years. Much has changed in that time. I am somewhat anxious, fearful of how my family will receive me. If only they could know the contents of my heart. I will forever pay for the mistakes I've made. Trusting the Lord will ease my way. I will subject myself to their mercy, the prodigal daughter returning in shameful sorrow.

August 22, 1852

I am currently in the home of a dear friend and sister in Zion, Emily Gartner. After spending the day wandering the streets of this new city, I was amazed by the progress that has been made in so short a time. Everywhere I looked, there were trees, flowers, and grass. The Saints are truly creating a paradise from this desert.

Filled with wonder and regret, I searched for those who might have news of my family. Most shook their heads, claiming they knew of no such clan. Despair afflicted me. When dusk began to settle, I bowed my head and pleaded for guidance. I felt someone's hand on my shoulder and looked up into the angelic face of Sister Emily. Sure that God had sent her to my side, I gratefully accepted the embrace of this dear woman.

She has brought me to her home, treating me with such kindness that I am at a loss to know how to repay her deeds. It puzzles me that she refrains from saying where my family is, claiming she will arrange for me to see them as soon as possible. I have given in to her motherly nature, trusting in her decision that I must first regain my strength.

After a warm bath, Sister Emily furnished me with a clean change of clothes and a hot meal. She then begged me to tell her of the time I've spent away. She sensed I was hesitant to speak in front of her husband and children and guided me to a small room near the kitchen, entreating me to unburden my soul. I told her all and she wept with me as I revealed the pain and suffering that were endured at the hands of Jedediah. I could scarce tell her of my sons' murder, being so overcome with grief at the memory. She stood, gathered me in her arms and promised that God would ease my troubled heart.

I will close for now, hoping to soon attain what has been desired for so long—the chance to reunite with my family.

August 23, 1852

Today will be remembered as one of the darkest in my life. Sister Emily has finally revealed where my mother now lies. Her words of comfort did not soften the searing pain as it descended upon me. How can I endure what has been lost to me? Oh, sweet Mother, if only you could know the contents of my heart. As I stood at your grave, staring at the cold stone that now bears your name, I felt as though my grief was more than I could bear.

Sister Emily has brought me back to her home, her attempts at consolation failing to ease the agony that has befallen me. Thinking I alone had suffered for the choices I have made, I was not prepared for the discovery that others paid a dear price as well.

Forgive me, Mother. If only I had the comfort of knowing we'll share the eternities. That promise is lost to me now as well—gone with the virtue that once was mine.

August 24, 1852

Tonight my heart rests easier, though the pain I bear is sharp indeed. Sister Emily's husband, Brother Warren, laid his hands upon my head and blessed me to find peace. I felt a calming within as he uttered these words.

Sister Emily has spent much of the day speaking with me. She told of how my former friend, Caroline Wicker, had helped to care for my mother in her final hours. That indeed, my mother mistook Caroline for myself, thinking I had returned. She died with a smile on her lips, clutching Caroline to her heart. I found little comfort in this news and cried bitter tears of pain. Leaving me to my grief, Sister Emily later returned to my side. She told me that the love my mother had for me did not die with her, and that she felt certain Mother had been with me through my trials. She further stated that all could be forgiven if I would turn from pride and renew my covenants with the Lord. As she spoke, the sweet Comforter bore witness of the truthfulness of her words. I will seek the faith that has been lost to me and embrace humility.

Tomorrow Brother Warren and his dear wife will drive me out to my brother's farm. It lies some five miles west of the city. There I hope to be accepted by my brothers, all that remains of my family. I will not blame them if they turn me away. I will not be a burden to them. I have been told there is a need for those who can teach. Whether I am accepted now as a Mahoney or not, I will seek a position with a school. Perhaps in some small way, I can repay what I've done by helping those around me.

August 25, 1852

I am writing this by candlelight in the place I shall call home for a short while. My heart warms still at the memory of this day. We arrived at the farm in the early afternoon, and I had but stepped down from the wagon when a tall man approached. Stunned, I saw that it was Jamie, grown to manhood in these four years that have passed.

Both of us stared for a time. Then we fell into each other's arms, sharing an embrace of joy and sorrow.

Jamie guided me to the house built with his own hands and introduced me to his wife, a convert from Denmark named Anna. With quiet joy, I smiled at the beautiful girl, observing that I will soon be an aunt. Welcoming me as a sister, she quickly set about preparing a meal, paying no heed to the discomfort she must surely feel. I offered to help, but was whisked away to greet Daniel.

As I gazed at my youngest brother, I was amazed by how he has grown. I feared he would turn from my embrace, but he nearly squeezed the life from me with his great arms. Both of my brothers told me there was naught to forgive when I beseeched their mercy for the pain I have caused them. Filled with warming love, I feel now that I have finally come home.

Kate sniffed, staring at the book in her hands.

"Here's your lunch," Sue said, moving toward the couch with a tray. "How's it going?"

"Good," Kate replied, blinking back tears.

"How close are you to finishing it?"

Carefully thumbing through the remaining pages, Kate showed her mother.

Sue smiled down at her daughter. "Is there anything else you need?"

Kate shook her head and reached for a sandwich. She hurriedly ate, then settled back to finish the journal.

September 25, 1852

I now live in a tiny room of a boarding house here in the City of the Great Salt Lake. From what Jamie tells me, he will be moving to the city as well. He has intentions of starting a studio, similar to the one Brother Foster had established in Nauvoo. He will sell the farm, with plans to build a new clapboard house on the outskirts of Salt Lake. Daniel will live with them for a time until Jamie deems our younger brother old enough to be on his own. Daniel seems intent on serving a mission for the Church. I will do what I can to help him in this endeavor.

It took much persuasion, but I finally convinced my brothers I could best use my talents as a teacher. Securing a position with Sister Mary Dilworth, I will be assisting this fine lady in the instruction of the youth of Zion.

In three days' time, I will be permitted to reenter the waters of baptism. Jamie has eagerly agreed to my request and will be the one to assist me in renewing this sacred ordinance. What a privilege to be given the chance to start fresh. Though I will always carry scars in my heart, I will not dwell on what has been lost, but focus on the future, placing myself as always in God's hands.

September 28, 1852

The feeling of joy attained on this day will not be soon forgotten. There are not words to describe the cleansing spirit that filled me as I was lowered into the water of the river called Jordan.

When I came forth by Jamie's hand, I felt sure our mother was near, rejoicing in this event. Chilled from the river, I was warmed by a sensation of love that has far exceeded anything I've ever known. As I was greeted by Brother Warren, Sister Emily, Daniel, and Jamie's dear wife, Anna, I felt as though I had been given wings to soar above the sorrows of this world. I thank thee, dear Father in Heaven, for not turning away from one such as I.

"Kate . . . are ya done yet?"

Kate glanced at her sister. "Not quite." Bothered by the frown on Sabrina's face, she marked her place and closed the journal. "Tell you what, though, I could use a little break. Bring down Uncle Wiggily. We'll play that game now."

Squealing with delight, Sabrina clapped her hands and hurried to retrieve the game. Nearly an hour later, after letting the five-year-old win, Kate picked up the journal again, determined to finish it. Scanning the pages after Molly's baptism, she was amazed by the change in her aunt. "What a rock," she commented after reading several entries. "Her testimony just keeps getting stronger." Impatient to see how David had come back into the young woman's life, she skipped ahead a few months, an entry in June of 1853 catching her eye.

June 14, 1853

Sister Emily came by to see me again this afternoon. She is determined to match me up with a man of the holy priesthood. After enduring another motherly speech on the joy that comes with marriage, I gently reminded her I have nothing to offer such a union. Barren as I am, I could never give children to a husband. I told her I am quite content to continue my life as such, teaching the children of others, looking forward to the time when I will be reunited with my own. Concerning this, Emily reminded me that the seal of eternity will not be mine without the priesthood. I am sure God will provide a way; it may come through the doctrine of plural marriage. My mother must surely be smiling in heaven to know I would submit to such a thing. But, if it means I will have my young sons with me in the eternities, I will not allow pride to stand in my way.

June 18, 1853

This has been a day of wonder, a time of sorrow and hope. I had journeyed to my mother's grave, bringing fresh flowers to replace those I'd brought last week. As I knelt down to arrange the colorful blooms, I heard a child crying nearby. I brushed the dust from my dress and glanced around. A young girl was lying near a grave, sobbing as though her heart would break. I quickly moved to her side and placed a hand on her trembling shoulder. She lifted her small face and stared, her deep blue eyes piercing through me. With hair as black as coal, skin as smooth as porcelain, the young girl struck a familiar chord within, though I could not place where I had seen the child before. When I asked why she was crying, she pointed to the grave and told me she missed her mother who had died and gone to heaven. As I glanced at the granite stone, I gasped, for I was gazing at the grave of a former friend and confidante, Caroline Wicker Miles.

The realization of who this girl was filled me at once with longing and distress. I gathered her close and tried to ease her pain as my own threatened to engulf me. When she quieted, she told me her mother had died before Christmas, after giving birth to a baby boy.

I asked her age and learned she had recently celebrated her fourth birthday, the age Zachariah would've been by now. She went on to tell me that her name was Shannon. Somewhat taken aback, I asked how she came to be known by that name. The young girl explained she had been named for the sister of her mother's dearest friend. She timidly smiled and asked if I knew her parents. Struggling for an answer, I heard someone approach. As I turned, the young girl called to her father, bouncing to her feet to race across the cemetery. Dread possessed me. What was I to say to this man from whom I'd fled five years ago?

I decided to leave, keeping my back to the only man I've ever loved. He called to me, wishing to thank me for staying with his small daughter. He moved closer and explained that she often ran off from the woman he had hired to watch his children.

I slowly turned to face David. He stared, neither of us daring to break the silence that separated us. He finally called me by name. Nodding, I didn't trust myself to speak. He asked if I was well. I answered that I was. He told me that Sister Emily had been by the mill where he worked. She had mentioned in passing that I had returned to the valley. Jamie had told me of David's marriage to Caroline. I had avoided both, fearing the pain it would cause us all.

David looked away and told me he had married Caroline soon after my mother's death. I assured him I did not need an explanation and apologized for leaving as I did that fateful night so long ago. He fixed his gaze upon me and asked if Jedediah had treated me well. Not wanting to cause him further distress, I did not answer.

I told him I was happier now than I had been in a very long time. I expressed my condolences concerning the loss of his wife, bid him farewell, and moved to leave the cemetery. I had but taken a step when he called to me. Turning, I gazed at the sorrowing man and his daughter. He asked if he could call upon me some afternoon, the hope in his eyes extending to the expression on his daughter's face. I implied that I would enjoy such a visit, then turned to leave before losing control of my fragile strength. Returning to my room, I gave in to the healing balm of tears, crying for the loss of a dear friend, the children who could have been mine, and for the husband lost to me because of my folly.

June 22, 1853

Reluctantly giving in to Jamie's request, I ventured to his studio today. He seated me on a cushioned chair, and excitedly gripped his new camera, asking me to smile. I did my best to please him; he is anxious to use my photograph as an advertisement, claiming my Irish beauty will gain him numerous customers. But, as I tried to smile, I couldn't keep my thoughts from straying to David. Poor Jamie, he tried to cheer me, chiding me for the dour expression his camera no doubt captured. As I forced a smile at last, he thanked me for my efforts, promising to give me a copy of the photograph when it is finished. He then invited me to dinner with his family, stating Daniel would be there as well. Agreeing, I hurried from the studio, wishing to be alone with my thoughts.

June 24, 1853

David came by the boarding house this afternoon. Both of us ill at ease, he finally got around to the reason behind his visit. He had come to ask me to attend a play with him that is currently being presented under the old bowery here in the City of the Great Salt Lake. A historical drama of song and dance, based on the 1847 emigrant trek from Winter Quarters to the Salt Lake Valley. Startled by his interest, both in myself and the theatrical production, I agreed, apprehensive of where this will eventually lead.

As we tried to make conversation, he told me more about his children, the two girls fathered by Truman, and the two Caroline and he had been blessed with. He claims them all as his own, loving them equally and without disdain. The older girls, Nancy and Louisa, are now eight and nine respectively, and from what I understand, have been quite good to help with Shannon and Jacob.

When he asked if I had children of my own, I closed my eyes, not knowing what to answer. I feared he would cease to desire my company if the truth were told, but I found I could not deceive him. I gazed into his questioning eyes and revealed the fate that had befallen my husband and sons. I further stated that I was unable to bear children following the difficult birth of little Daniel. He remained silent for a time. Believing I had upset him by my frankness, I rose from the chair, turning to leave the parlor. I quietly said I would understand if he chose to seek his company elsewhere, that as it stood, I had little to offer a man seeking a wife.

As I hurried to the stairs, I didn't hear him follow, and gasped with surprise when he gripped my shoulders firmly from behind. Spinning me around, he chastised me for ever doubting his affection and pulled me close, covering my mouth with his. The tenderness of his kiss brought tears to my eyes and peace to my heart. When he drew back, I gazed at him, seeking for words that would not come.

He blushed and apologized for his rash behavior. I hastily assured him that he had not offended me. Smiling shyly, he then kissed my cheek, stating he would be coming by with his buggy in two nights' time.

I cannot describe the emotions that plague me now. Longing desire and fearful suspense combined with the warming flow of vanquished love. Is it possible David and I can regain what once was between us? Time alone will tell.

June 30, 1853

I am failing to keep up with this record. All at once, my life seems as a whirlwind. David has been calling upon me with great regularity, giving Emily cause to smile when she chances to stop by for a visit. Returning her smile, I can only hope that what she seems so sure of will come to pass.

July 4, 1853

This was a grand day of celebration. David brought his children when he came for me early this morning. We gathered together with the other Saints as enthusiastic bands played joyous music from a pavilion built for this occasion. In between the music, games, and merry-making, speeches of fiery patriotism were offered by several Church leaders, including remarks from the Prophet Brigham Young.

Securing permission from the woman who runs the boarding house, I had used the kitchen to prepare a large hamper filled with food. We shared the lunch together, enjoying the music and games that continued throughout the afternoon. The evening ended with a fine display of fireworks. I was touched when Shannon chose to lay her tired head in my lap to quietly watch the final blasts of colorful glory exploding in the sky. Several gunshots were fired in the spirit of the holiday. Frightened, the four-year-old clung to me, seeking refuge from whatever evil had apparently befallen us. I quickly convinced her all was well and felt David's eyes upon me. I met his gaze and sensed he was pleased with how I had handled the situation. As he moved close, cradling tiny Jacob in his arms, I felt as though we were already a family, though indeed, we are not as yet.

Later, as David escorted me to the boarding house, he seemed nervous and hesitated in front of the door. Apparently making peace with himself, he drew me close for a lengthy kiss. I was embarrassed, fearing what his children would think who were observing from the buggy. Thus, I was unprepared for the question when it came. Dramatically falling to one knee, he took my hand in his, asking me to become his wife.

Startled, I begged him to rise to his feet. He grinned and refused, claiming he would remain in that position until I agreed to his request. Aware that we had attracted an audience, I quickly responded. Barely had the words of acceptance left my lips when David whooped and threw his hat into the air. He grabbed me and danced us around, the crowd laughing and cheering, becoming especially loud when he sealed our engagement with a kiss.

So now, at long last, I am to become the wife of David Miles. We will begin our lives together in two weeks' time. I can scarce

*believe all that has transpired since my return to Salt Lake Valley.
Ironic, the journey this journal contains.*

*I will treasure this record kept by my hand, a reminder of the
hard-earned testimony I hope to retain. Ever it will be a struggle,
for this life was not meant to be otherwise. Yet, I know we are
entitled to righteous joy. We are in fact our Father's children, and
we have but to ask for His assistance if the burdens are heavy that
we carry.*

*As this is the final page of a book that has been a true and
faithful friend, it seems fitting I begin a new journal; a sign of the
fresh path my life now takes. I close this record much wiser than I
was at its start.*

> *Faithfully yours in Zion,*
> *Molly Mahoney Taylor, soon to be Mrs. David Miles*

Kate closed the journal and wiped at her eyes. Glancing up, she
saw that Paige had stepped down into the room.

"Supper's about ready," Paige said softly, moving to the couch.
Kate silently handed the journal to her aunt. "Have you finished it?"

Nodding, Kate quietly reflected on the life of Molly Mahoney.

"So, what's the verdict, thumbs up or down?"

"Definitely thumbs up," Kate replied with a smile. "Mom said
you were planning on typing it. I want a copy."

"Count on it," Paige responded, helping her niece off the
couch. She clutched the journal in one hand and steadied Kate
with the other, carefully guiding the young woman to the stairs.

Chapter Forty-Six

As Sue and Paige made their way from the garden carrying the fresh vegetables Paige wanted to send with the Ericksons, Sue suddenly pulled her sister-in-law back, leaning against the side of the brick house.

"What . . ." Paige bit off her sentence as the other woman motioned for her to be quiet. Looking in the direction of Sue's pointing finger, her eyes widened. Kate and Randy had moved outside and were sitting in the back porch swing just around the corner. Paige smiled and gave her sister-in-law a knowing wink, then silently indicated that they could walk around to the front. Nodding, Sue followed her lead.

"Those two sure make a cute couple," Paige said, her eyes twinkling.

"I know," Sue sighed, carefully balancing the zucchini squash that had been stacked in her arms.

Paige stopped, turning to look at her sister-in-law. "You don't sound too thrilled," she commented.

"I am, about Kate and Randy, anyway. It's the other people in Kate's life that I worry about. Jace and Linda. To be honest, I'm a little worried."

"Why?"

"They've both had such a hold on her. And when we take Kate back to Bozeman tomorrow, I'm sure they'll both be right there to welcome her home."

Paige frowned. "I suppose that's a possibility, but Kate has changed so much since the accident."

"True. But what happens when she comes in contact with her former music, clothes, and friends? What will keep her from slipping back into who she was before?"

"Have you talked to her about any of this?"

"Not yet," Sue sighed. "I've wanted to. I just don't want to upset her right now."

"I think she's strong enough to handle just about anything."

"Even Jace's letter?" Sue asked, continuing toward the house.

"What letter?" Paige followed Sue to the front door.

"The one he sent while she was in the coma. He called two or three times. Linda called every other day. I told Kate about the phone calls, but I haven't had the courage to give her the letter. It's still in my purse."

"Sue, you have to be honest with her. She'll have to come to terms with these people. With her past."

Sue nodded, entering the house as Paige held the door.

"Maybe the girls in your branch could help."

"Maybe," Sue agreed, heading toward the kitchen. "Kate's made fun of them for so long, I'm not sure they'll want anything to do with her."

"She has you. That should balance things out."

"I hope so, Paige. It would kill me if after all of this she . . ."

"Don't even think it. It might be rough going for a while, but I've seen something in Kate's eyes that wasn't there before. She has a testimony to fall back on now."

". . . anyway, there must be other journals that Molly kept. Uncle Stan and Mom said they'd never heard of any. So, I was wondering . . ."

"If my mom had stumbled onto them," Randy said, finishing Kate's sentence.

"Yeah, something like that," Kate said with a smile. "Would you mind checking it out for me?"

"No problem. It'll give me an excuse to keep in touch. That reminds me . . ." He reached into the back pocket of his jeans and pulled out a slip of paper. "Here's my home address and phone number. Mom can keep you posted on my whereabouts if you ever decide to write to me while I'm gone."

Kate accepted the paper, holding it in her hand. "I'm sure I could manage to drop you a line once in a while," she teased. "I hear you already have my number and address in Bozeman."

"Uh, yeah. Your mom was kind enough to give it to me in the hospital when you were still playing 'Sleeping Beauty,'" he teased. "For a while there, I was afraid you'd sleep right past my departure date. Which reminds me, how about that musical number for my farewell?"

"You're persistent, aren't you? You'll make a wonderful missionary."

"Thank you. Now, are you going to come through for me?"

"I'm still thinking about it."

"Maybe this will help." Leaning close, he gently kissed her. They were startled by the electricity that flowed between them. As they drew back from each other, Kate blushed and glanced down at her hands.

"Sorry, I shouldn't have done that," Randy apologized. "But I really care for you, Kate."

Looking up, Kate smiled. Randy returned the smile, then slowly stood. He offered his hand and helped her to her feet.

"Well, I guess I'd better head back to Heber. It's getting late. My mother'll be having a fit."

"Don't forget to ask her to check into those missing journals."

"I sense a deal in the making."

"Okay. I'll sing at your farewell."

"I'd say it's a fair exchange," he replied with a grin.

"You'll have to let me know which Sunday."

"Not a problem," he replied, guiding her back to the house.

"Here you are," Sue said, entering the main floor bedroom that Kate had been using since her return from the hospital.

Glancing up from the bed, Kate smiled at her mother. "I guess today's adventures have caught up with me. I've had it."

"It has been a busy day," Sue agreed. She closed the door behind her and moved to the bed, sitting down on the edge.

"What's up?"

"Well, there are just some things I think we need to discuss before we head home."

"Okay."

"I know I said something about this before . . . in the hospital. But I want you to know again how sorry I am about all of this."

"Mom, what happened was an accident. I'm not blaming anybody. In fact, I'm kind of glad it happened."

"Honey, it wouldn't have happened if I'd listened to you. You could've died because I shut you out. I don't know how I can ever make that up to you."

"It wasn't your fault, okay?" Kate insisted, sitting up. "We both said some things we didn't mean."

"But, maybe if I'd handled things differently . . ."

"I haven't exactly made things easy for you. It was my big mouth that got us into trouble."

"Well, I want you to know that from now on, I will always try to listen."

"Now, there's something else I need to talk to you about."

"Okay. Let's hear it."

"This came for you while you were in the coma."

Taking the letter, Kate gazed at the familiar handwriting. "Jace," she observed quietly, glancing at her mother.

"It's been in my purse. I haven't read it. I just wasn't sure I wanted you to."

"Mom, it's okay . . ."

"No, it's not. I should've given it to you earlier."

Kate stared at her mother, then focused on the letter. She ripped it open, pulling the folded page from the envelope. Scanning the contents, she shuddered, then handed it to her mother to read.

"Honey, I don't have to read it."

"Go ahead. I can't believe I ever felt anything for that jerk."

Nervously swallowing, Sue began reading.

Hey babe,

If your mama, the hag-woman, ever gives this to you, I'll be in total shock. I called the other day and thought she was gonna hang up on me!

When ya gonna haul that firm little tush of yours outta bed? (Can you believe I said that, knowin' what my goal for the past two years has been?) Our little get-togethers just aren't the same without ya. Linda got so high the other night, we thought she'd never come down. I guess she's worried about ya. We all are. Some vacation. I told ya to stay here with me. I would've shown ya a better time than your family did! Guess it'll have to wait until ya come home. Hurry up, sweet cheeks. A guy like me can't wait forever!

Jace

Sue's hand trembled as she handed the letter back to her daughter.

Taking the page, Kate shredded it into tiny pieces and leaned to drop it and the envelope into the small garbage container next to her bed. "Mom, I want you to know I will never have anything to do with Jace again. I don't ever want to end up with a Jedediah!"

"A what?" Sue asked, relief showing in her face.

"A guy like the one Molly married the first time around. I want something totally different than I did before. The Church is true, Mom! I feel it inside, all of those things you used to tell me about. It all makes sense now. I've still got some changes to make, and there are some things I'll have to take care of," she said, "but I can do it. Especially if you'll help me."

"You can always count on that, sweetheart," Sue answered, leaning to kiss her daughter's forehead.

Smiling at her mother, Kate slowly nodded, filled with the sweet realization that a loving Father in Heaven would be watching over her as well.

CHAPTER FORTY-SEVEN

Your light *is* still on. Stan thought he saw it when he headed upstairs." Paige entered the room and smiled at her niece.

"Yeah. I don't have enough ambition to pull myself out of bed to flip it off," Kate replied.

"If you're ready to turn in, I can get it for you," Paige offered. "You want to call it a night?"

Shrugging, Kate frowned.

Paige moved to the bed and gazed down at the troubled girl. "Is something wrong?"

"I don't know. Maybe. I guess it's a combination of everything." Kate glanced up at her aunt. "I'm worried about what's waiting for me in Bozeman. And for some reason, my leg is killing me tonight. Plus, I can't stop thinking about the dream I had during the coma."

"I see. Well, I can get you some Tylenol for the pain. As for Bozeman, take it one day at a time. You'll be all right. I'm not saying it'll be easy, but you'll get through it. Just remember, you're not in this thing alone."

Kate nodded and glanced down at her hands.

Sensing her niece needed to talk, Paige eased herself down onto the edge of the bed. "What's bothering you about the dream?"

Kate looked up to meet her aunt's inquiring gaze. "The same thing that's bugged me from the beginning. It all seemed so real . . ."

"I know. I'll admit, it's kind of thrown the rest of us too.

Especially when you found that hidden compartment in Grandma Colleen's trunk. I just about swallowed my teeth. Good thing they were firmly attached," she joked, grinning at her niece.

"You don't have dentures yet?" Kate half-heartedly kidded.

"Hardly," Paige said dryly. "However, I do have a theory about dreams."

"What?"

"I believe that sometimes we can receive inspiration or even messages in them."

Kate stared at her aunt. "You think maybe I was given a message?"

"Maybe. Do you remember the dream Lehi had about the tree of life, the one Nephi recorded in the Book of Mormon?"

"Kind of. I think we discussed it once in one of my Primary classes a few years ago. It was Merrie Miss B. I remember Sister Rhoads tried to draw it on the chalkboard."

"And?"

"And I sort of made fun of her artwork and cracked up the rest of the class," Kate admitted, blushing. "I really don't remember anything else."

"You ought to read it sometime in the near future. It's in First Nephi," she added, smiling thoughtfully at Kate. "For now, let's just say that it's filled with symbolism. Lehi was given an analogy for life. He saw an iron rod that would guide his family out of the mists of darkness, toward the tree of life."

"What exactly was the tree of life?"

"That's what Nephi wanted to know. After his father told them about the dream, Nephi sensed it contained a special message for his family. So, he prayed about it. He wanted to know what the symbols his father saw meant."

"I remember some of this now. Wasn't there a tall building filled with people . . . in the dream, I mean?"

"Yes. Do you remember what the building represented?"

Concentrating, Kate finally shook her head.

"Nephi was told it was the pride of the world, and the people inside were those who mock the faithful journeying to the tree of life."

"Like Jace and Linda . . . and the old me," Kate said glumly.

"Something like that," Paige answered, smiling kindly at her niece.

"So, what was the tree of life?"

"The love of God. It's offered freely to those who are strong enough to walk the straight and narrow path of righteousness. The iron rod represented the word of God, or the scriptures. They were given to us to guide us past the mists of darkness, or the temptations of Satan."

"Wow! This is giving me goose bumps."

"It's the same feeling I had when you told us about your dream."

"And this other dream, the one you're talking about . . . it's all in the Book of Mormon?"

"Yes."

Kate shook her head and sighed. "Sounds like I've got some reading to catch up on."

"Oh, maybe just a little," Paige teased, patting Kate's hand.

"So, back to this theory of yours. Do you really think I was given a message?"

"I'm almost positive. It happens, Kate. I remember when my grandmother was very ill, I was about your age. She kept drifting in and out. We'd go to the hospital to see her, and she would claim Grandpa had been there visiting."

"Your grandpa?"

"Yeah. He had died ten years before."

"Whoa! Did she really see him?"

"Well, at the time, we thought she was hallucinating because of the illness. Then one night, my mother had a dream that Grandma had come to see her. She told my mother it was her time to go, and to not worry or grieve too much because she would be with Grandpa now. Mom woke up just as the phone rang. It was the hospital calling to let her know Grandma had passed away."

Absorbing this, Kate stared at her aunt.

"That dream brought my mother a lot of comfort in the days that followed. Every time she thought her heart would break, she'd remember what Grandma had said about being with Grandpa. It really helped her through a difficult time in her life."

"Kind of like me, now," Kate said softly.

"I think so, sweetheart. We've all been so worried about you, about the direction you were heading in life. Maybe some of our ancestors were, too. I'm sure they love you just as much as we do. You're special, Kate. You have so much potential. I look at you and see leadership qualities, intelligence, determination, and talent. But, for a while there, we were so afraid you were throwing it all away, seeking after . . ."

"The mists of darkness?"

Nodding, Paige smiled. "I think what had worried your mother more than anything was the fear that you would be lost to us . . . on an eternal scale."

"That was what had upset Grandma Colleen most about Molly. I mean, here was a lady who had suffered through so much, and the only time I saw her give up was when Molly ran off with Jedediah." Shaking her head, Kate frowned. "And, like a total idiot, I put my own mother through the same thing."

"Don't be so hard on yourself. We all make mistakes. Learn from them. Then strive to do better. That's part of why we're here—to grow from the experiences we have. If it was always smooth sailing, we wouldn't learn very much." Rising, Paige leaned down to kiss Kate's cheek. "You're heading in the right direction now. Keep your chin up and use what you learned from that dream. And remember, all of us are pulling for you." She turned and left the room.

CHAPTER FORTY-EIGHT

Nearly an hour later, as the Tylenol eased the throbbing in her leg, Kate fell asleep. Drifting quietly through a myriad of hazy images, she eventually found herself in a large meadow filled with beautiful flowers. She turned and saw a lake of brilliant blue. Making her way through the tall grass, she approached the white sand lining the lake's edge. Leaning against a large rock, she gazed with wonder at the breathtaking beauty that surrounded her.

A small object bobbing in the water caught her attention. She moved to the shore's edge and knelt, reaching for the floating shape. She gripped it tightly in her hand and stood, staring at the same piece of driftwood she had thrown out into Jackson Lake weeks ago. As she focused on the driftwood, several thoughts went through her mind. "I was wrong," she said aloud. "Boundaries are important. They keep us from drifting aimlessly through life."

"Well said, Katie-girl," a familiar voice said brightly.

Stunned, Kate dropped the piece of driftwood and turned to stare at two women dressed in magnificent white robes. "Grandma Colleen . . . Aunt Molly!" Squealing with delight, she ran into their waiting arms, embracing first Colleen, then Molly. As Kate pulled away from her aunt, she blinked back hot tears. "I found your journal," she said in a hushed voice.

"I know, Katie. I was hoping you would. I hope it helped. We couldn't bear to lose you. There is much you will accomplish in your life for good, if you so choose it."

Kate shifted her gaze to her grandmother. "I never thought I'd handle it when you died," she said softly.

"Just as we grieved, seeing the road you were determined to take in life. We'd near given up hope of reaching you, your heart was so hardened."

"Remember, Kate, you must be wary of the perils that exist in the world today," Molly said. "Set an example for those who waver."

"And now, dear girl, we must leave you for a time."

"No, Grandma, please . . . there's so much I want to ask you. Please stay with me . . ."

"Katie, our parting may seem long to you now, but you will see it was no time at all. Live your life that we may greet you when your journey on earth is through."

Tears blurred Kate's vision as the two women faded from sight. She turned to stare across the lake. "I won't let you down," she whispered. "I'm glad I share your name."

Waking with a start, Kate slowly sat up and wiped at her eyes. She had been crying! She flipped on the lamp beside her bed and gazed at the alarm clock. Three-thirty-six. Contemplating the dream, she reached for the new journal Paige had given her, turned to a clean page and began to write.

CHAPTER FORTY-NINE

Greg loaded the final suitcase, grunting as he forced the back door of the Explorer shut.

"Got it?" Stan asked.

"Yeah," Greg replied with a grin. "I forgot how much luggage these women have to have to survive."

"Don't I know it," Stan responded, slapping his brother-in-law on the back.

Greg turned to face the other man. "Stan, I don't know how to thank you guys for everything . . ."

"Now, that's enough of that. Like I said earlier, if it'd been the other way around, you would've been there for us."

Nodding, Greg silently agreed.

"Well, I guess we're ready to leave," Sue said, walking across the lawn to the driveway. She winced as her brother squeezed her tightly.

"Keep in touch," Stan demanded, giving her another squeeze.

"We plan to," Sue gasped, relieved when he released her. She glanced toward the house, smiling as Tyler and Sabrina raced toward the car.

"Where's Kate?" Greg asked, moving around to the driver's side.

"She'll be right out. Paige wanted to talk to her for a minute. You know how those two are."

"Unfortunately," Greg said, reaching for the sunglasses that were sitting on the dashboard. "I guess we can cut them a little slack under the circumstances," he added, smiling indulgently.

Curbing a smile of her own, Sue stepped back to help Sabrina with her seat belt.

Inside the house, Paige sat next to Kate on the living room sofa. She set her niece's journal on an end table and beside it, placed a shoe box.

"Did you have a chance to read it?" Kate nervously asked, glancing at the journal.

"Yes. I hid downstairs for a few minutes. That was quite a dream you had last night, young lady."

Flushing, Kate stared at the floor.

"Thank you for sharing it with me," Paige added, sensing Kate's discomfort. "Sounds like you've got more people in your corner than you've ever realized."

Kate smiled, meeting her aunt's loving gaze.

"Just remember, no matter what life hits you with, you are a special daughter of our Heavenly Father. Anything's possible if you have enough faith." She reached behind the arm of the sofa and picked up the shoe box. Handing it to Kate, she smiled. "We took a vote last night. We all decided you should have this."

Puzzled, Kate lifted the lid from the box. Blinking rapidly, she pulled out Colleen Mahoney's mirror and brush set. "Oh, Aunt Paige. I can't believe this! Really?"

Paige nodded. "We can't think of anyone who has more right to it than you. And I'm sure Grandma Colleen would be very happy to know her namesake has the set. Take care of it, and the name you've inherited."

Unable to reply, Kate reverently replaced the set back inside of the shoe box.

"Well, I guess I'd better help you outside before your father starts laying on the horn." Taking the box from her niece, she helped the teenager stand. She handed Kate the crutches, then retrieved the journal from the end table.

"Aunt Paige," Kate said softly, leaning on her crutches. "Thanks for everything."

"You're more than welcome. Now, let's go." Slipping an arm around her niece's waist, she gave Kate an intense squeeze.

"Remember, you'll be coming back down in a month for Randy's farewell. We'll talk more then."

"Deal. And you're right, we'd better head outside. Dad'll be having a fit."

"I doubt that," Paige countered, carrying the journal and box with one hand while she steadied Kate with the other. "I have a feeling that man is going to spoil you rotten. Honestly! The way he dotes on you lately."

"I know," Kate said with a grin. "Pretty great, huh?"

Paige nodded in agreement, guiding her to the door.

Sue and Paige worked together to help Kate up into the back seat of the Explorer. As the car backed out of the driveway, Kate shifted around to wave to Paige, Stan, and her cousins. Sensing her mother's lingering gaze, she looked up and returned the concerned smile. She sighed contentedly, overwhelmed by a surge of love for her family. She didn't even mind when Sabrina leaned against her shoulder, seeking a soft surface for a much-needed nap. A feeling of warmth penetrated her heart as her sister snuggled close. Reflecting on all that had transpired during the summer, Kate stared out the window, eager to start the journey home.

Cheri Nel Jackson Crane

About the Author

Music, sports, community and church service, and lots of family time can't seem to keep Cheri Crane from writing. A native of Idaho Falls, Cheri Nel Jackson Crane and her husband, Kennon, live in Montpelier, Idaho, with their three sons.

Cheri plays guitar and piano by ear, writes songs, loves racquetball, baseball, and volleyball, and she enjoys cooking. Besides these, she is in a Young Women presidency and heads a local chapter of the American Diabetes Association.